Praise for *New York Times* bestselling author Maisey Yates

"Yates' new Gold Valley series begins with a sassy, romantic and sexy story about two characters whose chemistry is off the charts."
—*RT Book Reviews* on *Smooth-Talking Cowboy* (Top Pick)

"The banter between the Dodge siblings is loads of fun, and adding Dallas (Bennett's surprise son) to the mix raises that humor up a notch or two."
—*RT Book Reviews* on *Untamed Cowboy* (Top Pick)

"Fans of Robyn Carr and RaeAnne Thayne will enjoy [Yates's] small-town romance."
—*Booklist* on *Part Time Cowboy*

"Passionate, energetic and jam-packed with personality."
—*USATODAY.com*'s *Happy Ever After* blog on *Part Time Cowboy*

"[A] story with emotional depth, intense heartache and love that is hard fought for and eventually won.... This is a book readers will be telling their friends about."
—*RT Book Reviews* on *Brokedown Cowboy*

"Yates's thrilling seventh Copper Ridge contemporary proves that friendship can evolve into scintillating romance.... This is a surefire winner not to be missed."
—*Publishers Weekly* on *Slow Burn Cowboy* (starred review)

"This fast-paced, sensual novel will leave readers believing in the healing power of love."
—*Publishers Weekly* on *Down Home Cowboy*

MAISEY YATES

Unbroken Cowboy

Recycling programs for this product may not exist in your area.

ISBN-13: 978-1-335-04112-8
ISBN-13: 978-1-335-99946-7 [Walmart Exclusive edition]

Unbroken Cowboy

Copyright © 2019 by Maisey Yates

www.HQNBooks.com

Printed in U.S.A.

For Nicole. You didn't shout, "Full Yates!" at me
even once while I wrote this.
A true testament to our friendship.
Especially given this book contains a raccoon.

CHAPTER ONE

Beatrix Leighton was a friend to all living things.

She cared for creatures large and small, domestic and wild, both in her job at Gold Valley Veterinary Clinic and in her everyday life.

Whenever she found a wounded critter on the side of the road she always stopped and tried to help it. If ever she found a sickly mouse or a sad, stranded kitten, she nursed it back to health.

She never lost her cool or brought harm to any being.

But she was close, very close, to administering grievous bodily injury to one *extremely* irritating cowboy who was—no doubt about it—the worst patient she had ever tended to in her life.

Not that Dane had asked her to tend to him, as he was the first to point out, often.

But if she didn't, what was going to happen to him? Who else could care for him?

She had a special place in her heart for Dane. She always had. From the first moment she'd met him. She'd known him for so many years now it had settled into being part of who she was. She loved him. And it was as much a part of her as her love of nature, animals and pie.

Something so ingrained in her fabric didn't require

her to be conscious of it at all times, or to live with expectation on it. It simply was.

As simple and plain as the fact that Dane saw her as a sister, and yet she loved him still.

Well, most days she loved him. Today he was being an ass.

But the care and keeping of Dane was currently a responsibility she couldn't turn away from.

She lived in a cabin on the property of Grassroots Winery, happily tucked away in the woods, and currently Dane was the only person occupying the main house.

His sister, Lindy, had moved to Get Out of Dodge—the dude ranch owned by the Dodge family, which sat on the outskirts of Gold Valley—when she and Wyatt Dodge had gotten married, and when Dane had been horrifically injured eight months ago during a championship rodeo competition, it had made the most sense to move him into that house.

And there he had stayed ever since. With Bea on the property basically taking the place of his sister, when the last thing she felt for this man at all was *sisterly*.

It, along with his grumpiness, was getting old.

The grump she'd been able to cope with. After all, he was incapacitated and stuck indoors. Bea had made sure that she checked in with him now and again just to be certain he was doing okay, but his unwillingness to follow doctor's orders and his inability to be even remotely civil was amplifying, and Bea was a hair's breadth away from clubbing him fiercely with his own crutch.

She supposed she should be grateful that he was

on crutches at all. But he was overdoing it. He had just begun transitioning from his wheelchair and doing physical therapy to get walking again a week ago. But from the moment he had stood up, he had refused to get back into his chair and he never admitted when he was tired.

Today he'd been God knew where the whole day. Then she'd heard he'd been out in the field making sure the grapes weren't going to die in an upcoming frost and then she'd heard through the workers that he'd *fallen down* because his leg had given out and the bastard hadn't even come in then.

He wasn't doing the prescribed exercises from the physical therapist. He was *literally* trying to walk it off.

It drove her absolutely insane.

The fact that she didn't need to be there—the fact that no one had actually asked her to take him on—occasionally did occur to her.

But then, she had not asked her heart to fall resolutely and ridiculously in love with her former sister-in-law's brother all those years ago, and yet it had.

So here she was. And here he was.

Being a total jerk.

"Bea, I'm fine."

"You're not fine," she snapped, looking at where he was sprawled out on the couch, appearing as if he had just run a marathon.

A stupid marathon of idiocy through a vineyard *on crutches*.

As soon as he had been able to get even a little bit mobile, he had been on his feet. And he had been trying to get back into what he called fighting shape.

Bea was actually shocked at just how close he was to at least looking like he was back in fighting shape. His muscles weren't nearly as diminished as she would have expected. His thighs still thick and muscular, his stomach flat, his chest broad, and his arms...

If anything could entice a person to write poetry about forearms, it would be Dane Parker's very loaded-looking guns.

"Take a pain pill," she said, standing there holding a glass of water out, with a pill flat in her other outstretched palm.

"I don't need a pain pill," he growled.

She wanted to punch his sculpted, handsome face. Right in the scar that he'd gotten in his accident. That still hadn't marred his beauty. No, it made him more roguish if anything. With his blue eyes and blond hair, he could easily trick someone into believing he was angelic.

The scar made it much clearer that he was more of a fallen angel.

"I'm going to put it in a piece of cheese and trick you into eating it," she said.

"I'm not a schnauzer," he said.

"Then stop acting like one." She didn't know if he was particularly acting like a schnauzer. Actually, in her experience schnauzers were much better patients. In her experience, basically everything was a better patient.

"Bea..."

"Dane," she said, perilously close to stamping her foot. "Lindy asked me to check in on you."

"Lindy needs to realize that just because she's my older sister doesn't mean that I'm not a grown-ass man."

"A grown-ass man who got trampled near to pieces because he insists on earning money by engaging in…a measuring contest for private parts."

Her cheeks heated intensely and she tried to keep her expression steady.

"For private parts?" he repeated.

"You heard me," she repeated, the glass of water and the pill still held determinedly out in front of her.

"I did hear you," he said. "I just didn't realize that you were in the third grade." He shook his head. "Private parts."

"Stop it," she said.

"I don't want to take a damn pain pill," he responded.

"Then drink some damn water." She slammed the glass down on the coffee table in front of him and stood there expectantly.

"I want a beer."

"Yeah, great," she said. "Drink a beer, don't hydrate."

"I'm fine," he said again. But he did sit up and lean forward, picking up the glass of water.

"You need to be careful with yourself," she said. "If you overdo it then it's entirely possible you'll set back some of your progress. You don't want to cause any internal bleeding or anything like that."

"I have been stuck in here, sitting on my ass, going on eight months. I'm over it."

Bea sighed and took a seat in the chair across the room from him. She really did feel for him. She did. A man like Dane was…almost impossible to contain. It was one of the things she admired so much about him. She always had.

She remembered vividly the first time she had met him. He'd looked so mature and compelling to her. A *man*.

He had been twenty, and when she looked back on pictures of him then, it surprised her how young he looked, since to her eleven-year-old self he had seemed extremely mature. He had such confidence and swagger, he was already riding professionally in the rodeo, and the stories he had told had been…amazing.

Her parents had hated him on sight. They'd hated everything about the woman that their oldest son, Damien, had chosen to marry, including her family. Trailer trash, that was what her mother had labeled them. Social climbing gold digger had been her father's take.

Lindy had tried. She'd done her best to fit in and please her future in-laws, but Dane… He was every inch who he was. And nothing more.

And Lindy had made it abundantly clear that her brother was part of her life. They didn't have a great relationship with their mother, and Lindy had stood firm with Damien on the inclusion of Dane at holidays and birthdays.

For Bea it had been…

He had been an instant obsession.

Bea had always felt like an outsider in her family. And there was something about the way Dane inhabited his skin that had made her want to get closer to him, and made her envy him all at the same time. Over the years that had…morphed. Into an extremely sincere and fatal-feeling crush.

A crush that was so abundantly and clearly futile it was painful. It had been easy to pretend that maybe there had been hope. Especially when Lindy and Damien had divorced.

Maybe it was a strange way to look at it, but she had been partly convinced that one reason Dane had so resolutely seen her as a younger sister was because he was her brother's brother-in-law. They were sort of family by marriage, and she had imagined that it kept her in a strange protected bubble.

With the divorce, she had been worried that it might mean she would never see him anymore, but given the nature of Lindy and Damien's divorce...

Her brother was a cheating louse. And in the years since, she had done what she could to have a relationship with him. Particularly since he and his new wife had a baby, and that baby was Bea's niece.

But Lindy had been in her life since she'd been a little girl, and she felt just as much like a sister to her as Damien felt like a brother. She hadn't been able to shake that connection just because they weren't legally sisters anymore.

And that meant that she did still see Dane. Almost as much as she had before. When he passed back through town, he would always join them for dinner, often making a point of saying hi.

But these past months...she'd seen him more than she ever had. And his disinterest in her could not have been made more apparent.

She had spent a goodly amount of time physically caring for him. And he was...unmoved.

During Christmas the previous month he'd been downright cantankerous when she'd attempted to get him to join a dinner that Lindy had thrown right there at the winery for family and friends.

And if he felt...anything special for her at all he would have been there.

She knew, because she would basically walk across broken glass for him. Crawl across it maybe even. Do the Electric Slide across broken glass.

Really, she would do a lot of things across broken glass for him.

He wouldn't even take a pain pill for her.

"Have you thought about taking that job at Get Out of Dodge that Wyatt offered you?"

He flicked a glance at her, those blue eyes sending an all-too-familiar shiver through her body.

"It isn't my goal to work on another man's land."

"He's your brother-in-law," Bea pointed out. "And may I say a trade up from the last one."

Dane snorted. "No argument from me. I like Wyatt, he's a decent guy. I mean, once I got over the fact that I knew way too much about him and his past exploits to be entirely comfortable with him sleeping with my sister, I could acknowledge he was a good guy."

"He's not just sleeping with your sister," Bea said, not quite sure how she managed to keep her face from catching on fire. "He's married to her."

She'd rather never talk about anyone sleeping with *anyone* around Dane.

"Yeah, so was your brother. He still cheated."

"Wyatt won't cheat," Bea said.

"You think you're a good judge of that kind of thing?"

She thought about it for a moment. The fact of the

matter was, Bea had absolutely no experience with men. But she had a fair amount of experience watching people. She was the kind of person who blended easily into the background. The person at the party who would be in the corner on her hands and knees making friends with the dog instead of chatting with people. And that meant she had a lot of time to form opinions.

All growing up she had moved—reluctantly—in fairly rarefied circles. At least by the standards of Logan County. Her family was wealthy and consequently she had spent a decent amount of time around powerful men. And then there was her mother. Who had never been faithful, not through all the years of her marriage. Bea had quite a few opinions about cheaters, in actual fact.

"Damien is spoiled," Bea said. "He blames all of his problems on other people, and he doesn't know how to be told no. He also gets tunnel vision and thinks he's the most important person in the world. He can't even remember there's another person when he's in one of those moments. Wyatt… He's different. Totally different. And he waited a long time to get married. I think because he was waiting till he could be the best kind of husband. So yeah, I think I know."

"Well, your vote of confidence means a lot."

"Why do I get the feeling you're being sarcastic?"

"Because I am." Dane shook his head. "Your problem is that you've never met a stray you didn't like. You're too giving."

That made her want to choke him. He acted like she was a child, and she was not a child.

Bea clucked her tongue. "You're right about that. I

haven't ever met a stray I didn't like. There are no bad animals, Dane. Animals want to be fed, safe and warm. Animals are only interested in having basic needs met. And if you do that, they love you. Humans on the other hand are innately selfish and some of them are bad."

"Some animals are bad."

"They aren't," she insisted.

"What about sharks?"

"If you don't go into the water looking like a fish you'll never have a problem with sharks."

Dane shook his head. "I'm not debating the finer points of animals and their morality with you."

"No, but you are doing a great job of changing the subject. Are you going to take the job with Wyatt?"

"I don't have anything else to do."

"I imagine you can keep on doing work here." Lindy hadn't asked Bea to broach the topic about the job, but Bea knew it was weighing on her. And Bea wanted to help. Lindy wanted Dane to take the job at Get Out of Dodge in part because she didn't want Dane to further isolate himself over at the winery, and in other part because she was afraid that without supervision he was going to work himself too hard, whereas Wyatt could tailor the tasks he meted out to his brother-in-law as needed.

Dane did not look at all cheered by the prospect of working on his brother-in-law's ranch.

She supposed a man like him… She could understand that.

Bea just wanted to live. She loved her little cabin in the woods, loved the sanctuary that she had carved out for herself and her animals. She had learned, when she was a little girl, to keep her head down, to avoid the notice of her parents so that she wouldn't draw any negative attention to herself.

They could never understand why she was happier outside than inside the high-polished marble halls of their home in the winery. Could never understand why she didn't like the parties that they threw, or why she didn't get along with the acceptable children of the families they preferred to spend time with.

But she didn't.

Her solution was to be sunny, cheerful and generally out-of-the-way. If she was going to be unacceptable, she found it was best to be unacceptable in an unobtrusive way.

As an adult, she had a few friends, and she had her family—both by blood and marriage, though the marriage was dissolved now—and she loved them very much. They saw her behavior as somewhat haphazard and often in need of commentary. She smiled and then did what she wanted anyway.

No one ever seemed to notice.

Dane wasn't like that. He was a man who had forged his own way. His own destiny. He didn't like easy, and he didn't like unobtrusive. She admired that about him, even if it made her want to beat him over the head with one of the heavy hardbound books that were stacked on the coffee table.

"Just think about it, Dane," she said. "Lindy is worried about you. And I understand that it irritates you that she's…" She tried to choose her words carefully. She was getting frustrated and she was forgetting that Dane was like any other wounded animal.

She just had to figure out how to handle him with the kind of care that he needed. And she had an idea.

"Do this for her," she said. "She's worried about you. And if you… If you do this, she's likely to ease up. Eventually, you'll be back on your feet and…"

The look he gave her was skeptical at best. "Right. Suddenly, you're very concerned for Lindy's well-being."

"I am. We are…family, kind of," Bea said, almost choking on the words, because if Lindy was family, then Dane was family, and she had just never felt familial to him. "And I care."

The fact of the matter was, whether or not she felt sisterly toward him didn't change the fact that he felt brotherly toward her. And right about now she wasn't above using that to her advantage. There had to be some advantage in it. Because there wasn't in any other corner of that painful reality.

"And I appreciate that," he said, his tone so gentle and placating it got her hackles up yet again.

He talked to her like she was a kid. The little sister she didn't want to be to him.

But if she was gaining ground, she couldn't really afford to be tetchy about it right now.

"Great. Then appreciate it by doing something for your sister. She's been letting you stay here…"

"I don't really like to rehash all the charity my sister has given me. I have my own money. I can take care of myself."

"No one doubts that. But this house is empty, and there's no reason for you not to be in it."

"You could be in it," he said.

"I don't want to be in it," Bea said.

"I've never understood why you had such an aversion to this place."

"Probably for the same reason you have an aversion to working on another man's land. There are just some things that don't suit us, right?"

"I expect so."

"So will you do this? Will you help Lindy feel more at ease?"

"Sure. If it will get her off my back, then I'll do it."

He didn't say it, but she had a feeling that the unspoken words were: *if it will get you off my back, then I'll do it.*

Bea was nothing if not relentless, and she was not above using it to her advantage when the occasion called for it. She had been described as a dog with a bone on more than one occasion.

She really didn't find that as offensive as some people might. Dogs were loyal. Much more so than most humans.

"Thank you," she said, leaning forward, and without thinking, pressing her hand over the top of his and squeezing.

Their eyes locked, that startling blue punching a hole in her chest and leaving her breathless. Suddenly, that rough, masculine hand beneath hers felt like it was burning through her skin.

She jerked her hand away and rubbed it on her jeans, trying to make the feeling go away. She had made a mistake touching him. She was always making mistakes with him.

That initial startle in her chest was beginning to settle, and she looked at him clearly for the first time since. And saw that he was oblivious to the whole thing.

Because of course.

That simple touch had lit her on fire from the inside out, and he had felt nothing at all.

But hey, she had convinced him to take the job.

Maybe she wasn't like a little sister to him after all.

Maybe she was more like a faithful retriever.

That was even worse. Or at the very least it was the depressing same.

But she was helping him. And she supposed caring about anything else was silly.

Dane was getting better and that was what mattered.

Her feelings were a dead end. Dane didn't want her, and even if he did…it wasn't like she wanted to get married or anything like that. Not when she'd seen just how miserable marriage made people. Her feelings were pointless, and they were just going to have to stay buried. Like always.

DANE PARKER CURSED the pain that rolled through his body, as he pulled his truck into the driveway of Get Out of Dodge. This damned injury was the one thing he had never been able to use sheer force of will to push through.

Yet.

It made him a little bit sorry he hadn't taken the pain pill that Bea had given him last night.

Or, *tried* to give him.

But he was sick of it. Sick to death of the whole damned regimen. He just wanted to be up and on his feet. He wanted to find normal again.

It was becoming abundantly clear that normal was a hell of a long way off, and taking a pain pill and sliding into obscurity was only a reminder of that. A reminder he was in no way interested in.

He just wanted it to be over.

Bodies were a bitch.

But he was determined to make sure his was at least *his* bitch.

To the best of his ability, anyway. He got out of the truck and grimaced when his foot made contact with the uneven gravel drive. The impact, the slight twist in his ankle when the rock rolled beneath his boot… all things he would never have noticed before an angry bull had made it his mission to grind Dane's body into the arena dirt like powder.

He gritted his teeth, walking over to the house, the shooting pain going up his thigh, rattling around the screw that held his bones together enough to make a typical grown man cry.

Fortunately, he was something other than a typical grown man. He was a bull rider. And that meant he wasn't going to cry over a little bit of pain.

But all this silence, this stagnant existence…was worse than the pain.

He wanted that life again. That rush. The roar of the crowd and the hot pulse of adrenaline coursing through his veins.

He wasn't going to get any of that here.

He shoved his hands in his pockets, doing his best to shove his hand down as far as possible and discreetly offer some support to his compromised thigh muscle as he made his way up the stairs, using his other hand to cling tight to the railing. Lindy was going to ream him for not being on his crutches and he wasn't in the mood.

If he was going to talk to his brother-in-law about doing work, then he sure as hell wasn't going to show up looking like a damned cripple.

As soon as he reached the front door he pictured Bea again, standing there holding a pill in his face. Right now it was like the mirage of an oasis in the middle of the desert.

But a pain pill wasn't water, and he didn't have to give in. Because pain wasn't going to kill him.

It was just pain.

Still, when he knocked on the door, he did it maybe a little bit more firmly than was strictly necessary. But it helped a little of the burning feeling in his chest, so maybe it had been necessary.

It took a couple of minutes, but his sister jerked the door open, looking disheveled and red cheeked. The sight knocked him back on his heels, or would have if he could afford to let go of the railing he was bracing himself on. Lindy was never red cheeked. And she was never disheveled.

It didn't take a genius to figure out that she had been messing around with her husband.

"Hey," she said, looking breathless, smiling. Then, her smile quickly faded away as she looked him up and down. "Dane…"

"I don't need a lecture," he said.

"Then why do you do things that are so lecture-able?"

"I can walk," he said, brushing past her and limping into the house, forcing himself to walk as straight as possible as he made his way into the kitchen and sat down at the table. He tried to keep the look of relief off his face as he sat. He would be okay by tomorrow. It galled him to admit it, but he really had overdone it yesterday. Apparently, being pissed at injuries didn't make them lie down and behave.

"Yes," she said dryly. "Clearly."

"You need to quit sending poor Bea to do your dirty work," he said.

"I didn't send Bea to do anything," Lindy said.

"Right," he said dryly. "So, you don't have her babysitting me because she's close and you're living all the way over here."

Lindy rolled her eyes. "No," Lindy said. "Honestly, Dane, it's a good thing your head is so hard, because I think it kept you from sustaining more serious injuries than you might have. But you know, she cares about you."

"Right," Dane said.

"Nobody *makes* Bea do anything," Lindy continued.

"Sure," he said, sounding as unconvinced as he felt.

Bea was…sweet. The kid sister he'd never had, really. He had always liked her, from the moment he had first met her when Lindy had started dating Bea's older brother, Damien. He could not say the same for Damien, who he'd always felt a little bit of skepticism toward. Had a hell of a lot of guilt when it came to everything that had gone down later. Because he was the one who had introduced Damien to Lindy in the first place.

Damien had done a great job managing Dane's career in the rodeo in the early years. Had gotten him a lot of good endorsement deals, and had helped him make a decent amount of money.

But that was all business connections. And just because he was a good guy when he was out with the boys and a good manager didn't mean he made a good husband. Didn't mean he was actually a good man.

That had been a lesson learned the hard way.

Of course, the two of them had been married for ten years—it wasn't like it had all gone bad right away. No, it had taken a while.

Still, Dane felt a certain measure of responsibility for it all. Like he had somehow let it happen.

Well, he had.

"Look," Lindy said. "I know she seems soft." Her words jerked his thoughts back to Bea. "But you know, she would heal a creature whether or not it wanted to be, and I have a feeling that you fall right under that heading."

"Great. Now I'm a wounded creature."

"I call it like I see it," Lindy said. "Anyway, why are you here?"

"I'm here to take that job offer," Dane said.

"Good," Lindy said, not looking overly happy.

"Wait a minute, now you're mad about this?"

"To be perfectly honest with you I was hoping that you would come and tell me that you couldn't take the job because you needed more rest."

"Why did you offer then?"

She sighed heavily. "Wyatt wanted me to."

"I've been resting for eight months. I can't take any more of this."

"But what if it's what you need in order to heal right?"

"I'm about to lose my damned mind sitting in that house by myself. So, either you have me do the work here or I am going to be doing it at the winery. But I have to do something."

He hated this. Not just the sitting still. The obscurity. The silence.

He'd spent a lifetime making something of himself. Making himself matter.

And now he was just down-and-out. Washed-up. And any number of words that lived in his worst nightmares.

"Okay," she said. "I mean, that is why Wyatt and I talked about having you here. Because I knew that you had to be going nuts."

"Lindy," he said, suddenly feeling weary. "You know how we grew up. With nothing. A damned lot of nothing. We've both managed to make something of our lives. Of ourselves. How would you feel if you just suddenly couldn't... If nothing worked anymore. If you lost all the power that you had to feel any kind of control in your life."

"I'd probably be as big of a pain in the ass as you are," she said, her tone surprisingly gentle. He didn't trust Lindy when she sounded gentle. It wasn't like her. "But just because I understand," she continued, "doesn't mean it's the best thing for you."

He had to disagree with that. Because Lindy couldn't talk about what the best thing was, since she had never spent eight months restricted like he had. He was used to being able to do whatever the hell he wanted. He left

home at eighteen and had done just that for the past
thirteen years.

Had it been only thirteen years? It felt like a whole
lifetime. And the past eight months felt like another. An
eternity. In hell, as far as he was concerned.

"Are you going to let me work here or not?"

"Yes," Lindy said. Her face softened, and that was
just as frightening and off-putting as when her tone
had gentled. Because it really did make him feel like
the sad schnauzer he had told Bea he wasn't last night.
A pathetic creature to be pitied.

It reminded him of the boy he'd been. Before he'd
found a way to make glory cover up the emptiness inside of him, the cheers of the crowd drowning out the
hideous crying and pleading that had come out of his
weak, boyish body the day his father had driven off
for the last time.

If you make it onto TV, maybe I'll see you there.

But I love you.

And there had been no response to that at all.

That wasn't who he was, not anymore. He wasn't a
man anyone walked away from.

At least he hadn't been. Now...what the hell was he?

"Good," he said. "I assume that you want me to talk
to your husband about what I might be doing? I also
know he's here because it was very obvious to me that
you were in the middle of something when I showed
up."

Lindy's face turned bright red. "No, we weren't."

He shook his head. "Believe me, having been caught
in my fair share of compromising situations, I know
when I've caught someone else."

"You're such a heathen," she said crisply.

Not lately. But he didn't say that out loud.

That was the other thing. Eight months of hospital-ization, wheelchair confinement, surgery, screws, halos sticking out of his leg…

He hadn't gotten laid in over eight months.

A phenomenon that had not occurred ever in his life from the moment he had first become sexually active.

Dane Parker did not go to bed alone unless he chose to.

And he did not often choose to.

There hadn't even been any opportunity in the past six months.

And frankly, with things like they were…

Physical labor was his best bet right now. Anything to make this time pass. Anything to get him back out there. He was so close to being off his crutches perma-nently. And after that…well, after that he'd be back in the saddle. Then back on the bull.

There wasn't another option.

"Yes, I'll go get Wyatt," she said.

"You know this is only temporary," he said. "Until things go back to normal."

"Dane…"

Dane ground his teeth together. The look of pity on his sister's face bothered him more than any of the physical pain in his body ever could. That look like he might be out of touch. Like she might know exactly what was happening with his bones, better than he did.

"It'll be fine." No argument was made, because his tone had left no room for one. Lindy could be fierce, no denying it. But they were cut from the same stubborn-ass cloth, and he knew his sister knew well enough when there wasn't going to be a discussion.

"Okay," she said, turning away again. "It's just temporary."

Because ever since he'd picked himself up off the ground after watching his dad drive off into the distance, he'd made a decision. A decision that he'd get what he wanted, come hell or high water. And in all the years since it had been true. From football glory in high school to the rodeo later on.

Bright lights and on TV, and look at him now, Dad.

Dammit all, this wouldn't be any different.

CHAPTER TWO

DANE MANAGED TO get himself down to Get Out of Dodge and reporting for duty by 6:00 a.m. It was no mean feat. His bones did not like to work when it was that cold out. Which just pissed him off. He didn't know what to do with a body that wouldn't bend to his will. He wasn't used to that. Hell no.

When he had decided that he wanted to train to be a bull rider, he'd done it. Whatever he wanted to do, he'd always been able to. From playing football in high school, to transitioning to rodeo work.

It was one of the very few things in the world he could control. He wasn't made for studying, was never going to get the kind of grades that would have earned him a scholarship to get into college. He was never going to be able to change his stars that way.

But physically, physically he had been able to achieve whatever he wanted.

He'd been able to excel.

He'd been able to seduce.

His body was the most valuable tool that he possessed.

And now it was broken.

But he was at work. And he was on time. It was the most insultingly simple goal that he ever set in his life.

Still, he walked into the mess hall, ignoring the shooting pain in his leg, and looked around. His sister and Wyatt weren't there, but Wyatt's brother Grant and his fiancée, McKenna, were there, as was Luke Hollister, surprisingly. Luke had bought his own ranch more than a year ago, and typically didn't put work in at Get Out of Dodge anymore. Though, he had grown up on the ranch, and was a part of the Dodge family, not by blood, but by choice. So, it wasn't too surprising, Dane supposed.

He tipped his hat and began to walk toward the table. "Good morning," he said.

"Good morning," Grant said, grinning.

It was a good thing to see Grant Dodge smile. And had been unusual for a long damned time. After he lost his wife years ago, he'd settled into a pretty firm, serious space. But since McKenna, that had changed.

Dane had never put much stock in the idea of romance, or long-term relationships. But he couldn't deny that Lindy's marriage to Wyatt had changed her for good. And he also couldn't deny that Grant meeting McKenna had changed some things in his life.

Of course, he couldn't ignore the fact that it was their first long-term relationships that had broken them to begin with.

That about said it all, Dane figured.

He walked over to get himself a cup of coffee, and the door opened behind him.

In came Bennett—Grant and Wyatt's younger brother—his wife, Kaylee, and their son, Dallas.

Now, the only person that was missing was Jamie Dodge, the youngest, and the only girl.

"What's going on?"

He didn't expect to see Luke or Bennett here at the start of a workday. Much less, Bennett's entire clan.

"We have a big project going on today," Grant said. "Completely refencing the south pasture. Which means all hands on deck."

"Great," Dane said.

He was eager to get moving, and if moving meant a huge-ass project, all the better.

He wondered if he should be taking pain pills like Bea had suggested. But if he had done that, he wouldn't have been able to drive himself. And what was he going to do? Limp down to Bea's cabin at the crack of dawn and ask her to drive him like he was a dependent?

Already, Bea was taking care of him to a degree he found uncomfortable, and if it were anyone else he would have told them to back off.

But Bea was not anyone else. Bea was her own sort of creature. Strong and stubborn, all wrapped in sunshine. Sometimes all that light hurt his eyes. And he did his fair share of growling at her. But she just shined him on, cheerfully going about his care and keeping.

When she wasn't lecturing him.

He poured himself a black coffee and walked as straight as he could over to the table, ignoring the pain that was…everywhere.

His every movement seemed to list his extensive injuries, loud and clear. The broken femur that had left his thigh open, his artery pouring blood onto the arena dirt. The shattered knee that was full of bolts and screws. Broken ribs that had taken a shot at his liver and left it bruised. Severe concussion. The hoof he'd taken to the cheek that had laid his face open.

The bull had basically used him as a welcome mat, wiping his feet all the hell over him, and stomping a few times for good measure.

That was one of the more shocking things about it. He'd had...dammit, hundreds of rides, where nothing happened.

He'd been thrown before. He'd been stomped before, it just hadn't resulted in any serious injuries. So it was a crazy-ass thing that all it had taken was one throw that had gone wrong. One bull that refused to be lured by the bullfighters.

And he'd gone all out on Dane.

And left him with this...shell that he walked around in. It didn't feel like him. In his head, he was Dane Parker, champion bull rider. But this was not Dane Parker's body. Hell no.

There was breakfast, and the small talk was kept to a minimum. Dane was grateful for the eggs and bacon. Frankly, he was not eating like this at the house. But he didn't want to tell Lindy that. Basically, he didn't want to complain about anything, because he didn't want anyone babysitting him. And if sometimes he got up and drank beer for breakfast...that was his business. He was taking care of himself, and that meant he would do it how he saw fit.

But the bacon...that was welcome.

Bea would come and cook for him. He knew that.

He didn't *want* Bea to come and cook for him.

She already doted on him, and as Lindy had put it, it was much like she was caring for any other wounded creature. Well, really, it was like having another sister right there.

During breakfast, Wyatt and Lindy walked into the mess hall, all smiles and holding hands. Honestly, if he weren't so happy for his sister he might gag.

"Too good to eat with the riffraff?" Dane asked.

"We have an agreement," Wyatt said. "I have to cook her breakfast. I can't pawn it off."

"He has to cook bacon for me. It has to be his bacon."

"Stop there," Dane said. "This is edging into double entendre territory, and I don't want any part of that. I am a wounded man. Weak. Compromised. That could kill me."

Lindy smiled sweetly. "If you're too weak, then perhaps you shouldn't work today."

He didn't respond to that. He just treated her to a look that would have made lesser men and beasts tremble. But Lindy was neither man nor beast, and she certainly didn't tremble beneath the angry gaze of her younger brother.

Jamie showed up a while later, and after they finished breakfast, they piled into a couple of different trucks, heading out toward the south pasture. His every attempt at grabbing a box of tools, or roll of fencing, was met by someone else grabbing it from right in front of him.

By the time lunch rolled around, he didn't know what pissed him off more, the fact that he was relegated to doing fiddly wire work, attaching the fence to the posts, or the fact that it actually hurt to do such menial work.

Dane opened up a cooler and produced a sandwich, wrapped up tight in plastic wrap, and a can of Coke and sat down as gingerly as he could on the tailgate. Wyatt sat across from him, on the other open tailgate, while Bennett stood, Dallas sat in the dirt alongside Luke and Jamie crouched against the fence line, hunched over her sandwich like a feral animal on a kill.

"You going to let me do some work?" he asked, directing that at Wyatt, keeping his tone low.

"You're working," Wyatt said.

"I'm hardly doing anything," Dane said, keeping his tone conversational. "And you know it."

"I have to keep your sister from killing me," Wyatt said, as if that was an explanation of some kind. "That's my ultimate goal in life. You know, along with keeping her happy."

"I appreciate that," Dane responded. "But she's not my keeper. And neither are you."

"There's no harm in going easy on yourself when you've had an injury. You were in a wheelchair a couple of months ago. Be reasonable about what you can expect from yourself right now."

"Bullshit. You would be reasonable if this were you?" Dane ignored his aches and pains and took a bite of his sandwich.

"Hell no. You and I both know that rodeo riders aren't built for reason. But I'm not in your position. And that means that I get to hand down advice from on high."

"I don't want your advice."

"We're brothers," Wyatt said, throwing the word around easily. "That means I have some advice to give, and you should listen."

Dane wanted to throw a punch, but right about now

he knew he'd just get his ass beat. So he opted for being a total and complete jerk. "You're not the first brother I've had by marriage, Wyatt. I didn't care much for the first one. Don't make me disown you too."

Wyatt chuckled, taking a bite of his own sandwich. "You won't. You won't because I'm good to your sister, and you know it."

"Sure. But that doesn't mean I can't hate you."

"You won't."

"It isn't that I don't appreciate the job," he said. "But I don't need you to babysit me. I can do more than just hammer grommets into the wire."

Wyatt shrugged and took another bite of the sandwich. "If you feel great at the end of today, then I'll listen to you next time. But for now, we're going to do it my way. Because this is the thing, Dane, if you don't want me to act like your brother, then I'm going to act like your boss. And that means regardless of the reason that I've assigned you a certain task, you have to do it."

"Motherfucker," Dane said.

Wyatt cleared his throat. "Sister."

Dane shot him an evil look. "I will kill you."

"Then you won't have a job, and your sister will be widowed. She'll be mad."

"She'd get over it."

A companionable silence settled between them. Somehow, threats of grievous injury had made things not quite so tense. He didn't know how that worked. Only that it did.

Or maybe it wasn't the threats. Maybe it was the surroundings. The vivid green of the pasture, fading into the rich grove of evergreens that had claimed space on the sides of the imposing mountains that stood sentry around the ranch.

"How are things?" Dane asked. "I mean, how does she like living here?"

"She seems to like it. I do have to make the bacon though. You could always ask her yourself."

"Yeah." But if he asked Lindy that, Lindy would ask how he was doing. And she would get that look on her face. And however much he thought Wyatt managing his activities was a load of crap, it would only be worse if Lindy was hanging around, or had any reason to get extra concerned.

"It was tough," Wyatt said suddenly. "Accepting that it was time for me to retire. But, there was just a point where…I didn't think my body could handle being rattled around one more time. I was so damn jacked up that there was just… Hell, man. I was just about done. I knew that if I got jarred one more time I wasn't going to be able to walk straight for the rest of forever. I didn't like having to accept that. You spend all those years throwing yourself around on the back of those animals and telling yourself you're invincible. Having to face the fact that you're just a guy in his thirties is a bummer."

"We're not the same," Dane said. "Because I probably already won't walk straight ever again. But that doesn't mean I can't ride. Hell, if I can get back on, at this point, there is no reason not to. I'm screwed. I'm not walking away from this job without permanent damage. Might as well go all in."

"You think you can?"

"Why the hell not?"

"That was a bad accident," Wyatt said, as if Dane wasn't sitting there made of the pain from that accident.

"Yeah, no kidding. But you know what else? I don't have to *walk* straight to be able to ride. So, I figure… Give it some time. Maybe even a whole year…"

Wyatt sighed. "Okay. Let's start with this. Let's start with the fence. If you feel fine at the end of the day I'll back off."

"Good."

"And then you can get back to me tomorrow and tell you how you actually feel. And we'll make a new plan from there."

Wyatt shoved the last bit of his sandwich into his mouth and brushed his hands off on his jeans. It took every last ounce of Dane's strength not to flip his brother-in-law the middle finger.

Wyatt thought because he was a couple of years older than him that he knew everything. But he didn't know how stubborn Dane was, not yet. But he would.

Hell yeah, he would.

BEA RETURNED FROM her shift at Valley Veterinary with a mission. Bennett Dodge, her boss, had told her he'd found out about a bunch of chickens that needed a place to stay, and Bea was more than willing to accommodate if she could.

Of course, when she walked into her house, she realized that Evan, her increasingly chubby raccoon, had managed to jimmy the window to her living area open and slip his fat-bottomed self inside, and she could only cringe at the horror she knew might await her.

Her little cabin was cozy, and as neat as it could be,

considering it was a very small space that had to contain supplies both for her and her eclectic and ever-rotating array of animals.

But this particular animal was…well, his own animal.

There were a few open cabinets, and some Cheerios on the floor, along with a neatly shredded box. But it was what she might find in her bedroom that truly frightened her.

Evan had a particular fondness for underwear.

And if Evan could steal her entire collection of panties, Evan would. The little raccoon she had rescued all those months ago had seemed benign then. But he was a giant pain in the butt now.

Still, she loved him, and she wouldn't ever have things any different. It was just…

Evan in her house unsupervised was never the ideal scenario.

She stepped around the Cheerios, crunching a couple under her feet as she stepped through the small kitchen and living area. Then she pushed open her bedroom door the rest of the way. "Evan," she hissed.

There was no movement, and no response, but the drawer to her dresser was partway open.

"Evan!"

She heard a rustling sound, and she gritted her teeth, walking over to her closet and pulling the door open. There she discovered Evan, with a stash of Cheerios and two pairs of underwear.

"You're a naughty raccoon, Evan," she said, reaching down and stealing her panties back. She would have to take them over to the main house with the rest of her laundry. She loved animals, but even she had some limits. And, wearing underwear that had been handled by a raccoon was that limit.

Evan was completely unashamed, and he remained where he was in her closet, happily shoving Cheerios into his whiskered face. He paused just long enough to look up at Bea, his nose twitching.

"I hope you think about what you've done," she said, shaking her head and reaching down, scooping him up and depositing him back in the main area of her house, closing her bedroom door behind her. Evan wobbled over to the Cheerios on the floor, and she decided that she was just going to have to give up that battle. The cereal was the raccoon's now. There would be no reclaiming it.

She opened up her fridge and found the prepared portion of food that she had for Evan—today it was gut-loaded crickets—setting it down on the floor in his spot. In defiance of her, he continued to eat the Cheerios until none remained.

"It does not have as much nutrition as your actual food. I hope you know."

He was unimpressed.

"You're supposed to be on a special diet," she said. "Balance, Evan!"

He ignored her, sniffing the ground and licking up crumbs.

She sighed and went across the room to look at her terrariums. The blue-bellied skink she had found looking poorly a couple of weeks ago seemed fine now, and she couldn't really figure out what had been wrong with him. But rest and access to food seemed to have solved most of his issues. Pretty soon, she would go ahead and release him in some wetlands.

She didn't have as many animals right now as she liked to, didn't have as many as she ultimately hoped to have someday.

She missed Mabel terribly sometimes. The old dog had been her constant companion from the time she was sixteen. A balm for her terrible loneliness from being the odd one out in her family. The weird girl at school. Having lost the one person she'd thought might understand her.

But given the amount of time she spent working, plus, at this point, having Evan, there was just no real fair way to have a dog in her life at the moment.

Still, Evan and the assorted reptiles and amphibians were okay for now.

She looked in on Tara, her box turtle, who was missing a leg and would not be headed back out to a wild pond any time soon.

And that reminded her, she needed to go out and check the state of her coop.

She had never used the chicken coop, which was next to the cabin, so she didn't know if it was actually ready to contain chickens.

But Bennett had said he didn't know of anyone who would be willing to take ten chickens on short notice. Except for Bea.

Bea was willing to take any animal, on any notice, but the question would be whether or not she had the facility.

She looked in the box of Cheerios on the floor, then thought better of touching it, and reached into her cereal cabinet and pulled out an alternate box, opening up the Honey Bunches of Oats and snacking on them mindlessly as she wandered outside, heading toward the coop.

The ground was soft, moss and leaves carpeting the floor. With all that moisture, the dampness was a potential problem she could see now. She winced, looking at the wood that propped up the old coop. It was… badly compromised. A bit damaged.

It would need a lot of fixing up to take the chickens.

She took her phone out and dialed Bennett's number. "How long until the chickens have to be moved?"

She was met with a chuckle on the other end. "Hi, Beatrix," he said. "I think you have about seven or eight days until the chickens would be headed your direction. Is there something wrong?"

"Nothing is wrong. I just have to mount a full-scale chicken coop restoration project."

"If it's too difficult…"

"No," she said. "I would love to have them. I've been wanting chickens. Really."

And she had a new rule about limiting herself to rescues only, because otherwise she would be overrun. It felt reasonable. And if an entire passel of rescue chickens happened your way, you had to seize on it. Because rescue chickens were a rare and valuable thing.

At least, she assumed so.

"Well, as long as that's all right."

"It's more than all right," she said. "It'll be great."

"All right," he said. "I'll talk to you later."

"Bye," she said. She looked around at the coop and tapped her cheek. It wasn't like she couldn't do the renovation herself. She was pretty handy with that kind of thing. Though, her work was much more determined amateur that it was skilled worker.

And mostly, the big concern was keeping up with the classes she was taking online for her vet tech certificate.

But she didn't want to say anything about that to Bennett. Kaylee had been the one who had originally encouraged her to take work at the clinic. But she wasn't completely sure if a full-time position at Valley Veterinary was what she wanted, and she didn't know how to articulate her feelings on the matter. She was afraid that if she did… Well, everyone would do what they *did* to her.

It would be *Advise Beatrix Hour.* Everyone would give their two cents on what she should do when and with what, and what was practical. Like she didn't understand how the world worked at all.

It wasn't fair for her to be irritated about that since her method of getting through life had always been to keep her head down and quietly do what she wanted while smiling serenely and making no waves.

But the constant deluge of advice was starting to grate, and she had no idea when that had started to change.

Whatever the reason, she didn't want anyone interfering. She didn't want Bennett or Kaylee feeling like they needed to check in with her or offer a hand. She was going to do it on her own.

She heard the sound of a truck engine rumbling up the road, and could only think of one thing.

Dane was home.

She picked her way through the damp moss, ignoring the way the dew splashed up and soaked into her jeans as she wandered up to the driveway. She cut across the gravel, heading the most direct way to the house.

She had grown up on this property, she knew every pathway and passage, every hollow and hiding place.

She had spent most of her time outdoors on this land. She loved it. With all of her soul. It was part of her family legacy.

Except… It wasn't really. In many ways. Not hers.

But that was a whole kettle of fish she wasn't even going to look in right now. Anyway, it didn't matter. Because Lindy had gotten the land in her divorce from Bea's brother, and now it was…well, much more shared between everyone.

It was hard for her to imagine what it would have been like if Damien had ended up with the place. He probably would have gotten rid of the little cabin down by the river, the one that she called home.

The cabin was her refuge. It had been lodging for winery employees for a while, Liam Donnelly, first. And then Michael Fulsome, who she tried not to think of because it only made her feel sad and abandoned all over again.

But once he'd gone, the cabin had become a refuge and a rebellion for her. She'd moved in at sixteen and had loved it from the moment she had.

It was spare. It had a woodstove, and a very meager shower. The toilet worked.

That was all Bea needed.

She had a feeling that this was another thing that made her family and friends find her mysterious or even hapless. That she chose to live how she did. The deliberateness of the choice—of all her choices—seemed lost on them.

But then, she'd never bothered to try to make it otherwise.

There was something about that little space that was completely under her control that made her feel…safe in a way the large, sprawling home at the winery she'd grown up in had never felt.

There were so many places to hide in a house like that. So many places to hide secrets.

The cabin was like a den, and she loved it.

The feeling that she got when she approached the large house had changed over the past few years, and again over the past several months, with Dane living there. It was amazing how Dane's presence had wiped away years of childhood trepidation that she had associated with the place.

That house was where she'd first learned why she felt so wrong. Why she didn't feel like a Leighton. That house was where she'd had it underscored to her, again and again. That she was nothing but an obligation to Jamison Leighton.

A redheaded cuckoo in the nest.

One who hadn't even been wanted by her own, real, redheaded father.

A confirmation for her that no matter what, no matter who, there was something fundamentally unsticky about her as a person. People just seemed to detach from her so easily. Which made it that much more important for her to act as she did.

The way that she interacted with everyone—even her friends—was to often just let them talk even when she disagreed, so that she would never have to confront the rejection of her real heart.

Just thinking about it made her feel like hiding.

But now, Dane was in that house. And that made her heart swell with anticipation.

She came to the clearing, to the edge of the lawn, just as Dane got out of his truck.

When his foot connected with the ground, his face contorted with pain, and it was all Bea could do to keep herself from rushing after him. He wouldn't want that. He really, really wouldn't.

She waited a moment, hanging back, and as soon as he made his way into the house, she scampered on after him.

He had barely closed the front door behind him when she knocked. He jerked it open, his expression very carefully flat. "I'm fine," he said.

"I didn't ask," she responded, breezing in past him.

He shut the door behind her. "Well, you were going to ask."

Oh, he was obnoxious. "I wasn't," she insisted.

"Really?" He crossed his arms. "You had a personality transplant since the last time we spoke?"

"Mmm," she said. "A revelation."

"Go on."

"I hate you."

He arched a brow. "Really?"

The corner of her lips twitched as she saw his own do the same, amusement coursing through her as he fought not to smile.

"Yes," she said gravely. "I can't stand the sight of

you. I wouldn't care if you dropped dead right here in front of me."

"Beatrix, I have half a mind to do it just to prove that you're a liar." The way he looked at her, those eyes glittering with humor, made her stomach take a sharp drop and roll. It was exhilarating in a way. To talk to him this way.

What she knew about herself and Dane Parker was that it would never be…well, never what she'd dreamed it might be when she was young and silly, and didn't understand that men like him didn't fall for girls like her. There was a freedom in that.

A freedom that allowed her to enjoy this moment, without worrying what it might mean later.

"All right," he said. "What are you here for?"

"How was work?" She grinned broadly at him.

"Ridiculous," he said, heading toward the kitchen, trying as hard as he possibly could to conceal his limp. He was doing a terrible job.

"What do you need?" she asked.

He looked at her like he was going to argue, and then, the fight seemed to go out of him. "Beer."

"Go sit in the living room," she said, waving a hand.

"You don't have to ask me twice."

"Are you hungry?" She was. She might as well get something for him too.

"Is there something easy?" he called out.

"I'm sure there will be something."

She opened the fridge and took out one beer, and one Coke, then she began to rummage around for food. There was quite a bit in the way of leftovers that had been sent from the ranch. She figured the easiest would be reheating chili.

She set about to do just that, arranging two bowls of chili on a tray, along with the drinks, before heading back into the living room.

"Okay," she said. "Now you can tell me about your day."

"I thought you hated me."

"It has waned slightly in the past few moments. Tell me."

He groaned when he bit into the chili, and groaned again when he took a long drink of the beer. She just... watched him. Watched the way his lips closed around the bottle, the way his throat worked as he took a sip. She could not put words to the way he appealed to her. She couldn't explain it, couldn't justify it. But it was real. And it was strong. And it was quite unlike anything she'd ever felt for anyone else. She never really felt anything for anyone else. From the moment she'd met him he'd been her crush. It was just that over the years it had grown in intensity.

In physicality.

She swallowed hard. Then took a bite of her own chili.

"Wyatt is going too easy on me," he said.

"Really? Because you look like he hit you with a tire iron, and then kicked you in the knee screw."

Dane choked out a laugh at that. "He did not kick me in the knee screw."

"Well, that's how you look."

He set his spoon down and pushed his bowl back. And she wanted, so much, to lean forward and smooth the lines in his forehead out with her thumb. "I'm frustrated."

Everything in her softened. "You also just need time."

"I don't want time. And I don't want to work surrounded by a bunch of people who are…babysitting me."

She looked at Dane, at all that leashed energy. And she thought of Mabel. Her old dog. Dane would be unhappy to know he'd made her think of Mabel. But she was smart enough to keep it to herself.

Mabel had been a herding dog, and at the end of her life, a herding dog with no herd.

She'd had so much of a drive to do something, to be of use, and nothing to apply herself to.

Bea had consulted a trainer who had told her that she needed to give Mabel a job. Something simple. Something that the old girl could handle. Not taking care of herds of sheep, but just wandering the perimeter of the property. Something to keep her mind engaged, something to make her feel useful.

Dane needed to feel useful.

Dane needed a perimeter to walk. Something that would give him purpose without pushing him too hard.

"I have a proposition for you," she said.

"Go on," he said.

"I need some help. Around the cabin. Bennett just told me about a bunch of rescue chickens…"

He held his hand up. "No," he said. "That is not a thing."

"It *is* a thing."

He shook his head. "It isn't."

"I don't know what to tell you, Dane," she said, keeping her tone steady and very serious, "I have access to ten rescue chickens, and the fact that the rescue chickens *exist* suggests that rescue chickens are a real thing."

"I refuse," he said, shaking his head.

"With or without your refusal, the rescue chickens need a place to stay. And I need to get the chicken coop into shape. But I'm…"

She took a deep breath, and she made a very calculated decision. She needed Dane to feel useful. She needed him to feel like he was in charge of something. Not being watched over by her, by Lindy, by Wyatt. Anyone.

"I'm going back to school," she said. "Or I guess going to school for the first time of my own choice. And I just don't have time. I don't have time to repair the coop, keep up on my lessons, go to work at the clinic… I don't have time."

"I didn't know you were doing school."

"I haven't told anyone. And I don't want anyone to know. So this…this is going to be between us. I won't tell anyone that you're working extra, you don't tell anyone that I'm doing school stuff."

"Why don't you want anyone to know?"

"It's… I don't know. I don't know if…anyone would understand why I want it. I've never done anything like this before. Maybe I can't do it."

"Why wouldn't you be able to do it?"

"You know me. I never did very well in school. I'm a… I'm a daydreamer. I don't… It's hard for me. But this has been different. I'm doing courses online and it's going okay. But I can't get a chicken coop repaired and work, and take care of Evan…"

"Oh yeah, how is Evan?"

"He demolished a box of Cheerios earlier, but that's neither here nor there." She leaned forward. "Will you help me?"

"Bea…"

"For the chickens, Dane."

"I do not care about the chickens. But I'll help you, Bea."

His blue eyes connected with hers and she felt it, clear down to…well, to everywhere. He might not have agreed to take a pain pill for her. But he was willing to help her with this.

It mattered.

And for a moment she was going to let it matter far more than it actually did. She knew he was just being nice. She knew he was just doing what any older brother's former brother-in-law would do.

But it made her feel special. And that was close enough to what she really wanted to feel.

So she would take it.

CHAPTER THREE

BEA HAD PUT in a full day at Valley Veterinary, and was feeling tired, but satisfied. She didn't have to work at the clinic while she studied. She had more than enough money to cover her living expenses thanks to her trust fund, but she also felt she couldn't afford *not* to.

It gave her the opportunity to give practical application to the things she was studying. Although, practical application wasn't her issue.

She was good with animals. She had a natural affinity with them.

Of course, she didn't have experience with vaccinations, surgeries, or any of the technical things she was learning about. But later, when she was further along in the program, she would talk to Bennett about the possibility of doing some observations.

"I think Lindy is planning on having everyone over for dinner tonight," Kaylee said, as they began to lock up the facility. "Do you want to come?"

Bea hesitated. She probably needed to make sure that Evan wasn't wreaking havoc on her cabin. That window was another thing she needed to get fixed. She didn't mind having him in the house sometimes, but the fact that he had endless access was an issue. Still, if everyone was going to be there…

She hadn't seen her friend Jamie in a while, or her friend McKenna, who was now engaged to Grant Dodge.

She would pretend her excitement had nothing to do with the fact that Dane might be there. Particularly since he had put in a full day of work at the Dodge ranch today.

"Sure," she said, trying to sound casual. "I'd love to."

She followed Bennett and Kaylee until they forked off, heading back to their own house, probably to pick up Dallas, and she continued on toward Get Out of Dodge. Her heart fluttered, and she pressed her palm to her chest, breathing deeply as she stared out at the scenery, the gently curving two-lane road winding through the trees.

She didn't need to be fluttery and ridiculous over Dane. She saw him every day right now.

When she had been younger... Well, when she had gone a couple of months at a time without seeing him, the physical response to his presence had always been intense. Her heart would slam against her chest, like there was an angry bull in there, trying to kick its way out.

It wasn't that bad when he'd been around for a while.

More butterflies than angry bulls. But there was still a reaction. And for the life of her, she couldn't do anything to eliminate it entirely.

In many ways, she wasn't bothered by it.

She enjoyed the feeling. She liked being with him.

It was just...

It was good as long as she didn't get mired in the impossibility of it. And wanting it to be more than it was.

If she could just enjoy being around him, and not worry about the future, then everything was fine.

She pulled onto the ranch property, and down the gravel road that led to the main house. Jamie Dodge was sitting on the porch of the expansive log home, her feet kicked out in front of her.

Bea parked and got out. "Hi," she said, bounding up the steps toward her friend.

Jamie smiled. "Hi. I didn't realize you were coming tonight."

"Kaylee just invited me. I didn't realize there was dinner."

"It was impromptu. There were leftovers from one of the guest dinners, and Lindy wanted to get rid of them all with the family." Jamie hesitated for a minute. "Plus, Dane was looking really tired by the end of work today and Lindy was worried. I think she wants to keep an eye on him."

Jamie was always hesitant to mention Dane around Bea, which was uncharacteristic for Jamie in all other things, since Jamie never shied away from anything. But with Dane it was like she never wanted to bring up the topic at all. Bea hadn't had a lot of friends growing up. She had always preferred the company of animals to people, but even she knew it was a little bit strange not to talk about crushes and things with a friend. But she didn't know if Jamie was averse to the topic in general, or if it had something to do with the fact that Bea gave off the sense that she didn't want to discuss Dane.

Or maybe it was Jamie's own lack of experience with men.

And Bea didn't especially want to talk about him.

Because the problem was in terms of practicality—it was a crush. A thing that wouldn't go anywhere, ever.

But in terms of her emotions...

It felt real. Like something fragile and sacred, in a weird way. The only place her feelings for Dane lived was inside her and the idea of talking about it with someone, giggling, or whatever it was you were supposed to do, didn't appeal to Bea at all.

"Is he okay?" Bea asked, keeping her tone low.

"Just in pain," Jamie said. "I've watched Wyatt have a lot of minor injuries over the years. Limp around for a few weeks. This is just nothing like that. It's terrible."

"I know," Bea said. Silence fell between them. "Have you started work with the Daltons yet?"

Jamie had taken a job over at another ranch, doing rehabilitation and training with retired rodeo horses.

"Not yet," Jamie said. "Wyatt is still being an obstinate tool about it. He has issues with Gabe, and I don't blame him. But, I'm a little bit offended that he doesn't think I can handle myself around an asinine rodeo cowboy. I was literally raised with them."

"He's an older brother," Bea said. "They're like that. I mean, I hear."

The corner of Jamie's mouth tipped upward and she swept her dark braid back over her shoulder. "You have an older brother."

"Yes, but my older brother is...useless as an older brother."

Damien was so much older than her, she had never felt particularly close to him. But it was more than that. Sabrina was quite a bit older than Bea was too, and they were very different. But still, she loved her older sister.

Sabrina was always smooth, polished. The only time that had ever been untrue was when Liam Donnelly had broken her heart when she was seventeen, and she'd had a very public meltdown over it. But even that, Bea hardly remembered.

At least, at eleven, she hadn't been able to understand her sister's heartbreak. Not really.

She knew that age and personality didn't have anything to do with whether or not you felt close to your siblings. It was all about how much she wanted to reach out, or not. Much like her mother, much like the man she'd grown up calling Father, Damien just hadn't had any use for her.

It was so completely different from Jamie's family. The way that they rallied around each other. The way that they cared.

She felt so happy that Lindy had been able to marry into a family like that this time. She had certainly gotten the short end of the stick marrying into the Leighton family, at least, in Bea's opinion.

Her family was all cold, stiff ceremony, proclamations about good behavior. For years, their father hadn't spoken to Sabrina because of that meltdown she'd had in front of all their friends and family.

She couldn't imagine a member of the Dodge clan disowning another. They were imperfect, they were noisy and they fought. But they loved, most of all.

But Bea wasn't really part of it. Not really. She was friends with Jamie, she still felt like Lindy was her sister, in spite of the fact that she had divorced Beatrix's brother and married someone else. But none of this was really hers in that way.

Another thing for her to stand on the perimeter of. But at least this was something she liked.

"Well, mine are very much fully functional and obnoxious, if you would like to borrow one."

"I'm good. Thanks."

"Anything new with you?"

She should tell Jamie about the vet tech program. That she was hoping to take a position at Bennett's place. After all, she would be working with Jamie's brother, hopefully. But something stopped her. She just felt so silly talking about that kind of thing.

Felt so silly admitting what she wanted.

It brought her back to times when she'd felt small, standing in Jamison Leighton's office, with his disapproving stare boring into her as he questioned why her grades were so poor. Why she didn't finish her homework. And why she spent every afternoon outside climbing trees and rescuing baby birds, putting them in shoeboxes, when she should be applying herself to something that mattered.

She had never known how to tell him that animals were what mattered to her. And there was never going to be a career path for her that involved sitting indoors.

Because when he didn't care about something, he was quick to make it seem small and unimportant. And she couldn't fathom opening up her heart and sharing all the things she *did* care about, so that he could minimize those too. Tell her why they didn't matter.

Why the way she saw the world wasn't important at all.

Maybe that was why it was so difficult to talk about things now.

That and the one time she'd found someone she thought might care...

She'd discovered how small and unimportant she was in a new way. One that hurt far worse than Jamison's cold detachment.

"I'm getting some chickens," she said. "So that's exciting."

Jamie rolled her eyes. "Chickens."

"Chickens are useful," she insisted. "Last time we talked about my animal collection, you told me that you didn't understand useless animals like rabbits."

"You don't really want the chickens because they're useful though," Jamie said.

"Not especially. They're very cute."

Jamie shook her head and laughed. "Horses are enough for me."

"I'm happy to let you have all the horses. I like all animals, but I do prefer the small ones."

Jamie's lips twitched. "Except for Dane? He's a very large animal."

"And I'm not doing a very good job caring for him," Bea said, sidestepping any potential double meaning her friend was trying to walk her into.

"I have a feeling you're doing as good a job as anyone can do. Men like that are hardheaded," Jamie added, with exceeding confidence.

Bea had known—at least as much as she could know with intuition and scattered comments—that Jamie had about the same level of experience with men that she did.

But Jamie was a totally different type of person. She was confident and outspoken. She didn't go through life hoping to be invisible. She went in with guns blazing, to every situation, and never seemed to be at a loss.

Bea admired it in a way, though privately wondered if her own method of baiting metaphorical flies with honey worked a bit better.

"It's a good thing his head is so hard," she said, as she followed Jamie into the house. "Otherwise his brains might have fallen out completely."

There was laughter and conversation filling the living area of the house, and it continued, even when she and Jamie walked in. But her eyes found Dane immediately, and he looked up from his beer, his eyes meeting hers, a small smile on his lips.

She took that, held it close. Even if she shouldn't.

But it was right next to all the other things that she never talked about or showed anyone else, so it was safe.

She was greeted almost immediately by Lindy, who grabbed her and gave her a quick hug before ushering her into the kitchen to fill up her plate with chips, a hamburger and baked beans.

"How is everything going at the house?" Lindy asked.

She knew she meant how was Dane.

"Good," she said. "How was everything at the winery today?"

"Good," Lindy responded. "It's a little bit strange. I go there to work, then come back here. Dane is working here, and going back home to the winery." She paused for a moment. "Bea, does it bother you that he's in the house?"

"Why would it bother me?" Bea asked.

"Because you're out in that little cabin. And I feel

like… You grew up in that house. Maybe it should be yours."

Horror hit Bea in the chest, spreading out like ice. "No," Bea said. "No. I did my time in that mausoleum. Thank you very much."

"Okay. I just wanted to make sure. It's the Leighton family home and…"

But Bea wasn't actually a Leighton.

There were only four people on earth who knew. Jamison, her mother, her real father and her.

When her mother had told her, it had almost been a relief. Because suddenly it made sense why she didn't fit in.

And that it was Michael Fulsome made so much sense to her. She'd forged a connection with the quiet, reclusive winery worker when she was thirteen. And at sixteen she'd discovered he was her biological father.

It made her feel whole. Brought her a connection to herself she hadn't felt before.

Because those same things she'd witnessed in him lived inside of her. A wildness. A desire to roam.

That piece of herself that felt suffocated by those walls and marble floors. That part that didn't want to get lost in rows of grapevines, but in dense forest and endless mountains.

Until he'd left. Because money given to him by Jamison had mattered more.

The fact of the matter was the winery and the property were far more suited to Lindy than it would ever be to Bea. Sabrina still worked at the winery, but she wouldn't want to live there. She lived on her husband's ranch.

Which was perfect for her. Bea wanted the life she'd made for herself. Simple, humble. Full of creatures and freedom.

"I'm happy in the cabin," Bea said. "Really. It's perfect for me. I'm just one person."

"So is Dane," Lindy said.

"You have to fit him and his ego into one place," Bea said, smiling. "The cabin isn't up for it."

Not to mention all of the equipment that he needed to keep him safe. But, she wasn't going to mention that. Because he really wouldn't like her throwing out the reminder that he was injured. And even though he couldn't hear her, that mattered to her.

He would have agreed about his ego.

"True," Lindy said, grabbing her own full plate, and leading the way out into the living room.

Bennett, Kaylee and Dallas had arrived, and they had a full house, including Luke and Olivia Hollister, and their baby girl. Bea naturally sat back and faded into watching everyone interact.

Voices rose up and filled the warm space, the log home absorbing the sound and holding it in around them.

She enjoyed it. She found it comforting and interesting. She liked being around all the happiness. She also would've been happier if there was a dog around that she could have snuck potato chips to.

She looked around and noticed that Dane didn't look very good at all. He wasn't participating in the conversation. He was just eating. He looked like he was in pain. And she didn't like that at all.

Unlike her, Dane never faded into the background.

Not before the accident. He had always been the focal point in any room he was in. Happy to lead the charge telling stories about his exploits on the rodeo circuit, making everyone laugh.

He was a natural charmer, and it was something that Bea had always admired about him. Because the only thing she had ever turned naturally was beast, not man.

She stood from where she was sitting and edged her way over to where Dane was on the couch. There was a small wedge of blank space next to him, and she hesitated, before sitting there.

Then, she took a breath, and did.

Her knee brushed up against his thigh, and the air she had just taken in rushed out of her completely. He didn't seem to notice. But he did look at her, unperturbed.

"Are you okay?" she asked, keeping her voice low.

His blue eyes cooled slightly. "That seems to be the only question anyone wants to ask me."

"You look tired," she said.

"I'm fine. I'm just not used to working these kinds of hours anymore. But it's fine."

"I might need you to come look at my chicken coop before it gets dark."

He huffed out a laugh. "Beatrix, that sounds like a particularly ridiculous pickup line."

Her face got hot, shame prickling over her. Because it had not been a pickup line, but him suggesting it might be made her feel exposed. And worse, him laughing about it, as if it were ridiculous, wounded her. It shouldn't.

"I'm just saying. I could use some help. And… You

can come by and look, and then go get some rest. But, no one has to know that you're tired."

He gave her a long look. "I'm fine. But if you need me to come and look at the chicken coop…"

"I do," she said. "The rescue chickens are coming in just five days."

"We can't have homeless rescue chickens. They'll need to be rescued from the rescue."

"That's kind of what I was thinking."

That little burst of shame shifted and expanded into something else. Pride. Because he was taking her help. And he might rather have her punch him in the injured thigh than admit it, but he did seem to be taking it.

"Thanks for dinner," Dane said, looking at his brother-in-law. "Bea needs some help out at the cabin before it gets dark, so I think it's time for us to head out."

The way he said *us* made Bea's stomach kick a little bit, and she was instantly irritated at her body's nonsense. This was a little white lie of her own making. She could hardly go getting worked up about it.

"I'm not actually going to let you look at the chicken coop," she said softly once they were outside.

"Bea," he said. "I can handle coming out to look at the chicken coop."

She crossed her arms and planted her feet resolutely, staring him down. Which felt a little silly since she barely came up to his chin. "You looked like you were about to pass out."

"It was just a lot of noise. Sometimes… I don't know. I don't know what all makes it bad like that. But, some of it is just pretending it's not bad. If I show even a hint of what I'm feeling, then Wyatt is going to make sure that I actually can't do any work at the ranch, and Lindy is going to lock me in the basement until I'm healed. And not let me move at all."

"So what? So what if they did? Is it the worst thing to get taken care of?"

"Yeah," he said. "Like that it is. I left home when I was eighteen, Bea. No one has ever taken care of me. I mean Lindy… She was my older sister. But, she hooked up with Damien pretty early on, and she was involved in that. I'm happy for her. I mean, I was. I was happy she escaped. But my next goal was to escape. And I had to make sure that it happened myself. We made it. Lindy and I. We didn't just stay like our mother. No one fussed over me then, they don't need to do it now."

"Is that what this is about? Being mad that Lindy wants to watch over you now when she didn't before?" Bea knew all about being angry about the past. Mostly, she was the least angry person around. But she also understood what it felt like to feel isolated while surrounded by people.

To feel like you were somehow alone, no matter how good the intentions of those around you were.

"No. But I made a whole life based on doing what I felt in my gut was the right thing to do. I don't need somebody to step in now and try to handle everything."

"Okay. In that case, come and look at the chicken coop. But if something hurts, please feel free to cuss about it and make a big show of how terrible it feels."

"You're not going to try to manage me?"

The question made Bea blink. She was so used to

feeling managed by those around her it hadn't occurred to her she could make…anyone else feel that way.

Though she supposed she was managing him a little bit. But it was all with good intentions. Just making him think he was getting his way a little bit more successfully than Lindy was.

But she didn't say that.

"I've taken care of a lot of wounded animals," she began. "And each one heals its own way. But, none of them hold their pain in. If it hurts, growl about it."

Dane lifted a brow, the slowly sinking sun casting a gold wash over his face, illuminating the light whiskers around his jaw. The way he was looking at her now… It made her heart trip over itself. Because it wasn't really neutral, or cool. Not at all. "You know I'm not one of your creatures, right?"

"Of course," she said. "I only meant…"

"I'm a man, Bea. Not a dog." He lowered his head as he said that, and the wind kicked up, tangling his sharp, masculine scent around her. His skin, the sweat from the day's work. Something twisted, low and deep inside of her.

Desire.

It was embarrassing, to be that close to him feeling this. If he could read her mind…

Well, it would be embarrassing for several reasons. The first of which being that it would probably horrify him. The second of which being that it would only betray her lack of experience.

Because while the desire coursing through her was hot and sharp, the actual focus of the desires was a little bit fuzzy.

"I know that," she said, knowing that she sounded a little bit breathless. "If you were... If you were a dog I would just scratch behind the ears and tell you to go lie down."

His lips curved and she felt it. Somewhere deep inside her. "You're welcome to try that."

Just the thought of touching him, particularly the thought of touching him like that, after their thighs had just been so close together made her feel like she'd pressed her face against a campfire.

"Don't say things you don't mean," she said, taking a step back for him, her breathing labored. *She* was embarrassing. Everything about her and her response to him was embarrassing.

"Let's go," he said, his voice rough. "It's getting late." And she could tell that he was getting tired. His voice certainly wasn't rough for the same reasons that her own throat was tight, and her words strangled.

She nodded, and headed out toward her truck. It was a big vehicle for somebody her size, she knew, but it was practical. She often picked up animals that she found on the side of the road, and sometimes she needed the space. She also often needed it for supplies for the cabin, or for the animals.

Dane got into his own truck, and Bea led the way down the highway and toward the little turnoff before the official winery entrance that led to her cabin. Dane parked behind her, and Bea rounded to the front of the house, relieved when she saw that the window was shut.

"What are you doing?"

"I had to make sure that Evan hadn't snuck back inside while I was gone."

"How does Evan get inside?" he asked.

"The latch is loose on my window," she said. "He's able to work it open and then he slips in. Usually, he just gets into the pantry, but sometimes he…" She was not in a position to be talking about her underwear with Dane Parker. She cleared her throat. "He gets into other things. I would rather not have a raccoon disaster to clean up."

"I can fix that too," he said.

"Really?"

"Whatever you need, Bea. You've been helping me, and it sounds to me like you're pretty busy. I'd hate to think that you were helping me at the expense of your own place."

It was so weird to have him paying so much attention to her. He'd always been nice. But he'd been distant. He'd been…well, at the rodeo. Visiting Lindy when he came back into town. Going out drinking.

The past few months had forced him to slow down, and she was kind of in his path as a result.

"You're not causing me to neglect anything. But you know, with the studying… It would definitely be helpful for you to do this."

He nodded. "Well, show me the chicken coop."

She led him back around behind the cabin, down the little narrow path that led to the little coop.

"I've never used it," she said. "There's a bunch of rot, and the chicken wire is damaged in a few places. But for the most part, I think the fencing is salvageable."

"Yeah, this is something I can fiddle with over the next few days. It really shouldn't take much time."

"I don't want you to overtax yourself."

"Beatrix," he said. "The point of coming over here was to get away from being micromanaged."

"Fine. I won't micromanage you."

"See that you don't."

She stared at him for a while, as he tried to navigate the soft, uneven ground. As he appraised the chicken coop and grimaced as he shifted his weight from one leg to the other. "Is it so bad to have a whole bunch of people care about you?" she asked.

"No," he said. "That's not... That's not the issue."

"I think the issue is that you're a stubborn ass," she said, kicking a stone and looking at him defiantly.

"Really?"

"Yes. You're in denial about what your body can and can't do, and I kind of get that, Dane, but at a certain point, you just have to deal with the fact that you're not invincible. That's the thing you were in denial about the entire time you were riding. This was always a risk. Always. And now you have to...deal with it."

"I would actually rather if you told me to go lie down and scratch me behind the ears," he bit out.

"That's ridiculous. Why would anyone tell a man to do that?" she asked stiffly.

"I wonder if any of these methods work on you?" he asked. "Go lie down, Bea." And before she could react, he reached out and tucked her hair behind her ear, rubbing the sensitive skin back there with the tips of his fingers.

He was scratching her behind the ears.

She felt it between her legs.

Oh...

"Good girl," he said softly.

She jerked back, going stiff, her entire body feeling like it was shot through with fire.

He looked amused with himself, and he thought it was funny. Because he was acting like she was a kid sister, and he could just touch her like that, and it wouldn't mean anything. And she wouldn't feel anything. But of course, neither would he. Why would he? It was appalling. And horrible.

But not more horrible than the fact that what she really wanted to do was lean into his touch, and beg him for more. Even this teasing, condescending touch that should enrage her left her on fire in ways that made her feel...

Small.

It all made her feel very small. That he had so much power over her, and she had so little. And he didn't even know it.

She was so very tired of wanting affection, wanting caring, from people who didn't want to give it to her.

"Maybe I will go lie down," she said. "You can... You can come over tomorrow and work on the chicken coop."

"Did you want to come up to the house for a little bit?"

"No," she said. "You can get your own beer tonight."

"Beatrix..."

She knew he had no idea why she was upset, and that she was being confusing. She also knew that she didn't care. Not right now. Not when she felt electrified and she knew that he wouldn't have any clue why what he'd done was painful.

"Okay," he said. "I'll see you tomorrow."

"Okay. Tomorrow."

Then she dashed into the cabin. As soon as she cracked the door open, Evan appeared, scampering in behind her. She closed the door, locking it, which made her feel like a silly, immature girl. It wasn't like Dane was going to come in after her.

Bea looked down at Evan, who was gazing at her expectantly. Then she sighed and opened up the fridge, digging for his food.

There. She had Evan to take care of, anyway.

And tomorrow was going to have to take care of itself, because tonight she was just too exhausted to cope with it.

Reluctantly, slowly, she reached up and touched the place where Dane had touched her.

It didn't feel warm. It didn't feel different.

But she felt different.

And she didn't know how long it would take for that feeling to go away.

CHAPTER FOUR

IT WAS CHICKEN coop day. Dane felt oddly relieved by that. Mostly because he was ready to get something done that was both useful and not under the watch of Lindy or Wyatt.

He'd been doing work on the winery for the past few weeks, but the fact of the matter was, it had been busywork. He'd had no real goal beyond moving around and doing something with the feeling of futile restlessness that was churning in his gut.

And by the end of the day he'd been completely and totally wiped out. All for nothing.

But Bea needed the coop. For her…chickens. There was a chicken deadline.

Hell, it was good to feel useful. And it wasn't really about the chickens. It was about Bea.

She was special. Hell, she was about the only person to successfully make him laugh in the last eight months.

He could still see her cheerily telling him she hated him that day in the house.

Only Bea.

He drove down the dirt road that led to Bea's little cabin, tucked back in the wood on the winery property. It was surrounded by trees, with a river at the back. Beyond that was more land that had once belonged to the Leighton family. Fields that had now gone fallow. Totally unused.

It seemed wrong to let a piece of land just sit there like that. Not that he had any real call to an opinion on that. He didn't even own a house. He traveled so much that there had never been any point to him having a permanent residence. He'd stay with Lindy when he was in town, or in a place on the property, the cabin Bea lived in now, before she'd lived there.

He knew nothing about managing a property long-term. Hell, he knew nothing about…sitting long-term. Which was where he'd been for the past eight months, and he didn't like it at all.

The little cabin came into view, and so did Bea, who was standing out front, wearing an ankle-length dress, a small basket in her hand. Her head was bent down low, the sun creating a fiery halo around her riot of chin-length curls. She stooped down in the grass, setting the basket down.

He couldn't see what she was doing, but he already knew it was creature-related.

Her lips were moving. If he had to guess, she wasn't singing to herself, but talking to whatever animal she'd spotted in the grass.

For some reason, he couldn't look away from her. It was like the light had wrapped itself around each strand of hair and set her on fire, her skin glowing like a mythical fairy.

There really wasn't another person quite like Bea.

She sometimes seemed like she was from another world.

She straightened, and looked up, her eyes meeting his, a cheery smile crossing her face.

He parked the truck and got out, grimacing when he stepped down, bracing himself on the door.

"What were you talking to?" he asked.

"A robin," she said. "I was afraid he might be injured but he seems okay." As if on cue, the bird hopped, revealing himself over the blades of grass, then took flight, fluttering into the nearest pine. "He should be careful. Evan would probably find him to be a decent snack."

"Are you an actual cartoon princess?"

She tilted her head to the side. "What?"

"That birds don't even fly away from you."

She laughed. "No. He was after a worm, I think. Birds are funny like that. Sometimes they hop when they could easily fly away, and I don't really understand why."

"That sounds like a metaphor."

"Mmm. But it isn't. It's just birds." The breeze came up and ruffled her curls, and a soft smile curved her lips.

He found it hard to look away.

"What's in the basket?" he asked.

"Pie. Alison Donnelly brought it from Copper Ridge for the tasting room, and there was extra leftover at the end of yesterday. I figured maybe you could use some sustenance, for your chicken coop building."

"I'll never say no to pie."

"Me either."

He rounded to the back of his truck and got his toolbox, slamming the truck door when he walked by it again. Bea trailed after him as he walked down the path toward the coop.

"What are you going to do first?" she asked.

"Well, I'm going to take measurements and get an idea for what we actually need to buy."

Her brow wrinkled. "Right."

"I can pay for the supplies, Bea," he said.

The woman worked part-time at a veterinary clinic and was taking college courses. He doubted she could afford random repair expenses. He, on the other hand, had almost no expenses and a hell of a lot of money socked away in a bank account.

It was something he could do, along with the repair work.

Her laugh, airy and sweet, cut through the morning air. "I have money, Dane. I'm not going to enlist your help to fix the thing and then make you pay."

"How do you have money?" he asked.

She lifted a shoulder. "It's a trust fund situation."

"Your dad gave you money," he said, unable to imagine Jamison Leighton doing anything of the sort. He didn't know Bea's father well, but because of Lindy he'd met the man on more than one occasion, and he had Lindy's accounts of what a rigid ass the old man was.

Bea cleared her throat. "It was something that was set up a long time ago. But yes. It's from my parents."

He looked past her, at the cabin. He couldn't imagine... well, anyone, coming into a trust fund and choosing to use it—or not use it—like this.

"I'm surprised your dad would have had all that to spare from the family fortune, considering that Lindy ended up with the winery."

"Well, that was all part of Damien's inheritance. He might have lost the winery but he still got some money. He's fine."

"I really never worry about him."

Bea huffed out a laugh. "Sometimes I do. But, he seems happy. I guess that's... It's hard. I love Lindy. But, I do care about my brother."

"Of course you do," Dane said.

Though, in his world, there really was no *of course*. There was no real family loyalty to fall back on. Not in the traditional sense. His father had left. Never looked back. His mother... Well, she was wrapped up in her own stuff.

He and Lindy were all each other had. So, on that level he could understand loyalty to a sibling. But even then, it was different. It was them against the world. And that was another scenario entirely.

"She's done so much more with Grassroots than he ever would have though. He would have used it to make passive income. She's made it into a dream. And I really appreciate it."

"You never feel like any part of it should be yours?"

Bea wrinkled her nose. "You know, she asked me that yesterday. I wonder if she's ever asked Sabrina."

"I'm not sure about that. But then, I imagine Sabrina has quite enough on her plate with running the tasting room in Copper Ridge and taking care of the business at the Donnelly ranch."

"Maybe," Bea said. "I'm happy with what I have."

"Except you aren't," Dane said.

He walked over to the chicken coop and began to take measurements. Checking out which sections of wood were completely shot and which might still have a chance at being salvaged.

"What does that mean?" she asked.

"The vet tech thing," he said, by way of explanation. "You're obviously not completely happy with where you're at or you wouldn't be trying for anything new."

"I guess so. But I just meant… That's the only thing I really use any of my money for. For the vet tech thing. I'm not sure what else I want to do. I want to do something. That's part of the problem with sharing about school. I really do want something different. But it hasn't all come together yet."

"You don't have any ideas?"

She frowned. "I mean, I could keep working at Valley Veterinary. I could get a full-time position. But that doesn't feel like…it."

"You have time to figure it out, I guess."

Bea had a whole bunch of opportunity spread out in front of her. As for him, his days of building toward anything more were likely over. Even if he did get back on the circuit, chances were he wasn't going to be more successful than he'd been when he was completely able-bodied.

The whole thing was a damned mess. Bea had time, and opportunity. Two good legs.

It was a damn good place to be.

"I'm going to head down to the feed store," he said. "Do you want to come with me?"

"Yes," she said.

"I'll drive," he said.

She squinted, looking at him skeptically. "Are you sure you don't want me to drive?"

"I'll drive."

He wrote down his measurements and took the toolbox and the measuring tape back to the truck. Bea scrambled into the cab on the passenger side. He backed out of the driveway, and before long the two of them were headed down the two-lane highway that would take them into Gold Valley.

It was a strange thing to drive down these familiar streets with the perspective he had now. He remembered well being a child and going down the same road in his mother's car. Looking at all the facades on the brick buildings and mentally inserting dollar signs above every door. Whether or not it was a place they could go.

Bellisima and Gold Valley Inn, two of the nicest restaurants in town, were out of the question, always. Mustard Seed had been an occasional treat, but something that they didn't do often. When he'd gotten his first summer job, Dane had spent every Friday there. After every football game. A chocolate shake and a burger. It was when he'd first truly understood the way that money and prestige would allow him to take control of his life.

Because when he was a hero on the football field, he had mattered.

Before that, he had just been fatherless trailer trash.

And he was realistic—no matter how well a kid played for a small school like Gold Valley High, it wasn't going to translate to college success or any kind of professional career. But it had given him a taste of what it might mean to pursue something like that.

That was where the rodeo came in.

It had been such a small thing back then. Enjoying

being someone people worshipped. Enjoying being able to buy a burger when he felt like it.

And he got sucked right into the circuit. And frankly, into Damien Leighton's circle.

The man was a brilliant agent. He had brokered some great endorsement deals for Dane. And had married Dane's sister.

That had all been great for a little while. Until he realized what an asshole he was.

He cut ties with him after that. Of course he had.

No matter how lucrative the partnership was, he wasn't going to stay chummy with the man who had cheated on his sister.

Of course, he probably didn't have any endorsement deals on the horizon now. Nobody wanted a busted-up cowboy advertising anything.

It made him feel like he was floating through black space, with nothing to anchor him.

He focused on the restaurants again. On the fact that none of them were off-limits to him now.

He could shop anywhere he pleased in Gold Valley and beyond.

He supposed he should be happy with that achievement. With the fact that he'd accomplished something. Changed his situation.

But he hadn't been done.

He wasn't done.

They breezed through the main part of town, around the corner and out toward Big R, where he knew he would be able to get everything they needed.

He parked in the lot, and the two of them got out,

walking with a good chunk of space between them into the store.

Bea went straight for the box with the heat lamp over it in the front, casting what looked to him to be a wistful glance at the baby chicks inside.

"You're about to get chickens," he reminded her.

"But baby chicks are so cute."

"And likely to be eaten by Evan."

She shot him a very mean look. "He would not."

"He's a raccoon, Bea. They aren't vegetarians."

She looked angry. "Well, I know that, Dane. I feed him." Her face suddenly got a very worried look. "I hope he doesn't harass the chickens."

"I'll make sure to build the coop with extra reinforcements," he said, his tone placating.

"Good," she said. "I don't want to rescue the chickens only to have them devoured."

"Nobody wants that," he said gravely.

"It would be an *extremely* poor rescue."

"No argument from me."

She wandered away from the chicks, following him over to where the lumber was. He picked up a flat cart along the way, something to put the two-by-fours on.

"Thank you for helping," she said.

"Thank you for giving me something to do."

"I just don't want to give you too much to do."

"I'll tell you what," he said slowly. "You told me about the vet tech program, even though you hadn't told anyone else. I would rather saw through my own wrist than talk to Wyatt or Lindy about any of my pain. But I will tell you if I need to quit for the day. I promise. I have to find a balance with how much I can take sitting around."

She nodded. "I understand that. I really do. I know you're not just being difficult."

"No. Not *just*."

"You're a little difficult," she pressed.

"I don't like sitting around."

He braced himself on the cart, and dragged a plank off the shelf, depositing it onto the platform with a clatter. He was not going to waste any energy picking those boards up. He was already doing mental gymnastics, trying to figure out how he was going to handle it when they were back at the coop. He looked at Bea, and saw that her eyes were full of concern.

"I've got it," he said. "As long as you let me figure out some work-arounds without freaking out."

"I won't freak out," she said.

"I don't remember what it's like to not have a goal," he said. "I've had one since I was eighteen. And I followed it ruthlessly. It's frustrating. My goal is to be better. And I can't make that happen. I just… I don't have any damned experience with not being able to make something do what I want."

"I do. It's called literally my entire childhood."

There was a slight edge to her voice, and he wasn't used to hearing that from Bea. Ever. She was saccharine if she was anything.

"What was it like? Growing up in that house?"

He finished with the wood, then went down to procure a roll of chicken wire. He looked over at Bea, who was chewing her lip. Like she was considering what to say.

She tucked her hair behind her ear. "I used to play hide-and-seek with myself a lot. It was big. The house. That was good. But, it was hard to move as slowly as my father expected me to. I just wanted to be outside. I didn't want to learn to play the piano. I didn't want to study. I didn't want to... I didn't want to be the daughter they wanted me to be. For a long time, Sabrina was perfect. Obviously that didn't last. And they had that falling-out. But at first... They compared me all the time. And you know Sabrina. She's beautiful. Blonde, and with hair that doesn't do..." Bea plucked at a curl. "This. And she seemed to find behaving herself so easy. She did exactly what they wanted. Until she didn't. And then it was an explosion. I just never... I never even tried. I couldn't. But I also never melted down at a party. So I was always treated like I was this...innocuous disappointment. Not really a help or a hindrance. There's something very particular about that. It's suffocating."

"I can't imagine," he said.

"I think you had it harder."

"I only can't imagine because my mother just didn't care," he said. "And there was no expectation at all about how I might behave. She didn't even have any expectations for herself."

"Your dad left," she said, softly.

"Dads leave," he said, trying to keep his voice casual. *See you on TV...*

If he had, he'd never told Dane. And Dane had the echo stuck in his head all these years. He'd tell himself he didn't picture his dad sitting in a bar watching the championships.

Didn't wonder if he told people that was his son.

He gritted his teeth.

"I always wished I didn't care," Bea said. "But I just...went off by myself and tried to do things quietly. On my own terms, but small. Rescuing birds in shoeboxes and hiding them in my room. Climbing out the window and running around in the forest behind the winery instead of actually doing my schoolwork. I always admired the fact that you didn't seem to care."

"What do you mean?"

"I just remember the first time I met you. And you said a swear word. In front of my parents. And in front of me. And when my mother looked at you disapprovingly, and my father looked shocked... You didn't care. I kind of wished that I could bottle that and put it inside me somehow."

He looked down at Bea, and he was stunned into silence by the admiration in her eyes. He didn't feel like he had done a damn thing to earn it. He didn't do anything that Bea valued. At least, he hadn't thought so. She was kind. Considerate to people and animals. And somehow, she admired him. He was... He was selfish by comparison. That was the nicest word for it.

"Bea," he said, "you care about people. And maybe that comes with caring what they think. I don't really know how that works. But you shouldn't trade that for any kind of confidence you think I might have. Ever."

Bea tilted her head to the side, her golden-brown eyes appraising him. "You care about people."

"Which people?" he asked.

He continued on collecting materials. And if the edge of the damn chicken wire cut into his hand, he went ahead and ignored it. Anyway, his thigh hurt worse.

"You care about Lindy. If you didn't, you wouldn't be here all the time. And you know what, you wouldn't feel so terrible about her micromanaging you. Because you would just tell her to…" She hesitated for a moment. "Well, jump in a lake."

The corner of his mouth hitched upward. "I probably wouldn't phrase it that way. But I take your point."

"No, I know exactly how you would phrase it," she said, her cheeks turning slightly pink.

Come to think of it, he had never heard Bea swear in a very serious way. The realization amused him.

"There are plenty of people like me. Who are cynical and selfish. The world needs more people like you."

"Women in their early twenties with trust funds who live in forests?"

"I wasn't thinking that specifically. But, if that's how you want to look at it."

"You're not as selfish as you think you are," she said.

"I think I might not be as nice as you think I am though."

Bea made an exasperated sound and walked ahead of him, and Dane continued to lean heavily on the cart as they wandered through the aisles.

By the time they got up to the front of the store his thigh was throbbing like a son of a bitch, but when they got back to Bea's place he would take some Tylenol. Something that wouldn't knock him out, but might take the edge off.

That better be enough, or he was going to break his leg off and chuck it over a mountain.

Okay, maybe not. But he wanted to sometimes.

Karen, the owner of the store, was working the register, all flannel and practicality, smile tight and reserved mostly for animals. He heard a thumping sound coming from behind the counter, and that was when he noticed there was a dog lying on a blanket there.

Bea noticed as soon as she approached, and immediately sprang to action, crouched down and stroked the rather pathetic-looking animal.

It was shaggy, and all gray in the face. Some kind of Australian shepherd mix, probably, though he was no expert on dogs. Still, it was a common enough dog to see running around on ranches.

He'd never had pets. Not as a kid, not as an adult.

"He's so sweet," Bea said. "What's his name?"

"This is Joe," Karen said, that tight-lipped smile stretched as far as it could go. "His owner was an older man, a customer of mine. He died a couple of days ago, and he doesn't have any family that can take Joe. They were going to take him to the pound, but I figured I would bring him here. My papillons have been harassing him though and he is an old man. It's all a little bit too much for him."

Bea's whole face went soft, her eyes liquid. "Poor guy," she said, stroking the old man behind the ears. "So he needs a place to stay?"

"Well, I can't keep him in the store indefinitely, even if I wanted to." Karen's voice gentled for a moment. "Anyway, he wouldn't be very happy."

"No," Bea said, looking around. "He was used to having a companion all the time. And he lost him. Now he's here…"

Her voice was practically trembling. Dane could only marvel at the amount of compassion she carried around in that petite frame. The sheer amount of caring. He couldn't remember the last time he'd cared about anything that much. Every single thing in the vicinity of Bea seemed to get a full dose of that heart, of that compassion.

"I can take him," Bea said softly. "I have so much property. And…well, Dane's home most of the time."

Dane shot Bea a look, then looked back at Karen, who was studying him. "I'm living in my sister's house at the winery," Dane said, feeling the need to explain that he was not bunking down with Bea.

The judgment in the older woman's face faded slowly. Hell, he couldn't blame her for being instantly judgmental. He would judge himself.

"I am working at Wyatt's place now."

"Joe could go," Bea said, insistent now. "And lie on a blanket and watch you work. I bet he would feel much happier than being here all day. There are always so many people at Get Out of Dodge."

"Bea," he said, "I've never actually had a dog."

"I'll take care of it," Bea said.

"Then you'll feed it, and walk it?" he asked, his tone dry.

"Well, you can walk him. I mean, let's face it, Dane, you're not going to move much faster than the dog. He probably has arthritis, and you have…"

"Fine," Dane said. "I guess we'll take the chicken coop supplies and the dog."

"A bad leg."

"Bea, I cut you off for a reason."

"And I finished." She grinned up at him. And God help him, he couldn't find it in him to disappoint her.

He didn't know what forest magic she possessed. It was damn sure something. There wasn't another person on earth who could possibly railroad him into this. It was Bea, all the way.

Back in the truck, with the dog—who Dane had lifted into the vehicle, in spite of his screaming leg—who had firmly settled between himself and Bea, Dane could only wonder what the hell had become of his life.

"I know I can't take every animal," Bea said once they were back on the road.

"I didn't say anything."

"But you were thinking it," Bea said. "Everyone thinks that. Even if they don't say it."

He sighed heavily. "Beatrix, I'm not here to tell you what to do. I don't care how many animals you take in."

"I mean, if I kept going I'd end up with a whole animal sanctuary." She suddenly reached across the space, her hand locking around his coat sleeve. "Dane! I could start an animal sanctuary!"

He blinked and looked over at her quickly, then back at the road. "Like a... What would it be?"

"I've been to them before. Like breed rescues for specific kinds of dogs. Or there's a place a few hours away that takes in farm animals that came from abusive situations, or who lost their homes because of fire or foreclosure. I could have one here. There are always animals in need. I should know. I seem to trip over them."

"Well, that is true," he said, slowly.

One thing he'd started to realize about Bea in the past few weeks was that there was a grit beneath her sunny exterior that most people didn't seem to notice. He'd yet to see her falter when she'd set her mind to something. And that included when she locked horns with him.

"It would be really expensive," she said.

"You have a trust fund, don't you?"

"I do," she said, sounding even more determined. "And I can use it on whatever I want. I don't want a fancy house or cars or clothes. I want to do something. I want purpose. And my schooling would be so helpful for this, because I could do minor procedures and administer vaccines and any number of things!"

"That is true," he agreed.

"It just seems crazy," she said, sounding more enthusiastic with each word.

"Yeah, but you're a little crazy. And I mean that with full affection."

Bea looked over at him, around their furry companion, and scrunched her nose. "Thank you."

"I'm a little crazy too," he said. "A man doesn't ride bulls for a living without being a little bit screwed in the head."

She huffed out a laugh. "No argument from me there."

"If you're going to be the crazy...well, any-animal-you-happen-to-run-across lady, you might as well be all in."

The smile that earned him filled the cab of his truck with sunshine. He didn't think he'd ever seen a person happier than Beatrix Leighton in this moment. He didn't think he'd ever seen someone with that kind of pure passion. "I could do that," she said. "I mean, I could really do it."

"You could. You can have your very own wildlife refuge."

He could practically feel her vibrating on the other side of the cab now. "A wildlife refuge. Bea's Refuge. Where animals can heal and recover from trauma… and…and things. Some of them could live their lives out there safely and happily and maybe others could even find permanent homes."

"Sounds good, Bea."

"Okay," she said. "We should do it. I'll need a plan."

He barked a laugh. "Something tells me you have one already."

"Okay, I kind of do. But I'm going to need to enlist your help. On the side of the property my cabin is on there are structures that might be salvageable. We'll need shelters and fences. I'll need your help to oversee that."

"Hey, I'm indisposed and at your service."

There was so much excitement in her voice, so much passion, and it was…infectious. He hadn't had a goal, not a real one since his accident. Sure, there was the *go back in time and not have this injury* goal. Which is just slightly less realistic that the *heal instantaneously* goal.

But this felt like something. Something real. Something he could do while he waited, while he took that time that everyone was so quick to remind him he needed to take.

Hell, he had spun his trailer park upbringing into gold by getting involved in the rodeo, he didn't see why he couldn't work this out too. Elbow grease, determination and charm could get a man a long way. He had all that, and he was confident he could make it work in this instance the way he'd used it earlier in life.

It was the thing that gave him purpose. The thing that made him feel alive.

Helping Bea with this might be the best damn thing for him.

"I guess I'll have more work to do," he said.

"Yes," Bea said. "Yes indeed. I'm going to put you to work."

CHAPTER FIVE

"WHAT IN THE hell is that?"

Dane looked down at the dog who had been his constant companion for the past two days, and asked himself a similar question. Though, he had to admit, even if it was just himself, that the utter shock on Wyatt's face almost made the whole unexpected turn of events worth it.

Not that the dog was any trouble. He mostly wandered from his food bowl to his bed—both things that he and Bea had acquired at Big R before taking the dog home—and back again.

This was the first day he had brought Joe to Get Out of Dodge. He expected that the dog would do much the same here. Migrate between the food bowl that Dane had brought with him, and the bed, that he had also brought.

"This is Joe," Dane said.

"I didn't know you had a dog."

He shrugged. "I didn't have a dog. Now I do."

A dog that was going to end up a permanent resident of Bea's sanctuary once Dane was healed. Because he sure as hell wasn't home often enough to care for a dog. No matter how likable the dog might be. Lindy popped out of the house a moment later, a grin on her face, which shifted when she saw Joe. "What's that?"

"I just asked the very same question. Apparently, Beatrix got Dane a dog."

Lindy exploded with laughter. "She got you a dog!"

"It's a long story. I'm helping her with…some things. We ended up going over to Big R two days ago, and Joe was there. His owner just passed, and the poor dog didn't have anywhere to go. And you know Bea."

"And she thought you needed an old dog?" now Lindy asked.

"Yes," Dane said. "She did. Something about me needing to learn to care for other beings."

"Well, that's very nice of her."

Dane sighed heavily. "It was very Bea of her. She tries to take care of everything. And I think in this case she decided that this would take care of me and the dog."

"You don't agree?" Wyatt asked.

"I don't…*not* agree. I mean, he's a nice dog. But I've never had a dog before."

Lindy frowned. "Does this mean there's a dog living in my house?"

Wyatt wrapped his arm around his wife's shoulders. "It's not your house anymore."

"Yes," Lindy said to her husband, lifting his arm up off her shoulders and stepping away from him. "I own that house. That means it's my house. And Dane didn't ask if he could bring a dog into it."

"Beatrix has brought Evan into it," Dane said, watching his sister's expression closely.

Lindy blinked, and he could tell that fraction of a response meant she was awash in horror. "She has not."

"She has," Dane said. "She fed him cereal at the table."

Her lips twitched. This was worth…well, everything. To be here in this moment, torturing his older sister. "I think you're making that up."

He shook his head. "I'm not making it up. Okay," Dane said. "So she didn't so much feed him cereal at the table as he got into a cereal box that was still sitting on the table. That's splitting hairs."

Lindy made a groaning sound and slapped her hand over her eyes. "This is ridiculous. You're all ridiculous. It sounds like anarchy over there."

"Animal anarchy," Dane agreed.

He wondered what his sister would think of Bea using the property for a sanctuary. They'd have to discuss it, but not until Bea was ready to present an actual plan. Lindy would need a plan. A full plan with graphs and things, because that's just how she was.

"In all seriousness, Lindy," he said, because he was starting to feel more and more protective of Bea. It was a strange feeling, but not totally shocking, he supposed. Bea took care of him, whether he wanted her to or not. That he wanted to return the favor seemed fair enough.

He'd started the joke, but Lindy should know better than to think Bea was going to let animals run wild over her property. "You know that Bea isn't taking advantage of anything. She loves you, and she respects you."

"No, I… I know. She just…is irrepressible sometimes."

"She's determined," Dane said. "Stubborn. And I think the difference between those two things and irrepressible matters. What she does, she *decides* to do."

Lindy frowned slightly. "I… No, you're right. I'm

sorry. I didn't…realize I made it sound that way. It's just easy to…to think of her as a kid still."

"She's not," Dane said, unsure of where the conviction had come from.

Lindy's eyes narrowed. "No, she isn't. But she's still young."

He had no idea what his sister was implying with what had sounded like a warning, and he chose not to turn it over too much. "But not a kid. Believe me, as someone who's had all that determination pointed at him like a laser cannon over the past few weeks, I am more aware of what she's capable of than most."

Lindy shook her head. "I hope you enjoy the dog."

"The dog is fine," Dane said.

Though, he had to admit that it was kind of nice to have something to talk to at night when he was sitting there in the recliner. Even if it couldn't talk back. Or probably understand him. But he got the sense that it was nice for the dog too. The old guy just sat there and let him go on. Sometimes it even looked at him.

For a man who had been feeling pretty solitary for the past eight months it was kind of nice.

Maybe Bea was onto something after all.

He wondered sometimes if she was roundly underestimated. If people saw things like the way that she rescued impractical creatures and thought of her as impractical. Rather than someone who was…

Caring like she did must be awfully damned heavy. And yet, even with all of that her smile often seemed effortless.

It was easy to think of her as a kind of bubbly, effervescent sprite who tripped around gathering furry creatures here and there.

But he realized in that moment what a mistaken thought that was.

He pictured her again, the way he had seen her the other day, kneeling down in the grass, looking at the little robin.

She had thought the bird was hurt. And there had been no way that her conscience would allow her to pass it by.

He didn't know very many people who felt that strongly about...much of anything.

Bea watched. And she cared.

And better than that she acted on her feelings.

"And how are you?" Lindy asked, her gaze getting pointed. He remembered what Bea had said about that too. About how the way he responded to that concern from Lindy proved that he wasn't entirely selfish. He liked that interpretation of it.

But he also supposed that meant he could bend just a little bit more on the subject. That he didn't need to be quite so difficult.

"Sore sometimes," he said. "But, I've been all right. After the workdays. And I've even been doing a little bit around Bea's cabin. Don't yell at me for that."

He could tell that Lindy was trying not to yell at him.

"As long as you're feeling okay," she said.

"I swear to you," he said. "I'm not trying to do anything to mess up my body. I want to be back and functional as soon as possible, and I understand that abusing myself isn't going to help me accomplish that."

"That's very sensible," Lindy said, clasping and un-
clasping her hands.

"Sometimes I'm sensible."

She shook her head. "No, you aren't."

"I really am," he said. "I managed to have the good
sense to get where I am in life now, didn't I?"

Lindy bit her lip. It was Wyatt who said the words
that she was holding back. "You mean, trampled by a
bull?"

"But for the grace of God, Dodge. And anyway, you
know that's not what I meant. I was sensible enough to
get my ass up out of poverty, wasn't I?"

"Yes, you did," Lindy said.

"I'm not going to just sit down now. That's the thing
you have to understand. I'm being careful. But I'm a
man who knows what he wants. And I'm a man who's
determined to get it."

After the conversation, he and Joe, and Joe's various
supplies, wandered over to the field to begin the day's
work. And if Dane naturally walked a little bit slower
so that he didn't tire Joe out, then that was fine. He
didn't want the dog to end up stiff and uncomfortable.

It was just for the dog.

That was all.

BEA SPENT THE whole day thinking a little bit too much
about how Dane and Joe were doing. She thought about
them, even while she went over to Valley Veterinary
for her shift.

Bennett was out in the field, but Kaylee was there,
seeing to her usual workload.

They had just finished doing a general physical on

Clarence, a particularly cute dachshund, with a hand-some and attentive owner. The kind of man that—if Bea weren't such a goner for Dane—might have interested her. He was so clearly an animal person. She thought of the way that Dane had reacted to Joe. They seemed to be bumping along well together, but Dane was clearly not sure about what to do with a pet in the general sense.

But he was trying. Just the memory of how he was trying made her smile.

"What are you thinking about?" Kaylee asked, work-ing at sterilizing instruments on a metal tray in the exam room. Beatrix was checking stock and in general get-ting familiar with what all the standard equipment was.

"What?" Bea asked.

"Your eyes went large. Like they do when you see an animal you like."

"Oh." Bea shook her head. "I wasn't thinking about an animal."

"Really?" Kaylee asked. "Were you thinking about Michael?"

That must be Clarence's owner. Bea frowned. "He seems very nice."

"Yes," Kaylee said. "He is. He's also seeing some-one pretty seriously."

"Well," Bea said. "Good for him."

"I thought so, considering I tried to date him for about five minutes but couldn't actually make it work because I was so hung up on Bennett."

Bea blinked, uncomfortable with the strange paral-lels in the moment. Between Bennett and Kaylee, and herself and Dane.

Of course, the primary difference there would be that Dane was never going to be interested in her back.

"Well, I'm glad he found someone."

"You'll find someone too," Kaylee said.

Bea loved Kaylee. A whole lot. But the fact that she was assuming she knew what Bea was thinking grated on her.

"Well, if nothing else, you know that I'll always find some*thing*," Bea said. "It's my talent."

She could let the conversation die there and continue to let Kaylee think she was aimless. Waiting for a man or animal to come along, like she wasn't doing things in her life. That was how she usually handled people.

But maybe…maybe she needed to stop. As safe spaces for that kind of thing went, Kaylee was a good beginning.

"Kaylee," she said slowly. "I am thinking of starting up an animal sanctuary."

Kaylee paused, a wet cloth held steady in her hands. Her eyes went wide. "An animal sanctuary. That sounds like a really big undertaking."

"It will be," Bea said, heartened by the fact that Kaylee hadn't told her not to. By the fact that she hadn't laughed. That she hadn't told Bea it was impossible.

"It will be a lot of work, but it's something I'm up for. Though, you know, an animal sanctuary won't exactly fund itself." Bea's trust fund would do it. But, with that in mind, she would need a job for her daily expenses even more.

"No," Kaylee said softly. "That kind of thing isn't known for being very lucrative."

Bea shook her head. "No. And I don't need it to be.

Eventually, I'll have to figure out donors and things. But, only eventually. I'll be able to sustain it for a few years. Maybe I could get some part-time work to supplement though." She squared her shoulders and steeled herself for the rest. "I'm taking an online course through Western Oregon University. To become a vet tech."

"Bea," Kaylee said. "That's fantastic."

Instantly, relief flooded her. Of course Kaylee didn't think it was silly. Of course Kaylee thought she could do it. Because Kaylee saw her with animals. And if there was one thing that Bea did very well with, visibly, it was animals.

"I have to pass it first," Bea said. "And there's a lot of…technical questions and things. A lot of technical things to learn. I know I don't have to tell you that, because you went fully to veterinary school. So. But, I just… It's much easier for me to study like this. Out of a classroom, I mean. I didn't ever do very well in school. Not that I did terribly or anything but, you know, average. The idea of continuing school was always daunting to me. But I really want to do this. And… I thought I might try."

"You would have a full-time job here. If that's what you want. I couldn't imagine someone more capable, someone more compassionate taking care of my patients. And I know you're going to do a fantastic job. Everything you do here is great."

"Yes," Bea said. "But I haven't assisted with the surgery yet."

"We do get a few. But, this is a small-town practice, and while we definitely do have our emergencies, mostly we get our regulars in for checkups and vaccines. It's rewarding to take care of them."

"I get that feeling. I haven't told anyone else. About the vet tech thing. Well, no one except for Dane."

"You've been spending a lot of time with him," she mused.

"Well, we're living on the same property. And he's going to help me with the sanctuary. With building plans. And all of that."

"Wow," Kaylee said. "That's pretty big. I mean, he doesn't have a whole lot of capacity physically right now, does he?"

"He's getting better," Bea said. "But it's very generous of him to offer himself like this. He's really supportive. And…"

She realized that she was getting borderline poetic. About a man who she really had no business being poetic about.

"You know," Bea said quickly. "As a brother."

"He was never *your* brother-in-law," Kaylee said, shaking her head.

"It doesn't matter. That's the foundation of our relationship. Him being Damien's brother-in-law. I mean, that's…how he knows me. Basically a younger sister."

"But that's not how you feel about him. And you weren't thinking about Michael, were you?"

Bea was feeling safer right now with Kaylee than she could remember feeling with anyone. So far, Kaylee had listened to her talk about school, and about the sanctuary. And she hadn't made her feel stupid. Hadn't made her feel wrong. Not at all. "I know that nothing's going to happen between us. I do know that. I think

Lindy knows that I have a crush on him. But that's all it is. It's a crush. I admire him. I don't really aspire to the whole marriage thing, not really. Not now. I mean if I were going to, obviously I'd like a man like him, but I… Not him. I'm not stupid."

Foolishly hopeful, maybe. But, not stupid.

"Bea, there's nothing stupid about caring for someone. And honestly… Relationships change. Look at Bennett and me. I loved Bennett. For almost half my life. And he didn't look at me the way that I looked at him in all that time. Not until… Not until he did."

"What changed?" Bea asked. Because no matter that it was a stupid thing to do, she wanted to know. She wanted to know because she wanted it. Even if she shouldn't.

"The wind? The way that my hair looked? The way that his heart beat. I don't know. I don't know the answer to any of it. Maybe it was him. Maybe it was me. Maybe it was just life. But somehow… Well, I kissed him. I kissed him and he didn't seem to think it was the worst thing. And then I propositioned him."

"You propositioned Bennett?"

"Yes," Kaylee said, smiling faintly. "It was not…one of my finer moments. It was a little bit desperate. But that was all when his son had just shown up, and Bennett's whole life was thrown into turmoil." She frowned. "Well, I guess that's the answer. Sometimes, when everything around you is different, you see the people around you differently too."

"I guess," Bea said.

Except, that made Bea feel unspeakably depressed. Because everything around Dane had changed. He couldn't ride anymore. He was housebound at Lindy's. Bea was taking care of him. They saw each other more now than they ever had.

There had been no magical change. Not at all.

Of course, she hadn't kissed him. Or propositioned him. But... Surely Kaylee had had some indicator that making a move wouldn't be met with...abject horror or something.

Also, she imagined that Kaylee had kissed a man before she'd kissed Bennett. Had probably even slept with a man.

Bea had not done either thing. And the idea of crossing a physical line with Dane when he had given absolutely no indication that...

The very idea made her want to crawl beneath one of the blue felt and metal chairs in the waiting room and hide for the rest of her life.

"I'm just saying. Sometimes things change. People change."

"So you recommend long-term hopeless crushes then?"

"Oh, hell no," Kaylee said. "But then, I tried just about everything to get over him."

Well, so Bea could confirm with that statement that Kaylee had a heck of a lot more experience than she did.

"What if I just...don't want to? What if I just want..."

"Well, that's the other thing. If things don't shift around him and change his heart, then count on the fact that they'll shift around you and change yours. If you want him...you can always make a move."

Bea had no idea what making a move on Dane would even look like. Or what the point would be. She didn't expect love and devotion or forever from Dane.

"You're taking control of your life with going to school. Why not with this? New job. New boyfriend."

The very idea of having a boyfriend made Bea feel bemused. Dane seemed…too hard and sharp-edged to be anything as soft-sounding as a boyfriend. What would that be like? To be with him. In…any kind of romantic capacity.

She couldn't imagine it. Which was funny because she'd had feelings for him for so much of her life and yet she just…had never imagined being with him was possible. So she didn't think about what-if.

Talking with Kaylee made her think about all kinds of things.

"Maybe," Bea agreed. "But I suppose before I do anything I need to pass this class."

CHAPTER SIX

THE NEXT DAY was Bea's day off, and Lindy asked her to come to the winery and help with a large group coming in for a bachelorette party.

When Bea arrived at the main dining room, she had a strong sense of déjà vu. Not only was Lindy in the office, so was Sabrina, Bea's older sister, and it was so rare that the three of them were ever together anymore at the winery that it felt a little bit like old times. Back when Lindy had lived here, and Sabrina hadn't been consumed with the tasting room. Back before either of them had gotten married, and given a significant portion of their free time over to their husbands.

Back before Dane had been injured.

She could almost see him walking through the door, healthy and smiling. The way he had been.

It was interesting to have a good memory at this place. And it didn't surprise her entirely that the good memories centered around the time when Lindy had taken over the winery. Not when the Leighton family had been in charge.

"The tasting room in Copper Ridge is busy all through tourist season now," Sabrina said, happily. "It's even kind of busy outside tourist season. All of your expansion endeavors seem to be paying off."

Lindy nearly preened. Except of course, she didn't need to. Since her blond hair was pulled smoothly into place, her appearance was immaculate. She dressed casually more often than she ever used to, since life on the ranch was hardly conducive to a life spent in high heels. But when she came into the winery, she was still perfectly pressed Lindy. Sabrina was the same.

Bea felt small and frazzled by comparison. She knew her hair was doing what her hair did. She kept it short because it was so thick that if she ever let it get longer than her shoulders she could break a comb in it. But she had to keep it at least chin-length so that she could scrape the curls back into a ponytail if she needed it out of her face.

Still, she never looked as poised as Lindy or Sabrina did when they put their hair up. Her hair never looked sleek and glossy. Just unruly, and vaguely like a spiraled carrot.

Normally, she didn't care. Not at all. And she certainly didn't waste time on comparison. Though, sometimes it hit her, stark and clear, that she was the cuckoo in the nest. A metaphor she might have liked—given her affinity for animals—were it not for the connotations. That she didn't belong. That she wasn't one of them. She'd felt that way long before she'd discovered the truth about her paternity, and in the years since she'd learned the truth it had been driven home undeniably. All in all, she mused while watching the two perfectly polished women discuss business, it wasn't that much of a surprise that she wasn't a Leighton. Not really.

Sabrina might be kind and caring, and a lot of fun, but she knew how to hone herself into a necessary image when need be. Damien was the consummate networker. It was why he had gone into business representing rodeo riders and garnering endorsement deals. A hint of rebellion toward their parents by getting involved in something somewhat lowborn, as they would see it, but he had gone on to be so successful at it they could hardly stay angry.

Though, she imagined they had been angry about his losing the winery, but she wasn't privy to conversations like that.

Bea was the loan fuzzy peg in a set of sleek holes. And she'd decided to make space outside of those holes because what was the point of trying to fit when she already knew she didn't?

"You're not working my brother to death, are you?" Lindy asked, and it took Bea a moment to realize that Lindy was talking to her.

"Me? No. He offered to help me with my chicken coop."

"Your chicken coop?" Lindy asked, eyes narrowed.

"Yes. There's one right around my cabin. I thought how handy, because I got offered some rescue chickens."

"You were offered chickens."

"Yes."

"So you're going to have chickens at your cabin."

It occurred to Bea then that this was Lindy's property. She knew that. The manicured section of the winery felt very much Lindy. But that wild, overgrown space that Bea inhabited felt very much hers. She had meant it when she had told Lindy that she didn't want the big house at the winery for herself. But she realized that she did think of parts of the property as her own. She always had, to a degree.

Those spaces that no one ever walked but her. They had always seemed like Bea's sanctuary.

She was really going to have to talk to Lindy about the animal refuge. The very idea terrified her.

The whole of the grounds belonged to Lindy now, thanks to that infidelity clause in the prenuptial agreement she had signed with Bea's brother.

A foolish thing for him to sign, since there was clearly nothing but infidelity in the marriages of the Leighton family.

As Bea stood, a living testament.

"You won't even hear them. My cabin is set back so far… No one will ever know."

"I suppose so," Lindy said, her tone wary. "But the chickens are not allowed in my house."

"Why would I ever bring chickens into your house?"

"Dane said that you brought Evan into the house."

Bea frowned. She was going to punch Dane next time she saw him. Okay, she wasn't going to punch Dane. But it made her feel better to think it.

"I have *never* brought Evan into the house."

Lindy let out an exasperated sigh. "Then my brother is a liar. But you did give him a dog. And he has the dog in the house."

Yes," Bea said. "But that's normal."

"And you acknowledge that raccoons in the house are not normal."

Bea thought of the frequency with which Evan inhabited her house.

"It's not normal," she conceded. "And I know to keep my eccentricity confined to my own space."

"What made you think of getting him a dog?" Lindy asked. "Out of curiosity."

Bea shifted. "There wasn't a lot of thought that went into it. Not really. I mean, you know how it is for me. Animals just kind of find me. And this animal happened to find Dane and me at the same time. I thought the dog would be a good companion for him."

"So you didn't give my brother a dog. You *coerced* him into rescuing a dog. You have a strange kind of magic, Bea," Lindy said.

"Lindy," she said, before she could think too terribly hard about it. "Did you mean what you said about me and the house on the winery property? You know, since my family used to own it. And, all of that."

Lindy frowned. "Of course I meant that. I mean it for both of you," she said, looking at Bea and Sabrina.

"Okay. Well, I don't want the house—"

"If you ever feel like you want more of a say in the business…"

"I don't," Bea said. "I'm not really going to be doing as much at the winery in the future. It's just not where my particular interests or strengths are at. I don't dislike it, but…"

"You're not really a wine drinker."

"No. And I like being outside. And I don't like nylons."

"Nobody likes nylons," Sabrina said.

"Well, I'm going to make life choices that ensure I can avoid them forever. I don't want any of the business. I just want use of the section of property behind my cabin. Across the river."

"I mean…" Lindy frowned. "We don't use it."

"I know," Bea said. "So I thought that maybe since you don't I might be able to."

"What do you want to use it for?" Lindy asked.

"This is the part that you probably won't like. I want to use it for an animal sanctuary."

Lindy blinked. "Isn't it…kind of already one? Isn't there already a raccoon wandering my winery?"

Bea sighed, and tried to keep herself serene. "I think Evan primarily wanders the woods behind the winery. But, yes."

"How would this be different?" Lindy pressed.

Bea had spent all last night weaving plans in her head but she didn't have a ton of practice with explaining her plans to people. That part of herself felt more than rusty after years of disuse.

"I would be renovating some existing structures and building some new ones. We would probably need more direct access to those pastures. And it would be… Well, people would know that I was taking animals. Instead of me just happening upon them."

"That is very much a you problem," Sabrina pointed out.

"I would have to think about it," Lindy said. "I mean, it would probably be pretty separate from the rest of the winery. But I worked really hard to make this place a certain…"

"You want it to be fancy. And I understand that. I promise I won't get my…Beatrix-ness all over it. I just want the one spot. I suppose I could get my own plot of land. Or I could buy that section from you. Maybe we could partition it off."

Bea understood that for Lindy the idea of class was

sticky. Bea had been born into money and she'd never cared one way or the other what anyone thought. Lindy had been born without and had spent a lot of years trying to prove she was good enough. In that way, Bea could relate, even though her particular point of insecurity wasn't people worrying about how classy she was.

It came from the same place though.

From being afraid to feel small.

Bea could be sympathetic to that.

Lindy sighed. "I don't feel good about that either. I'm not using that part of the property, and I don't want to profit off it. It's just the proximity of animals and the tasting room and all of that."

"I really do think it's far enough away. You haven't ever seen Evan over here, have you?"

"No," Lindy conceded.

"And anyway, the other animals won't be free-range like he is. There's not much I can do about a raccoon. But I'm going to keep the chickens very secure, in part because of Evan. Anyway, Lindy, you know there's animals all over the place out here. You probably have bears wandering through the grapevines every other night. It's just that you don't know about them."

Lindy's eyes went wide, a small crease denting her forehead as her brows shot upward. "You think I have bears wandering through the grapevines?"

Bea nodded. "You totally do. You should ask Wyatt if you can borrow a game camera and set it out here overnight."

"Everything here is so well kept." Lindy pressed a hand to her chest, as if she were looking for pearls to clutch.

"That doesn't matter. Animals don't care if it's manicured or not. If there is space available, they're going to occupy it."

"Okay, I take your point. Anything out here... We are going to have some animals."

"Plus, there's the river that runs through the property. That's a big-time animal magnet."

"Of course. It's just that I never really thought about that before." Bea didn't understand how you couldn't think of something like that, but she wasn't going to press the issue.

Sabrina's face seemed to light up, then her lips twisted into a half smile. "It would really irritate Dad. To know that not only did Lindy end up with the winery, but Bea started a full-on animal sanctuary on the property. When he never even let you have pets growing up."

Such a fundamental way her father had never understood her. That she needed that extra companionship. Would have given anything to have a dog to follow her around the property.

Or maybe...maybe it was a chicken-and-egg situation. Maybe she wouldn't have needed the dog so bad if her dad was the kind of dad who could understand that she did. It was impossible to say.

"If it doesn't work then I can shut down the operation. Or, I can refuse certain animals that end up being too much trouble. Or have too much smell."

"Smell," Lindy repeated.

"Well, farm animals *are* farm animals," Bea said.

Lindy looked aggrieved. "You know that I'm never going to be able to shut down your animal sanctuary once it's open."

Bea's lips twitched. "Well, yes, I kind of do know that."

"Beatrix," Lindy said, shaking her head. "I didn't know you were evil."

"She has that Leighton stubbornness," Sabrina said, and Bea felt gratified that her sister, at least, looked entertained.

But of course, Bea didn't have Leighton stubbornness. It was just her sister didn't know that.

All of Bea's openness from a moment before suddenly felt silly. And so did she. She wasn't who anyone thought she was.

She tucked her hair behind her ear. "Anyway. You don't need to make a decision right now. I'm not expecting you to. But…"

"But you want this," Lindy said softly. "And if you want it then I support you."

"I guess it's the closest thing to a dream that I even have. And I didn't really know that I wanted to do it. Dane was teasing me and… Well, that was when we started talking about it."

Lindy's eyes narrowed. "You and Dane were talking about it?"

"Yes," she said.

"I didn't know he had an interest in…that kind of thing."

Bea had a feeling that what Lindy meant was she didn't know that Dane ever talked to her. Which was fair enough. He hadn't much. Not before the accident. They had done a lot more talking to each other since then. They had been around each other a lot more.

And she wasn't ten years old anymore.

"Well, I will definitely consider it. More than consider it. I want to do it. Because I really appreciate your heart, Bea. And I think that it's only fair that you get some use out of this property. I just have to…"

"I understand," Bea said. "The winery is your dream. And you've worked really hard to make it into everything you have."

Lindy's hesitation didn't come from being a snob. Not like her parents. It wasn't about that. She had legitimate concerns with whether or not a rescued cow fit in anywhere on the property of an upscale winery, and Bea got that.

Bea spent the rest of the day alternating between trying to keep her focus on work, and spinning wild fantasies about the sanctuary. And then worrying about whether or not she was taking on too many new things at once. She had never considered herself a very ambitious person. In comparison with the rest of her family, she had always felt out of step that way. So it was weird to suddenly want so much. All at once. She had just never considered herself like that, and she was beginning to wonder if she was gnawing on something she was never going to be able to fight through.

By the time she was finished with the relatively easy work in the winery dining room her brain felt crispy from the tedium and from being indoors. And seeing the window to her cabin's living room thrown wide open when she got home did not help her mood one bit.

"Evan," she growled, then stomped into the house. The pantry was ransacked. Torn granola bags, decimated cereal boxes and shredded candy wrappers had been left in Evan's terrible wake.

And the door to her room was open.

She gritted her teeth, irritation creeping up her spine and rolling over her shoulders.

"You…grimy…snack bandit," she muttered as she began to make her way through the room.

When she got to her room, she saw a ringtail disappearing out the window, which he could obviously *also* open now.

She dashed to the open window and saw Evan scuttling away with some of her *intimate clothing*.

"Evan, you jerk!"

She dashed out of her bedroom, and out the front door, rounding to the side and going after him. He was fat, and not the fastest moving creature, but even so, he had disappeared quickly enough into the trees. She held on to the skirt of her white dress, holding it up, and charged into the woods after him.

CHAPTER SEVEN

DANE HAD A date with a chicken coop, and he couldn't find Bea anywhere. She wasn't answering her phone, and that wasn't like her.

He parked his truck in front of the house. Her truck was there. He walked up slowly to the front door of the cabin, and noticed it was cracked open. He pressed his hand against the rough wood and pushed it open.

And saw the mess that was strewn out everywhere. It looked like the place had been burglarized. For a second, his heart seized up, fear clawing at his chest. Had something happened to her?

The thought made him feel murderous. Made him forget his leg hurt at all. If someone had come into this place and done harm to Bea in any fashion, he'd show that bastard just what he was made of. Metal rods, muscle and rage.

And the man who dared cross Dane wouldn't like it.

He couldn't imagine anyone choosing to rob Bea's cabin. But he supposed Bea herself could have been a target, if not any of her earthly possessions.

The idea made adrenaline and fury spike through him.

He went toward her bedroom, where her dresser was completely pulled apart, and the window was open.

And then he remembered.

Evan.

Evan liked to get into the house and steal food and in general make a mess. The raccoon could get through the windows, he and Bea had discussed that, and Dane had even gotten some locks for them a couple of days ago. Of course, he hadn't gotten around to installing them.

And then he heard shouting, filtering through the trees. It didn't sound like terror. It sounded a whole lot like feral rage.

Dane chuckled and walked out of Bea's bedroom, making his way out the front door and heading toward the sound of the indignant yelling.

The sound of rushing water mingled with Bea's yelling, and Dane smiled a little bit broader.

Bea sounded as if she was fit to be tied, and he couldn't remember ever hearing her sound that angry. She was such an even-tempered person. Not low-key, necessarily, but her emotions tended to reside on the positive end of the spectrum. She got frustrated with him sometimes, but she didn't yell.

Hearing her yell at an animal was particularly amusing.

He rambled down the path, dodging rocks and roots as he did. Then he came through the grove of trees and stopped.

There she was, in the river. She was clutching a scrap of fabric in one hand, and glaring across the rest of the river at what looked like Evan on the opposing bank.

There were other scraps of fabric floating in this still part of the water, and she seemed to be actively attempting to collect them.

Her curls hung in her face, one damp spiral in the center of her forehead. And her dress...

A white summer dress that was now soaking wet and clinging to her body.

And the thing that shocked him into absolute stillness was that it was *such* a damn body.

He had never... He had never realized that Beatrix Leighton had a body like a back road.

He had never given much consideration to her body before, in all honesty. But it was impossible not to *now*, with that sodden, see-through dress hanging on her every curve. The material was translucent, and the water was...

Well, the water was cold, obviously.

And she was...

He felt a growing warmth in his gut, interest stirring in his...

Hell no. *Hell no.*

There were bridges too far, and then there were bridges to *fucking nowhere*.

And this was the latter. This was untenable. This was him being an absolute asshole because he hadn't seen a naked woman in the flesh in more than eight months.

And here was one, supple and naked and *damn those breasts* right in front of him.

He had never, ever felt any kind of below-the-belt stirring for Beatrix Leighton. It was an aberration. An abomination. It was...

Bea suddenly let out a squeak and sank, the water crawling up to her jawline.

Without giving it a thought, Dane leaped forward, unable to stop himself.

"Are you all right?" he asked, wading in, the water biting its way up his thighs, till it hit his jackass of a groin.

"Dane?" She looked up at him from the water.

He gritted his teeth against the cold. "Yeah."

"I slipped," she said simply.

Talking to her would surely fix this madness. Because once he was fully cognizant of the fact that she was Bea all of these feelings would go away.

"Why are you in the river?" he asked.

"Evan stole my…" She seemed to be searching for words. "Evan stole my clothes."

"Evan stole your clothes?"

"Yes."

He frowned. "Well."

"And the little bandit flung them into the river when he saw I was going to catch him. Now I'm trying to get them."

"I see that." More of it than he'd bargained for.

"Except it's so slippery." She began to swim, her dress flowing out around her, visible through the dark water as she went toward one of the pieces of fabric that floated on the surface.

And he was just staring. Like an asshole.

He charged forward, figuring forcing his body into a shocked state of cold was better than standing there working up an inappropriate boner for a woman who was practically his younger sister.

His boots were filled with frigid liquid, and he could feel them sloshing even beneath the surface. He was a dumbass. And now he was a dumbass with wet jeans and wet boots.

"What are you doing?" she asked.

"Helping," he bit out.

"Appreciated," she said. "Except I was the only one who was wet. And now you're wet too."

"Thank you," he gritted out. "I am aware."

He lurched forward, reaching out and grabbing the pale peach fabric floating on the surface. And it was only just as he closed his hand around it that he realized what he was grabbing.

A pair of flimsy. Lacy. Panties.

Bea's panties.

He did his best not to react. Which was a damned trick, since it was like he'd been reaching out to grab an innocuous stick only to find out it had fangs.

He turned around, and Bea was suddenly there, mostly submerged still, and thank God. But she was looking up at him with utterly pink cheeks, water clinging to her lashes, her lips shining and full and somehow incredibly noticeable.

"I think those are mine," she said.

He bit the inside of his cheek. "Well, I assumed they weren't Evan's."

"Thank you," she said, straightening, and reaching out her hand.

And giving him an up-close view of what he had seen from the bank earlier.

She didn't know. Obviously. Didn't realize that he could see the outline of what appeared to be a very thin white bra underneath the white dress. That he could see the exact size and shape of her breasts, and the way that her nipples had pulled into points. Because of the cold.

He dragged his eyes back up to hers, unable to believe that this was happening to him right now.

"A man sees a damsel in distress, it's the least he can do. If you ever get tied to any railroad tracks, I'll be there to help out with that too."

Bea rolled her eyes. "Evan doesn't have thumbs, Dane. He's not going to be tying me to the railroad tracks any time soon."

"Who knows?" Dane said, backing away. "The little bastard can obviously open windows."

"That is true." She was still standing there, arm stretched toward him. "May I have my underwear back now?"

Dammit.

He shoved them into her hand. "I don't have any use for them."

She slunk back down into the water and paddled back toward shore, and Dane stayed firmly waist deep in the cold water while she got out, that white dress clinging just as tightly to her ass as it had been to the rest of her.

Well, who the hell knew *Beatrix Leighton* had curves like that.

He certainly hadn't, because he had never looked at them before. Because why would he? What kind of pervert would he be if he did?

On the other hand. He was also a man. And this was kind of an extraordinary circumstance. One where he had been celibate for quite some time. One where she was prancing around like a wood nymph in a transparent dress.

He would defy any man to behave better than he was right now.

He wasn't even misbehaving. He was observing. Observing that he could see the color of her pale skin beneath the dress as it tangled around her legs. Observing that her ass was perfectly rounded, and just the kind of ass that a man could take a big handful of while he held her tight.

An *observation*.

Along with the observation that she had a sweet, narrow waist and... She turned to the side, yeah. Those breasts.

"I need to go get changed before we start...doing the chicken coop."

"I'm probably going to have to do the same," he said.

"Come on," she said.

"Okay," he said slowly, not wanting to leave the punishing shelter of the water, because the fact that his dick was submerged at the moment was probably the only reason he didn't have a hard-on.

The discomfort of the wet denim, and the biting cold of the water was the exact combination he needed right now.

But he also wasn't going to ostentatiously stand in a creek like there was something wrong. He wasn't going to show her that anything was wrong.

So he got up out of the water, training his gaze away from her body. But it was tough, because her eyes fell down to his lower half, amusement tugging at the corners of her lips as she looked at the wet denim.

Great. Glad she was so damned amused.

He was not amused.

"I have a mess to clean up in my house," she said, reaching up and fluffing her curls, then shaking her head out like a small, woodland animal, droplets flying around her. Then she smiled. Like she was pure innocence.

With a body that looked like a sure path to damnation.

"I saw." He pushed the words through his tightened throat.

"I was going to invite you over for dinner, since you're helping with the chicken coop. But, now all of my food is… Well, I don't know what survived the ransack." She looked thoughtful for a moment. "We could eat Evan for dinner."

He huffed a laugh. "Yeah. Like I believe that."

"I *am* about mad enough to roast him at this point." She shot an evil look across the river, and his gaze caught a drop of water slowly rolling down the side of her neck. To her collarbone. Down to her…

"Beatrix," he gritted out. "Why don't you go get dressed?"

She blinked. "I'm dressed, I'm just…"

She looked down, and he could see the moment she realized that her dress had gone see-through. "Oh. I…" She backed away. "I'll see you later."

She took off through the trees, and Dane just stood there, wondering how the hell the world seemed to be straight all around him when he felt like it had shifted beneath his feet.

CHAPTER EIGHT

BEA WAS ONLY mildly dented by the time she emerged
from her cabin again, feeling sheepish and red-faced
and hoping that she could possibly face Dane again
after the transparent dress incident. It would have been
better if she hadn't realized. But, she'd just been standing there talking at him with all of her…everything
plainly visible.

And he had been…she couldn't put a name to what
he'd been. Stoic. But firm about her needing to go and
get decent. And just so…flat. It was strange. She'd never
seen him look like that before, his lips set into a grim
line, his eyes cool and unfocused.

She didn't know how she felt about any of it. Just
weird. And wound up. And mostly like she wanted to
hide in her cabin for the rest of the evening. But they
had a chicken coop to refurbish.

She cast her eye over the pantry, unsure of what to
grab. It wasn't like Evan had gotten into everything,
but he had done a fair number on the pantry and after
her little embarrassment, she wasn't feeling particularly
hungry, anyway.

She felt… She didn't even know how to describe
it. She had never been even close to naked in front of
a man before, and now Dane had seen…some things.

And his response had been so tense. Which, she got. He was obviously embarrassed for both of them, and really, he should be.

She felt…

Like a naughty child who had been sent to her room. And actually, that bothered her more than the nudity.

She was a *woman*. She wasn't a child. And he had looked at her like she was… It was so dispassionate. So negative and…

She was wrong. Again. Like everything about her was wrong.

She gave up on food and clambered outside, heading toward the chicken coop, where Dane already was. Joe was lying down beside him, on his blanket, which Dane dragged everywhere with them. Not a big surprise considering Dane was turning into a softy where Joe was concerned.

There was also a cooler beside him, and that did surprise her. Because somehow, he had managed to get changed and collect something in the time it had taken her to change into something that was not translucent, and to steel her courage and come back outside.

"What's that?" she asked, pointing to the basket.

"Food," he said simply.

"What food?"

"Dinner. Nothing fancy. I had some leftover fried chicken. It's cold, but there is macaroni salad and some biscuits in the cooler too."

"Dane," she said, lowering her brows, "you want me to eat chicken while we build a house for rescue chickens?"

He tapped his chin. "Now that you mention it, that

does seem… Well, it seems right to me. I'm sacrificing my time to the chickens. They can sacrifice something to me."

"Sacrificing some time is hardly the same as sacrificing a thigh."

"Hell, woman," he said, gesturing toward his leg. "I
am sacrificing a thigh to do this. My leg has seen better days."

"I guess so." She laughed. And it felt…well, normal
at least. Not entirely back on their normal footing, but
then, she wasn't sure what their normal footing was.

They weren't exactly friends. They weren't really
family. She'd had a crush on him for most of her life,
and he'd been something of a distant, benevolent sym-
bol during that time.

But there was something about his accident that had
made them a lot more like equals, and neither of them
seemed to quite know what to do with that at any given
time.

But at least this didn't feel horrifying in the way the
inadvertent exposure an hour or so ago had. At least
this felt companionable and comfortable.

Not so much like she had lost her protective outer
shell and left herself exposed to censure and the ele-
ments.

"I can fix your windows tonight," Dane said, conver-
sationally as he began to unroll a spool of chicken wire.

"That might be nice," Bea said.

"Do you think Evan is going to come back today?"

"That's very hard to say. He's cheeky, but he also
knows when he's in trouble. And he's kind of…partly
rehabilitated into the wild."

"Right. And just domestic enough to be a pain in the ass."

"Yes." She didn't tell him that she also fed Evan every night. So, odds were he would be back to check and see if she still liked him enough to give him a treat.

And of course she did.

Stupid animal.

Without talking, she and Dane worked on the chicken wire, stretching it over one of the new sections of coop he had built earlier in the week. They were very nearly done. After this, there was only the brand-new door to put on. The old one had been completely unsalvageable. It had rusted hinges, plus it hung crooked. She needed to be able to get in and out easily. But, she also needed Evan to not be able to get in or out easily.

"I bought a couple of locks for the windows when I went into town earlier," Dane said, once they were finished with the chicken wire.

"Thank you," she said. "Locks have never really been a concern out here."

"Yes, the only kind of burglar you have to worry about is a strange, furry kind."

"True," she said.

Dane sat down on a part of the ground that was slightly raised, groaning as he did.

"You must be tired," she said, suddenly realizing how much of an effort he had put in today. He had been at Get Out of Dodge earlier, and then he had come here. And engaged in a water rescue for her underwear. She had been so lost in her own embarrassment she hadn't fully realized that the whole endeavor had probably physically taxed Dane.

Which could explain his reaction to it all.

Which meant maybe he hadn't been angry.

Maybe he'd felt nothing.

Somehow, that was worse and she didn't even know why.

He grabbed the cooler and opened it, pulling out a piece of chicken and biting into it ferociously. She sidled up to him and picked through the pieces till she found a leg, sitting with the cooler between them and starting on her own dinner.

Joe approached on unsteady legs, and looked at Dane, clearly expecting some food.

"No chicken bones," Bea said.

"Really?" Dane asked. "Why not?"

"They splinter. They're bad for dogs."

He shook his head. "You're going to have to give me a list of things that are bad for dogs," he said. "Because I really don't know anything about them."

"I can do that," she said. "He can have some chicken skin though," Bea said, peeling a little bit off the drumstick and offering it to the dog.

"You're going to spoil him," Dane said, his tone disapproving.

"Are you telling me you haven't already fed him food off your plate?"

"No," Dane said while steadily peeling a piece of skin from his chicken breast. "Of course not." He tossed the scrap to the dog, and then winked at her.

Her heart flipped, her stomach tightening. Normally at this moment, Dane would look away. Or he would say something that would remind her that he didn't feel any of this, regardless of what she felt.

Except, he was still looking at her.

And the light in his eyes was strange. She suddenly felt self-conscious about her lips. They felt conspicuous and dry all of a sudden, and she had no idea what she was supposed to do.

She ignored it.

For one breath.

Two.

And then, she had to do something. She had to lick them. *She had to.*

She darted her tongue out and did it quickly, but she noticed when his eyes dropped down and followed the movement.

Something fizzled in the air between them, like a sparkler. But when she looked there was nothing there. It was invisible. Something that seemed to exist on another wavelength. In the air first, beneath her skin the second.

And then Dane drew back. Sharply.

He pushed into a standing position. He took one more bite of the chicken and threw it back in the cooler. "It's time to get the locks put on," he said.

She nodded, feeling slow and strange, and like she didn't fully understand what had just happened.

Her fingertips tingled. Her lips tingled.

The tips of her breasts tingled.

Dane went back to his truck and acquired the tools, silently setting to work on the locks. Bea hung back outside, not sure why she felt compelled to keep her distance from Dane. Not sure about much of anything.

It wasn't until after Dane had loaded up his tools,

his cooler and his dog, and driven away that Bea had realized.

That maybe, just maybe, what she had experienced wasn't only inside *her*.

But that maybe he had felt it too.

She had no idea what to think of that.

No idea at all.

CHAPTER NINE

THE NEXT DAY, Jamie Dodge was looking for recruits to go out to the Dalton ranch with her and meet a few of the new horses that she would be working with in the next few weeks.

Bea and McKenna had happily volunteered. Mostly, Bea had volunteered because it was her day off and she knew that Dane would be coming over to put the chicken coop door on, and a good portion of her wanted to avoid Dane right now.

She wasn't even sure entirely of why.

Just that she felt weird and embarrassed and wanted to delay seeing him.

Which was something she had never wanted to do before. Not ever.

Bea had driven herself to the ranch, but then they had all loaded up into Jamie's truck and headed out on the road to the Daltons.

"This is nice," McKenna commented. "We haven't all gotten together for a while."

"Because you're obsessed with my brother," Jamie said dryly.

"I'm engaged to your brother," McKenna shot back. "That's a little bit different."

"Then are you *not* obsessed with him?"

McKenna laughed. "Oh no. I am."

Bea knew that Jamie liked teasing McKenna, but in reality she was thrilled that McKenna and Grant had ended up getting together. Grant had been widowed eight years ago. The fact that he was happy now was something that made the entire Dodge family happy.

"What have you been up to, Bea?" Jamie asked.

Studying. Working at the winery. Working at the vet. Having strange, electrically charged moments with Dane Parker.

"Not much," she said simply.

"But I haven't really seen you around the ranch," Jamie pressed.

"I'm getting those chickens," she said absently.

"And the theoretical chickens are that time-consuming?"

"Sometimes," Bea said, shifting uncomfortably in the bench seat.

"How is Dane?" McKenna asked, pointedly.

Jamie didn't ask about Dane, out of respect, it seemed to Bea. McKenna always did. Because McKenna didn't ever seem to mind ruffling feathers.

"Everybody always asks me about him," Bea said, feeling a little bit snappish and ruffled of feather, even though that wasn't exactly fair.

She looked over at McKenna, whose dark brows had shot upward.

"Sorry," she said. "I don't think I've ever seen you grumpy before."

Bea frowned. "I'm not grumpy."

"You sound a little grumpy," Jamie agreed with McKenna.

"I'm not," she insisted. "I'm just…taking a break from Dane."

"Did something happen?" McKenna asked, suddenly sounding far too interested for Bea's peace of mind.

"Why would you think something happened?"

The problem was, that nothing had happened. And yet, something had. Or maybe Bea was crazy and she was making things up. That was the problem. She didn't know.

"Bea," McKenna said, "is everything okay with you?"

"Everything is fine," she said.

"Did Dane do something? Do we need to beat him up?" Jamie asked.

Bea was starting to get annoyed with herself too. Because McKenna was concerned, and she was being a good friend and Bea was just…so over being protected. So over being coddled. If Dane needed punching, Bea could do it herself.

"It's probably nothing," Bea said, feeling like she wanted to unzip her skin and escape the truck. Escape her body.

"You're one of the most easygoing people I know," McKenna said. "And the kindest. You literally bought me a jacket when I had nothing. I was a stranger to you, Bea, and you bought me clothes. You don't get worked up over nothing. That's not you. So whatever it is you're feeling, don't try to convince yourself that it isn't happening."

Bea looked over at McKenna. She wasn't a whole lot older than herself or Jamie, but McKenna had lived a lot more life in a similar amount of years. She was tough, and she was extremely knowledgeable about the workings of men and women. Which made Bea wonder if she had been severely misusing her as a resource. Except Bea hadn't thought she would need a resource. She had never been trying to actively make anything happen with Dane.

It was so outside the realm of possibility it was laughable.

She had spent a lot of years following him around like a puppy, and maybe in the beginning she had wondered if she could be with him, but mostly, she had always realized that her admiration of him was just that. Admiration.

"Nothing really happened," Bea mumbled. "That's the problem."

"Tell me about the nothing," McKenna said.

"Well," Bea said slowly. "It was just a look. He looked me and… It was different. Somehow, it was different. I don't know why. But it was like there was an electrical storm. Or something."

"That's not nothing," McKenna said. "Maybe he's attracted to you."

"I don't… I don't think so," Bea said, her face going hot all over.

"Beatrix," McKenna said, using her full name, which people only ever seemed to do when they were being terribly serious with her. "I've only known you for a few months, but in that time it has become abundantly clear to me that you are a lost cause for that man. So my question to you is this—do you want to be with him?"

Bea gritted her teeth. "It's completely off-the-wall and unlikely."

"I didn't ask you if it was likely. Or probable. Or even

possible. In a perfect world, where you didn't have to worry about anything. Where everything would turn out perfectly no matter what you tried... Is he a thing you would try?"

"I... Yes."

"Then what are you going to do about it?"

McKenna said that like it was simple. Like Bea wouldn't be opening herself up to humiliation, and like it wasn't something she'd gone over and over again in her head. Dane wasn't looking for a commitment. And she had no idea how she could ever be with him, then not be with him. How she could see him all the time if they'd ever...

"I intend to keep doing what I've *been* doing," Bea responded tartly. "Ignoring it and hoping it'll go away."

"You haven't been ignoring it," McKenna said. "You're basically baiting him like he's a stubborn animal and you're a piece of cheese."

"I am not a piece of cheese," she said, grumpily. "I mean, I'm not acting like a piece of cheese."

"You've been caring for him for months."

"Because I care *about* him," Bea said simply.

"That's really sweet," McKenna said. "But that's not all it is. It's not platonic. And I don't see why you should have to accept that. I don't see why you should keep acting like his nurse or...or God forbid his sister."

"Because he's important to me," Bea said. "And no matter what happens with him he's basically part of my family."

"Except he isn't family," McKenna pointed out.

"McKenna," Jamie said, after having been noticeably

silent for the whole trip over. "I think what you don't understand is what Dane is."

Jamie turned the truck to the left, off the main road and up a paved driveway that Bea knew would carry them toward the impressive, immaculate Dalton ranch. Bea focused on the lawns, the white fences, the glorious white barns with green roofing.

Because if she didn't she might yell at Jamie.

Jamie acting like she knew about Dane. About men like Dane. Because why? Because she lived with rodeo riders like it made her an expert?

She was just as big of a virgin as Bea was and she was always going around talking like, of the two of them, she knew more.

Jamie claiming to be an expert on men because she shared a house with rodeo guys was as stupid as Bea claiming an expertise on sex because she'd watched crickets mate.

"What do you mean I don't understand what he is?" McKenna said. "He's a man. And no offense, but I think I know more about men than you."

"He's a *bull rider*," Jamie said. "And I'm related to one of them. I know all about them. We're about to go to the house of one of those men. I think he happens to be your father?"

McKenna waved a hand. "Sure," she said, meaning Hank Dalton, who McKenna had just discovered was her father a few months ago. It was that connection that had first brought her to Gold Valley. Hank had been reluctant to embrace the daughter he hadn't realized he'd had, the result of an extramarital affair he'd engaged in back before he and his wife had gotten their relationship on track.

"You're saying that all bull riders are like my father?" McKenna asked.

"Yes," Jamie said. "No offense, because he seems like a really nice man."

"None taken," McKenna said. "But Wyatt seems to be a pretty good husband, I have to say."

"It doesn't matter. The odds are bad with those guys. Believe me. I've completely had the mystique of the cowboy destroyed. Living with a whole bunch of them will do that."

McKenna muttered something and Jamie shot her a look.

"What was that?" Jamie asked.

"I don't think that's entirely true, Jamie," McKenna said, her tone crisp.

"It is absolutely true."

Bea looked out the front window of the truck and saw a rangy figure moving across the manicured property toward them. Gabe Dalton.

"So *my* brother is just boring to you?" McKenna asked, her tone exceedingly leading as she referenced her newfound half brother.

"Gabe Dalton is nothing but a work partner to me," Jamie said. "When I do find somebody to date it's going to be someone a hell of a lot different from these assholes."

Jamie got out of the truck and began to walk across the grounds toward Gabe, leaving the two of them in the dust. McKenna looked over at Bea. "Don't worry about what she says. I don't know what her deal is. But you know my assumption would be that she protests too much."

"Sometimes it's hard to talk about those things. Especially if you're not used to being able to," Bea said slowly. "And Jamie… Jamie likes to think she knows everything. It makes her feel safe, I guess."

"I get that," McKenna said. "I've been the very queen of self-protection for years. It's only since Grant that I actually changed at all." McKenna frowned. "It's not only Grant, you know. It's you. You and Jamie and your friendship. I don't mean to come at you with tons of advice or act superior or anything. I just want you to be happy, because you've helped make me happy."

A warm glow expanded in Bea's chest. She loved McKenna, and she loved that the way Bea cared for her in the beginning had meant something. It was something Bea knew how to do well. How to care for people. How to care for creatures.

"I've had feelings for Dane for half my life," Bea said. "And you know… You know he's made it clear in a lot of ways that he doesn't have similar feelings to me. But I still… It won't go away. I've pushed it down and tried not to think about it. Tried not to talk about it all this time. Having him look at me like that…"

"I think you should take a chance on him," McKenna said. "If he's not interested, what's the worst that could happen?"

"He never speaks to me again?"

"This isn't high school, Bea," McKenna said gently. "And I don't want to… I don't want to offend you. And I feel like Jamie would probably box my ears if she heard me say this. But you know… It's not that big of a deal.

Making a move. Having it rejected. I feel like you've never done it, and that makes it all feel huge. But it doesn't have to. It doesn't have to feel fatal. Or permanent. You can just…see what happens."

"Well, that's the problem. I have a lot of feelings, but I also don't think I want to get married or anything."

"Bea," McKenna said. "Middle ground. You know, you could just sleep with the man for a while and enjoy him. You want him. Why not?"

The idea slapped Bea right in the face. "I… Well. I don't know. I guess because feelings and…"

"You should like the guy you're sleeping with," McKenna said. "I've lived with men I didn't like very much because I thought I needed to be with them to survive. I needed a partner, and I was scared to be alone. Well, you're not alone. You have money and security. A place to live. Dane would be a decadent extra, and then when you're done with him, you can still be friends."

Well, that sounded a lot better than what her parents had always done. Tormenting and hurting each other. Infinitely better to the way Damien had been with Lindy. That sounded sophisticated and reasonable and like something Bea really would like to be.

"You have experience with the still friends thing?" Bea asked.

McKenna hesitated. "Well. No. But I dated a lot of jerks. But I really, really liked Grant and I went into it with that intention."

"But you ended up with him," Bea said.

"Well, yes," McKenna said, shrugging. "I really didn't expect to though. He was difficult. He was really wounded after losing his wife. And I understand that. He loved her very much. I had to get in there and be understanding of the fact that he might not be able to feel the same way about me. And you know what? He doesn't. We have a different relationship. We have our own relationship. Our own kind of love. It's certainly not less. It's…intense and wonderful. I never thought I could have love like this. But I only got it because I took the chance in the first place."

Bea nodded slowly, but said nothing. She watched as Jamie stood and made stilted conversation with Gabe. And worried that for her, it would be much the same that it was for Jamie. That the risks would never seem worth it, and that in fact the possibility of having something destroyed or rejected would be a lot more fatal to her.

Though the advice session had been better than Bea had anticipated. Bea was beginning to understand that sometimes talking about things was actually helpful. McKenna certainly hadn't made her feel small. She'd opened something up in Bea's mind.

"I suppose we should go intervene," McKenna said. "Jamie asked us here with her for a reason, I'm sure."

"Probably to keep Wyatt off her back," Bea said. "He's been touchy about her spending time with Gabe."

"But Jamie hates cowboys so much," McKenna said, her tone dry. "And she definitely knows her own mind, and just exactly what she's doing. Wyatt has absolutely nothing to worry about."

Bea worried a little bit about her friend. Jamie was brash and bold, and so many things that Bea wasn't. Bea, for her part, had always seen herself as soft. As vulnerable and easily wounded. It was why she'd always hidden away, why she'd let herself be invisible.

Jamie, Bea knew, was no less vulnerable. She just didn't know it.

And it terrified Bea that her friend might have no idea the kind of hurt she could get herself into.

Gabe tipped his cowboy hat up and smiled down at Jamie, and Bea immediately felt protective. Yes, it was a very serious worry.

"Yes," Bea said. "We had definitely better go… intervene."

"What are you going to do about Dane?" McKenna pressed.

"Hope that one of *you* will intervene?" Bea asked.

McKenna laughed. "I don't think you need someone to intervene," she said. "I think you need someone to give you a push."

CHAPTER TEN

BY THE TIME Dane limped into the bar the day after the River Incident—as he'd begun calling it in his head, in hopes it would superimpose itself over images of her body like a giant censor bar—he didn't know what the hell to call the feelings rolling around inside of himself. Hell, mostly. Just a little bit of hell that had gotten into his bloodstream and seemed to be spreading throughout his whole traitorous body.

He couldn't stop picturing the way Bea had looked at him while they were sitting there by the chicken coop. She had been delicately nibbling the chicken at first, and that had been…something of a strange distraction. One that should not have meant anything to him, but it did.

He had been distracted. By her teeth, by her lips. By the little smacking sounds she made.

What the hell of a psychopath was interested in the *smacking sounds* a woman made when she ate chicken?

A sexually deprived one.

A deviant.

But it had only gotten worse. A hell of a lot worse. Because then that little rabbit had looked at him.

Her eyes were so wide, so luminous and just plain fascinating. He had wanted to stare. And keep on staring. And then something had changed on her face. Color had crept into her cheeks, and he had realized something.

Beatrix Leighton was looking at him like he was a man.

And he had seen her down in the river only an hour earlier, and had been made very aware of the fact that she was a woman.

Tension had wound around them, thick and intense, and he'd had so many questions that he wasn't even sure he wanted the answers to. Like if this was the first time she had looked at him and seen a man, or if she had for some time.

He was left wondering if he had ever really looked at her at all.

Seriously. Closely.

There, in the sinking sunlight she had been beautiful.

A pretty little halo around all those curls, light spiraling through them like flecks of gold. Her lips were pink and full and lovely, and he'd wondered what they would taste like.

A moment of insanity that was now branded into his brain.

Absolute insanity.

He knew only one solution to that. And that was to drink it away. He had not wanted to risk drinking at home. Not because he'd do anything to Bea.

But drunk. Alone in his bed. With his body acting like this…

God knew what he might be tempted to fantasize about.

Last night had been tough enough, but he'd managed. Today it had all grown, the images of her body—her lithe body—all glistening in the water plaguing him. And he was pretty sure his brain was adding details.

And yeah, now he was out without a DD, but Lindy would come and get him. Hell, Lindy would probably take him in for the night, and help him avoid the winery altogether.

He didn't trust himself. Not now. Not while he was so clearly crazy.

He walked slowly across the distressed wooden floor, picking through the crowded place. It was a Friday night, and it was packed all to hell. Laz, the owner of Gold Valley Saloon, was behind the bar mixing drinks. But, Dane didn't require his skill. He just required whiskey straight out of a bottle.

"Hey," Dane said, flattening his hands on the distressed countertop. "I need a double."

"Is that all?" Laz asked, looking at him a little bit too keenly.

"To start with."

He laughed and shook his head, finishing up the drink he was shaking and sliding it across the bar to a man whose hands were as smooth as the suit jacket he was wearing.

"Nothing fruity in mine," Dane said under his breath.

"Don't go chasing off my customers by being a dick," Laz said.

"I would never do that," Dane said.

"Yeah," Laz replied. "You would."

He turned and acquired a bottle of whiskey, pouring a healthy measure into a tumbler for Dane. "Cheers," Dane said, lifting it to his lips.

Laz shook his head and went to take the next order. And Dane set about drinking.

"Drinking alone, Parker?"

Dane turned and saw Gabe Dalton standing there leaning against the counter. "I was," he responded.

"Looking for a partner?"

"No," Dane responded.

A smile hitched up Gabe's lips and he took a seat at the vacant bar stool next to him. "Well, consider me drinking adjacent."

Dane snorted. "Excellent."

"How's the leg?" Gabe asked.

"Great," Dane replied. "Spent the day training for a half marathon." He drained the rest of the glass. "Laz," he said. "More for me, and some for this asshole."

"Careful," Gabe said. "That feels perilously close to you drinking *with* me."

"Nope," Dane replied. "You going to ride this season?"

"Thinking about it."

"Only thinking about it?"

Gabe lifted a shoulder. "Things are picking up out of the ranch. I have a few new endeavors happening there. Also, a sister."

"Yeah," Dane said. "That's what I heard." It had been a minor scandal in the community when Hank Dalton's adult daughter had suddenly appeared.

"All things considered it might not be a great year to spend half of it traveling."

Dane shook his head. "I would. In a heartbeat."

Especially right now. He needed to…well, *get the hell out of Dodge*, quite frankly.

"It's things like what happened to you that make me think it might be time to be done," he said casually.

Gabe Dalton rode saddle bronc. So while their paths crossed, given that they often competed at the same events, they didn't totally move in the same crowd.

"Well, now," Dane said. "In fairness, if you get stomped by your animal, it doesn't have horns and it weighs a hell of a lot less."

"Still," Gabe said. "It just has to hit you in the right place."

"True enough."

"My brothers are all doing other things. Not particularly interested in helping me around the ranch. Smoke jumpers."

Dane had heard that. But he figured he'd let Gabe talk. Since the asshole was clearly intent on talking. "Trading in one dumbass endeavor for another?"

"Basically."

"I heard you hired Jamie Dodge for something over at the ranch."

Gabe chuckled. Laz brought their drinks over at that moment, and Gabe lifted the tumbler to his lips. "Was Wyatt blistering your ears with threats of skinning me?"

"No," Dane said. "My sister mentioned it."

"Wyatt was none too happy with the situation." Gabe scanned the room behind them, resting his elbow on the wall, his gaze sharp. Pointed. Looking for a woman, if Dane had to guess. Not a particular woman. Just a woman. Even if he wasn't particularly, it was habit. Lots of months spent on the road, nights spent in bars, where a man could meet a buckle bunny any night of the week who might make that motel bed seem less lonely. Dane could remember that all too well, though it was distant enough now it felt like someone else's life.

He missed it. If he were still living it there was no way he'd be dealing with the Beatrix situation now.

Gabe continued. "Wyatt doesn't trust me."

"Should he?"

Gabe lifted a brow and took another drink. "He doesn't have to have any association with me. Whether or not *he* should trust me seems immaterial."

"It's a sister thing," Dane said slowly.

"I have one of those," Gabe said.

"You've had one for a couple of months. It's not quite the same." That turned his thoughts back to Bea. She was basically a sister. Or she should be. She was certainly a sister as far as Lindy was concerned, and Lindy would not hesitate to lay waste to Dane's entire being should he behave inappropriately toward her.

"I promise I don't have any grand plans to debauch Jamie Dodge. I want her help."

"Still. Just thought you'd want to know. All the Dodge brothers would kill you. And I would help."

"You're not much of a threat to me right now," Gabe said, looking him up and down. Dane scowled and drained his tumbler again.

"Are you drinking to dull the pain or drinking to forget a woman?"

"The pain," Dane bit out. "I've forgotten women." Damn he wished that were true. He remembered Bea. He remembered Bea all too well.

"What the hell does that mean?"

Dane treated Gabe to a flat look, deeply regretful that he had opened his mouth about this particular topic.

But things seemed fuzzy around the edges and he had lost his hold on why exactly he should regret saying something like this.

"I've been convalescing," he said.

Gabe nearly choked. "You've been down-and-out for about eight months."

"I'm aware."

Gabe took a drink. "That sounds like hell."

"Least hell is hot. This is nothing."

He tapped the top of his glass and Laz refilled.

"Well, you're in a bar," Gabe said. "I expect you could find a hookup here."

"If that's an offer, Gabe, it's awfully sweet, but I'm pretty firmly team tits."

Gabe laughed. "Not an offer."

Dane looked around the bar, not just to see what Gabe might be seeing, like he had done earlier. But really looked. For himself. There were a lot of women in there he didn't recognize, which was frankly about where his standards were at. But none of them…caught him. None of them held him.

None of them had a wild riot of curls and wide, innocent eyes.

He doubted any of them would crawl around in the grass to have a conversation with a robin. And he didn't know why in the hell that should matter to him.

Not that he should be thinking of her while he was thinking about sex.

Putting that word into his brain and mixing it with thoughts of Bea was like the impact of a moving train. Particularly when mixed with alcohol, which lowered his ability to stop all those roaring images.

How would she look up at him as he were to touch her face? If he were to bend down and kiss her mouth?

Hell no.

He was supposed to come out and drink and forget about all that. There were women here. There was no reason why he couldn't get something going with a woman here. No reason in hell.

This was some kind of bullshit.

"I don't think it's happening tonight," Dane said, resolutely turning away, putting his focus on the back of the bar. He just wouldn't think about sex at all.

Which was, of course, now all he could think about.

The rest of the night was a blur, and he could barely remember calling Lindy and slurring out that he needed to get picked up. Sometime around when he and Gabe Dalton had taken control of the jukebox and asked the patrons of the bar to save a horse and ride a cowboy.

And he only barely registered his sister's judgmental comments after she loaded him into the truck.

And then later when she deposited him on the bed in the guest room.

When he woke up the next morning he had a splitting headache, and the tiny sliver of light that was filtering through the curtain felt as deliberate as it did evil.

When the door to the bedroom flung open, he knew that sliver of sunlight had in fact been deliberate. His sister was a damned witch.

"Good morning, sunshine," she said. "Wyatt is making bacon."

"I don't give a fuck," Dane said, covering up his head and trying to escape the pounding sensation in his head. Trying to get an accurate sense for what the hell time and place it was.

Then everything came flooding back to him with alarming clarity. Drinking with Gabe Dalton. Making an ass of himself at the bar. And Bea.

"You partied pretty hard last night."

"And you didn't. Which is why you're up being obnoxious this morning."

"I'm an old married lady," she said cheerfully, crossing the room and flinging the curtains open.

Dane cursed a blue streak, his own voice joining in with the light to add to the pounding in his head.

"You're kind of a pansy, Parker," Lindy said. "Since when can't you handle a night out drinking?"

"Since it's been eight months since I've done anything?"

"Don't tell me you haven't been drinking alone in my house."

"I have. But not quite to that degree."

"So what were you doing out with Gabe Dalton?"

"I wasn't with him. I happened to run into him." He dragged a hand over his face. "I need coffee. I can't be talking to you like this."

"How weird. I can talk to you like this just fine."

"Get out," Dane said."

Lindy hummed cheerfully and took her time meandering out of the room. Then she closed the door firmly behind her, and Dane sat up, going into the bathroom and splashing his face with water before heading to the kitchen, where his brother-in-law was busily cooking bacon.

Lindy handed him a cup of coffee, at least being a little bit nice beneath all of her obnoxiousness now.

"You want to talk about it?" she asked, settling against the table and pressing her fingertips against the rim of her mug, peering over it with wide blue eyes.

"No."

"Come on, Dane. It'll be like old times. When you used to get in trouble in high school, and I used to find you hungover. And then we would talk."

"I don't think that ever happened."

Lindy looked at him with full seriousness. "You were often hungover in high school."

"But we didn't talk," Dane said.

"Yes, we did. But mostly about how we were going to hide your hangover from mom. Who didn't really want to put up with yours since she had one of her own."

He shook his head. "How did we turn out so normal?"

Wyatt made a wheezing sound that he turned into a deliberate cough as he labored over the bacon. Both Dane and Lindy shot him a look.

"Anyway. I thought you were doing better."

"I am," Dane said. "I went out drinking. I haven't done that in forever. Not since the accident. Progress."

"Progress to coping with things in an unhealthy way?"

"I'm fine."

She had no idea what he had gone out drinking to avoid. If she thought it was all about his injury and his career... Well, he wished it were.

"Have you talked to Mom at all lately?" Well damn. Suddenly he had a feeling she wasn't asking about his injuries. "I know that… She tried after the accident. Has she… Has she been around much since?"

"I've seen her three times," Dane said.

"Does that bother you?"

Dane laughed. "Hell no. Three times is honestly pretty impressive for her."

"Have you ever… Have you ever heard from Dad?"

Rage streaked through Dane's gut. Hot and fierce, and he couldn't even quite say why it was so immediate. He never thought about that old bastard. Not ever. That he could have such an extreme, intense response to just the mention of him was…not really a pleasant revelation.

But then…wasn't that the best lie he could tell himself? That he never thought of him. That he never wondered if the old man watched him on TV. That his career had nothing at all to do with those parting words.

Maybe I'll see you on TV.

But I love you.

Dane's *I love you* hadn't gotten a response. *TV* was the last word.

He'd never heard from him. Not ever. He'd rode and rode, won championships, made a name for himself. Soaked up all the glory from strangers and told himself that was all he ever wanted.

That it didn't matter if his dad ever saw. If he ever knew.

If his dad watched…it meant he knew he was injured. And even then, nothing.

"No," Dane said. "Why would I have?"

"Because you got injured. And anyone who watches rodeo knows that. You know Dad always did."

"He probably stopped once I started doing it. In the grand tradition of never watching anything one of his kids did."

Lindy's lips twisted upward in wry humor. "I mean, that is a possibility."

"I don't care about Dad," Dane said. "Not at all."

"Sure," Lindy said. "Me neither."

That sweet, calm tone in her voice irritated him. Maybe because he knew she didn't really believe him. And she was trying to be gentle and nice because she was afraid…well, she seemed to be afraid that he wasn't coping.

But why would he care about their dad? He hadn't seen the bastard since he was thirteen years old. Why would any of it matter?

"You're early for work today," Wyatt pointed out.

"You're an asshole today."

"I'm an asshole every day," Wyatt said.

"You two are a match made in heaven," Dane said.

"That we are," Wyatt agreed. "You up to working?"

Yes, he was. He was up to staying the hell away from the winery. The hell away from Bea. The hell away from all of that weirdness that he really didn't want to cope with.

"Yes. I beg you. Give me something to do. I shouldn't be left to my own devices. Clearly."

"Now there's something we can agree on," Lindy said.

"Well, then you might have some fun using the paint stripper today."

"Power tools I am definitely good with."

"I'll meet you outside," Wyatt said, and Dane had the

distinct impression he was being set up by his brother-in-law, who left the kitchen.

The determined set of Lindy's face when he turned toward her confirmed it. "Real talk, Parker," she said. "What's going on?"

"I thought I'd see if I could have some of my life back. You know. Drink. Meet a woman." Any woman but the one back on the winery property.

"Dane," Lindy said. "You can't jump back into life before your body is ready to."

"My body is fine on that score, Lindy."

She stuck her tongue out and made a gagging sound. "Ew. I don't care about that. I didn't mean that specifically. I just meant you can't expect to just get back on the...bull, in this instance."

"I haven't done anything stupid." Not too stupid, anyway. He'd fallen down working on the winery once, but he hadn't touched Bea in spite of the fact that she currently made his blood hot. So he figured that balanced out.

"But you're tempted to," Lindy said softly.

He gritted his teeth. "Yeah, well, I'm tempted to do a lot of things."

"You do most of them."

He laughed, hollow and hard. "Not these days."

She had no idea. No idea at all.

"I guess that's growing up."

"No, that's being forced into solitude for eight months. I will be back. But it won't be for him. It'll be for me. Because this life... It doesn't work for me."

"What? Living at the winery, working with your

brother-in-law? Is it that bad, Dane? We have everything we need. It's nothing like when we were kids."

He gritted his teeth. "It's not mine."

"What do you mean it isn't yours?"

He shrugged. "I didn't build it."

"Then I suppose the winery isn't mine."

"Oh, you know that isn't true," Dane said. "It might have originally been owned by the Leighton family, but they didn't do half with it what you did. You did build it. You built it up and made it better. That would be like me saying just because I didn't start the rodeo I didn't build my career."

Lindy laughed. "Well, not just like that. But I can appreciate where you're coming from. I guess."

"Are you going to let Bea start that sanctuary?" he asked.

"What?" She blinked. "That's quite the subject change."

He shook his head. "It's not. It's the thing she wants to build, Lindy. It's her dream. It matters to her."

"You know I'm going to relent and let her do it."

"I don't see why it's a relenting thing."

"Because I have… It's my winery," she said. "You just said it. And…"

"And you're still scared of being unconventional?"

Lindy frowned. "I am not. I married my ex-husband's former client. I live on a dude ranch. I'm not scared of being unconventional."

"Just a little bit."

"Well, you're afraid of having to sit around here and sort out your feelings."

It was his turn to scowl. "I'm not afraid."

"Yes, you are. You're afraid that if you sit here for

too long you might have to sort some things out. Because as long as you keep moving, you get to hook up with women you'll never see again, stay in motels you'll never have to sleep in again. You're running, Dane. And that's really what you want to do."

"No," he said, standing up and shaking his head. "That's where you're wrong. I'm not running. Any more than you are hiding at the winery. That's what it's like. It would be like asking you to give that up. Your life's work."

"And the very idea of that used to terrify me," Lindy said. "Because the winery was everything I was. It was everything I had. I had such a hard time with Mom. She could never let it go. That I had decided to marry Damien. That I was so weak I had to take a man's money. You know how she felt about that. She thought she was right and good because she refused to take anything from Dad. Because she turned him away enough times that he quit coming back altogether. She thought that I was wrong. And so I clung to all of my reasonings. To everything I had achieved with that marriage, because it was all that I had. But it's not all I have now. And if I lost the winery tomorrow my life would still be full. I don't want to lose it. It's important to me, and it matters. But it's not everything now. I'm sorry that you're injured. I'm sorry. But, if you let life around here mean more to you then maybe it wouldn't hurt so much, the fact that you lost that other life. Maybe you wouldn't need it quite so badly."

As far as he could tell, life here was a disaster for him. Working at his brother-in-law's ranch, lusting after the much-younger-and-sweeter Bea and living in his sister's house. About the only thing that seemed to mean anything right now was the sanctuary. Because at least that was building something. But that was with Bea, and it didn't feel sane at the moment.

"Next time," Dane said, turning to head out of the mess hall. "Just ask me about my leg."

He turned and left his sister sitting there, ignoring the pain shooting through his leg and the heaviness in his chest as he went outside and went to work.

CHAPTER ELEVEN

BEA HAD SPENT the day researching permits.

She was going to have to get some in order to start the sanctuary, she knew that much. And she would need building permits for the barns. Also, there were various hoops to jump through when it came to gaining non-profit status. By the time she was finished looking at all of that she was exhausted.

But she also had studying to do, so that meant she couldn't be done.

Not for the first time she wondered if she was an idiot for deciding to open the sanctuary before she finished getting her certification.

But the more she thought about it, the more she felt like everything fit together. She was getting her training, and she already knew enough to provide basic medical care. It was a lot to take on, but if she waited, she might miss out on some animals in need.

She had spent a good portion of the morning on the phone with a woman who ran a dog rescue that she had volunteered at in the past. They talked a lot about her start-up costs and the ways that she went about running the facility, and the various grants that she had gotten over the years.

Beatrix felt empowered and determined. But still also a little bit sleepy.

For someone who had avoided this kind of work for most of her life, she'd sure gone and thrown herself in the deep end now.

Like she was making up for lost time.

She flopped down on her bed and opened up her animal anatomy textbook. There was a test coming up on the subject, and while Beatrix had a pretty innate sense for what hurt on an animal and what it might mean, she certainly hadn't known the scientific names for everything.

She did now.

She read until her stomach started to growl, and she was about to get up when she heard the sound of a hammer coming from outside. She pushed her bedroom window open and looked out, into the trees, where she saw Dane attacking the chicken coop.

"I didn't know you were coming today," she shouted.

"It needs to get finished," he said. "Aren't your chickens coming soon?"

"Yes," she responded. "But I thought you might want a day off." The wind blew straight through the window, crisp pine and earth filling her senses. She pushed her curls off her face and peered through the trees at Dane.

"I'll take a day off when this is finished," he shouted back.

Beatrix frowned and shut the window, heading toward the kitchen and snagging an apple. She paused, went back and took another one out of the bowl. Dane might be hungry too. An apple wasn't going to get either of them very far, but it was better than nothing.

She pushed the front door open and jogged down the path that wound behind the cabin and to the chicken coop. He was studying the door, a level set on top of the door frame. The bubbles were off center and he was tweaking and adjusting, the muscles in his forearms shifting as he did.

She swallowed hard. "I appreciate this. But I really don't want you to overwork yourself."

He shot her a deadly glare. "I just need everyone to stop trying to baby me."

She frowned. "You don't look so good."

"I had a rough night. I was hungover. But that's not really related to whether or not I should take it easy."

She blinked. "It's four in the afternoon."

"I worked at Get Out of Dodge all day."

"And so you immediately thought you should come attach a door to my chicken coop." He was a fool. But he was here. She appreciated that.

"Yes," he said. "I did."

She sighed and took a few steps toward him, holding the apple out. He jerked backward, his eyes narrowing, chin tilting down as his shoulders rose up. Like she'd held a spider out toward him and not a nice piece of fruit.

"Apple?" she asked.

In fractions, his shoulders lowered, his posture going back to its typical set. "In my remembrance of the story it's not Snow White who goes around offering apples."

She frowned, trying to parse the meaning of that. "Do you think I'm trying to poison you?"

He didn't say anything. He reached out and took the

fruit from her, taking a slow, deliberate bite that she felt somehow. "Not poison."

"Tempt?" She shrugged. "It's the only other thing I can think of that an apple is famous for."

He huffed out a laugh, then set the apple down on the top of his toolbox and continued to work.

She watched in silence for a moment, until she couldn't stand it anymore. Until just looking at his movements had started creating a strange sensation beneath her skin. "I'm going to start applying for permits on Monday."

He flicked her a glance. "Did Lindy agree to your plan?"

Beatrix bit the inside of her cheek. "Not exactly. But, acquiring permits can be a pretty lengthy process, so I figure I had better get started on paperwork now."

"Do you need any help?"

She bristled slightly. "Dane, I said that I was moving forward getting permits. You think I need help filling out basic paperwork?"

"I'm trying to be helpful," he said. "The fact of the matter is I might need to do some work that's not quite so intense the next few days. I kind of did a number on myself recently. A little bit of paperwork might be what the doctor ordered."

Beatrix felt slightly mollified by that. "I suppose that could be helpful. I do have a lot to do." And more sit-down-and-read time might send her over the edge.

"Just send over the things that you found," he said, waving a hand. "I'm sure your info is solid, I can just put it all together. Unless you're afraid the dumb rodeo rider can't figure it out."

"Not even a little," she said. "Thank you." She felt

mildly surprised that he so easily accepted that she knew what she was talking about. What she was doing.

It occurred to her then that Dane never really gave her advice.

It was kind of a stunning realization.

He had never treated her like an adult *or* a child really. He treated her…well, like no one else. He didn't talk down to her. He didn't act like the things she did with the animals were some delightful quirk to be indulged or ignored depending on the moment.

She remembered a couple of Christmases ago when she'd found three baby green herons that had been thrown out of their nest. It had been Dane who had immediately helped her get the supplies she needed to get the poor little birds hydrated.

It had been Dane who had abandoned the conversation that had been going on. Dane who had treated it like a serious situation.

He could also be an ass. Dismissive and stubborn. But not more to her than he was to anyone else.

She cleared her throat, but Dane didn't look up from his work. "My dad used to talk business over dinner. Constantly. And there were invariably issues with permits during the period of time when they were expanding the winery. My dad is not fond of the way the county runs, and he'll be the first to tell you that." She shifted. "I absorbed a lot of that. Even though I thought it was boring at the time. I'm surprised how much of it I remember now, actually."

Dane shook his head. "I don't know anything about all that. I've never had to…learn about it. All I've ever had to do is fling myself around on the back of a wild animal and hope that the thing couldn't get me off. And then if he did, that he didn't step on me."

"Don't say it like that," she said. "Like it didn't take skill. Or determination. It did."

She realized another thing when those words rolled off her tongue. That Dane was one of the few people she really got to take care of. And even though he was surly about it, he let her.

He picked up the fruit again and took another bite. She found herself captivated by the way his mouth moved when he chewed. The way his Adam's apple moved up and down. There were so many things in her life that she had wanted. And she had gone about getting them in different ways.

Beatrix had never liked the word *impossible*, and yet she had stuck it easily onto Dane.

But he didn't treat her like everyone else did. He didn't treat her like *anyone* else did.

And she didn't feel for him the way she felt for anyone else.

He looked over at her, as if he had just suddenly realized she was staring. The air between them got thick again, and she wondered for a moment why it was that this had happened twice while they'd been eating. It seemed weird.

But she couldn't explain it away either.

She didn't want to.

She had wanted to run from it the other day. In fact, she had. She had positioned herself so that she could take shelter by running errands with McKenna and Jamie. Because the moment she had thought the attraction between the two of them might in some way go both ways it had startled her.

Her feelings for Dane had been one of those closely cherished secrets that she liked. One that concerned only her. Because she had decided quite some time ago that nothing would ever happen between them.

She remembered what Kaylee had said. That something would change. Whether with him or not, something would shift. Like the wind turning the tide.

This was a change. Because three days ago nothing like this had ever happened between them. They never had a long, silent moment that felt anything but comfortable. This wasn't comfortable. It was charged.

Bea had no experience with men, but she had experience with Dane. She had experience in her own body. She was smart enough to know when things were different.

Working with animals meant being conscious of body language. Animals couldn't speak, so you had to look for signs in other ways. Dane's body language was different right now.

He was tense. And he was watching her. Like she might be a predator. It was the most abnormal experience of her entire life.

That she, Beatrix Leighton, might seem even remotely predatory to a man like Dane Parker. She was going to need some time to process that.

Or maybe she wouldn't process it. Maybe she would just look at him.

She took a step forward without really thinking, and he lowered his hand, the hammer still in it. "Beatrix," he said, his voice taking on a warning tone.

He was warning her. About what? She wanted to know. She very much wanted to know.

"Why don't I hold this steady while you finish hanging it," she said, curving her fingers around the door frame and standing there.

A muscle in his jaw twitched, and he cleared his throat. "Right. Sure."

He moved to straighten out the chicken wire and their fingertips brushed. Beatrix felt it like a kick straight to her stomach, when those rough, calloused fingers made contact with hers. The air seemed to rush out of Dane in one hard gust. And that he had a reaction at all was fascinating.

She looked down at his hands and felt much the same. They were scarred, hard and, she knew now, rough against her skin.

And this time, when they touched, he reacted too. She remembered a couple of weeks ago when she'd handed him that pain pill, and she'd reacted like this to them touching then, but he hadn't.

Something had changed. Something had shifted.

He worked silently, quickly, and she took the opportunity to stare at him.

The way his forehead creased as he concentrated on getting everything just so.

The way the corners of his eyes crinkled as he concentrated, his sun-weathered skin enticing and fascinating. An endless map of the expressions he'd made in the past. A key to who he was.

She wanted to know him better all of a sudden.

Really know him. Not just the man she had always

looked up to and admired. But the man who had fallen off the bull. The man who had been trampled.

The actual man, and not the aspirational figure.

He continued on his work, finishing up quickly, then calling Joe back toward the truck without saying much.

"Are you going?" she asked.

"I better," he said. "I'm bushed."

"Do you want to stay and get some dinner?"

He shook his head. "No, thanks."

"Should I go over to the house with you and help you get dinner?"

"I'm fine," he said.

"You look like you need someone to bring you a beer." And frankly, she wanted to keep advancing on him. If she was a predator.

"Beatrix," he said. "I'm tired. I want to go home. Alone."

She blinked twice, and watched his retreating figure as he got into the truck and started the engine.

He was running away. He was running away, and that fact would wound her if it didn't lead her to a couple of different conclusions. The first being that you didn't run from something if it didn't scare you.

Bea had never thought of herself as being particularly scary.

Which meant that it wasn't her. It was that thing that had changed.

And that made her even more certain than she had been before that Dane Parker was attracted to her. And he was...

Well, he was doing something. Protecting her from it? Maybe.

She had spent an awfully long time protecting herself from it.

And not acting on it would be a continuation of that. But she was doing things now. She was committing to this sanctuary and advocating for it. She was getting the vet tech certification. She was…

She wasn't letting all of it live inside of her anymore. She wanted more. She wanted people to see her as more. She'd spent a lot of years being perfectly content with her invisibility, but the problem with invisibility was that it was useful until it wasn't. If she really wanted to be treated differently then she had to act differently. And ask for something different.

Maybe that would extend to Dane too.

One thing was certain, when Beatrix Leighton set her mind to something she found a way to make it happen.

She just had to decide what exactly she was going to set her mind on.

CHAPTER TWELVE

Here's a link to the forms I found, plus some other info.

DANE LOOKED DOWN at his texts, his thumb hovering over the link attached to the message Bea had sent, when another message followed immediately.

Also my chickens are coming.

He hadn't spoken to Bea since last night. He'd just needed a break. From the tension that had sprung up between the two of them. Tension that had gotten so strong and thick that he didn't think it was even a question anymore.

They both felt it. But God knew there was no point doing a damned thing about it.

She was Bea. *Beatrix*, for heaven's sake.

He said that to himself like it should mean something, and for the life of him his body couldn't figure out anymore why the hell that should dissuade him.

He was saying no. That was enough.

He picked up his phone and responded.

Congrats on the chickens. I'll look into these permits right away.

He didn't get a response immediately, so he clicked the link to the paperwork, realizing quickly he wasn't going to be able to do this work on his phone.

His sister had a computer that was still in the house, and he'd been using it for his own purposes when necessary. Not that he often had use for a computer. He sat down and typed the web address into the browser, and started to go through all the information. It was pretty straightforward. Except they'd need a name for the sanctuary, they'd have to register it, get a tax ID number and get it all registered with the secretary of state. But there was no reason they couldn't get this started at the same time.

He could fill the forms out online, but he was going to have to submit them in person.

Because why would anyone want to make the process smoother?

He sighed and printed the forms off, getting a pen and sitting down at the coffee table in the living room with a beer in his hand. He went through checking boxes and entering information.

Doing as many estimates as he could based on what he and Bea had talked about before. He filled in as much as he could, but he was going to have to talk to Bea. He was going to have to see her.

He thought of how she'd been last night with the sun shining over her, and her face glowing like a damned angel. And oh, Lord it hadn't been heavenly things on his mind when he'd looked at that mouth of hers.

He wanted to make her fall. And that's what it would be. Sweet Beatrix Leighton getting down and dirty with him.

No. No way in hell. Or heaven. Or Gold Valley.

Anywhere.

Funny how doing paperwork didn't seem so bad when the alternative was dealing with Bea and whatever the hell weirdness there was there.

He was exhausted after the week of hard work too, but he was a damn sight better than he'd been even over a week ago, when he had taken a fall out in the grapevines.

So at least there was that.

He put his pen down and rubbed his temples, and noticed he had another text.

The chickens are here.

He smiled.

Congratulations.

Do you want to come and see the chickens?

Do I need to see the chickens?

You are a very large part of the reason they ended up being rescued.

He chuckled. That was Bea. Her being so very in character made it easy to forget that things had gotten so upside down with them recently. It was easy to forget the past week had happened at all. This was the Bea he knew. Texting him easily, no tension in the words.

He should go see the chickens. There was no reason

not to. And he and Bea were going to have to see each other eventually, anyway.

Sure. I will come see your chickens. And I have some questions for you.

He reached for his truck keys, then paused. He decided that he was going to walk down to the cabin. He was feeling better, anyway.

"Come on, Joe," he said, rallying his old companion to come with him. He would walk slowly.

For Joe.

He held the forms and pen in his hand, leaving behind crutches. He hadn't been using them, and while sometimes he relied on them to get over uneven ground, he didn't like to use them as a matter of course.

Joe limped along with him, and Dane made sure to keep an easy pace. One that happened to be gentler on his leg too.

It was nice out, the early spring air getting warm, reminding him of that time of year when it was getting to be close to ride time. When everything started to get busy and his whole life reduced to adrenaline-fueled punches when the gates burst open and the crowds cheered his name.

Long wild nights in bars and very late mornings tangled up in hotel sheets. Not always alone. Sometimes with a woman, usually with hangovers from hell. Often with both.

Glory that settled like stale confetti on a barroom floor. A celebration while it floated all around, drifting to the earth.

Trash once it landed.

This moment seemed in sharp contrast to those memories. It was quiet. With nothing but the golden sun high in the sky and the smell of sweet grass and early blooming flowers. A carpet of purple and orange beginning to spread out in the green field.

He couldn't remember the last time he had really stopped and noticed something like wildflowers. For him that wasn't what this time of year was about. It was about saddling up, about getting ready to go on the road again. Getting in his souped-up truck and migrating from town to town.

Filling his bank account. Win after win.

Each ride, each dollar, a brick in the fortress he built up for himself. The one that kept him from going back to where he'd come from.

The thing that separated Dane Parker, rodeo star, from Dane Parker, fatherless trailer trash.

But he couldn't do that now. Not anymore.

And the idea should fill him with terror. It had for the past eight months. A waking nightmare that followed him around. But he didn't feel full of horror now.

He didn't recognize the man walking across the field now, a limp in his step and a slow, stiff dog at his side.

No, he didn't know that man. But what struck him was that he wasn't deeply unhappy in the moment either.

He wouldn't call it happy either, but it was something else he hadn't experienced in recent memory.

Peaceful.

Bea's little cabin came into view, and his stomach tensed up.

He hadn't expected that. But he pushed it down and

continued walking on. Stopping to let Joe sniff around, probably smelling Evan's scent.

"If you see him," Dane said, looking down at Joe, "you have my permission to eat him."

Joe only looked back up at him, his tail swinging back and forth a couple of times.

"You wouldn't eat him, would you?" Dane asked. "You'd probably make friends with him."

The door opened and Bea came running out, a short floral dress whipping around her thighs, a pair of simple white sandals on her feet. He wondered if her toenails were painted. Which was about the dumbest and most inexplicable thing he'd ever wondered.

And he realized he was a damned fool.

He had imagined that everything would feel right back to the way that it was, but it didn't. That just because he was aware it was happening, it meant he could make it stop.

He'd seen her that day, standing in the river. Really seen her. He didn't know how to make the image go away.

He curled his hands into fists, keeping himself steady where he stood.

"Come and see!" she said, leading the way down the path toward the coop.

He followed slowly, careful to keep his distance, and Bea seemed happy to not wait for him. He was okay with that.

And there they were. The group of rescue chickens that had frankly started most of his troubles. Chickens and a raccoon.

And a bull.

Really. His entire life had been upended by a group of animals, if he thought too deeply about it.

"They're settling in," Beatrix said, looking luminously happy, staring at a group of nine little brown chickens and one multicolored rooster, who was strutting around with all the confidence of…well, of a cock really.

"Yes, they are," Dane responded.

"And that is the first of what I hope to be many successful official rescues."

"I think you've conducted a great many successful rescues," he said, his tone dry.

"I guess," she said, waving her hand. "But, the chickens spurred on the whole idea for the sanctuary. So, the chickens are significant."

"Yes. Very significant rescue chickens."

He watched them scratch and cluck around the little space, and he was surprised by how…accomplished he felt. They were just chickens.

Hell, he *ate* chickens.

But he'd helped fix up the coop, and now they were here. He'd built something, changed something, even with the way his body was right now.

"Thanks, Bea," he said, his voice rough.

She looked up at him, confusion shimmering in her eyes. "For what?"

"For giving me this."

"You built the coop for me," she said, smiling up at him.

"No, I think you let me do it for me. Thanks."

It was like a thread whipped up on the wind and

wrapped around them both, tightened, drew them both together.

But he resisted it.

He had to resist it.

He took a step away from her.

She cleared her throat. "Come with me. I want to show you some of the other parts of the property I want to use."

He thought about saying no. Thought about telling her they needed to see to the paperwork. Instead, he set the forms and pen down on a stump by the chicken coop.

"Sure. Lead the way."

He followed her down a trail that—thankfully—led off to the right, and not straight on ahead toward the river, because he didn't think that he could handle revisiting that particular crime scene. The fence around the field seemed in pretty good shape, which was good news as far as Dane was concerned. There would need to be some fixing here and there, but hopefully nothing too intensive.

Bea wedged open a big metal gate that definitely needed some repairs to make it functional, and the two of them entered the field. There was a barn off in the distance, and Beatrix went on ahead of him, her dress blowing up dangerously around her thighs, and he found that he had a difficult time tearing his gaze away, no matter that he should.

She looked at him over her shoulder, just a glance, but it felt like a hit straight to the solar plexus. Not unlike getting stomped on by a bull, now that he thought about it. The whole last twenty minutes of his life were like a strange out-of-body experience.

Or maybe it was the whole of the last eight months and it was all coming to a head right now.

Nothing felt quite like it should, and he didn't feel half so angry as he expected to feel about it either. Not right now. Not out in this field all alone with a beautiful woman.

But she was *Beatrix*. She wasn't just a beautiful woman, that was the problem. She was Beatrix, and no matter how beautiful she was she would remain Beatrix. And he would still be Dane.

"Is this thing even structurally sound?" he asked when they approached the old barn.

"All of the barns were structurally sound when Lindy had them revamped a few years ago. I mean, all the ones that she did revamp. This one she didn't, for obvious reasons. It's so far away from the rest of the winery facilities that there just isn't any point doing anything with it. At least, nothing related to Grassroots."

"We're going to need to make a back access into the property," Dane commented, mostly because he was looking for something to say.

"Yes," Beatrix agreed. "That would definitely be a good idea."

She started to pull on the barn door, but it didn't budge. She looked up at him, those eyes hitting him with that blunt force again. "Would you give me a hand?"

"Am I not too much of an invalid to open a heavy door like that?"

She squished her lips down into a firm line and

squinted. "Only you can answer that question, Dane. I can't answer it for you."

"Well, I guess the only thing I can do is try." He made his way over to the barn and gripped the edge of the door, pushing it until it gave, taking deep, sure steps that created a biting pain that ate its way up his thigh-bone as he did. But he ignored that and kept on pushing, because it would take only a couple of more steps for it to be open all the way.

When he looked up, he found himself standing right in front of Beatrix. Her lips curved into a smile. "I guess you could do it."

"I reckon," he said, walking inside the barn and looking around. It was dry inside, and that was a good sign. There was no lingering smell of rot or mildew, or anything like that, which might indicate the roof had leaked or there was water damage. He appreciated that because that meant most of the repairs for the place would be aesthetic.

"It's in surprisingly good shape, actually," he said looking around.

"It is," Beatrix said, moving into the center of the room. "That's very good news."

He turned a slow circle, looking at the empty space. "So what exactly are you thinking you're going to keep in the barn?"

"Horses, maybe. Although, I have a feeling that any horses I get will be quickly moved on to somebody like Gabe Dalton. There's a lot of help for horses. But you never know. I'm going to need shelters for pigs, sheep, goats. Probably a lot of goats."

"You think?"

"Yes," she responded. "Goats are a pain in the ass. They eat everything, and they can be escape artists. I imagine that a lot of people get goats only to find out that they are not quite worth the trouble."

"But you think they're worth the trouble," he said.

She shrugged. "Someone has to."

All that determination and caring in that slim-built, petite frame, and what he wanted more than anything in that moment was to know why.

"Why is that, Beatrix?"

She paused and turned around in the dim space, a slight crease wrinkling her forehead.

"I guess… You know it started out as a simple thing that I could do. My parents were unhappy. They were unhappy from the first time I can remember. My house felt unhappy. Damien was always angry and difficult. Him running off to manage rodeo riders didn't exactly thrill my parents. But then, he also earned a lot of money, so that was a bit of a difficult position for my father."

"And he married Lindy."

Beatrix nodded. "Yes," she said. "He did. He married Lindy, and they didn't approve of that either. And then Sabrina… You know, the whole thing with Liam Donnelly back then. When he left and broke her heart, and Sabrina found out it was because my father had paid for Liam to go away… She lost it. Completely. In public and embarrassed my dad in front of his friends. After that they were barely on speaking terms. Walking through my house was like trying to navigate through a roomful of delicate figurines that would be easy to break. Literally and figuratively, really. And I was… I was not the right person to be thrust into that situation. I never wanted to be at the center of conflict. It scared me, and I felt…so much stress, trying to figure out how to be the person that my father wanted me to be."

"But you couldn't be."

"No," she said, not sadly. Just simply. "And I didn't want to be either. I couldn't fix that house, but sometimes I could fix little birds that had hit the window, or one time a mouse whose leg had been caught in a trap in the kitchen."

The thought of wild, young Bea with her red curls in a tangle, and her face set to an expression of determination rescuing mice her parents had actively been trying to exterminate made it feel like there was something heavy and large sitting on top of his chest. "You rescued the mice that your parents caught in a trap?"

She nodded. "I did. I didn't tell them, of course."

"No, I would imagine not."

"It just started out as something that I could do. A difference that I could make, however small. And after a while, I started to kind of…identify with those creatures. They were small, and to a great many people they were useless. But I cared. I…I wouldn't want anything to go through life feeling uncared for."

There was something vulnerable in those words. But something strong too. That Bea took her pain and turned it outward, turned it into helping.

"Beatrix," he said her name slowly. "Do you feel uncared for?"

Her eyes widened, the corners of her mouth tilting down, then up again. "No. Not now. I don't now." She reiterated. "I feel…like I've made a great family. I feel like I found a place where I can be important. Working at the clinic, helping Lindy with the winery. Helping you…"

"Do you always need to be helping someone?"

"There's nothing wrong with that," she said.

"I don't suppose," he responded. "You can build a sanctuary, Bea, and the fact that you want to is a pretty amazing thing. But you don't have to *be* a sanctuary for everyone around you to make them care for you. We all care for you."

The soft, sweet smile on her face felt electric. Lit up places inside him that had only been lit up by pain for months.

"Thank you," she said. It took a breath for the moment to go from sweet to thick. Even with all that space between them, the broad expanse of hay-covered floor, he could feel a change. She shifted and looked down, and he held his ground. Didn't move forward. Didn't move back. He figured the best he could do was pretend it wasn't happening.

"We should go back," she said softly. "I should look in on the chickens and give them some feed. Plus, maybe we should make sure Joe didn't eat any of them?"

"Joe doesn't strike me as a vicious chicken killer."

"You never know."

"What we probably really need to do is make sure that Evan hasn't created any drama."

"Well, that is probably true," Beatrix said. She rushed past him, and her sweet floral scent caught on to him and held and it immobilized him for a moment. She was gone, having scampered through the barn door, leaving the broad rectangle empty, the sun shining in like a punch square into the darkness that surrounded him.

And he just stood. For that one brief moment he didn't feel anything except desire. There was no pain in his entire body for the space of a breath. There was only her scent, and his deep, biting need to go after her. Take hold of her. Do something they would both regret.

He gritted his teeth and took steps that were heavier than were strictly necessary as he went back toward her. Embracing the pain in his body as he went, because it was better than the desire.

Is it?

His fogged-up brain said different.

Bea looked like salvation somehow. Like touching her might make him whole.

But he couldn't. He wouldn't.

Suddenly the sun didn't seem quite so bright. Didn't feel as warm.

Bea was far enough ahead of him now that he couldn't make out the details of those long pale legs, they were just an impression. So there was that, at least.

When they got back, he picked up the forms he had intended to give her at the start. "Did you want to take a look at these?"

"Oh," she said, tucking her hair behind her ear. "Sure."

"If you don't want to…"

"I do," she said. "I do. Let's go inside."

Well, he hadn't really anticipated that. "Come on, Joe," he said, calling the old dog from where he was lying in front of the chicken coop, keeping vigil. He would use the old guy as a chaperone, if he needed to.

"Thank you for doing this," she said, ushering him

inside, and then moving hurriedly into the kitchen. "Do you want some tea?"

"No. I don't want tea."

"I don't have beer," she said. "I'm sorry."

"That doesn't really surprise me. I didn't take you for a beer drinker."

"I *do* drink," she said, as if that made her edgy or dangerous.

"You little rebel," he said, doing his best to lighten the mood between them, which had twisted into something decidedly strange.

She fumbled around, putting a teakettle on the stove, her delicate hands turning the burner on, taking a teacup and a tea bag from her cupboard. Again, someone might think from her movements that Bea herself was haphazard, but there was purpose in everything, and he knew there was purpose in this too.

Knew that she was probably fighting against that same current that he was so aware of right now too.

He'd wanted women and not had them before, hell, that had happened plenty of times. Because the timing was wrong or any number of reasons. He'd also wanted and had plenty of women, so this shouldn't feel new or difficult to battle at all.

Maybe it was the celibacy. That was the one wild card in this mix.

He could wonder what was wrong with him, but really it wasn't too mystifying.

Bea was a woman, after all. He might have spent a hell of a long time ignoring it, but he'd had it…kind of thrust at him and now it was all he could see.

That part of his body was not injured, thank you very

much, and he felt the ability to desire a woman plenty. But the idea of taking his clothes off with someone, of testing out his prowess with an injured back and leg and scars all over his body… Well, that was another thing entirely.

He wasn't anything now. He had no fame, no glory and no hope of getting it back any time soon. Nothing to make him important at all.

If he hooked up, he'd be bringing the woman back to his sister's house.

Taking a risk of being some kind of pity lay. Well, that he hadn't been willing to do.

The idea of being Bea's pity lay was even worse.

But watching the way she was reacting now, he didn't think it was that.

Because if she had been trying to offer comfort and he had indicated that he didn't want that kind of comfort, she would have been normal now. Relaxed, now that the issue was resolved. But she wasn't.

No, she was caught up in the same electricity he was. And she was avoiding it the same as he was too.

After she got the water on, he held the papers out to her, and she took them, looking over them. "It looks good to me."

"I need to know what your official business name is going to be. We need to get it registered and submit our information to the state to get certified as a nonprofit."

She nodded once. "Got it."

"I can conduct the meetings for you, but you're going to have to sign the final papers. I don't mind doing some of the initial dropping off."

"Okay," she said, nodding.

She passed the papers back to him and their fingers brushed. Dane gritted his teeth, taking a step back. "On second thought, I will have something. A glass of water."

"Sure," Beatrix said, overly bright as she bounded toward the cabinet and opened it, taking hold of a glass and fumbling with it. It slipped through her fingers and crashed onto the floor, spraying shards everywhere.

She cursed mildly, and Dane added a harsh one over the top of it. He set the papers down on her little dining table and lunged forward at the same time she did, both of them reaching for the small broom that was leaned up against the counter. They wrapped their hands around it at the same time, and the motion brought their faces close enough that they were sharing the same air.

"I've got it," she said softly.

"I'll get it," he said, his voice barely rising above a whisper.

"No," she said. "You should sit. You should sit, and you can just ask me... Ask me what you need to know for the form, and I'll tell you... And..."

Her words died, and he realized she had moved closer to him. Just a fraction.

The air seemed to stretch between them, tighten, get closer. She lifted a hand, the one that wasn't wrapped around the broom, her fingertips trembling as she reached forward and brushed the tips of them against the base of his throat, where he knew his pulse was pounding heavy. She rested them there, didn't move them away.

And he didn't step back.

Because right then it felt inevitable. Right then it felt

like he had been on a path toward this moment ever since he had decided to walk out his front door and head down to her cabin.

He didn't move away.

Instead, he moved closer.

She looked up at him, her eyes wide, her pale pink lips parting before she licked them. Slowly. Her pink tongue leaving them wet and irresistible.

His groin felt thick and heavy, his stomach tense. A whole mess of animals had upended his life and landed him right in this moment, but of all the things that had happened to him in the last few months, this one felt good. It felt necessary.

He didn't feel like a victim standing here right now. Didn't feel like a rag doll being tossed around on the back of an angry animal. No. He felt like a man.

He reached out, gripped her chin between his thumb and forefinger and held her face steady. She moved in, slowly. Slowly.

And then her mouth met his.

IT WAS HER first kiss. But that didn't matter.

It was Dane. That was all that mattered. That was all that really mattered.

Dane, the man she'd fantasized about a hundred times—maybe a thousand times—doing this very thing. But this was so much brighter and more vivid than a fantasy could ever be. Color and texture and taste. The rough whiskers on his face, the heat of his breath, the way those big, sure hands cupped her face as his lips moved slowly over hers.

She took a step and the shattered glass crunched

beneath her feet, but she didn't care. She didn't care at all. She wanted to breathe in this moment for as long as she could, broken glass be damned. To exist just like this, with his lips against hers, for as long as she possibly could.

She leaned forward, wrapped her fingers around the fabric of his T-shirt and clung to him, holding them both steady, because she was afraid she might fall if she didn't.

Her knees were weak. Like in a book or a movie.

She hadn't known that kissing could really, *literally*, make your knees weak. Or that touching a man you wanted could make you feel like you were burning up, like you had a fever. Could make you feel hollow and restless and desperate for what came next…

Even if what came next scared her a little.

It was Dane.

She trusted Dane.

With her secrets. With her body.

Dane.

She breathed his name on a whispered sigh as she moved to take their kiss deeper, and found herself being set back, glass crunching beneath her feet yet again.

"I should go," he said, his voice rough.

"No!" The denial burst out of her, and she found herself reaching forward to grab his shirt again. "No," she said again, this time a little less crazy and desperate.

She didn't feel any less crazy and desperate.

"I have to go, Bea."

"You don't. You could stay."

The look he gave her burned her down to the soles of her feet. "I can't."

"If you're worried about… I didn't misunderstand. I mean I know that if you stayed we would…"

"Dammit, Bea," he bit out. "We can't. You know that."

"Why? I'm not stupid. I know you don't want… I don't want…" She stumbled over her words because it all seemed stupid. To say something as inane as she knew they wouldn't get married. Even saying it made her feel like a silly virgin.

She was a virgin, there wasn't really any glossing over that. But she didn't have to seem silly.

She did know though. For all that everyone saw her as soft and naive, she wasn't. She'd carried a torch for Dane for a long time but she'd also realistically seen how marriage worked. Her brother was a cheater. Her mother was a cheater.

Her father was…she didn't even know.

That was the legacy of love and marriage in her family. Truly, she didn't want any part of it.

Some companionship though. Sex. She wanted that. With him. Why couldn't she have that? McKenna made it sound simple, and possible. And Bea wanted it.

"I'm going to leave again," he said. "Get back out on the road and get back to my life. I know it won't be this year, but I will. Next year, I bet you. And then what, Bea?"

"I…" His words hurt. Not just because he was rejecting her, but because in that moment she saw what he couldn't. That he was a man lying to himself.

That for all that Lindy and everyone protected her, they'd been protecting Dane even more. She among them. In that moment she wasn't sure it had been a kindness but there was no way to tell the truth now without it just sounding like she was using it to get her way.

"You mean a lot to me. You've helped me a lot. I appreciate that. But it can't change. We can't change."

"You kissed me back," she said. She didn't know what else to say.

"I also stopped," he said. "You're important to me. I'm not going to hurt you."

"You think you can hurt me because you think I'm a child, is that it?"

"Hell…no, Bea, that's not it. But we've been spending a lot of time together, and…you like to take care of what you see as wounded. It makes you feel good. But I'm not here to be a pity fuck, do you understand me? Not for you or anyone."

That Dane could possibly be wounded by her motivations shocked her into total silence. A pity…*pity*. As if she hadn't wanted him for most of her life. But she didn't know how to say that either. It got all tangled inside of her head and before she could speak he took a step away from her and headed toward the door. Then he let out a hard breath, and walked out, leaving her standing there, numb.

She grabbed hold of the broom and started to sweep up the broken glass, feeling like she was looking at a strange metaphor glittering down in her dustpan.

She'd taken a chance on a fantasy, and it had shattered right in front of her. But not for the reasons she'd imagined it might. She'd imagined it wouldn't work if Dane didn't want her, but she'd never thought that he might want her and say no anyway.

That he'd think she pitied him.

She heard scratching at the door, and she knew it wasn't Dane returning to apologize. She opened it and

Evan ran in, shuffling between her legs and heading straight for his food bowl.

She sighed and shut the door firmly behind him. Evan was watching her intently, his glittering shoe-button eyes appraising her every movement.

Evan, she decided, could wait. Evan was the cause of some of her current troubles.

She fed Tara, and then made a show of moving slowly toward the fridge. Evan quickly raised and lowered his front feet, his nails clicking on the linoleum, his face hopeful.

She sighed heavily and bent down, scratching him behind the ears. She opened up the fridge and got his dinner and deposited it into his bowl. At which point he lost interest in her completely.

She patted Evan one more time and was rewarded with no response beyond the cursory twitch of his tail.

She thought about what Dane had said. About the way she wanted to care for things.

It was true. She had been caring for him like she did her animals. It was what she did. It was how she connected with people. She took care of them. It had certainly worked with McKenna. She had bought McKenna a coat and they had become friends.

She had been taking care of Dane, and it was how they had gotten closer.

But it was more than that. It was. And no matter what he said to try to make it seem different, she wasn't going to let him. It wasn't just circumstances or her feeling sorry for him.

Something *had* changed.

She had kissed Dane Parker. Even if it was only once.

And she…well, she wasn't going to just accept what he'd said.

He could turn it around any way he wanted but it didn't change the reality of the situation. It didn't change the fact that he was doing what everyone else did to her all the time. He was putting her in her place. Assuming he knew what was best for her.

But this was different. He was doing it because he was afraid.

Of her.

"Evan, if you destroy my house I will throw all your food away," she said, rushing back to the bedroom and opening up—fittingly—her underwear drawer.

If Dane didn't want her, that was fine. She was a big girl, and she could handle herself.

But that was the thing.

She could handle herself. And she would be damned if she let this idiotic cowboy protect her from what she wanted.

From what they both wanted.

She was a woman. And she knew her mind, her body and her heart.

And no, she wasn't Dane's first choice. Being here wasn't his first choice.

But this was where he was now. And maybe…maybe they could have this now.

Whether or not he actually wanted it she didn't know. But she would have some respect. And it was going to start with him.

CHAPTER THIRTEEN

DANE HAD FELT like Joseph running from temptation by the time he had left Beatrix's cabin that night. He'd had a neighbor who had taken him to church sometimes when he was a kid, and he remembered a story about another man's wife coming after Joseph, and Joseph running from temptation so quickly he'd left his coat behind.

If Bea had grabbed on to him, he would have left his damn coat behind.

He didn't know why it was like this all of a sudden. All he knew was that moment down by the river had shifted things, and he couldn't seem to shift them back. He couldn't unsee something that he had seen. And it was like his eyes had been opened for the first time. Now all he could see was how much she'd changed in the past few years. How beautiful she was.

He had already begun to change the way that he saw her as a person. Not as sunlight, as a fairy creature. Not a sexless wood nymph flitting around the forest. But as a flesh and blood woman who would probably open her own vein to save even the smallest of creatures. She had passion. She had heart and determination, and it didn't come from her parents, who didn't seem to care about anything more than themselves.

Her mother had been reckless, had betrayed her marriage often, a fact everyone in both the towns of Copper Ridge and Gold Valley had known about, though everyone had been circumspect about the rumors out of deference to Jamison Leighton, Beatrix's father. He had always been concerned with image. Above all else.

Beatrix cared. Not about her own circumstances, not about what people thought. About living things. About people and animals and the world around her.

She was shot through with steel, and not because anyone had put a screw in her kneecap. No, she was strong and defiant in soundless ways that all these loud people around her seemed to miss. He thought back to the other day when Lindy had made those comments about Beatrix letting animals roam free in the winery. And how much it had annoyed him. How clearly he had seen then the way people misunderstood her.

The way everyone treated her like she was out of step, or needed advice, when he wondered if they would all be better off walking in her footsteps and taking advice from her.

Bea was unconventional, but that was a mistake to think it was an accident. She was what she was because she fought for it. Even if she did it with quiet stubbornness.

No one in his life had ever cared what he did. That made rebellion pretty easy. There was no risk in it. Lindy had just brought up the drinking he had done in high school. Yeah, he'd gone out and gotten hammered after football games with friends.

Had fooled around with whatever cheerleader was in the mood to play, and he'd continued living his life that way. For himself. A life that no one had ever opposed, because no one had cared enough.

Bea had lived in this house at the winery that seemed to him to be a giant box of a mansion that they'd tried to confine her in, and she wouldn't allow it.

But it seemed to him that few people appreciated quiet strength. Or the intelligence of a woman who had found a way to end up living the life she wanted when there had been no one around her to push her toward that goal.

Yeah, all that had changed first.

And then there was her body.

That was a hell of a worry.

Damn, that kiss.

It had made him feel alive.

But he couldn't. He couldn't do it.

Because though she was strong, and though she was stubborn, she still sweet. And a hell of a lot more innocent than he was. At least in that way. He would bet money on it. He hadn't been around all the time, and during the years when he had been traveling on the circuit, it had been intermittent enough that it was possible Beatrix had dated off and on, though never anyone long-term or he would have at least known about that.

Either way, she wasn't him.

And he and Bea were…in a very complicated way, like family. If something happened between the two of them and they went their separate ways—which they inevitably would—they would still have to see each other all the time.

Dane made a habit of hooking up with strangers so

he didn't have to deal with messy emotions associated with that kind of behavior.

Traveling, it was very easy to do just that.

Bea and all the complications associated with her were his own personal nightmare.

No. There was no way in hell they could ever be a thing. He walked into the living area of the house and saw his phone sitting on the coffee table, going through two of its very last buzzes on a phone call before it went dark again.

"Dammit," he muttered, walking up to the table, wondering who the hell was calling him at this hour. He picked it up, and saw a number he didn't recognize. One that wasn't local. He sighed and when a red number appeared by the voice mail spot he swiped his thumb over it. Lifted it to his ear.

The voice on the other end that came through the phone was a man's. It sounded familiar somehow, and he couldn't quite figure out why.

"Hi there," the message played. And then, it all became clear. "This is… This is your dad. I saw your accident on TV. I was wondering… If you were going to get back to riding ever. I always did enjoy watching it. You…you can give me a call back if you want."

Dane dropped the phone like it was a snake. He didn't care that it crashed on the coffee table, and damn near took a chunk out of the wood. He didn't care if the message hadn't finished playing.

His dad had called him. His dad.

He'd watched him. All this time he'd watched him. And he'd known that Dane had been injured for the past eight damn months and said nothing. No, of course he was getting in touch now when the season was ramping up.

He'd watched him. His dad had watched him.

His heart felt like it might explode. Rage, some other emotion, he didn't know. He'd wanted—so badly—for the rodeo to be about something other than his father. But standing there now, his body vibrating, he knew that it had always been about him.

Look at me, Dad. Look at me now.

Do you love me now?

He looked around the living room and saw his crutches leaning against the wall. He shoved them over, anger pouring adrenaline through him. "Yeah," he said, reeling back and resting too much weight on his injured leg, making him grit his teeth with pain. "Look at me now."

There was a knock on the front door and Dane froze.

He swore to God if that man was standing on his front porch he wouldn't be responsible for what happened next. There was a rifle in the house, and at the moment, Dane had half a mind to use it.

He walked to the door as fast as he could, gritting his teeth against the pain that was now his constant companion, and jerked it open. The anger in him fizzled away, shifted and twisted down low in his gut, giving way to a different kind of heat.

It was Bea. Looking up at him with a strange and determined look on her face. "Can I come in?"

"It's not a good time."

"Seriously?" she asked, frowning at him. "That's the line you're going to give me?"

"It's not a line, Bea."

"Sounds like one to me."

"Bea…"

"I am not leaving. I am not leaving until you tell me what the hell is going on. I deserve that much."

Damn her and her stubbornness. He might admire it when it came to patching up baby birds, but he didn't much like it when it was applied to him. "Come in," he said, stepping away from the door and allowing her entry.

"Dane…"

"My dad just called," he said, the word scraping his throat raw.

Bea blinked. "He…*what*? Your…your dad."

"My dad just called and he asked if I was going to be getting back on the circuit any time soon. He likes to watch me ride."

"Your dad. Who you don't talk to."

"Who doesn't talk to me. It's not like *I* abandoned *him* when I was a kid."

"No," Bea said. "Of course not."

"He called me," Dane said, anger still writhing around inside of him. Anger at everything. At his body, at the phone call, at Beatrix for changing one of the few things that had felt steady and nice in this whole damned world.

"What am I supposed to do with that? I mean, what the hell? He's never given any indication that he even knew I was alive and now suddenly he wants to know if I'm going to be getting back on the circuit after my injury. Like I… Like that mattered to him. Like the rodeo mattered. And he never… He never said. I haven't seen him since I was a kid. He never made contact, not once, during all this time, and he does it now."

Bea approached him, her expression cautious, and he fought the urge to step back. Mostly because he was just so damned angry he couldn't stand demonstrating that she affected him on top of it.

Couldn't stand the idea of changing his reaction to her. So, he stood there, to spite himself. To spite her. To spite everything.

Except, she didn't look like she felt the spite at all.

"You don't have to do anything with it," she said. "You can ignore it. You can ignore him. There's no reason in hell that you shouldn't have to. You don't owe him anything."

"Really? That's what you think? You don't think that I should be caring or compassionate and try to figure out why he… Why he did what he did, and why he called now?"

"If you want to," Beatrix said. "If you want to. But you know, genetics doesn't mean you owe him anything. Genetics doesn't mean anything. You don't owe him anything any more than I owe my dad… He gave me this house. He was here. But he wasn't interested in me. He was interested in the daughter he thought I should be. The one he wished he'd had instead of me."

There was something ferocious behind those words, something fierce in her eyes. And he liked it.

He took a step away from her then, pushing his hands through his hair. "I'm not going out riding this season, anyway. So it doesn't matter. And that's the only time my old man sees me, so, what the hell am I supposed to do with that? He watched me, Bea. All this time.

My dad had a connection with me, and I didn't have one with him. And I have no idea what the hell to do with this."

He was at a loss. He had been at a damned loss for eight months and he hated it. He wasn't a man who did passive. He wasn't a man who knew how to let the world defeat him, and there just wasn't any damn thing he could do about the situation he found himself in now. Not about the shit with his dad, not about the shit with his body. He just didn't know what the hell he was supposed to do.

He turned and hot, sharp pain shot through his thigh. He swore, picking a knickknack up from the coffee table—a leftover from his sister—and throwing it against the wall to spite…anything. Anything he could.

"Dane," she snapped. "Sit down before you injure your damned leg."

That stopped him for a moment, because Bea in a fury was an unusual thing. But she was definitely in one with him.

"Don't order me around."

"Then don't act like an asshole," she shot back.

There was an anger radiating off Bea that surprised him. He was pushing her, and he knew it, but he had never seen her angry. Not like this. She had definitely been short with him before, but this was different. Completely different.

She practically shimmered with her rage right now, and he had a feeling it was about a hell of a lot more than their present conversation, though he wasn't sure he wanted to know exactly what it was about. Not at all.

She was also beautiful like this. With her cheeks

red, her hair wild and as ferocious as she was. Her eyes glittered with passion, and even though it was a whole different kind of passion than he was used to having a woman direct at him, it was still a fascination.

And it made him think of that kiss. That kiss that was still there simmering on his lips. He might be on fire with anger right now, but Bea was incandescent with it.

Which made him wonder just how passionate she was in other ways. Other places.

The exact last thing he should wonder.

He needed distance, and his head wasn't functioning well enough for her to get it. So he said the first thing he could think of. For his own benefit if not for her.

"You don't have to hover over me all the time," he bit out. "You're not my damn sister, Bea."

BEA WAS ABOUT to lose her mind. She had already experienced some kind of whiplash, coming here hoping to seduce him and finding him like this.

And now he was accusing her of being his sister.

Dane had no idea. No idea at all. She remembered what it had been like to walk into the hospital and see him after that injury. Looking like he was dead.

And he didn't know that she had to lie to get in there. That she had to claim to be his sister. And she had to care for him like a sister. That's what she'd been doing. All this time. And she was tired of it. She didn't love him like someone loved a brother. She loved him like a woman loved a man. Wanted him that way.

And she was sick of it. Sick of keeping constant vigil by him like a concerned family member when that was not what she was.

He was hurting. Hurting emotionally, but it was a lot of the same as it had been that day in the hospital, and she was sick of being able to offer only this kind of comfort. She wanted to touch him. That was what he needed. She wanted to soothe him in a completely different way than she was allowed to. And she was tired of it.

So, so very tired of it. Of everything. Of him being so beautiful and so out of reach. Of wanting all these things she couldn't have. Of feeling like everything—absolutely everything—she wanted was something she somehow couldn't or shouldn't have.

A shame to push down deep and go unacknowledged. She couldn't do it. Not anymore. Not with him. And what the hell did it matter, anyway? He wasn't going to be what she wanted him to be, what she wished deep down he could be, so who cared what he thought?

Right now staring down into the gorgeous futility that was Dane Parker, she found she didn't care at all.

She'd come here to get him to listen. To get him to understand that she wasn't some fragile flower. Wasn't a glass that was going to shatter on the floor.

Telling him wasn't enough.

She'd have to show him.

"Sit down," she said again, heat like a prickling rash over her skin.

"Or what?"

There was only one answer. Only one thing to do.

And that was to follow through with what she came here for in the first place.

It took her a moment to realize she was actually acting on it, not just thinking about it. It was the mo-

ment her fingertips connected with his cheek that she
became fully aware of it. When that heat and lightning
flowed through her fingertips like a powerful shock
wave. When she felt that hot, smooth skin made prickly
in places by the evening growth of beard.

That was when she fully realized what she was
doing. And that was when she knew there was no turning back. She leaned in, her eyes meeting his, and there
was a fierceness there in his expression, but he didn't
tell her to stop.

Probably because he didn't believe she would do it.
Because he'd put a stop to it last time, so she wouldn't
be brave enough to do it again. But he was wrong.

And she was brave.

She closed the distance between them and pressed
her mouth to his.

And ignited a fire between them both.

The taste of his lips was an explosion. She was
rocked. His mouth was hot and firm and if it wasn't
like her fantasies she didn't really know or care. Fantasy didn't matter, not when the reality was here. Not
when it was everything. She cupped his face with both
hands and angled herself slightly so that she could part
her lips, his lower one between hers as she pressed herself more firmly against him. He wobbled off balance,
wrapping his arm around her waist as if to steady them
both, falling against the wall as she kept on.

She was dizzy. She was pretty sure she was going to
fall apart. Right there in his arms.

She wanted to absorb this moment. Take in everything. That scent that was so familiar to her, so very

him. His skin, which wasn't familiar to her by touch, but she wanted it to be. The taste of him.

Everything.

This wasn't like that sweet kiss back at the cabin.

She would never have called that kiss sweet. Not until this one.

This was something else.

He was kissing her back, like a man possessed. Like he was trying to consume her.

She wished he would.

She whimpered and shifted, pressing her breasts hard against that firm, muscled wall of his chest. His hold tightened on her, just a bit. Just enough. She was on fire with wanting him. And she could happily live in the moment for as long as she could, except there was a restlessness growing and expanding low in her stomach and she didn't know what she would do if she couldn't have more, couldn't have everything.

Touching his face was no longer enough. The thought of touching his whole body was such an intense, potent thought that the very idea made her groan, made her roll her hips forward.

And she felt it.

Dane Parker was hard for her. *For her.*

And that was about the moment she found herself being pushed backward. She wobbled on her feet, breathing hard and heavy, her whole body trembling.

She felt like she had a fever, but she wasn't sick. She felt hollow, and unsatisfied, and a sense of yawning desperation that she didn't know quite what to do with.

"Beatrix," he said, his voice low. "You need to stop."

"Why?"

"I already told you," he ground out.

"You didn't tell me anything. You never have."

"I told you earlier…"

"Yes, you did. You told me. You told me all about what you thought I wanted and what I didn't want. And what I could handle and what I couldn't. Well, you don't know me like you think you do, Dane Parker, and that's never been clearer to me than it is right now."

"Beatrix…"

"You *did* want to kiss me," she insisted, because dammit she wasn't going to let him pretend it was nothing. Pretend he'd had no feelings about it at all. "You liked kissing me."

"I'm a man," he said, his voice hard, tight. "It isn't a matter of me wanting to kiss you or liking it or not. You put an offer out."

"I don't know what that means," she said, her heart pounding so hard she felt dizzy. Felt sick.

"I haven't had sex in eight months," he said, the biting, bald words piercing her skin. "It wouldn't matter who you were. You go offering yourself up like that, my body is going to respond. But you and I both know that's not going to work between the two of us, Beatrix."

"Why not?" she asked, taking a step forward.

"Because you'd get hurt."

"Oh really? Why do you think that is?"

"You're a nice girl." His tone was so maddeningly even, so horrendously superior.

"What makes me a *nice girl*?" she pressed, shoving at his chest. "First of all, Dane Parker, I am not a girl. I'm a woman. If you hadn't noticed."

"Oh, I fucking noticed, Beatrix. About the time that you were standing in front of me naked the other day."

It was her turn to take a step back. "I wasn't naked."

"I could see through your dress." The way he was looking at her made her feel like he could see through her clothes now. Maybe even more than that. Like he could see straight into her.

She lifted herself up a couple of inches and tried to hold herself steady, tried not to look upset. "Well, then you were clearly able to observe the fact that I'm a woman. The fact that it makes you angry seems to be a you problem."

"No, it would quickly become a *you* problem," he said, his eyes full of fury now. "Because you think you want to help me scratch an itch, but you don't actually understand what you're getting yourself into."

"Shut up," she said, trembling with anger now. "You're the only person who has never talked down to me. You're the only person who's ever really treated me like I knew what I was talking about. You've never acted like the way that I took care of animals was silly. And you supported me when I decided I wanted to do the animal sanctuary. I don't understand why now... Why now you would go and act like everyone else. Why now you would go ahead and treat me like a kid who doesn't know what she wants."

"Because in this case I think you are a kid who doesn't know what you want. I'm sorry if that hurts your feelings. But I have shit that I'm dealing with right now, and I don't need your drama along with it."

"I didn't give you drama, I gave you a kiss."

"With you, honey, it's the same damn thing."

"Great," she responded. "But I don't think it's about protecting me. Because I'm not weak. And I'm not a child. And you get so angry at all of us for caring about you, Dane. But you don't know what it was like to walk into that hospital room and see you lying there looking like you were dead. Do you know what it did to Lindy? Do you have any idea what it did to me? I'm sorry that I was worried about you. I'm sorry that I… That all of my caring has gotten in the way of you having everything the way that you wanted. And I'm very sorry that suddenly I didn't behave exactly in the way that makes you comfortable. That you couldn't just use me for comfort anymore."

"Bullshit," he shot back. "I didn't help you build your chicken coop and get on board with the idea of your animal sanctuary for my own comfort. Don't go acting like a martyr now because you didn't get your way."

"You're just being an asshole."

"And you're being a spoiled brat. If you want to have some fun and get laid, go right ahead. I don't give a damn, Beatrix. You're right. You are a grown woman. But I'm too much man for you to handle, and you should go find someone more your speed."

"You think you know what my speed is? You think you have any… You don't know me, Dane. Obviously."

She was almost blind with rage. She couldn't remember ever feeling so…so angry. And she knew she had been this angry before. Angry at all kinds of different people in her life and not quite knowing what to do or how to say it. Being caught between the desire to remain invisible and the desire to be seen, to be understood. Right now she wasn't caught between anything.

Because she had taken care of this man for months and now he was doing the very thing that he hadn't done before. He was writing her off. Minimizing her. Taking his anger out on her when she had been the one who had actually tried to help him. She'd been endlessly indulgent of him. Had tried her very best to help him heal, to make him feel like a man in the process, to never minimize him.

And he was going and treating her like a child when he was the one person who should know that she wasn't.

Not because he had seen her naked in the water, but because he had seen the way that she worked. She had let him in. Had told him all about her dreams. And he had said that they were valuable. That he understood.

But apparently only up to a point. Only up until he was running scared.

"You're too much of a man for me, Dane?" she asked, vibrating with anger. "That's interesting. Because I don't see it that way."

"Because you don't know better."

"Oh, that's not why. It's because all I see in front of me is a scared little boy. You're in denial. And you can say that you're angry because your dad called you, but it's more than that."

"You don't know anything about it."

"Did one phone call from your father upset you?" She took a step forward and pushed against his chest. "Congratulations. Your dad called you once and hurt your feelings. My dad hurts my feelings every time we talk. That's my entire life. My whole relationship with that man. Buck up. Deal the fuck with it, Dane Parker. Because God knows I have. For my entire life.

I figured out how to be exactly what I wanted to be, exactly what I could be, getting no help from anyone, least of all the people around me, who all act like I'm easily wounded. But look at me. I'm standing here, and I don't have a limp."

"I didn't exactly choose to throw myself under a raging bull, Beatrix."

"You threw yourself on top of one, and you knew this might happen."

"Something might happen any time I walk out a door. I was hardly trying to get myself hurt."

"Maybe you weren't," she bit out. "But you're sure as hell choosing to wallow in it."

"Once this is all over…"

"What? What do you mean over?" she asked, horrified by herself now. By the words she knew were coming next. But she couldn't stop them either. She refused to stop them. "Do you honestly think that you're going to get back on the bull next year?" she exploded.

Bea had never hurt a person on purpose in her whole life. She was careful. Always. If she went against her parents' wishes she did it so quietly that by the time they realized what she'd done they'd likely forgotten they'd ever asked her to do any different. But she wanted to hurt him. Wanted to hurt him the way he'd hurt her.

"You're in your thirties. You only had a couple good years left, anyway. You know that. Somewhere inside you know that. I think the thing that really pisses you off about your dad calling you is that you know that the answer to whether or not you're going back is no. That's the real reason that you're upset. Because he asked you the direct question that everybody else is too tactful to ask. But be honest with yourself. Really honest."

He took a step back from her, his movements stiff, and she knew he was hurting. She also knew he'd never admit it.

"You don't know what you're talking about," he said, his entire face tight with anger now. She didn't think she'd ever seen him this angry. At least, certainly not directed at her.

She liked it. She liked it because it wasn't careful. She liked it because it wasn't safe.

She was so tired of the two of them being careful. That's all they ever were. Careful around each other. She had been careful to never do something crazy like she had back in the cabin. Careful never to kiss him even though she'd wanted to. And he had been careful to never hurt her. But she was over it. And maybe if she made him angry enough he would be too.

"I don't know what I'm talking about? You have been sitting on your ass for the last eight months feeling sorry for yourself. Making no decisions. Not doing a damn thing. Because you're just sitting here in denial. Hoping that one morning you're going to wake up and everything is going to magically be better. Let's face it. You're broken. And I know it. I know it because I was the one that went into that hospital room and saw you lying there like that. Like you were dead. I know it. I saw how bad it was. You were cushioned. By drugs. By this…silly idea that you have that someday it's all going to be back to normal. But it isn't and that's the thing that no one is telling you."

It was what she'd held back earlier, in the cabin. The

truth about him, the one he didn't want to see. She'd held it back because she was afraid of what it would make him think of her.

She didn't care now.

"Everyone's asking how you are," she continued. "And everyone's walking on eggshells because they're afraid to say *pull your head out of your ass and get a new plan for your life*. The old plan isn't going to work."

He made a sound that was halfway between a groan and a growl, and suddenly he was in her space. "I'm broken? Is that what you think?"

"Yes," she said, not letting her eyes leave him. "That's what *I know*."

"You think that because you take care of creatures that you have any idea what the hell is going on with me?"

"Yes," she shot back. "And if you were one of the creatures that I take care of I would've thrown your ass back into the forest by now and told you to make your own way. Because this is the truth of it. You can't have your old life back, Dane. You have to find a new one. So yeah, they should let you work harder. Wyatt and Lindy. Because they should get that by now. That *this* is your life. That's what terrifies you. Deep down you know I'm right."

"I can't have my life back?" The words were spoken softly, so evenly, that she realized he'd actually topped out on his rage. He had gone from yelling to a whisper, and that was even more terrifying than the yelling.

"I'm so broken that I'm suddenly easy enough for you to handle?"

"No," she said, rage spiking through her, spurring

her on. She reached out and grabbed a handful of his shirt, her heart thundering hard, giddiness mingling with the rage and making it difficult for her to breathe. Difficult for her to think. "I'm just saying that everybody's wrong about me too. I'm woman enough to handle you exactly as you are. And I think you're scared of that too, because it's just one more thing that's out of your control now. I'm not doing what you want me to do, and that's the real thing that bothers you. You're scared, Dane Parker. But you being chickenshit isn't my problem." And she closed the gap between them again, kissing him until his arm wrapped tightly around her and he reversed their positions, slamming her up against the wall with brute force that she wasn't sure he'd intended.

"You think I'm scared of you?" he asked, his voice rough, his whiskers rough on her cheek as he pressed his face against hers, his breath hot on her ear.

She was exhilarated. And terrified.

"Is that it, baby girl? You think I'm scared of you?"

"Y-yes," she said, a tremble in her voice.

"You're right about one thing," he said. "I am tired of sitting around and doing fucking nothing." She found herself crushed against his chest, his mouth hard on hers. He tasted like Dane, and fury, and in all the fantasies she'd ever had about this happening between them, it hadn't been like this.

He hadn't been so rough. So hard and angry. Her heart hadn't been pounding so hard that it seemed like it was trying to escape her chest. It felt like he was punishing her, and fair enough, because she had tried to punish him. But then somehow, someway, over the course of the kiss, it transformed.

It deepened, his tongue sliding against her mouth, demanding entry that she gave easily, willingly. It started to melt away the raw edges of the anger as it went harder, pulling something else out from inside of her. Creating within her a need so yawning and deep it felt like nothing she'd ever experienced. He tried to pull away, and she didn't let him; instead, she bracketed his face with her hands and kept the kiss going. Because whatever it was, she didn't want to lose the magic. Whatever was happening, she didn't want it to end. "I'll show you," he whispered against her lips.

"I'll show *you*," she whispered back, grabbing at his T-shirt, yanking it up over his head. She wasn't a little girl. And she wasn't here to be protected. There weren't words to express that. She'd already tried it. With anger, with spite, because he had hurt her. This was all that was left. It was all that she could give.

She broke the kiss for a moment and took a step back, looking at his torso, looking at what she had done.

She half expected him to pick her up and carry her to the front door before tossing her outside, but he didn't. He just stood there, letting her look at his body. She reached out, putting her hand on his bare chest, desire making her feel weak, making that place between her legs feel slick and hollow, her breasts feel heavy. She had never associated these kinds of feelings with anger before, but with Dane it was never that simple.

Because there would always be years surrounding her feelings for him. It would always go beyond the moment. He'd started to matter to her more than ten years ago and for her, this wasn't a shift, wasn't anything new, so much as it was an evolution. It was that anger that had allowed for another barrier to be stripped away. She had a feeling that for Dane, the first one had been stripped away down by the river and their anger had only stripped it down further. His reaction was showing her just how vulnerable he was. And this was her chance to show him how strong she was in return.

His face...oh, his face made her hurt. The sculpted line of his jaw, his perfectly curved lips that could look so inviting when he smiled and so forbidding when he frowned. The cleft in his chin that had another dent right next to it, a scar from who knew what or when. The new marks on his face, through his eyebrow, from the accident.

And his eyes. Lit with blue flame. Hot. For her.

He pressed his hand over hers and she felt the way his heartbeat raged beneath her palm.

His body was hard, the rough, masculine hair that covered his muscles there and down to his abs was fascinating to her. And he was... He was beautiful. So beautiful that it hurt. And every scar, every line on his body that showed the pain he'd been through made him all the more compelling. It was a road map to what had brought them to this moment.

Because maybe for the two of them it wasn't inevitable. Maybe this moment, this interruption in his life, had been necessary to bring it about.

This brokenness.

And she wouldn't have wished it on him. But she couldn't wish herself out of this moment either.

Not when it was everything she had ever wanted.

"Beatrix," he said, his voice hoarse.

"I don't care," she whispered. "I don't care if you have scars. And I don't care if you ever ride again. I mean, for you maybe. But, that's not why I want you."

"Don't," he bit out.

"Why are you fighting?" she asked. "Why? Everything is awful anyway, right? This could be good. It could be." She believed it. With all of herself. And more to the point she wanted it. She wanted it, and she was ready to take it. Ready to have this moment, whatever happened next. It was important. Because if she didn't want to be treated like she was invisible anymore, like she was a harmless child, then she had to quit acting like it.

He growled, and then his hands were in her hair, his mouth hungry on hers as he pressed her more firmly against the wall, the ridge of his arousal insistent between her legs. She rolled her hips forward, the sensation it created making her head fall back, making her gasp.

They made no sense at all outside this house, but this house was the only place that mattered. At least right now. And how fitting for her to be making out with a rodeo rider up against the wall in the house where she had been told over and over again that she was wrong. She didn't know her own mind. This same room where her mother had told her that her father—the man who had made her feel so insignificant for all of her life—wasn't even her father. That she was nothing more than the evidence of a regrettable mistake her mother had made all those years ago.

That she was nothing. That what she wanted was nothing. That she was wrong.

Well, this felt right. And it was what she wanted. And it was for her.

Because what she wanted mattered, dammit. From the sanctuary to Dane. It mattered.

His kiss was hot and hungry, desperate, matching everything she felt inside her, and she felt…liberated. Because what she felt wasn't wrong or strange—how could it be? When he seemed to feel exactly the same. For this moment, he did.

And in that moment, she didn't care so much what he thought. Not when she had given and given all this time and now she finally had the one thing she had wanted for longer than she could remember right in front of her.

"Show me," she taunted. "Show me that you aren't broken, then."

CHAPTER FOURTEEN

DANE SMOOTHED HIS hand down her back and cupped her butt, hauling her up against him and groaning as he lifted her off the ground and began to walk her back down the hall, toward the room that she knew he was staying in.

Part of her wanted to tell him to stop. Not to hurt himself. But there was another part of her that didn't want to give him that. They had both pushed each other past the point of no return, and she didn't want to give to him now. No, she wanted to keep taking, and see what he would take right back. He shoved open the bedroom door and threw her down on the bed, his eyes blazing. "Is that really what you want? Is this what you want? I tried to protect you earlier but if you insist..."

She looked at him, six feet two inches of angry, muscular cowboy, scarred and breathing hard from the exertion it had taken him to carry her down the hall, which probably only made him angrier.

Yes. This was exactly what she wanted. Dane. All of him. Not babying her, and treating her like she was fragile.

She wanted the man that she had been fascinated by for all these years, not some careful, muted version because he was treating her like a child.

No, she was a woman, and she damn well deserved for him to treat her like one.

"Bullshit," she said, on a roll now of using words she never did. "You were protecting you, Dane. Not me. I can handle everything you've got."

She grabbed the hem of her T-shirt and pulled it up overhead before she could second-guess anything. The bra she had on beneath her top was thin and lacy, and she knew that he would be able to see the shadow of her nipples beneath the fabric. She leaned back on her elbows, staring at him, appraising his response.

He moved forward, pressing his knee down on the mattress, between her legs, his muscles shifting as he did. Excitement jolted her, nerves twining themselves around the edges of that excitement. But she chose to embrace them. The bigness of it. That tingling that centered itself between her legs, where she wanted him to touch her most.

"I wanted to do this at the river," he said, his voice impossibly rough now, so rough that she swore she could feel it skimming along her skin, over her sensitized nipples.

She bit the inside of her cheek to keep from making a sound, to keep from wiggling and twisting beneath his gaze like she wanted to. She wanted to adjust herself so that his thigh was pressed firmly between her legs, offering some relief to the restless need that rioted through her. But she also wanted to sit there like that. Still as anything. To see just what Dane wanted. What he wanted from *her*.

Because he *did* want her, that much was obvious.

He reached down and wrapped his strong masculine hand around the center of her bra and pulled hard, until it snapped, freeing it from her body and leaving her bare to the waist in front of him.

He licked his lips, his eyes moving over her body. "Hell yeah," he ground out, leaning down and kissing her neck, his chest brushing against her sensitized nipples, the heat and hardness of his body sending a shock wave of need through her. He pressed his palm between her shoulder blades and brought her more tightly against him before claiming her mouth, rough, deep and sensual. It went on and on and by the time they parted, Bea was shaking, her center turned to liquid.

She didn't know that wanting someone could feel like this. Like a sickness. Like she might die if she couldn't have him. All of him.

She had known what it was to feel an attraction for him, to want him in a very hazy, fantasy sense. But this was close and real. So much sharper than desire had ever been before. It was the sound of heavy breathing, and the feel of his fingers tangling in her hair; it was those rough hands moving up to cup her breasts, and a lightning bolt of desire when his thumbs skimmed over the tightened buds there.

She whimpered, pressing herself more firmly against him, wiggling until she brought that thigh between her legs where she had wanted him in the first place. She arched against him, seeking satisfaction for the ache that had settled at her core.

He drew his leg back, his expression hard, unreadable. "Not yet," he said.

"Well, that's crap," she responded, reaching up to

grab his head, lacing her fingers through his hair as she arched up to kiss him.

He tilted his head back. "You said you could handle it. Were you lying to me, baby girl?"

"I can handle you." She lifted her chin, her heart thundering. "Don't hold back."

"Sweetheart, you have a lot to learn. Sometimes holding back is half the fun." His hands moved slowly over her body, his expression immovable. Then he reached down, his fingertips drifting to the waistband of her jeans, one fingertip easing beneath the denim, slowly, slowly teasing her.

"What's wrong?" she asked. "Did you forget how?"

"If you're a brat it's only going to take longer," he said, stopping his movements.

She bit back a hiss and stilled, and that was when he started to move again. And then she decided she wasn't going to just sit and let him control things. She reached out, putting her own hands on his belt buckle.

"I don't see why we can't both play," she said, working the leather free and letting it fall slack. She tried to disguise the trembling in her fingers as she unsnapped the jeans, then unzipped them, staring at the bulge she could see there behind the stretched black fabric of his underwear.

She was not going to let herself get all virginal and nervous. She knew what she wanted. If it was ever going to happen, it was going to be with him. And that had always been the truth of it.

He was the man she wanted. And it didn't matter what the circumstances were. Sure, when she had been younger, a stupid teenage girl with a thousand silly fantasies, she had dreamed of marrying him. Of being in love with him.

She'd spun fantasies around that kind of thing when she was a kid, but what she wanted had changed. As she'd gotten older, she'd understood. Marriage was a terrible, horrible trap. Her parents had both been caught in it, and neither one had been happy.

Neither one able to escape.

And Bea didn't want to be owned by another person, not ever again.

This was what she wanted. Just this. This might just be what they both needed.

"Careful," he bit out.

"Why? Because I might be too much for you?"

Gritting her teeth, steeling her courage, she reached into his underwear and wrapped her hands around his very hard, very thick length. She fought to keep the look of surprise off her face. Fought to keep herself looking strong and steady and supremely relaxed.

"Shit," he said, his hips bucking forward, his whole body on high alert.

"Oh yes," she said, supreme satisfaction rolling over her as she slid her thumb over the length of him, copying the way he had teased her breasts. "I think *you're* afraid that I might be too much for you."

That was how she found herself being pressed onto her back, her jeans being dragged away from her body, until she was left in only a pair of flimsy panties that matched her now ruined bra. Dane kissed her collarbone, the plump curve of her breast, sliding his tongue down over one tightened bud before sucking her in deep.

"Oh," she said, shaky as he teased her with his hand,

with his mouth, as he moved his free hand down between her legs and pushed it beneath the lacy fabric, his middle finger driving down between her slick folds, over that sensitive place no one but her had ever touched. Her hips moved involuntarily, her whole body strung tight as he sucked and stroked, drawing the tension inside of her up tight like a bowstring.

She whimpered, completely at his mercy and unable to even be upset about it now, because it felt too damned good. Because it was Dane, and he was touching her and it was perfect.

He shifted, twisting his wrist and continuing to stroke her as he worked one finger inside of her, the invasion unexpected and foreign, causing her to gasp. But he kept on kissing her mouth and making her mindless, making her crazy, kept on driving her desire up higher, hotter, like he was stoking a campfire with slow, expert precision.

He worked a second finger inside of her and she whimpered, the feeling of fullness almost too much to bear, quickly swallowed up by need as he increased the pressure on his thumb, as he sucked her tongue deep into his mouth, and then turned their kiss slow, deep and steady, an easy devouring that made it seem like there was nothing else he wanted, and nowhere else to be. She began to shake, her internal muscles pulsing around his fingers, the threat of desire in her stomach pulled so tight she was sure it would break. Or that she would break. All of her.

She had told him she wasn't fragile, but she felt like a pane of glass, perilously close to shattering, the cracks around the edges working their way toward the center until she knew… Until she knew she wouldn't be able to sustain much more.

"Yes, baby," he whispered against her lips. "Beatrix."

And it was her name that sent her over the edge. Her name on his lips, and that wicked, knowing sound, and she shattered completely, pleasure pulsing through her body like a wave. But to her surprise, she felt stronger. Felt renewed. He moved away from her, taking his jeans off quickly, and it all happened so fast that she didn't know where to look.

At that strong, masculine evidence of his desire for her, which was more beautiful and terrifying than she could have imagined. At the angry, horrible scar on his leg that went from his thigh down past his knee in a tangled-up mess that made her wonder how the hell he walked at all.

To the condom that he pulled out of his bedside drawer, which brought her focus straight back to that part of him that she wanted most. He tore the packet open quickly and rolled it over his length, and Beatrix didn't have much time to think before she found herself being pressed back into the mattress, kissed again on her swollen lips, which felt raw and sensitive and like a strange kind of magic.

He pressed that head of his arousal against her body, flexed his hips forward and primed her slick flesh with it, until she was aroused again, until she was full up of need again, so soon after her release that it didn't feel possible. He rocked like that against her body until she was whimpering, until she was pushing back, until she was pleading with him against his mouth to put them both out of their misery.

When he pressed against the entrance of her body it burned almost immediately and she panicked. So afraid that he would notice, that he would stop, she pressed her hands against his backside and pushed her hips forward. "Please," she begged.

And on a growl, he slammed home, a swear word on his lips as he did.

Their eyes met and held, and she was forced to face up to the moment. It was Dane. Inside of her. Dane, the man that she had wanted for as long as she had known what wanting had meant.

She was getting what she wanted, and she realized she had no idea how to handle that when another person was involved.

It hurt, she supposed, having him stretch that untried flesh of hers, but the pain wasn't anything compared to the huge knot in her chest.

To the emotional echo in her body that she couldn't quite shake.

But then, she didn't have to. Because he was kissing her again. Because he was moving slowly inside her, gently at first, just enough to stoke the desire that had been lost during the intense invasion.

She clung to his shoulders, kept her eyes focused on the familiar curve of his jaw, the golden stubble that covered his skin, the way his familiar mouth was set into a firm line, like it always was when he concentrated.

And then that beautiful mouth kissed her again, and she was lost. She moved her hands up and down his back, over his muscles, over his scars. She wrapped her legs around him, arching against him, meeting his every thrust. That knot inside of her chest began to ease, as everything in her body began to unravel, the slow build of pleasure inside of her deeper this time, lower and more centered. It felt right. It felt natural. Nothing about it new or foreign. Like it was something she'd always known how to do, at least with him. It didn't feel like a virgin and a rake.

It just felt like Bea and Dane.

Like all the changes that had happened in the last few months had been leading to this moment, and like each and every one of those changes had been a lesson. How to do this. And how to be this for him. And so she let go of everything that scared her and held on to him. She wasn't afraid to cry out her pleasure, wasn't afraid to whisper in his ear.

"More," she demanded. "Harder."

And he obliged, bringing his hands down beneath her ass and lifting her up as he thrust down deep.

"Dane," she whispered. He shuddered above her, bracing himself on the mattress as he froze, his arousal pulsing deep inside of her as he growled against her neck. His big body shook, that last little pulse of desire releasing the tension inside of her, her climax shocking her as it gripped her, gripped him, and they held each other. She was somehow more in tune with this man, who she had been yelling at not long before, than she had ever felt with another human being.

She traced a line down his bicep, enjoying touching him like this. Feeling how strong he was. Just being able to touch him. He was naked and pressed against her, and just beautiful. She felt stronger and more powerful right then with this boneless, sated man on top of her than she ever had in her life.

He rolled over, away from her, on his back, his arm thrown over his face. She wondered what he was thinking. If it had been good for him. If he was angry at her now, if he had regrets or if he wanted to do it again.

She waited. Waited endless seconds for him to say something. And that was when she noticed that he was breathing deep, his chest rising and falling slowly, evenly.

"Dane," she said, slapping him on the chest.

He jerked partway up, his fingers flexing, then relaxing. "Yeah?"

She blinked at him. "Did you fall asleep?"

"Not really."

He had totally fallen asleep. She pushed against his shoulder. "You…you big stereotype."

"I'm sorry," he said, rolling onto his side and looking at her. "I haven't done that in a while. Knocked me out."

She should be annoyed probably. But instead something inside of her melted. Because Dane Parker was lying next to her in bed, naked, and he was looking at her like she was special. She didn't have any room inside her to be mad. Not at all. "I feel… I feel like I should maybe be offended by that."

"But you aren't," he pointed out.

"I might be. But I can't decide if I'm offended you fell asleep or offended that you only fell asleep because you haven't…done that in a while."

"Bea, I'll be right back."

He turned away from her, his broad, bare back filling her vision as he sat on the edge of the mattress and pushed himself up into a standing position.

From this vantage point she could see his butt.

It was a very nice butt. His whole body was gorgeous. Even the places that were marked by scars. Maybe especially those in some ways. She winced as she watched him begin to limp toward the bathroom door. Okay, so in that way she couldn't enjoy the scars at all. She watched him intently, making a point to look at the one on his leg again as best she could while he walked into the bathroom and closed the door behind him.

She flopped back on the bed, feeling sulky that he'd left.

She couldn't believe the past few minutes had happened. Couldn't believe it was her life. Dane Parker. Her Dane. He had… They had…

A smile curved her lips.

All she wanted was to do it again. With him. As soon as possible. She had waited a long damn time. She was twenty-four years old and she had never even kissed a man and now she had… Well, she had had the best sex anyone had probably ever had. It had been with the object of her most beloved fantasy. How could it be anything else?

She could do this. She could have a perfect affair with him. Physical. Raw like this. She wasn't a child. She was a woman, and she deserved to have this.

Dane returned then, the protection dealt with, and with him still naked. She gawked at him shamelessly, utterly and completely fascinated by his body. By the way his muscles moved when he did, by the way hair sprinkled over some of him, dark and thick on his chest, thinning out to a line as it went over his abs.

"Yes?" he asked.

"Nothing," she said. "I'm just looking at you."

"As long as I can return the favor."

"I don't want you to worry about me," she said, sitting up, completely unembarrassed to be naked in front of him. It felt right. It felt normal somehow. And even though what had happened tonight was sudden in some ways, in other ways it was years in the making. He might not see it that way, but she did. There had been a shift in their relationship also. A slow, steady turning that had been waiting for all of these things to lock into place. That seemed clear to her now. She only hoped it was something he understood too.

"I wasn't actually feeling that worried about you," he said.

"Oh," she said, a flush of pleasure overtaking her. "Good."

"Might have been good if we had a conversation *before* that happened."

"We did," she said. "It was just that we were yelling at each other."

He nodded slowly. "We might have talked about the fact that you were a virgin."

She laughed. "Did you not know?"

He looked sheepish, shrugging his shoulder. "Honestly, I figured you probably were. When I thought about it. Which wasn't very often."

"But you did think about it."

"It crossed my mind. Mainly around the time that I saw your breasts through your dress."

"You liked that."

"You're gorgeous," he said. He shook his head.

"I'd never even kissed a guy before you, you know." He cursed. "Are you flattered?"

"I'm…I'm… I know this is a change."

"More for you than for me," she said cheerfully.

"How is that? I wasn't a virgin."

"No," she said. "But you are the one that seemed to be unaware that one of us was an adult. I was never under the impression that you were a boy."

"I've known you were a woman this whole time, Bea. But it's a hell of a lot easier with someone like you to pretend that I don't."

She wrinkled her nose. "What do you mean by that? Someone like me?"

"You know. I've got a certain thing that I go for when it comes to physical relationships. It's not you."

"Well, but you think I'm attractive."

"Yes," he said. "That's not the thing here."

"Well then what's the thing?" She sat up straight, taking great joy when his eyes dipped down to her breasts and his body started to harden again. She felt her mouth curve upward.

"Don't do that," he said.

"What?"

"You have to be careful. You can't… You can't be tempting me to do it again. You're inexperienced and I could hurt you."

She was fascinated by the very idea. *"How?"*

"Bea, I swear…"

"I like it when you're bossy and naked."

"I thought we were having a conversation."

"If you can handle it," she said.

"I travel. And I like my relationships as transient as my lifestyle. If we were to do this…"

"We've done it," she said, waving her hand between their naked bodies. "It's too late."

"What happened tonight was a heat of the moment thing. I'm not going to lie to you and tell you that it didn't matter that it was you. It did. What I said about wanting any woman… That was bullshit. I went out drinking with Gabe Dalton and I didn't want any of the women there at that bar. Any one of them could've kissed me and I wouldn't have been tempted. I want you," he said. "The problem is that there's nowhere it can go."

"I don't want it to go anywhere," she said. "Plenty of women have physical-only affairs and they're completely fine with it. I don't see why I can't be one of them. Really. I couldn't exactly stay a virgin for the rest of my life. And let's be honest, Dane, I've had a bit of a crush on you for a long time."

He jerked back, his eyes going wide. "You have?"

Well, that wasn't the reaction she had expected. She tried to look cool and she waved a hand. "Yes. I mean, in that way that I've been somewhat sexually fascinated by you. But believe me, I'm no more interested in a relationship than you are. Look at my family. It's a disaster. I don't want anything to do with that kind of thing. My parents didn't do anything but hurt each other. Ever. That's all they do still. I'd never want to waste my life like that. Even more than that, I don't really want to be beholden to anyone. I grew up like that. Doing what my parents wanted, trying to be something they wanted me to be. I'm finding my freedom now. I spent so much of my life trying to be invisible, Dane. To hide my feelings. To hide what I wanted. I don't want to do that anymore. I want to have an affair with you. I want to set up the animal sanctuary. I want to live a life on my terms. I don't want to worry about what other people think."

"Yeah," he said. "But here's the thing. Lindy can't know."

"Why not?"

"She would skin me alive. She would absolutely skin me alive if she knew that I touched you, Bea, and I think you know that."

Bea made a ferocious sound. "Well, that's not fair. She got to sleep around with Wyatt."

"She *married* him."

"Fair enough," Bea said, "but she didn't intend to marry him. Why is she allowed to have sex and I'm not?"

"It's not you personally. It's you and me. I think it would stress her out. I think she would be worried about what that would do to…everything. You know how she is. She's a control freak."

"Yeah," Beatrix said. "I mean, seems to be a genetic thing."

"What does that mean?"

"You're not really less of one. You're just one in a different way. But you still are one."

"Let's just keep this between you and me. Not because you should be embarrassed. But because it would be better if we didn't have to answer to anyone else, don't you think?"

She had to admit, that was a fair enough point. But,

she also wanted to find a way to mention to Jamie that this had happened. Because she would absolutely love to see the look on her friend's face when she realized that Beatrix was the one who actually had more experience with men now.

"I'm sorry about what I said," she said, moving to the edge of the bed and getting up on her knees so that she was eye level with his collarbone. She wrapped her arms around his shoulders and pressed her breasts to his chest, and she could feel him getting hard against her. "I'm sorry."

"I'm sorry," he said. "I said a whole bunch of brainless stuff. You didn't deserve that. It wasn't about you. It was about me."

"What I said was mean," she said.

"It was true though," he said. "Wasn't it?"

She shifted uncomfortably and looked up at him. He wasn't looking at her.

"I'm not an idiot, Beatrix. I know all the things that you said. But I try not to think about it. And I keep thinking… We'll just see how it goes. But it's not changing."

"There are a lot of things you can do," she said. "You don't have to ride bulls to make a living."

"I don't need to make a living anymore, Beatrix. I'm like you. Independently wealthy."

"Well, except you didn't get it from your… From a parent."

She stumbled over the word *father*, because it was just tricky to know what to call Jamison Leighton anymore. He was her father, in that he had raised her as his own daughter. But then, being raised as Jamison

Leighton's daughter was sometimes more curse than blessing. "So you don't have to work. You can choose what you want."

He stood there and looked stunned for a minute. "I've never looked at it that way, I guess. I always did what I had to. What I had to make myself into something."

"I understand that."

"I guess I'm going to have to figure out what I want after this."

"Well," she said slowly, wiggling against him. He was fully hard now, that thick ridge of flesh pressed firmly against her midsection. "You don't have to plan too far ahead right now. Maybe just the next hour or so?"

His lips curved up. "An hour, huh?"

"If you *can*."

He chuckled and slid one fingertip slowly down the line of her spine, the callused skin making her shiver with desire. "I think that you are vastly underestimating what we might accomplish, Bea. You're tough. A hell of a lot tougher than I think anyone gives you credit for. But I know what I'm doing in bed. On that you're going to have to trust me."

"I guess so," she said, wiggling slightly, gratified by the groan that elicited from him. "Since you're the only man I've ever been with."

He bit out a curse, and she was gratified by that too. Because obviously Dane Parker was a little bit of a caveman. And for her part, she liked it.

"Oh, I don't think you'll have to take my word for it," he said. "Not by the time I'm through with you."

CHAPTER FIFTEEN

WHEN DANE WOKE up the next morning the first thing he thought was not about how sore his body felt. It was not about the ache in his thigh. He didn't just lie there, hoping that he was dreaming any kind of lingering pain, and when he snapped into full consciousness he would find that it had all been just a dream.

No, the first thought he had the next morning centered around the fact that he was hard. And the fact that there was a soft, very willing woman tucked up against him.

When they'd finished for the—maybe third time?— Bea had completely melted into his body, her delicious ass now pressed up against his erection. One of his hands was firmly wrapped around her breast, and for a full minute he just lay there and enjoyed those feelings. Her softness, those sweet feminine curves.

And the memories of last night.

He'd tried to put a limit on things, tried to be gentle with her, all things considered, but she had gotten frustrated with foreplay after a while and had tempted him beyond reason. And right about now he was thinking he'd like her to tempt him again.

He waited for there to be guilt too. But he didn't feel any.

Why should he? Beatrix was right. She was a grown woman. And she knew what she wanted. Hell, she'd proven that to him quite a few times last night.

She squirmed in his arms, turning over to face him, looking up at him sleepily. "Good morning," she murmured.

"Good morning," he returned.

He couldn't remember the last time he had done this. Woken up in bed with a woman. Not hungover. And on purpose.

He waited for it to freak him out. But it didn't. It was Beatrix. Whether they were working on a chicken coop or lying in bed naked together, it was Beatrix.

"Dammit," she said, letting her head fall back on the pillow, her curls rusty gold against the white pillowcase.

"What? Are you that disappointed to wake up and find me in bed with you?"

She covered her face and wailed through her hands. "Evan is in my house."

He laughed and pried her hands away and dropped a kiss onto her nose. "Well, God have mercy on your panties."

"At least I have one pair that will be okay."

"Sorry about your bra though."

She shot a narrow gaze at him. "You're not sorry about my bra."

He grinned, honestly shocked at the lightness in his chest. "I'm really not."

"You're a bad man, Dane Parker."

"I'm not," he said. "I'm a Boy Scout. A Boy Scout who has been on his best behavior for eight months. I didn't do a damned naughty thing until you kissed me, Beatrix Leighton. So who's the bad one?"

That seemed to amuse her, and he liked it.

"I'm supposed to work at the clinic today," she said. "But I need to go and feed the chickens. And I need to get Evan out of my house."

"Why did you leave Evan in your house?"

"Well, to be honest with you, I figured you would throw me out."

"That's not a lot of confidence in a seduction."

She cleared her throat, looking sheepish. "I wasn't really trying to seduce you."

"The matching bra and panties say otherwise, Bea."

"Well, it crossed my mind. But mostly I was coming to yell at you."

He nodded slowly. "You did that."

"I was going to tell you that I was a strong, independent woman who knew her own mind."

"You demonstrated that."

"And I figured if it led to sex then great."

"It did," he pointed out.

"But then, I guess I didn't really consider the logistics past that."

"Well, who can blame you. I find that logistics get a little bit fuzzy where sex is concerned."

"Apparently," she said.

"I have to go to Get Out of Dodge this morning. Hey, do you want to get a ride down with me? I'll drop you off at the clinic."

"Would that look…suspicious?"

"I don't think so, seeing as we live on the same property."

"True," she said.

She got out of bed, and he wanted to drag her back in. He was so hard it was painful. And she was…

How hadn't he noticed this? She wasn't just pretty. She wasn't just an easy port in a storm, or whatever the hell he had told himself at first when he had found himself attracted to her. She was exceptional.

Curvy and lush, her skin soft and delicious. And lord she was sweet.

One of his very favorite memories from last night involved tasting her between her legs until she shivered and shook and came apart. Though that led him to thinking about all the things they hadn't done. He hadn't had the chance to see that pretty mouth wrapped around *him*.

Oh yeah, they had some unfinished business, him and Beatrix Leighton. She started to collect her clothes and he watched, enjoying her movements as she went. Then she stopped suddenly and scurried back to the edge of the bed, pressing a kiss to his mouth, which shocked and delighted him.

"I just am really glad that I can kiss you now."

Then she continued collecting her clothes, pulling them on and covering up his view. He got dressed after that, made coffee for the two of them and then hurried her down to her cabin, where he fed the chickens while she saw to hurricane Evan. When he returned from the chicken coop he saw her scooting the raccoon out of her house.

"Evan exits," she announced. "Pursued by Bea."

He snorted a laugh. "How bad was it?"

"Box of Cheerios down," she said. "But all things considered it could be worse."

"I suppose so." He opened up the passenger door and held it for Bea, and she stared at him. "What?"

"You're being a gentleman."

"It's fitting I play the part of gentleman now, since I corrupted you last night." She got in as he said those words and he closed the door on her before she could argue with him about corruption, which he knew she was about to do.

He rounded to the driver's side of the truck and put his hand on the handle, then stopped, looking at her through the window. She was beautiful. And right now, she was his.

He didn't have anything in the whole damned world just now. His whole life had been reduced to rubble. But Bea made it seem like awfully pretty rubble.

His.

He'd never thought of a woman—a person—as his before. But she felt like it.

He didn't know if it was because he had so little right now, and she was something—something soft and lovely and wonderful—to hold on to. Maybe.

All he knew was that now that it had hit him, it had hit him hard.

But given the way he'd realized he was attracted to her, that made sense too. It really was like getting trampled by that bull all over again. Sudden. Irrevocable. And leaving new sensation echoing through his body he couldn't banish if he tried.

He shook the feeling off and opened the door, getting into the truck and starting the engine as he was treated to a lecture on how Bea had not been corrupted by him. Which he happily listened to all the way down to the clinic.

They pulled in to the driveway and before he could think better of it, he kissed her. Quick and light, but it left an impression on his lips and settled something heavy in his gut.

"I can come pick you up later, if you want."

"I bet Bennett can bring me to the ranch," she said, biting her lip and looking up at him. He wanted to kiss her again, but in the interest of not having to talk about their sex life to everyone he figured they shouldn't risk getting caught.

Not quite so quickly, anyway.

"I'll pick you up," he said. "How about I get you around 4:30 and we can go drop paperwork off in town for the permits."

"Okay," she said, her gaze colliding with his.

"You have to go," he said, his voice getting rough. "Because I'm going to end up making a spectacle of us."

Bea left him quickly after that and he drove on to the ranch, the reality sinking in that he had to leave the bubble they'd been in at the winery and actually interact with people.

For quite a few reasons, Dane had no idea how he was supposed to face his sister. The fact that he'd gotten a voice mail from their father was one thing. The fact that *he and Bea had slept together* was another.

One of those things he did have to talk to her about. The other one he planned on taking to the grave with him.

He could only hope that Lindy had gone over to the

winery rather than hanging around the ranch. And when he got there, it seemed that he was right.

He went to work straightaway, choosing to take an assignment deadheading flowers around the guest cabins with the new hires, rather than doing work with Grant or Wyatt.

By lunchtime, he was thinking he might have dodged having to see Lindy. But as he was about to grab his lunch in the mess hall and sit down at one of the long tables, she appeared, dressed immaculately for winery work and yet somehow…

Here.

"Hi," she said, smiling at him. She looked for a moment like she might come forward and get a hug, but then didn't.

"Hi," he returned.

"What's up?"

"Why do you think something's up? I'm on lunch break," he said, looking around the rustic mess hall, where some of the other hands had come in to grab their food.

"Right. You just look… Well, you look like you have something on your mind."

"Nope. Nothing. My mind is a hollow, empty shell."

He went over to where lunch was laid out and dished himself a bowl of chili, putting a heaping helping of sour cream and cheddar cheese on the top of it. Lindy opted for a salad.

"You don't usually eat in here," he observed.

"No," she agreed, sniffing delicately. "I don't. But I thought I would see if I could catch you today."

"Why is that?" He took a bite of food and his stomach growled, his body suddenly very aware of how hungry he was.

"Well, because I wanted to see how you were doing. And I don't mean your injuries, so don't get mad at me. It's just, you got pretty drunk the other night, and I wanted to make sure there was nothing going on that you didn't tell me about."

"As it happens, there *wasn't*," he lied. Because he was not going to get into the Bea situation. Lindy would skin him. Then she would kill him. And she would make sure that both things were done very, very slowly. "But there is something now. And I was going to talk to you about it—I was just game to avoid it for a while longer if I could."

Lindy frowned. "What?"

"Dad called me."

The frown flattened out, her eyes getting glassy. *"Our dad?"*

"The very one. The one we haven't seen in…I don't know…eighteen years, give or take."

"Oh," she said, looking down. It was so unusual to see Lindy looking at a loss.

He reached across the table and covered her hand with his. "I didn't call him back."

"Should you… Do we…"

"I don't know if I want to," he said.

"Yeah," Lindy responded.

"He was asking when I was going to get back out on the circuit. Because apparently he watches me ride."

"Well, that's…that's just manipulative," Lindy said. "He really called you?"

"Yeah," Dane said.

His sister looked so vulnerable then. Younger. Like she had forgotten, maybe, that she liked to position herself as the protector. But it was okay. Dane didn't mind doing the protecting.

"I'm still thinking about what I'm going to do. But I want you to know that whatever I decide… You don't have to get involved. You have enough on your plate."

"He didn't call me," Lindy said softly.

Dane hadn't realized until then that it might hurt Lindy. That their father had contacted him. He hadn't realized, because he didn't feel particularly honored.

"Bea said…" He looked up quickly and met his sister's eyes, then looked down. He hadn't meant to bring Bea up. "Beatrix said that I didn't have a responsibility to him. That just because someone is a parent doesn't mean you have to give them anything. Not when they gave nothing to you. And I think she has a point."

"You told Beatrix?"

"She came up to the house right after I got the voice mail."

He couldn't take Lindy's question in any way but suspicion. Which was ridiculous because there was no way Lindy would ever suspect that there was something happening with Bea and himself. He wouldn't have believed it even a week ago.

It was like he had different eyes all of a sudden. Or was looking at the world from a different view. The one that came from walking slow with an old dog. One that let him see wildflowers, and seasons changing, and Bea as a beautiful woman.

He didn't know what the hell magic she had over him right now. But for eight months his body had felt like a stranger's. And it certainly hadn't felt like…like a man's body.

Bea had made him feel like a man.

The way that she touched him. The way that her lips had moved over his. The way her fingertips had skimmed his face. The way she had rolled her hips up against him.

The way it had felt to be inside her. Knowing he was the only one.

There were ugly truths hovering around the edge of his life, truths about his injuries and his future. Truths he'd been ignoring for far, far too long because facing them had seemed impossible.

Because facing a hollow life he hadn't chosen seemed impossible.

Life didn't seem hollow right now.

Being with her had made him feel more alive than he'd felt in months. She made him feel alive in a way that only the rodeo ever had. To get his adrenaline to spike like that usually took a one-ton animal and a crowd full of people cheering his name.

Or one petite woman with a riot of curls and a soft, sweet mouth.

He realized that he'd been silent for far too long, and that Lindy was staring. "I think she's right, anyway," Dane said. "We don't owe him anything just because of genetics. And if he was a bad father, we wouldn't owe him even if he'd stuck around. I don't have to return his message just because he decided to call."

"I guess not."

"You don't agree?"

"Yes. I mean no. I mean, I don't think you owe him

something just because he decided to make contact. But I would be...curious."

Dane looked down at his half-eaten lunch for a long time. "For years I wondered if he was watching me, Lindy. He never gave me any indication that he was. No contact at all. Not since I was thirteen years old. The last time he came over, and then just didn't come back."

"Mom pushed him away," Lindy said. "She wouldn't even let him in the door that last time."

"No one would ever keep me away from my children," Dane said, shocked at the conviction in his words, mostly because he had never much thought about having children of his own. In fact, he'd actively avoided the thought. "Would anyone be able to keep you away from yours?"

Lindy blinked. "No. I don't suppose."

"I can't blame Mom. She has her own issues, and I'm angry enough about those. But I can't blame her for keeping Dad away. He didn't want to come in badly enough. He didn't want to fight for us. You know what he wanted? A son he could sit back and watch on TV without having to do anything. And he thinks... Hell, I don't know. If he had called me a few months ago it would have reinforced everything I had always wondered. If he was watching me. And it would've made me feel like what I'd done was worth it. Because that's what I wanted, Lindy. I wanted my old man to see me succeed. So much of what I did was for that. For him. A way to reach out to him and hope that I could earn this phone call. Now I have it, and I don't know if I wanted it at all." He shook his head. "I'm doing something here. Right now, I'm helping Beatrix set up the sanctuary. You know, if you're on board."

He thought of Bea again, of her soft skin and the way she had felt beneath his fingertips. He was doing more than just helping her set up a sanctuary, but that wasn't a conversation he was ready to have with anyone else yet.

"I'm on board," Lindy said. "I was never going to actually say no. The reality is that place belonged to Bea's family for years and I've never been entirely comfortable having ownership of the whole thing. The winery itself…that feels like mine. But the rest? Anyway, if it's something you're invested in…you have no idea how happy I am to know that something is interesting you right now."

She had no idea how interesting he found life at the moment. And it didn't have much to do with the animal sanctuary so much as the delectable founder of it.

"What made you change your… I mean, you seemed pretty hell-bent on getting back out there and I didn't want to say anything about it."

"Bea again. She yelled some sense into me." Among other things.

It was a strange thing, but something about being with her had thrown everything into a clearer focus. That sense of being adrift, of feeling like nothing was his was gone.

"I can't really imagine her…yelling."

"Oh, she's good at it," Dane said.

"I'll have to…ask her to demonstrate sometime since it seems to have provided you with some clarity."

He cleared his throat. "I spent a lot of months feeling like…nothing here was mine. But I've been making some changes. I don't know where they'll all take me. But sitting around on my ass wasn't helping fix anything. And neither was living in denial of what these injuries mean. I haven't even gotten close to getting on the back of a horse that won't throw me. The idea that I was going to get back into the rodeo, and at my age… I just didn't want to deal with the reality of it. With the fact that I couldn't have that back. But I'm working with Bea now and I'm enjoying myself and it…it gives me hope I'll find something else."

"Look at you," Lindy said, "you really are all grown up."

"I guess I just needed to come to terms with the idea of being in one place."

It wasn't a mystery to him why he felt that way. And it wasn't really the sanctuary. Or a phone call from his father bringing about clarity to why he'd done the things he had for so many years.

"Anyway," he said, his throat dry. "Who would take care of my dog if I left?"

Lindy laughed. "I'm sure that Bea would."

But who would take care of Bea? She tried to take care of everyone and everything around her, and people looked at her and saw it as a weakness. They gave her advice and treated her with indulgence. But who took care of her?

"Better that I'm here to do it," Dane said.

"Well, I'm not sorry to hear you say that."

"Lindy, I'm not sure that I've ever told you how much it means to me… The way that you were there for me. Not just now. But when we were growing up. We didn't have the best parents. Hell, we barely had parents. But I had you."

"I don't think I was all that great."

"You were. We made the best of life with what we had. I felt really guilty for introducing you to Damien for a long time."

"Oh, don't feel guilty about that. I loved him. I really did. And I got a lot of good out of that marriage, as hard as it was for me to admit that for a long time. Not just the winery. But Sabrina and Bea. Actually, Wyatt. That came through your connection with the rodeo and with Damien too. And he's…everything. I can't resent any of the steps that I took to get me into a relationship with him. I just can't. Sometimes you have to take a few falls to figure out what's worth standing up for."

Dane nodded slowly. "Yeah, it took a pretty big fall for me. But I think I'm getting there."

"Just be happy, Dane. I think that's something neither of our parents ever managed to be. I'm happy. You be happy. Don't let them have the final say on that. Don't let a rampaging bull have the final say on that."

"I won't. I'll figure what I want to do. I'll…I'll find the thing that gives me what riding used to. I know I will."

He stood up, and the pain in his leg, his knee, it didn't bother him so much. Not because it had faded any between yesterday and today, but because everything around him had changed. It meant something different now.

A lot like the way Lindy looked at her relationship with Damien, he supposed. It was the pain in life that sometimes brought you to the place you should have been all along.

He would prefer to walk without a limp, but without the limp he wouldn't have ended up in Bea's arms last night, and he couldn't resent that at all.

He scraped up the last bite of chili in his bowl and demolished it.

"I'll see you later," he said, heading outside. There were dark, gray clouds teasing the edges of the mountains, creeping toward the ranch, but Dane decided that he didn't mind the threat of rain so much.

It felt less like a threat and more like a promise.

That things left lying there on the ground would grow, no matter how unlikely it seemed.

He supposed that was another thing he'd been missing all this time. That he had a choice. He could be angry about where he was, or he could grow where he was planted.

And he was ready to grow.

CHAPTER SIXTEEN

WHEN DANE CAME to pick her up from the clinic Beatrix felt slightly giddy. She wasn't sure how to respond, and Kaylee and Bennett didn't seem to find it at all strange that Dane was coming to get her.

It did make sense, for all the reasons he had mentioned before.

The fact that the two of them lived on the same property being chief among those reasons. But she still felt strange about it. Like everyone would be able to see the significant shift that her relationship with Dane had undergone. But of course they couldn't. It wasn't like it was written across her face. It wasn't like there was a giant scrawl across her forehead that decreed she was *no longer a virgin* because *Dane Parker had shown her what sex was all about.*

The thought made her insides twist in a knot, a pang of tingling excitement blooming between her legs. She wondered if he had really shown her everything sex was about. Or if there would be more.

The idea was obsessing.

And he hadn't said anything to indicate that they wouldn't have sex again. In fact, he had seemed nothing if not into the idea this morning.

Well, she was basing that off the fact that he had

kissed her quite a few times, and that he hadn't turned into a grumpy asshole weirdo on her.

So she could only hope that that remained true.

He seemed happy to see her when he pulled up in his truck and that made her feel all warm inside.

"I thought after we dropped the paperwork off we could go grab some dinner at Mustard Seed."

Dinner. Together. In public. Which was probably no weirder than him getting her from the clinic, because they were friends or something. But it felt weird. And she felt…things. So many things. "Oh, we can go to dinner together?"

"I was thinking so."

"Do you think Joe will mind sitting in the back of your truck through that?"

"All Joe does is sit," Dane said. "He's going to lie down, whether he's in the truck or not. So, he might as well lie down there. And anyway, I'll probably end up bringing him french fries."

"That's very bad for him," Bea scolded.

"Yeah, but you would give them to him anyway."

"Probably," she said.

They looked at each other across the cab of the truck and he smiled. Her heart turned over when those blue eyes connected with hers, that fallen angel grin like a secret between them. She scooted to the center seat and buckled in there, eager to touch him.

"Careful not to distract me," he said, as she put her hand on his thigh.

Her heart fluttered around like a bird trying to decide which branch to land on. "Am I a distraction?"

"You have no idea."

"Well, that's fair enough. You've spent a lot of years distracting me." The admission made her face hot.

"How many?" he asked.

"Stop it," she said. "That's mean."

"It's not mean," he responded. "Come on, Bea, I'm a man reduced. I have a bum leg and my career is over. Tell me what I need to hear."

"I thought you were attractive for quite some time," she said crisply.

"How attractive?"

"Dane Parker!" she shouted.

"Beatrix Leighton," he said, smiling. "Tell me, and later I will reward you for being such a good girl."

She narrowed her eyes. "And what will you do if I don't?"

His smile turned decidedly wicked. "Then I'll punish you for being a bad girl."

Those words made something dark and pleasant bloom inside of her stomach. "Well, I'm not sure which one I want."

"I'll tell you what," he said. "We'll try both."

Pleasure zipped through her, centering itself between her thighs. "I don't hate that idea. And it might please you to know that I first thought about kissing you when I was sixteen."

He coughed. "That makes me feel dirty somehow."

"Why?" She was feeling cheerful because she'd finally succeeded in gaining the upper hand on him. "You didn't think about kissing me."

"It's true," he responded. "I didn't think about kissing you until that day down at the river. We have Evan to thank for that."

"Who knew that my raccoon was the secret to me getting laid."

"Who knew indeed."

"I want you to know," she said, schooling her voice into the most pragmatic possible. "I am completely aware that what we are having is a fling. And that it won't last forever. I'm completely willing and able to participate and go back to being friends when it's through."

The idea made her feel exceedingly depressed, but she wouldn't tell him that.

"Is that so?" he asked.

She nodded. "I know that I was a… That I was inexperienced."

"Completely," he pointed out.

"Fine. Completely lacking in experience."

"You were a virgin."

She let her head fall back against the seat. "Stop it."

"I'm enjoying it," he responded. "Apparently, I'm possessive. I didn't realize that until you."

That put a total stop to her entire thread of conversation. She blinked. "You're possessive? Of me?"

"I am," he said, as they pulled into the parking lot for the county office. "And I can't quite recall ever feeling this way before. You're something else, Beatrix Leighton. And I don't need you to make bargains with me or tell me what you can and can't handle. You're not going to scare me off."

The words hit low in her stomach and twisted. She had never scared anyone off before, but she had certainly been an insufficient reason for people to stay around. She had been an obligation. And she refused to become either one to Dane.

"Thank you," she said. "But I just wanted to make sure you knew that I'm a big girl and I can handle myself."

"I'm well aware of that, Beatrix. But I find it a lot more fun when I'm the one handling you."

She shoved aside depressing thoughts and followed him into the county office, where the two of them waited to drop off their paperwork and get further instruction on what they would need to do to get everything approved. It didn't take long for them to finish, and they went back to the truck and drove a few blocks down to the Mustard Seed diner.

The building, which was routinely packed full of people and still hadn't expanded its seating, had been part of Gold Valley since the mid-1950s. It was a popular hangout for high school students, and every year as the school year wound to a close the graduates wrote their names on the windows in dry-erase marker.

The names were beginning to go up now in early spring—a clear sign of intense senioritis hitting earlier. Bea enjoyed looking at them. She had gone to high school in Copper Ridge, and hadn't partaken in the tradition.

"Did you write your name on the windows here?" she asked when the two of them sat down at the small white and silver flecked table.

"I sure did," Dane said. "As one of the leading football stars of my school I got a big slot to write my name. Girls wrote their names around mine."

"Really?"

He winked. "Really."

Lucinda, the owner of the diner, came by their table and made casual conversation with the two of them, her dark eyes darting between them, but no leading questions hovering on her lips. Still, Beatrix could tell that the woman had questions.

She and Dane ordered cheeseburgers and french fries and milkshakes.

"Now I really do feel like I'm in high school," he said.

"If we had gone to high school together you never would have talked to me," she said.

Dane laughed. "Of course—about a decade separates our high school experience."

"It doesn't matter. Kids are all the same." Bea looked around the diner and sighed. "I didn't have very many friends."

Dane frowned. "Why not?"

"I was weird. I went to science class with a vole in my backpack once."

"I don't believe that," Dane said.

"I did. I sat alone at lunch."

"Except for the vole?"

"I brought a vole once, Dane. Not every day."

A teenage waiter brought their food to the table and Bea grabbed hold of a fry and ate it quickly as a distraction tactic.

"Why is that, Bea? Because you're beautiful. And you're sweet. I can't imagine why anyone wouldn't want to be your friend."

The sincerity in his question was probably the nicest thing Bea had ever experienced.

"It isn't like I actively went out and tried to make friends. And anyway, I was Jamison Leighton's daughter. There was a wedge drawn between me and other people for that reason alone. People thought that I thought I was too good for them. In reality, I was just awkward and weird and I didn't know how to talk to them. And I was going through…things." She hesitated. "I found out something about myself when I was sixteen. And as uncomfortable as I already was, it just made it worse."

"What?"

She had never told anyone this. The only people who knew were her mother, her father and her biological father.

Sabrina didn't know. Damien didn't know. She had never told McKenna or Jamie. She'd shoved it down deep and never told anyone. Never told them how much it hurt.

But she could tell Dane. She'd told him about the vole in her backpack. He hadn't thought it was weird she was a virgin. He watched her with Evan on a daily basis, and that really would send most people running.

She could tell him this too.

They had a safe space here between them. Right now, he was here and so was she. And he was choosing to spend the time he had here with her.

She might not be top of an infinite list, but on the list of choices he had here in Gold Valley, she seemed to be in the number one spot.

That meant something.

"Jamison Leighton isn't my father," she said slowly.

"Bea…"

"Nobody knows this," she said, quietly. "Nobody.

Damien and Sabrina don't know I'm their half sister." Just saying the words made her eyes sting. She wouldn't tell him the story. Not the whole story. Because it was pathetic and awful and just thinking about it made her feel sick to her stomach. "I just… I already felt wrong. And anyway, I wasn't allowed to tell."

"You weren't allowed to tell, so you didn't?"

"I know," she said, her throat scratchy. "But I had already seen what happened when you opposed my father. Sabrina could be in the same room as him and he would barely say two words to her." She shifted. "Add to the fact that it turned out he wasn't actually my father and I just… I still don't know what to do with it. I still don't know how to think of him. He's the man who raised me, whether distant and unaffectionate or not. His is the name on my birth certificate. His is the money that I have, and the house that I grew up in. And I kind of resent him for that. Because if he didn't really want me that much then I don't know why he had to be the one that I had. Anyway, it just made all that hard. It made all of this hard."

"I would have wanted to know," he said. "Your secrets. And who you were. Why that weird girl brought a vole to science class."

Bea laughed and took a bite of her hamburger. "No, you wouldn't have. You've known me all this time and you've never wanted to know that."

He looked wounded, and she almost felt bad. But she knew she was right.

"That's not fair," he said. "I'm seven years older than you, Bea. I couldn't have thought of you as anything other than a kid when I met you. And yeah, it changed.

You changed. But it takes time to catch up with that sometimes. I think if we would have been the same age at the same school... It would've been different."

"No way, Mr. High School Quarterback. You would have been messing around with girls under the bleachers and going out for hamburgers, just like you always did. The only thing I was doing under the bleachers was catching lizards. If you didn't hang out with the weird girls when you were in high school, you wouldn't have hung out with me."

"You can't say that for sure," he pointed out.

"Yes, I can."

"No, you can't. Because none of them were you. And you're different."

Her heart twisted and she shoved her milkshake straw into her mouth and took a long sip. "It doesn't matter. Because you still would've been on to bigger and better things than me."

Dane paused for food, then sighed. "Yeah, well, talk about daddy issues. It was something I had to do. I loved being that football star, Bea. I loved having a reason to have my name written on that window all big. Because before I started playing football I wasn't anyone. Trailer trash. But once I found out that if you're good at something people care about, you start to matter, that changed everything. Every damn thing."

"Why didn't you try for college football?" she asked. "Why the rodeo?"

"First of all," he said. "I'm a big guy, but at a certain point, there's big and there's football big. I'm not fast enough to compensate for that either. But also... My dad didn't watch football. He used to watch the rodeo.

I thought… If he could see. If he could see what I was doing then I would matter to him. Turns out he was watching, all this time. All this time he was watching and… He didn't tell me till it was over. I hate him a little bit for that."

"Dane, you mattered to me no matter what you were doing. I didn't care about the rodeo stuff. I was proud of you the further your career went, but I didn't care. It wasn't what made you interesting to me. I had a crush on you way before you got super famous."

He chuckled. "I appreciate that. And just so you know, I might not have totally seen you as a woman until recently, but I always knew you were strong. I never saw you as Jamison Leighton's daughter. In fact, I never understood how such a cold bastard could raise such a special, caring person."

"I think it's because of my dad being cold that I feel the way I do."

"I'm not surprised by that. I think we both do pretty well in spite of the men that call themselves our fathers, what you think?"

Bea forced a smile. "I think that's true." They ate their food in relative silence, watching as the diner filled up with rowdy kids, who grabbed paint pens and began to scribble on the wall, before sitting down and ordering near identical dinners to Bea and Dane. When they finished, they got a cookie with their bill, for finishing every bite, Lucinda said, and they ate those on their way to the truck.

Beatrix jumped when her phone buzzed.

"Hello?"

"Hi, Beatrix," a familiar voice on the other end of the

line said. It took Beatrix a moment to place it. "This is Nancy at the border collie rescue. I just found out about a farm full of animals that are being removed from the house where the owners were arrested for drugs. They've been pretty severely neglected. I've got a couple of horses, pigs and five goats."

"I can take them," Bea said, quickly. "Well, I might talk to Gabe Dalton about the horses. But the goats and the pigs."

She felt Dane shift next to her.

"Great. Do you think you can arrange to have them picked up? I know it's a lot to ask, but I just found out, and I don't want them to be euthanized."

"No," Bea said. "Of course not. I can house them. I'm in the process of renovating, but I have enough space for them. And I will figure out a way to pick them up."

Bea hung up and quickly explained the call to Dane.

"Wyatt has horse trailers and things," Dane said. "I'm sure that he can help."

"Well, why don't you get in touch with Wyatt, and I'll see if we can get Gabe Dalton on board to help. I'm going to call Kaylee and Bennett and see if either of them can do some vet checks to see what we need."

They made phone calls on the drive back to the property, and after they had arranged for an early morning pickup of the animals with Wyatt's and Gabe's equipment, Bea led Dane out to the barn area.

"I think everything is fenced in properly here," Beatrix said. "But we might need to fashion a smaller shelter, one they can just go in and out of."

"They'll be fine for now," Dane said. "We can make do with the barn, I think."

"Yes, I think you're right." She smiled. "Thank you," she said. "For helping me make this possible."

Dane shook his head. "Bea, you're the one that's made this possible. It's you, honey. You've done it all."

"But you've done so much to help me and encourage me, while never making me feel like I didn't know what I was getting myself into. You really don't know how much I appreciate that."

The clouds that had been growing thicker and more ominous overhead broke open, and Bea felt a raindrop on her cheek. One on her arm.

"We'd better go back," she said. Her inclination was to run, because the rain was starting to fall hard and fast.

But she realized that Dane couldn't. She took hold of his hand and the two of them began to walk slowly through the field as the rain fell harder and harder.

They were getting soaking wet.

But they were getting wet together. And Bea didn't mind at all.

CHAPTER SEVENTEEN

RAIN WAS POURING down Dane's face. His back. Soaking through his shirt, his jeans, and he knew that Bea wasn't faring any better than that. But she was walking with him, her fingers linked with his, and he felt damned guilty for a moment. Because he was setting a pace that wasn't keeping her comfortable. She could have run ahead of him.

But she was choosing to hold his hand. Choosing to walk with him.

And he wanted her to.

Because it felt good. Because it felt right. By the time they got back inside the cabin they were soaking wet and freezing cold.

Bea shivered, a damp curl hanging in her face. He pushed it back and cupped her cheek. Then he leaned in slowly and captured her mouth with his. Raindrops clung to her lips, and he created heat and friction between them that banished the lingering chill.

She was incredible. This goddess who made him feel things he hadn't known he was capable of. Things that were deep and real and slow.

He had done his best to live life fast so that he couldn't stop and linger on small moments. So that he wouldn't think of pain from his past or worry overmuch about the future.

But with Bea he wanted to linger in small moments for as long as he could. Because those small moments seem to expand inside of him and become bigger. Become everything. Become air.

She slipped her tongue into his mouth, then nipped his lower lip lightly. He growled, and broke their kiss, cupping her face and staring down at her. At that lovely, familiar face that seemed new to him now.

Now that she was his lover.

She was like a treasure that he wanted to keep turning over and over again, that he wanted to keep staring at. Because every time he did he saw a new facet. Something he hadn't realized was there before.

It had been. All this time. He just hadn't stopped and looked long enough to appreciate it. But he was now.

She pressed her fingers beneath the waistband of his shirt, pushing the damp fabric up, her fingers splayed over his flat stomach.

"How are you still in such good shape?" she asked, her voice full of awe. Satisfaction kicked him right in the ego.

"I was alone in that house for a long time. I did a lot of searching on what kinds of exercises I could do. Because, dammit, I wasn't going to start from ground zero if I could help it."

Her brows knit together. "So you skipped a bunch of your physical therapy appointments but you worked out by yourself."

"Yes," he said, because it made perfect sense to him.

She sighed. "That sounds like you."

He laughed and grabbed hold of her shirt, also sodden from the rain, and jerked it over her head. "Does it?"

She breathed in deep, her full breasts rising up over the cups of the black bra she was wearing. "Yes," she said.

"Does this sound like me too?" He grabbed hold of her bra, but this time he unhooked it deftly in the back with one hand before pulling it off with the other.

"Thank God you didn't tear that one," she said. "I don't have an endless supply."

"You wouldn't have been mad at me if I would've torn it," he said, watching the color mount in her cheeks.

"Yes, I would have. I've got to spend my money on important things like feed for all the animals I have coming in soon. I can't be wasting it on lingerie."

"Honey, if you don't want to wear lingerie, that's fine by me. I'm happy to look at you naked."

He reached out and cupped her breasts, sliding his thumbs over her nipples, gratified by the little squeak of pleasure she made as he pinched her gently.

She really did have the prettiest body. "I definitely would have noticed you if we went to high school together," he said.

"Really?"

"You're stacked," he said, lowering his face and nuzzling the rounded curve of her breast with his cheek, before moving to capture her nipple between his lips, sucking on her. She grabbed hold of his head, holding him against her.

"I don't believe it," she said, sounding dizzy now. "But I don't mind the story."

Right then he was overwhelmed with gratitude over the fact that they hadn't gone to high school together. That there was time and space between their ages. Because he wouldn't have been a man who could have been there for her then. He was a man who had needed to leave. He'd needed those years running from his demons. He felt less like running now.

Standing here with her, he knew that the answers were in this room. With him. With her. But he had to go the long road to get there. And somehow, all that timing had clicked just right.

He knelt down in front of her, undoing her jeans and pushing the wet denim down her legs along with her panties, leaving her bare to his inspection. "You know you're beautiful, don't you?" he asked, pressing a kiss to her inner thigh.

She trembled beneath his mouth. "I…I can't say that I ever really thought about it."

"Never?"

"Animals don't care," she pointed out.

"I feel a lot like an animal right about now, Bea. And I care. In fact, I'm pretty damned obsessed." He cupped her ass, drew her forward to his mouth, so that he could taste her between her legs. She whimpered, grabbing hold of him as he went deep, satisfying himself on her flavor, on the sweet little noises of pleasure she made. She was a dream. She was his dream. One he'd had to wake up to have.

She grabbed hold of his wet shirt, peeling it over his head while he knelt in front of her.

"My turn," she said, breathless as she wiggled away from him and all but pounced on him where he knelt on the floor, undoing the buckle on his jeans and pushing the denim down his legs.

They were both naked then, their skin slick from the rain, cold. Beatrix pressed a kiss to his chest, his abs, lower.

"Bea…"

He grabbed hold of her hair, but she wasn't deterred, her eager tongue sliding along his length in an enthusiastic tasting. She made a deep, satisfied sound, and his arousal jerked, his stomach muscles tensing.

She pushed her hand against his chest and shoved him back, turning her ass toward him as she took him eagerly into her mouth. He chuckled, grabbing hold of her hips and swinging her around so that her center was poised over his mouth.

She was delicious, and he couldn't help himself. Didn't even want to. He hadn't been exaggerating when he'd said she made him feel like something that wasn't quite tame. But she wasn't tame either.

She was wild, his Bea.

And he wanted her to be utterly and totally wild with him.

He held on to her tightly, holding her against his mouth as she moaned and wiggled against him and continued to try to pleasure him with her mouth.

But the whole time he was doing his part to distract her. Torment her. Until she was shaking and shivering.

Until he could slide two fingers easily inside of her.

She shattered beneath his hands and his mouth, her internal muscles contracting around him as he continued to work his fingers in and out of her body. She collapsed against him, resting her head on his thigh.

"I didn't know that was a thing you could do," she said, her words shaky.

He laughed, in spite of the fact he was hard as iron and practically in pain. This was a fun kind of pain at least. "That just tells me I have a lot to show you."

"That wasn't fair," she said in protest.

"This isn't about fair," he said. "This is about desire. We can have whatever we want. There aren't limits on it. And anyway, as much as I enjoyed having your mouth on me, that's not how we're finishing this tonight."

He took hold of her waist and maneuvered her around again, so that their noses were touching. So that he could kiss her, deep and hard. When they parted, they were both breathless.

"You're strong," she said, fluttery and sweet, her hand resting lightly on his biceps. And he was just basic enough that the simple statement made him feel like he could lift a car.

For her, he probably could. Pain be damned.

"Yeah, well, I'm a lot sturdier on the floor."

She nodded. "That makes sense."

"Are you complaining?"

"I could never complain when we're like this."

"Well, you could. But it would be awfully ungrateful." He slapped her ass playfully and she yelped, clinging to him.

Dane reached over and took his wallet from his pants pocket, pulling a condom out. Then he wrapped his arm tightly around her waist and pulled her up with him so they were sitting. He pushed them both up off the ground, bracing himself heavily on the wall.

Bea helped, without him having to ask, without him

feeling like he had to. She clung to him while they propelled each other back toward her bedroom. Her bed was tiny, but he didn't mind. They stretched across the narrow mattress, clinging to each other, kissing, exploring each other's bodies with their hands.

Bea took to the task with a kind of giddy determination that made Dane's heart swell. The way her hands roamed over his chest, his back, his ass, her eager fingers wrapping around his cock.

She acted like he was her own personal candy store and she couldn't get enough. She wasn't gentle with him. And when she looked at him, it wasn't pity he saw in those beautiful golden eyes.

It was desire.

It was want, and need, even when her fingers skimmed over the scars on his knee, on his thigh.

For the first time, he didn't hate those scars.

He grabbed hold of the condom packet, tore it open, rolling it onto his length as quickly as possible while they kept on kissing. Then he lifted her up over him, positioning himself at the entrance to her body, flexing his hips upward, testing her readiness.

She gasped, bracing herself on his shoulder as he encouraged her to seat herself on him.

"Oh," she said.

"What?"

"You're showing me a couple of new things tonight."

He chuckled. "We're just getting started."

He bucked up into her and she let her head fall back, wild and beautiful as she found a rhythm of her own, tormenting and teasing them both.

"That's right, baby," he whispered, holding on to her

hips and encouraging her as she took control. She was wild and uninhibited, and the view he had of her body as she rode him made him crazy. He gritted his teeth to keep from coming because he wanted to draw this out for as long as possible. The way the light from her bedside lamp cast a glow around her damp curls, her pretty face, the gorgeous slope and curve of her breasts, her trim waist and full hips... The view of that patch of curls between her legs. This was the best ride of his life. And right now, it was the only one that mattered.

Bea led on instinct, and her instincts were good. She bit her lip, her hands skimming over his chest, down his abs, her fingernails leaving marks over his body as she rolled her hips forward and shuddered out her release.

And he couldn't take it anymore.

He flipped her over onto her back, pounding himself into her. It was a fire in his veins, his need for this woman. The way she made him feel.

His own release was violent, his need shaking them both as he came on a curse that felt a whole lot more like a prayer.

When it was over, she went limp against him, clinging to him.

A smile tugged the corner of his lips. "Did you fall asleep, Bea?" he asked, pushing her hair back from her cheek.

"No," she said, rubbing her face against the crook of his neck.

"I think you did, sweetie," he murmured. He kissed the top of her head and extricated himself so that he could go to the bathroom and dispose of the contraception. Then he went back to her, pulling her thin, plaid blanket up over them as he drew her over part of his body, wrapping his arms around her. She yawned, and he stroked his hands down her back, over and over again, relishing her softness.

Her breathing quickly became even and deep, and that along with the sound of rain on the tin roof of the cabin was the only noise left in the room.

Contentment washed over him. The sound of that rain, the sound of her breathing, was bigger, more real than cheers filling an arena had ever been.

He was more than happy right now.

Happy wasn't anything. He'd been happy before. He'd had moments of pretty damned great happiness, actually. He'd been triumphant. He'd been excited.

But right now he was content. And that was something he couldn't recall ever feeling before. Like somehow he'd found a home, not in a house, but in himself.

And it was because of her.

CHAPTER EIGHTEEN

DANE LAY AWAKE for most of the night, sleeping in fits and starts, and at about five in the morning he finally gave up. He got out of bed and pulled on his jeans, and nothing else. He didn't bother to look at his phone. He was enjoying this moment. He could appreciate why she liked the simplicity of the cabin. The quiet.

What he liked best about it was that it felt like their world, like there was no one and nothing else out there, and he really appreciated that more than anything.

He made a pot of coffee, and then put some eggs in a pan and started to scramble them. Dug around until he found some bacon.

He wondered what Bea would have to say about him cooking bacon on a day when they were supposed to take in rescue pigs.

A smile tugged the corner of his lips and he was tempted to start whistling. Him. Whistling. He didn't but the fact the temptation existed was weird enough.

When he was through making breakfast he peeked in at Bea, who was still asleep, and he didn't have the heart to wake her. So he ate by himself, sitting in a little armchair in her living area, until he heard a scratching sound at the door.

Joe was lying on the rug, having been let in late the

night before, so he wasn't the culprit. But Dane had a feeling he knew who was.

He opened up the front door and was met by Evan, who leaped backward when he saw Dane. He supposed if a small animal was expecting a small woman to answer the door, a large man might be off-putting.

"I guess you were waiting to get fed all this time, weren't you?"

Evan naturally didn't reply, but did come inside warily, where he took up a position by the fridge. Dane watched from the door, with his back to the outdoors as Evan did a small dance. His front feet lifting, then falling as he tried to express the urgent need he seemed to have for his dinner.

And after all, it was Dane's fault Evan had been out, anyway.

At least, that was the vibe he was getting from the indignant creature.

He heard the sound of vehicles pulling into the lot in front of Bea's cabin. And he realized that he and Bea had probably made a mistake not checking their messages again last night. They had ended up in bed early, and had been consumed with each other, and then asleep.

He imagined they had missed a few things.

He also knew exactly how it looked with him standing there, still not wearing a shirt, in Beatrix's doorway.

And it hit him then that he just didn't care. Not even a little.

They weren't going to hide this. He sure as hell wasn't.

And Bea was a grown woman who could do what she wanted. And she had clearly decided she wanted to do *him*.

Anyway, she was his. No point denying that. He might not have wanted to have the discussion, and he might have been happy to avoid the inevitable confrontation for a while. And he really hadn't wanted to do it when he was so obviously leaving Bea's bed, or with a whole audience.

But he wasn't embarrassed. And he sure as hell wasn't ashamed.

Still, he wouldn't mind wearing a shirt when he greeted everyone. Even though he realized they'd already seen him, he figured there was merit to at least making some pretense at being dressed.

He picked his T-shirt up off the living room floor and pulled it over his head before going back over to the door. By that point, the trucks, complete with trailers, had been parked, and Wyatt had gotten out of his truck, as had Lindy. Gabe Dalton was currently getting out of his truck, but that didn't matter so much, because Dane was being fixed with the evil eye from his sister.

"Good morning," Dane said. "Didn't expect you this early."

"I guess not," Lindy said. "Bea should have been. We all texted her last night."

"I'll get her," Dane said.

"Will you?" Lindy asked, her tone flat.

"Yeah," Dane said. "In a minute. You have the animals?"

"Yeah," Gabe supplied. "We brought the pigs and the goats. I'm going to go back in a minute and get the horses and take them back to my place."

"Good," Dane said.

"Is there an easy path to get them down to where you're going to house them?"

"We should be able to do it. Nothing a little bit of herding won't solve."

"I'll go get Bea," Lindy said.

"She's asleep," Dane said.

He was aware that Wyatt's gaze was getting stonier by the moment, and that Lindy was holding herself back from strangling him. Gabe Dalton was clearly unaffected by the situation. Which was something that Dane appreciated at the moment.

"I need to have a word with my sister for a second," Dane said, grabbing hold of Lindy's arm and pulling her over to the side. "Whatever you need to say to me, go ahead and say it, but don't you dare make Bea feel bad."

"Dane Parker," Lindy said, her teeth set on edge. "How dare you? She… She's had a crush on you forever and you…"

"You had a crush on Wyatt forever."

Lindy looked like she was tangled in her fury. "I did not have a… It isn't… I am the *same age* as my husband. Not only that, I had been married for ten years before. I knew what I was getting into."

"You think she doesn't? Lindy, how old do you think she is?"

"She's younger than you. And she's inexperienced."

"Lindy, I'm going to go out on a limb here and say that I know her better than you do."

"Being naked with someone doesn't mean you know them, Dane. As you know very well."

"And acting like someone's superior older sister

doesn't mean you know them," he said. "I don't mean mine. I mean hers."

"What are you doing with her?"

"What were you doing with Wyatt?"

"What does that have to do with anything?"

"Everything, Lindy," he bit out. "Why do you think it's fine for you to try to have a relationship but it isn't fine for her?"

"Because you and I both know she isn't going to get to have one with you. You're going to hurt her."

Anger streaked through Dane's veins, along with the sure and certain realization that he would rather cut his good leg off than hurt Bea. "I don't think that's what you're worried about," he said.

"Of course I am! I've known Bea since she was a kid, and I love her like a sister. I love you like a brother because you are my brother, but that doesn't mean I'm not realistic about who you are."

"You're worried about you," he said. "You're worried because you've made a life for yourself where everything is perfect again, and you don't want it disrupted. Because Bea and me having a different relationship will change things. Because if it goes bad it might make things hard for you."

"Is that what you think? That I'm that selfish?"

"No," he said, shaking his head. "I think you're that much of a control freak. You want your world the way you want it, and that's fine, Lindy, but you can't control what I want. You can't control what she wants. And you sure as hell can't get in the way of other people living their lives just because you want yours to stay the same."

Lindy visibly bristled. "So you're telling me, honestly, that this has nothing to do with the fact that you have been shut in for the past eight months and this girl worships the ground you walk on? Because she enthusiastically bought a ticket to the Dane Show and you've been missing your audience?" Rage spiked through him and he opened his mouth to tell her off, but Lindy pressed on, "You're telling me that this has absolutely nothing at all to do with the fact that she makes you feel good about yourself and your ego is in more desperate need of stroking than any other part of your body?"

Anger gripped Dane, because it wasn't like he hadn't asked himself the same questions but that was when the attraction was building. That was before. It was different than the reality. Because once he had actually touched Bea, once he had actually committed to what was happening between them, there had been no question left. He didn't want to use her in any way. He wanted her because she was...

She was damn near a miracle, and he was a man who'd had a shortage of those in his life.

"You're underestimating us both," he said, his voice rough.

"Am I?" Lindy asked. "Or do I just care about you both?"

He shook his head. "No. You think that I would do that to her, and you think she's stupid enough to get caught up in it."

"Because I know having feelings for a man makes you stupid," Lindy said. "That's the thing. I'm really glad that things worked out between Wyatt and me, but getting there nearly killed me. And I was thirty-four years old. She's not. She's twenty-four. She's never had her heart broken, and if she has to have it broken, dammit, Dane, I don't want it to be you."

"I don't want it to be either."

"You think you have…a future with her?"

Dane rocked back on his heels, his heart turning over. "From where I'm standing, Lindy, I can't imagine a future that she's not in. I don't know what all that means right now. But I know I've never felt this way about anyone else before. Maybe that doesn't make sense to you, because she's younger than me. Maybe it doesn't make sense because you think you know one thing about her and you think you know one thing about me. But if you put the two of us together and it doesn't make sense, then I'm just going to tell you, you don't really know either of us."

He turned and walked away from her, pausing in front of Wyatt and Gabe. "I'm going to go get Bea, and when I do, the first person to make an asinine comment is going to be on the receiving end of me testing out just how healed up I am."

Dane went in the house and expelled a harsh breath before walking back into the bedroom. Bea was only visible by a spiral curl, which was sticking out the top of the bedspread. He put his hand on her shoulder, rubbed it down her back. "Bea," he whispered. "It's time to get up, honey. The animals are here."

"Early?" she mumbled, sitting up and looking around bleary-eyed. She was also still naked, and the blankets had fallen down below her breasts. And Dane was only a man.

With great difficulty, he tore his eyes off her. "Yeah,

apparently there were texts and we missed them. And everybody saw me coming out of your house without a shirt on at 6:00 a.m."

She wrenched into a straight position. "What?"

"I handled it."

"What did you say?"

"I didn't deny anything. I'm not ashamed of what's happening between us. I'm sorry. I wanted to keep it a secret to keep things easy. But you know what? It doesn't matter to me what anybody thinks."

Color crept into Beatrix's cheeks. "Really?"

"Really. You're right. You're a grown woman. Everybody else got to fool around with who they wanted to fool around with. We can't?"

"Good point," Bea said, but her cheeks were only getting more and more pink.

"Bea," he said. "There's nothing to be embarrassed about."

"Well, maybe to you. But I've never done anything like this before."

"I'm not sure I have either. We'll figure it out together. We don't need anybody's interference. So if anyone says anything to you, I will be first in line to punch them in the face."

"I really do appreciate that," she said, slowly crawling from beneath the covers and digging through her dresser, pulling out a pair of jeans and a T-shirt.

Dane watched her get dressed, in absolutely no hurry to move along, and when she was through, he poured her a cup of coffee on their way out of the kitchen, putting his hand very intentionally on her lower back as the two of them walked out of the cabin.

He could feel her trying to shrink next to him, but he just stared everyone down. Daring them to make it an issue.

Gabe Dalton spoke first. "Where do you want us to put the animals?"

"I'll lead the way," Bea said.

Bea could practically feel Lindy's nervous energy in the air all around them while they dealt with the animals that morning. Bea was relieved to part ways with her and see to the care and settling of the animals, and she'd gotten the sense that Lindy was reluctant to leave.

And so, when the evening rolled around and Sabrina sent out a perky text that she happened to be in Gold Valley and was wondering if everyone wanted to get drinks, Bea wasn't overly surprised. She also had a feeling it was Lindy who had put her sister up to it. But Bea was determined to go about things the way that Dane said they would.

He was right. This was their life. It was their choice. And Bea had elected to have an affair with Dane like a grown, mature woman who didn't need anything else from the man. And if she wasn't worried about it then no one else should be either.

She ignored the little twist in her stomach that came when she thought of that. She was fine.

The past couple of nights with Dane had been the best of her life. He was so gorgeous and attentive, and he made her feel... It was like all these little pieces of herself that had seemed scattershot had suddenly joined together. Her wildness and her femininity, her desire to care, and her need to be cared for. It all fit in bed with him. Or on the floor of her cabin, as the case may have been. Because she had never felt more feral, or like more of a lady than she did naked in his arms. She had never felt more right.

This was why people needed to have love affairs, she concluded as she pulled her truck up to the front of the Gold Valley Saloon. Because it helped you discover things about yourself. Sexuality was important, and all that. She had shoved hers down for a very long time, and now she was embracing it. And by embracing it she had found a wholeness of self.

Dane was a conduit.

She wrinkled her nose as she stepped onto the sidewalk and peered into the window, scanning to see if Lindy and Sabrina were already there.

She could see, through the warped antique glass that they were in fact already there. As were Kaylee, McKenna and Jamie.

Beatrix had the sudden image of falling down in her chicken coop and being pecked to death by the hens.

She imagined the experience would not be terribly different than what was about to unfold here tonight.

But she was here to own it. Well, no, not just it. She was here to own *herself.*

She steeled herself and fluffed up her curls, straightening the floral dress she had chosen to wear before striding into the saloon. She kept her eyes facing forward as she marched to the bar. "Hi, Laz," she said. "Can I get some whiskey?"

He smiled, his dark eyes twinkling. "Bea." He shook his head. "Do you really want whiskey?"

"I do," she said. "And I don't need advice on what you think I should be drinking."

Laz did not seem off put by this. He chuckled. "It isn't that I'm questioning you, so much as making sure you're not wasting your money to make a point."

"Why would I do that?"

"I'm a bartender. I see people do a lot of things. I have a pretty good sense for it."

"Okay," she said. "How about a rum and Coke?"

"Heavy on the Coke?"

"Yeah," she said, tapping her fingers on the bar top and waiting. The true irritation here was that he wasn't wrong. She was trying to prove a point. And she was too much of a lightweight to really do it.

He delivered her drink and winked at her. "On the house."

"You don't have to do that," she said.

"I want to. It looks like you're at the center of something big," he said, gesturing over to the table of women.

"All right, I'll take the free drink. But since you're offering it, any advice on how to deal with well-meaning interfering friends?"

"Do it the same way you deal with well-meaning interfering bartenders. Tell them what you want."

Well, that went nicely with her general thought process. She was going to talk. She couldn't expect to be treated the way she wanted if she didn't tell people that what she wanted had changed.

Just like she'd done with Dane.

Beatrix took the drink and the advice under advisement as she went to the table. "Hi," she said, having a seat. "I didn't realize we were all coming out tonight."

"We're hangers-on," McKenna said, sneaking a glance over at Lindy. Lindy, for her part, looked agitated.

Bea was willing to bet very decent money that Lindy had planned to take her out and lecture her, and that anyone but Sabrina—who Bea imagined Lindy considered a sure thing when it came to being an ally—was considered a potential rogue agent.

Well, Bea was not going to allow Lindy to have the floor unopposed.

"I'm sleeping with Dane," Bea announced. "There, now you can stop looking so awkward, Lindy."

McKenna practically hooted with delight, Kaylee was grinning, Lindy looked like she wanted to crawl underneath the table, Sabrina seemed stoic.

Jamie was completely unreadable.

"That is why Lindy asked to go out with me tonight," Beatrix said. "And I imagine she felt irritated that you all complicated her intention to come out and have an intervention for me. So I figured I would just get that out of the way."

"When?" McKenna asked.

"Two days ago." Bea was enjoying the way everyone was looking at her. Like she was an unpredictable marvel. She didn't think she'd ever been an unpredictable marvel before. "It's very good sex," she continued.

Lindy looked like she might implode.

A little bit of embarrassment flashed through her at the thought. Because she couldn't think about it without imagining what it was like to be with him. And that was a bit intense.

"I'm not trying to have an intervention," Lindy said slowly. "But I did want to make sure that you were… okay."

"Dane would never hurt me," Bea said. "Why would you ask me that?"

"It's not that I think he would… Bea… He's…"

"He's older than you," Sabrina said. "And he's done a lot more living than you. I'm not criticizing him, it's just that things are a little bit imbalanced there."

"And that's different from either of your husbands… how?" Bea stared at them blandly. They both blinked back.

"Wyatt isn't older than me," Lindy said defensively. "Two years is nothing."

"Didn't you first try to sleep with Liam when you were seventeen?" Bea turned her focus to Sabrina. "And wasn't *he* in his twenties at the time?"

"That's different," Sabrina said. "First of all, because it was actually a really bad idea. And he broke my heart for a decade. It took us that long to figure things out. So it could be argued that even though it all came out in the end, it was a very, *very* bad idea for all the reasons I stated earlier and both of us had to go through a lot of pain."

"Well, I'm just using Dane for sex," Bea said cheerfully, taking a sip of her rum and Coke.

Lindy closed her eyes, as if in prayer. But Bea doubted she was praying.

McKenna laughed. "That's my girl."

"Did you encourage her to do this?" Lindy asked.

McKenna shrugged. "Maybe. Anyway, why not? You all get to have fun with your respective sexy cowboys and she doesn't? It's bull. She's not a kid."

"I'm not," Bea agreed. "In fact, that's why I wanted to get the Dane stuff out of the way. Because it doesn't matter. My sex life is my business. It always has been. You don't know me. You don't know what I've done or haven't done."

"Have you ever been with anyone else?" Lindy asked.

McKenna waved a hand. "Neither here nor there."

"It's *very much* here and there," Lindy said.

"Whatever. Also I want you to know, I've been going to school and working toward getting my certification to be a vet tech."

She was committed now. To sharing who she was. What she wanted from life. To showing them she was a person and not just their cheerful friend who lived in the woods.

Kaylee smiled. "And you're going to be a great one."

"I think so," Beatrix said, keeping her tone firm. "I'm mostly going to apply those skills to my animal sanctuary. I worked out a whole plan with Dane, and we started toward getting nonprofit status. He's been helping me with logistics like building, and taking some of the load while I keep studying for my final. But it's mostly all my idea. I managed to put it all together. I just… That's not something a kid does. I'm not a kid. I'm not less than any of you because I'm a couple of years younger. And I'm not… I'm not stupid. About anything. I know who I am, I know what I want. The sanctuary is the most important thing to me. These animals that we just took in are a great start. But once I can actually establish myself as an official nonprofit organization I should be able to take in a lot more animals and make a huge difference. I finally figured out what to do with my passion. And unfortunately, there's not a career track in high school for 'so you want to rescue animals.' But I figured one out. I'm going to chase that."

"Well, as much as I would love to have you at the clinic," Kaylee said, "I definitely understand you wanting to apply what you've learned at your own place."

"I might still do a couple days a week at the clinic," Beatrix said. "I need to gain experience, and it would be really great to work with your guidance. All of the things that I'm learning in this course are great, but I always figure things out faster when I can just do them."

McKenna smirked. "Are you currently in the process of figuring Dane out?"

Bea sniffed delicately. "Perhaps."

For their part, Lindy and Sabrina seemed stunned into silence.

"Good for you, Bea," McKenna said. "I can't think of anyone better to run an animal sanctuary. Or any kind of sanctuary. I don't think people understand how important caregivers are. But as somebody who spent her whole life without anyone caring for me, showing up in Gold Valley and having you show me the kindness that you did made so much difference. Kindness isn't weakness. I spent most of my life in and out of foster care and afraid to show real caring to anyone because I might get hurt. I know that it takes strength to open yourself up like you do and care for people. And care for animals, and care about anything."

Bea practically shimmered with warmth. "Thank you," she said.

The conversation took several different directions after that, and after a while Lindy moved and took a spot right next to Bea. "I'm sorry," Lindy said softly.

"For?"

"Dane said something to me earlier, and I didn't listen to him then. I should have. Because listening to McKenna talk tonight, listening to you talk, I realized he was…not wrong." Lindy took a deep breath. "He said that the reason I was upset about the two of you being together was that I was afraid of what it meant for me. That I was afraid… That I would have my life disrupted if something happened between you two. He's right. I was scared of him hurting you. Of the two of you not being able to be in the same room anymore. And what that would mean for my vision of this family that we have. And it's not fair. That's not really concern for either of you. It's concern for me. I feel… Bea, I love you. I really do. Like a sister. You are the kindest person that I know. McKenna's right. It's tempting to see that as a weakness. It isn't though. When I think about you, and how long I've known you… You've always gotten everything you wanted. Quiet and stubborn and determined. And suddenly you're over there doing exactly what you set out to do without any help from anybody. I'm not sure that I've ever fully appreciated what that says about you. I know I haven't. I'm sorry. You've always taken my interference with grace. And you've always been kinder to me about my clumsy advice than I deserve. I want you to be happy. If Dane makes you happy… Well, then I'm glad that you're with him."

"Thank you," Bea said.

"And I'm sorry about the sanctuary too. And that it took me a while to kind of get on board with it."

"I really do understand that."

Lindy grimaced. "That's something else I don't deserve. And more evidence of how strong you are. The way that you're able to understand where people are coming from."

Bea had never considered that a particular gift. In fact, she had never particularly considered herself gifted with people. Not considering how everything had happened with her father. Her biological father. That anyone here felt differently was… It was a revelation. The best kind.

"I love you," Bea said to Lindy. "You're wonderful. And you're like my sister. And nothing can change that. Even you divorcing my brother didn't change it."

"That's true," Lindy said.

In that moment, Beatrix really did feel strong. Because Lindy had been afraid of…losing her. And that made Beatrix feel good, even while she didn't want Lindy to feel that way. But it made her feel like she mattered. And it was something kind of marvelous.

Bea got up to get herself a basket of french fries and regular Coke so that all of the effects of the alcohol would vanish before she decided to drive home, and Jamie joined her at the bar. "So you did it," Jamie said. "Seriously. You're not just saying that?"

Bea scoffed. "Why would I just say that? And by *did it* do you mean I had sex? Or do you mean I made a move on Dane specifically."

"Both? All?"

Jamie was looking at her with quiet awe and Bea was struck by yet another strange shift. She knew more than Jamie. And Jamie couldn't pretend that wasn't true. Because Bea was quite certain Jamie had *never seen a penis*. Not the way that Bea had.

She felt… Well, she felt smug. "It's fun," Bea said lightly.

She turned to Laz and placed her order, and Jamie ordered the same.

"Fun?" Jamie pressed.

Bea sniffed. "Yes. I mean, that's the thing. There's no reason to be all uptight about it. I was for a while. I mean, I kept thinking that I had to know it could turn into something. But now I get it. It doesn't have to. We're just…having fun."

"Fun," Jamie repeated.

"Yes," Bea repeated again. "It's kind of…athletic. And…and…he's very attractive." Fun was perhaps not the best description for what she and Dane had. There was an intensity to it that really didn't encompass fun. But they did laugh sometimes. And Dane said the most outrageous and dirty things. And it felt good. So that was…definitely a way of putting it.

"I guess. That's kind of how men see it," Jamie said, a crease appearing between her brows. "Like a sport. Like roping or something. So, I'm not sure why a woman couldn't see it the same way."

"Exactly," Bea said.

"Good for you," Jamie said, nodding. "I mean, I know I said all of that about Dane, and bull riders and all of that. But you're right. If you know what you're getting into… Then I guess it doesn't really matter if a guy is going to stay with you or not."

Bea ignored the pang in her chest. "Right. And I went into it knowing exactly what I was doing."

"Right."

Bea wasn't sure exactly what Jamie was thinking of,

and she imagined that later she would worry that she had somehow encouraged her friend to do something rash, but for now, Beatrix was just enjoying the small little shifts happening in all the people around her. The ways that they were forced to see her. As someone capable. As an adult.

As someone who knew what she wanted and set about to get it.

Yes, that's who she was.

And if there was a little bit of a heaviness in her chest when she tried to explain the practicalities of her relationship with Dane, well, that was nothing she couldn't handle. She knew exactly who she was. And now, so did the people around her. She was going to focus on that being a win.

Because for the first time in her life, Beatrix Leighton felt respected by every single person sitting at the table.

And maybe she couldn't have everything. But she had that.

So she would take it.

CHAPTER NINETEEN

THE DODGES HAD been trying to rope Dane into a poker game for months, and he figured after Wyatt had put in so much time on Bea's sanctuary, today was the day he had to give in. And so he had, but that meant that of course he found himself now seated at a table with his brother-in-law, who was still clearly a little bit up in arms over the situation with Bea.

Gabe Dalton had also joined the game tonight, along with Bennett and Grant Dodge. Dane had never been to one of the games before, but he had the impression that Gabe wasn't a regular either. And had likely been invited because of the work they'd all put in together earlier. And maybe because Wyatt wanted to reinforce that he was large and grumpy, seeing as Jamie was about to start work officially at the Dalton ranch.

"I fold," Grant said, his face contorting in disgust. "This is terrible."

"What's terrible?" Wyatt asked, looking cheerful. "The fact that I'm taking money away from all you douchebags?"

"I think you cheat," Bennett said.

"I don't cheat," Wyatt said. "How would I cheat? I would have to be smart enough to count cards, and I think we all know I'm not smart enough to do that. If

I were, do you think that I would be ranching? Do you think I would have spent so many years abusing myself in the rodeo?"

"Yes," Bennett said. "Because that's just who you are."

Wyatt shrugged. "Whatever. You're all welcome to stay in, but you do have to match my bet."

"Out," Bennett said, throwing his cards down.

"Out," Dane agreed.

"I'm still in," Gabe said, clearly a man with a death wish.

Wyatt's mouth twitched. "Is that so?"

"It's so," Gabe replied.

"Well," Wyatt said, throwing a five into the pot. "I raise you."

Gabe threw the money into the pot, then looked down at his hand and up at Wyatt. "I call."

The moment stretched tense between them and Dane had a feeling there wasn't much keeping Wyatt from reaching across the table and wrapping his hand around Gabe's throat to make a few threats.

When they laid their hands down, Wyatt cursed a blue streak. "What are the odds of that?" he asked, gesturing down at Gabe's flush.

"Well, I'm not a card counter," Gabe said slowly. "So I can't give you odds. If I could, I probably wouldn't have been a bronc rider."

"If you'd had any balls you'd be a bull rider," Wyatt said.

"My balls are fine," Gabe said, sweeping the pot in his direction.

Wyatt looked murderous. "I move we break for beer," he said.

"Not me," Bennett replied. "I'm out, and Kaylee said that if she had to pick me up I was in trouble."

"Pansy-ass," Wyatt said.

Wyatt got up and headed toward the kitchen, clearly on a beer mission, and Bennett shook his head, following after his brother. That left Grant, Gabe and Dane sitting around the table.

"McKenna and I live a walk away—I can drink as much as I want."

"A couple beers is not putting me under the table," Gabe said.

Dane laughed. "Same."

"So, what are your plans?" Gabe asked, leveling his gaze at Dane. "Staying in town? What?"

"For now," Dane answered.

"She's a pretty girl," Gabe acknowledged.

Grant looked both interested in the topic shift, and somehow also annoyed with himself over the interest.

"She is," Dane agreed.

"But, you know, if you need extra work to keep yourself from getting bored, I was talking to a buddy of mine who was telling me there's a real need for agents. Damien Leighton quit, and anyway, when a lot of you dumped him, he stopped being such a hot commodity. Somebody with your connections... You'd be valuable to a lot of the guys, Dane. You know the kinds of endorsement deals that are good, you know what to avoid. Hell, I'd take your advice. If I wasn't too damned old to be out there doing it myself."

"I'm not any good with that kind of stuff," Dane said, the idea taking hold in his mind, in spite of himself.

The possibility was...

Well, it might be the answer. He could almost taste it. Being back there where the action was, connecting with the riders, with companies he'd worked with in the past. Using what he knew.

He'd be a key player in the industry again.

Important.

"You'd be great at it, come on. You don't spend as many years as you did on the circuit without picking stuff up, and you had some great sponsors. Did some great campaigns. My dad is connected out the ass—I could talk to him."

"Well, that begs the question, since it's your dad that's connected out the ass, why aren't you agenting?"

"I've got stuff happening at the ranch here. I'm more interested in that. But, I was just thinking that if you were a man looking for an occupation..."

"I'll think about it," Dane said.

"Think about what?" Wyatt asked, coming back into the room and sitting down at the table with a six-pack of beer.

"About agenting," Gabe said.

"Agenting?" Wyatt asked. "Like Damien used to do?"

"Yeah," Dane said. "I mean, it's not a terrible idea. I guess I wouldn't have to travel all the time. And... Well, I can't ride. But the rodeo is basically all I know." Suddenly, the idea didn't really seem silly at all. He hadn't thought of it because he'd been so obsessed with getting back on the bull. Mostly because he had been caught up in the idea of the glory of the rodeo. Because he had needed to think that his father was somewhere watching him ride on TV. Well, now he knew it was true and actually knowing that had changed something inside of him.

He could still do something that interested him, something for him.

Right now, he was busy with Bea's sanctuary, but he wouldn't always be. Eventually, she would be running most of that on her own, and while he might be able to support her, having something that he could do for himself would be good too. And anyway, he could choose how much of a workload he took on. Could choose how much traveling he wanted to do.

"What about Bea?" Wyatt asked.

Bennett and Grant looked at him, their heads snapping in his direction so hard they might have given themselves whiplash.

"I wouldn't be gone all the time," he said. "And anyway, I'll talk to her."

Wyatt blinked. "Are you... Are you in a relationship with her?"

"Yeah," Dane said. "I mean, I figure."

"I just figured you were messing around with her."

"I wouldn't do that," Dane said. "Not to her."

"Well, hell, man. Congratulations."

"Thanks," Dane said. "Can we quit talking about girls and get back to playing poker, please?"

Something felt settled inside of him now though. It all felt...good. Because he had a job, and he had a woman. And he had a place. Well, he and Beatrix would have to talk about all of it, but for the first time in a long time, Dane Parker felt like he wasn't living for a future he might not be able to have, or a past that he was trying to fix.

For now, where he was at made him happy. And that felt pretty damn good.

BEATRIX HAD TO travel to Eugene in order to take her final, and when Dane offered to take her she couldn't say no. It was strange, getting everything set up for the two of them to leave, like they were a couple. A *real* couple. They had been moving back and forth between her cabin and the house, though they had mostly been sleeping in her cabin because Beatrix was more comfortable there. And Dane didn't complain, even though the bed was cramped and his feet hung off the end.

Lindy had agreed to help take care of the animals, splitting the job with Sabrina, since the two of them would be over at the winery for work, anyway. And Beatrix was grateful. Especially since both of them were now being supportive of her situation with Dane. Over the course of the past few weeks everything had been going so great. They had the property inspected, and had been approved to construct a couple of new buildings, and to dig the back-access driveway, which they had started on immediately. They had also gotten their nonprofit approval through the state. And if Beatrix passed her final, she would have her certificate and be fully trained to take care of the animals in the best way possible.

Of course, she didn't need the certificate. Not really. It wasn't about needing it. It was about proving to herself that she could do it. And now everyone knew that she was doing it, so that made her feel even more edgy about the whole thing.

"What are you going to do while I take the test?" she asked when they pulled up to the lab on campus.

"I'm going to wait for you," he said. "It's only a ninety-minute final."

"You don't have to do that," she said. "You can go… see things. We're in the city."

He chuckled. "I guess so."

"It might be fun."

"I'm not really compelled to see anything here but you, Beatrix. You're why I'm here."

She wasn't sure she knew what to do with that. With the overwhelming support that he had shown to her.

"Thank you," she said, kissing him, which still kind of blew her mind. That she could kiss Dane Parker whenever she wanted. It was so strange, and wonderful. That he was a flesh and blood man beneath her fingertips rather than a fantasy in her mind.

All this time with him had been like a little dream. One she hadn't even known to have. Because of course she could never have imagined all of the things that he did to her in bed. Could never have imagined how much more raw and real being with him would actually be. It was so hot and close and intimate in ways that she had never anticipated. But then, she hadn't given a lot of thought to sex in a very specific way.

Sometimes it made her feel so good, so relaxed. And other times she felt a little bit broken when it was over. Like she just wanted to cry. But Dane would always smile. He'd always make a joke. And then that feeling would be over and she'd be back to feeling good again.

Right now, she felt a little broken, and she had no idea what to do with that. Because she had to go and take a final exam. She didn't have time to go feeling broken over Dane Parker. She wished he'd make a joke. But she supposed there wasn't time for that.

"I'll see you soon," she said.

"Good luck," he said. "And whether it goes well or not I'm taking you out to dinner."

"You don't have to," she said. "We can just drive back."

"Sweetheart," he said. "I have plans. And if you know what's good for you, you're not going to argue with me."

Beatrix went into the exam room, her heart pounding, her hands beginning to shake, but she had studied for this. She just needed to believe she could do it.

There was a man sitting outside in his truck who sure seemed to believe that she could. And a whole lot of people at home. And she supposed that was the other good thing about letting people know what she wanted.

She had people cheering for her.

That might not help give her the right answers, but it definitely got her through the test with a more positive feeling. When she exited the exam room, Dane was standing outside of his truck, leaning against the front, his hand behind his back.

"What are you doing?" she asked.

"I did end up going and exploring the big bad city," he said. "But this was all I found."

He produced a bouquet of roses from behind his back and Beatrix felt like someone had reached into her chest, grabbed hold of her heart and crumpled it.

"Dane…"

"Has anyone ever gotten you flowers before, Beatrix?"

"No," she said.

"You know, somehow I figured as much, considering that no other guy had ever kissed you before either. So, allow me to be another first."

"I don't even… I don't know what to say," she said,

her throat getting tight, something in her stomach feeling weird and trembly.

"Thank you, Dane," he said, "is a very appropriate response. Also appropriate, honey, if you can't think of anything to say, would be finding other ways to occupy your mouth later."

His foray into crassness was a relief. Because sex and all the dirty fun they had in bed she could handle—mostly—but flowers and him driving her to her test was proving to be a challenge.

It reached her emotions. Traitorous, hopeful things. It made it harder to think of this as temporary. It made her hope for more and…and more just wasn't possible.

She'd put more out of her head a long time ago. And she'd never imagined they could even have this much, so she had to be happy with it.

"Well, I might be able to do that, if we don't collapse at the end of the drive home."

"I don't think we will," he said. "I have another surprise for you."

They drove away from campus, until they were downtown, Bea feeling small among the tall, unfamiliar buildings. The traffic would have intimidated her, and she was glad that Dane was driving. When they pulled up, it was to the front of a hotel.

"I thought that you… I thought we were going to dinner."

"Yeah, well, we kind of are. Though, mostly we're going to have dinner come to us."

Dane got out of the truck and rounded to the back, grabbing a duffel bag from it, before moving to her side and opening the door for her.

"What is this?"

"We're spending the night, Beatrix. Since we made all those arrangements to have the animals looked in on today, I figured they would be fine overnight."

"Oh," she said, sliding out of the truck and finding herself captured in his arms.

A man in a dark-colored uniform approach them, and Dane passed him a dollar as the man got in the truck and drove it away.

"Parking is handled," Dane said. "Let's go."

She took his hand, feeling small and strange as they walked into the shiny lobby, with marble floors and gold fixtures. It didn't really look anything like Dane. And it definitely didn't look anything like her. She wasn't sure if she was nervous or excited. If she was happy or…

Really, she didn't know what she was.

She shifted nervously as she stood next to Dane while he checked in at the front desk. She couldn't remember the last time she'd gone to a hotel, and she had certainly never gone to one with a handsome man with an overnight bag and the very clear intention of having sex in the room.

The room was ready for them, and they took the elevator right up to one of the higher floors, with Bea clinging to his hand the whole time. He took out a key card and let them into the room, grabbing hold of the sign that was hanging on the inside of the door and putting it on the outside handle. "Do not disturb," he said.

"Well, we will need food," Bea said.

"Eventually," Dane said.

Bea looked around the room. The bed was covered in snow-white linens, all plush and soft-looking. And it was huge. They'd made love in a bed that size only once. Mostly, they'd been confined to the little twin bed in her cabin. And sometimes the floor. And once the bathtub, with promises issued to her that someday they would do it in the shower. When he wasn't afraid he would fall and reinjure himself, and wound them both.

It was a beautiful little fantasy, and the minute she put it into that column she felt much more at ease. Everything had started to feel so very serious and real earlier. It was a relief to be in a fantasy again.

And this really was more like a fantasy. Soft and gauzy and pretty. Removed from their regular lives.

"I'm afraid that Lindy is going to assassinate Evan," Bea said, walking into the room and sitting on the edge of the bed.

"Really?" he asked. "You think she's going to assassinate your raccoon."

"It's a legitimate concern that I have," Bea replied.

"Collateral damage," Dane said, setting the duffel bag down on the floor and stripping his shirt off. He walked over to the bed, kneeling down in front of Beatrix and gripping her chin, drawing her down for a kiss. She felt giddy, drunk even though she was sober as could be, and it was only three in the afternoon.

"I want you," he said. "And I want to have you quite a few times tonight. So, I guess we better start now."

She set her red roses down on the white bedspread and kissed him, and he rose up, pushing them both back onto the mattress. It was so soft, the bed so luxurious. And Dane was so hard and hot above her.

So beautiful. He was touching her face, and he pushed his hands beneath her shirt and began to touch her body. But she felt like he was touching her deeper somehow. Felt like her chest might crack open.

He kissed her slow and sweet, and there was none of his usual humor. There wasn't even the urgency that often colored their lovemaking.

There was a contentment to the way that he kissed her. Like he could do it forever. And it made her... It almost made her want to run away.

She wiggled beneath him, uncomfortable with the ache that was spreading through her chest. She was so much more comfortable with the ache between her legs. With wanting him.

She knew how to make that pain go away, but she had no idea what to do with the other.

He stripped her clothes from her body slowly, so very slowly, taking his time as he kissed the curve of her neck, her shoulder, her collarbone. He avoided the more obvious parts of her, instead moving straight through the centerline of her body, down to her stomach, stopping just above where she was wet and hungry for him. He kissed her inner thigh, her knee, down. Until she was shaking.

Until she felt like every kiss was a gunshot. Piercing her skin and going deep. Adding to that endless pain in her chest.

He stood, stripped the rest of his clothes off slowly.

Her mouth went dry.

She watched every shift and bunch of his muscles as he moved, the grace and strength in his body.

She could recognize now when he was in pain. When his leg was failing him, when his back hurt. He never said anything. But the way he held himself changed.

There was always a tenseness in his jaw, strain in his eyes. And she could see it there now, but he was standing tall. Looking down at her like she was more important than the pain.

She sat up, pressed her fingertips against the angry scar on his thigh and traced the line down to his knee, carefully avoiding that hard, insistent erection in front of her face, as he had ignored those parts of her. She explored the rest of him. Acres of smooth gorgeous skin, covered in hair, marred by scars. She kissed him. Kissed that dip right next to his hip bone, the ridges of his abs, his chest. The hollow of his muscular butt, down to his thigh and back up again. Until he was shaking. Until he was growling her name.

She wondered if he felt it in his chest too. Or if it was just her.

The thought made her eyes sting.

She didn't know why this felt different. Why it felt so deep.

Why they were teasing each other when they both knew what the other wanted.

They weren't talking.

The air between them was too thick for words.

He growled, hauling her up off the floor, his teeth set on edge, the tendons in his neck standing out. He made a rough sound as he brought her down onto the bed, her wrists contained in the firm grip of one of his large hands.

"You drive me absolutely crazy," he said.

He kissed her, as deep and animal as the sound that had just echoed inside of him. She arched up underneath him, begging him for more. For his possession. But he didn't give it. He teased her. Dragging that hard length through her slick folds until she was panting, gasping for more. Until she was all but sobbing with the desire to have him inside of her.

"Say it," he commanded.

"What?" she whimpered.

"Tell me where you want me."

Her eyes went wide, her stomach twisting. He wasn't teasing.

"Inside me," she begged. "Please."

There was no humor in his eyes, and there was no teasing in her answer. She was on the verge of tears. This was somehow them, the same as the rest of the sex had been. The same as the rest of their relationship had been. But there was something new to it, and it terrified her. She also didn't know how to stop it. Didn't think she could. Didn't think she wanted to.

Finally, he reached down and produced a condom from the duffel bag and rolled it onto himself slowly. He positioned himself between her legs, and when he entered her, it was not slow. It wasn't gentle. He slammed himself home in one easy thrust and she cried out with need for him. She clung to him, tears streaming down her face as he took her. As he took them both. Buried so deep she couldn't tell anymore where he ended and she began.

"Beatrix," he groaned as he shook and came. "Bea."

And then the wave broke over her, devastating, leaving her storm tossed in its wake. She clung to him so hard her fingernails bit into his skin, and she knew she should let go, but she couldn't.

When it was over, she sobbed out his name. And when she fell apart, he held her in his arms.

Then he pulled her against him, his hands moving over her curves. He kissed her, slow and tender, and it made her ache. Everywhere. But there was nowhere to run to. No animals to feed. No work to be done.

Dane wasn't in pain. There was nothing for her to do. No way for her to break the tension.

He moved his hands down, both large and firm and on her butt, and she waited for him to make a joke or something. But he didn't. He just looked at her. And breathed in deep, letting it out slow and long.

She lifted her hand and cupped his chin, the whiskers there bristly beneath her fingers. She intended to say something to ease the feelings that seemed to be growing, wrapping themselves around her like a creeping vine.

It was so weird to be with him like this. Out of the comfort of her cabin. Or even the discomfort of the house she'd grown up in. It made it more real somehow. That they'd stepped out of that life and were still with each other.

She wiggled and started to pull free of him, but he pressed a kiss to her shoulder and she stilled. The brush of his lips against her skin made her feel like she was home.

But that realization didn't take away the ache in her chest.

If anything, it made it worse.

CHAPTER TWENTY

WHEN DANE WOKE up the next morning his resolve was strengthened. Last night he'd spent all night in bed with Bea. They'd gotten up to eat, and she'd dressed because Bea had been insistent that it not look like they'd just finished ravishing each other at four in the afternoon. He hadn't seen the problem, but he'd deferred to her.

They'd eaten, and then he'd gone straight into dessert. Which was not something on the room service menu.

He smiled just thinking about it.

Bea was still sleeping, buried underneath a pile of plush white blankets. He wanted to give her everything. The life she deserved.

She sure deserved a hell of a lot more than shacking up with a guy who lived at his sister's place. But he had a plan for that.

He called downstairs and ordered breakfast, then climbed back beneath the covers with her, nuzzling her neck and running his hands over her curves. "I ordered bacon."

She stirred, rolling onto her back and looking at him with cloudy eyes. "What?"

"I ordered breakfast. It should be here soon."

"You can't be in bed with me when the food comes," she said.

"Why not?"

"It looks decadent," she said.

"Maybe it escaped your notice, Bea, but we are being decadent," he pointed out. "Plush hotel room. Good room service. Lots and lots of sex…"

"I don't have a lot of experience with that," she said.

"Me neither. At least, not in the sense of being classy. Other things…I've been a little indulgent with. But it still wasn't the same."

Bea sniffed and moved against him. He wrapped his arm around her, unsure if he should have reminded her about his past. But then, she knew who he was. That was important. There weren't secrets between them. Which meant that he needed to talk to her about the agent thing too. Soon.

The primary reason he had asked her to let him take her for the test was so that he could ambush her with something like this. With something special. Because he wanted her to understand what she meant to him. And more than that, he wanted to make some commitments. But they needed to work some things out. All good things, in his opinion. But, some things nonetheless.

"This bed is a lot nicer than the one back in your cabin," he pointed out.

"Well, there's more room," she agreed, shifting so that his thigh was between her legs, and all he could concentrate on was the feel of her body against him.

"I don't know what you've done to me," he said, brushing her hair off her face. "But I'm pretty obsessed with you. Just so you know."

She squirmed, looking uncomfortable, her cheeks turning pink. "I don't understand why you would be obsessed with me."

"I think knowing you has shown me how to have some purpose. Watching you put meaning into all kinds of things, into a baby robin, it's taught me something. About how when you care, happiness tends to follow."

"It's not always a happy thing to care," she said softly.

"But the fact of the matter is, it's a lot better than caring about nothing. It's a lot better than caring about just yourself. I think that was my biggest problem. Dealing with the accident aftermath. I love my sister. I always have. And I have a lot of good friends. I care about them. But I don't think I've ever cared about anyone as much as I cared about me. As much as I cared about proving that I meant something. To my father, mostly. A little bit to myself. To anybody that thought I wouldn't amount to anything. I was riding bulls at people, Beatrix. And when I lost that, I didn't know who I was. Because if I wasn't performing my success, I didn't feel it. If somebody couldn't see it then it must not be real. You've taught me a hell of a lot about doing. Just doing. Not for anyone's benefit, not for performance. Hell, you're the direct opposite of me in that way. You've been quietly achieving for years."

"Yeah," she said softly. "I suppose that's true. But then, people don't just immediately recognize everything you are because you decide that you want them to. I wanted a little of that glory. A little of that living out loud that you've always done."

"Maybe there's a middle ground. Maybe together we

can help each other find it. I mean, there's not much point in being with somebody who's just good at things you're already good at, is there?"

She was silent for a long moment. "I suppose, if you're looking at things that way, then… That is true."

"We need to figure out where we're going to sleep," he said.

She scrunched her face and he just wanted to kiss her and not have a discussion. "This bed seems pretty good to me."

"Not right now, Bea. The rest of the time. Because Lord knows I love being plastered up against you, but I can't do the twin bed for much longer. My whole body hurts in the morning, and hell, I don't know, maybe that's because of the sex. It's a workout I haven't had for a while. But I suspect also it might have something to do with the bed that my feet hang off the edge of."

Bea's movements became more agitated, and there was a knock on the door.

"Room service," the person said.

Beatrix scrambled out of bed and grabbed hold of her robe. Dane did the same, but moving much more slowly.

By the time he got to the door, Bea was back in bed, looking sheepish.

"You can bring it in here," Dane said, signing the bill quickly and sending the staff member on his way. Then he brought the trays right into bed with them and uncovered them, revealing eggs, bacon, biscuits and a plate of chocolate-covered strawberries.

He'd worked up a fantasy of Bea and strawberries, and checkout was at eleven. Which meant it was strawberry time now.

Bea grabbed hold of the carafe on the tray and poured herself some coffee into the basic white mug. Her lips twitched. "Fancy. Kind of."

"It seemed right."

They lay under the covers, picking at their food. And then he took a strawberry between his thumb and forefinger and brushed it against her lips. "Open up for me."

"That's not a breakfast food," she said.

"I don't care. You make me feel like chocolate-covered strawberries and sex in the morning, Bea. I don't care if it's the right time or the wrong time according to anyone or anything else. I just care about us."

She turned pink to the roots of her hair, but she obeyed him. And he watched those pretty pale lips close around the fruit, his body getting hard again.

"But the bed," he continued, trying to keep his resolve as firm as his dick. "I know that you love the cabin, Bea, but we've got the whole winery house just sitting there. And you might as well move in with me."

She went stiff. Still. "I don't like that house," she said.

"I understand that," he said. "But, I'm thinking practically. The sanctuary is going to be on the property, so living on the property makes the most sense."

"My cabin is fine."

"Yeah," Dane said. "For you."

"Yes," Beatrix agreed. "It's fine for me. I'm not sure what you think might be the issue with that."

"Because I would like to be with you," Dane said. "I would like to sleep with you at night. I would like to wake up with you in the morning. And in general, would like to share a living space with you."

She blinked, first slowly, then more rapidly. "I don't... I don't see why that's necessary."

"It's not necessary," Dane said. "But it's something that I want."

"Why?" Beatrix asked, frowning. "Do you want it because you're trying to take control of some...new life that you think you can have because you just...walked in and decided to?"

"No," he said. "I want it because I like being with you. This is about you and me. It's not about anything else."

"Bullshit," Beatrix said, sitting upright, her robe falling partway open and exposing the curve of her breast. Distracting him for a minute.

"My eyes are up here," she said. "And I never thought I would have to say that to you."

"Things change," he said. "Things have changed," he reiterated. "I don't think you understand that. I've changed. What I want has changed. The way I feel about you has changed. And now the way that we are carrying on, the way that our living arrangements are don't work for me."

"Well, maybe nothing's changed for me."

"I don't think that's true, baby, I really don't."

"Dane, I think that you just are desperate to find something to do. And I appreciate your throwing yourself into this whole sanctuary thing..."

"I have something else to do," he said.

"What?"

"Well, I was going to wait to bring this up because it's kind of a new thought, and what I really wanted to talk to you about was us moving in together, not this.

But since you asked. A couple of weeks ago Gabe Dalton brought up the idea of me getting into agenting. Like your brother used to do. And… I would be good at it. I have all the contacts, I actually know my business when it comes to the rodeo. When it comes to endorsement deals. I'm good with that. I think that you could keep me occupied, and… I don't need the recognition. But it would be nice to have something that feels like an accomplishment. It would be nice to have goals."

"So you're talking about traveling."

He lifted a shoulder. "Only a little bit. It doesn't have to be a ton. It's not like I'm going to be on the road all year or anything like that. And I don't have to take on more work than I can handle."

"Yeah, I actually understand how the job works, seeing as my brother did it. And, he made my sister-in-law's life miserable while he was doing it."

"It's not going to be like that."

"You know, it doesn't matter if it does. But I think that it's proof that you want this other life. And I'm not the right person to give it to you."

He frowned. "What the hell? We want the same life, Beatrix, I know we do. And I'm not proposing anything crazy. I just think that we're at the point where we should make some choices about our relationship. You know, in the interest of me not suffocating you in a single mattress."

"This isn't me," she said, scrambling out of bed and flinging her hands wide. "This fancy hotel room, and the winery house. And… And… I'm not a person that you want. I'm just not."

"Beatrix," he said, following suit. "I don't understand what's got you so upset."

"That's the other thing. You don't understand. You don't understand anything. Because just… You can't. You can't possibly understand. But you know, we could move in together, and we could move in to that awful house that I don't even like. And we could pretend that for a while everything was going to go great. But eventually, Dane… Eventually, you would follow the money. You're just going to go hard into agenting, and you're never going to be home. And you're going to forget about me."

He stared down at her, at the obvious distress on her delicate, beautiful face. "I'm not going to forget about you," he said slowly. "But I think we can both agree that it would be better for me if I had something that was mine. I want to help you with the sanctuary, Beatrix, I do. But, it's going to make us both crazy if that's all I'm doing."

"That's not the point. That wouldn't work either. You couldn't stay home and just do the sanctuary because I would just be an obligation to you. And you would resent me. You would keep me, but you wouldn't even want me."

"Why are you acting like those are the only options?"

"Because they are," she exploded. "Because that's all we're ever going to get. Because that's how things like this go."

"I don't understand what you're talking about right now, and you need to start explaining it to me, because there's no way I can win as long as we don't understand each other."

"At first maybe you wouldn't, and you might not

mean to. But things will change. Look how much they've changed just recently. They'll change again."

"Beatrix," he said. "Tell me."

"That's what he did," she said. "That's what my father did. Jamison Leighton offered him money to never talk to me and he took it. My own father took money and walked away from me when he was offered that. A cabin in the woods was fine, until he could have more. I don't know why… I don't know why you wouldn't feel the same."

CHAPTER TWENTY-ONE

BEA WAS SHAKING, and she felt silly and hysterical and completely on the verge of a nervous breakdown. But Dane didn't understand. And he was right, she hadn't told him, so maybe it wasn't fair. But he needed to understand.

She couldn't uproot her life in the cabin that meant so much to her. All that hard-won independence that she'd been forced to find at such a young age, when she had realized that she was going to have to make her own way, make things matter to herself, make herself matter, or she never would.

That was what her cabin represented. Her independence. Her own life. Happiness on her terms, rather than her parents'.

"My father's name is Michael Fulsome. And he used to work at Grassroots Winery. He kept the grounds and lived in a little cabin in the woods, by the river. He had a farm dog named Mabel. And she used to follow him around everywhere. He had a wide smile and a big red beard. And animals loved him. And I thought he was the nicest man that I had ever met. And I remember being a kid and thinking that if he would've been my father my life would've been a lot happier."

"Beatrix," he said, his voice and face going horribly soft, like she was a wounded animal, and she should know, because she had used that voice on more wounded animals and people than the average person ever would.

"Don't," she said. "Don't look at me like I'm damaged. I went through all of this by myself. I don't need you to feel bad for me now. But you do need to understand. I found out when I was sixteen that he was my father. I was… I was happy, Dane. Because suddenly I made sense. Who I was made sense. I was part of him, not Jamison Leighton, who didn't have a kind word for anyone. Who didn't have a smile for anything, much less children or animals. Michael was my father, and suddenly my world clicked into place. My mother told me. She told me to hurt me." Bea blinked back the tears that were building, making her nose feel prickly and her throat tight.

"Why would she do that?" Dane asked.

"Because she wanted me to be a certain thing, Dane. She wanted me to be her ally, her friend, I don't know. To get nails and hair done with her. To be a kind of wild force against my father—against Jamison, I mean—but I wasn't in the right way. And so she saw me as a weapon that she could use in a different way. Of course, she wanted Jamison to know that I wasn't his. And of course she wanted me to know it too."

"What happened after that?"

"I spent a summer at the winery with Michael. With him knowing. And me knowing. And I would go out and visit him every day at the vineyard. Asking questions. About his life. About why he loved animals. But never about my mother. Never about how he got involved with her. Never about why my father let him continue to work at the winery if he even suspected."

Bea shifted, trying to ease the pain that was building inside of her with every word. She knew the story already. She'd dealt with it. It didn't need to hurt this much.

It was what had taught her the lesson she'd carried forward ever since. That no matter what promises were made, they were only as certain as the present moment.

The future might bring better, bigger, more than Bea could ever hope to be.

"I didn't care about his relationship with my mother," she continued. "I just wanted to know who I was. I wanted to make sense of that. And I wanted to have a father who loved me. Because God knew Jamison didn't. But it was the happiest I'd ever been. Because suddenly all of that resentment made sense. Always feeling like I didn't fit made sense. Even my red hair made sense."

Dane reached out and put his hand on her cheek and she pulled away. "My father didn't like it. Jamison didn't like it. He was afraid, I think, of what I might do, of what might happen if more than just us knew that Michael was my father. As far as he was concerned the fact that I was a late-in-life surprise for them that came years after their other children, the fact that I looked different... Any rumors about that were unsubstantiated. My father wanted it kept that way. One day when I went down to visit Michael he was packing up. He was leaving. He said that he had to. That Jamison had sent him away. He left Mabel. He left Mabel to be with me. I went running into the house, and I screamed at Jamison, and I told him that I wouldn't let him send Michael away. I said that I loved him. And that he was my father. My real father. The only one that I cared about at all. That I didn't love Jamison. Not one bit."

Beatrix took a deep breath. "And do know what he said to me? He was cool and calm, like he always was. Like he wasn't hurt by any of the things that I'd said to him, or by the idea that I might not love him. He said he hadn't sent Michael away. But he said he'd given him an offer. And he offered him a substantial sum of money to agree to sign a gag order and never tell anyone that I was his daughter. And to always stay away from me. So what was the point? What was the point in being angry, or causing a scene the way that Sabrina had. In carrying on and ruining everything for everyone else?"

It was so hard to tell the story. So shameful and embarrassing. "That's when I moved in to the cabin. Michael was gone and it was empty, so why not? Sabrina and Damien didn't know. I was only sixteen. It was my quiet rebellion. And no one knew so my—Jamison—didn't care. I took Mabel and moved in to the little house and I made it mine. I made it safe."

She scrubbed at her stinging eyes, angry that emotion was right there at the surface, no matter how hard she tried. "My father chose money over me, Dane. As if a simple life in a cabin with a daughter wouldn't be enough. Well, I made it enough for me. I live in a tiny cabin with animals, and it's enough for me. It's my choice. I have money, I could do whatever I want. I choose this life. I don't know why it couldn't be enough for him. Maybe it was me. Maybe I wasn't enough."

Dane put his hand on her face, his thumb warm on her cheek, moving in slow circles. "Bea... Jamison must care about you. He gave you the trust fund. Just like he did the rest of his children."

"Not to Sabrina, because she embarrassed him," Bea said, her voice wobbling. "No, he gave money to me and he made it very clear why. When he called me into his office to tell me that it was passing into my control a couple of years ago I asked him that same question. I said why. Why are you giving money to me, when I'm not one of your children and we both know it. He said it was obligation. Because for all to see I was his daughter. Because I had never humiliated him or shamed him. And doing anything less would be a failure to those obligations. He fully claimed me as his. And that was what mattered. Then he gave me money. Not a hug. He didn't say that it was love that made me his father. He said it was obligation and appearances."

"Maybe that's all he knows how to give."

"I think it is. But I don't want it. And the best thing that I can think of to do is take that money and benefit animals. Do nothing to benefit myself. To stay exactly where I am and prove that it's enough. That even if I have Jamison Leighton's money that's the life that I'll choose. Because it's good enough for me."

"Bea, I didn't realize that the cabin meant so much to you. And I didn't realize that you'd been through all of that. But I have to tell you that any man who takes a payout to walk out of your life is a damned fool. The problem is not with you, sweetheart. It never was."

"Easy for you to say, Dane. You're the man who formed an entire career around proving to your father that you mattered."

"That's true, and I can't deny it. But I also know that

living to spite somebody else, to show somebody else what you are... It's empty in the end. And it's selfish. Because it's taking all of your hurt and everything that person did to you and putting it at the center of all that you are. And that doesn't give you a happy life. That I can promise you."

"Why can't I be selfish?" she asked. "No one else ever considered me first. Why can't *I* consider me first?"

"You can. Hell, honey, you should. We don't need to move in to the winery house. We just need to move a bigger bed into the cabin. And maybe we won't have a bunch of room to move around, but it's okay."

"Maybe I don't want you to move in to the cabin, Dane, did you think of that? I've made a life. A life that matters to me. A life that means something to me. And even if all of you see it as small, what you don't see is that it's mine. I fought to be happy with who I was. I fought to see the meaning in the things that I loved, when everything around me told me, with words and without, that it was small and silly and insignificant. I worked to be sure that it wasn't. Not for me."

"Beatrix," he said slowly, his blue eyes gazing into hers, melting her. Making that ache in her chest expand. It was all getting so big. So impossible. The sex this time had been terrifying. And the words that had followed it had been even worse. And all she wanted to do now was run away and hide. Go back to what was familiar. She didn't want to stay here and do this. She didn't think she could.

She was never supposed to have to deal with this.

It was supposed to be a fling. It was supposed to be

fun. But this wasn't fun. He wanted things from her. He was asking her to change. He was asking her to give him things. And she just didn't know... She didn't know.

"You matter to me," he said. "And I want to be able to give you a life. A life with me. We can...we can build something. I have my rodeo contacts and I can use that to give us the life we should have."

"You have one foot out the door, that's all it is. You can call it whatever you want, and say you're building something for me, but it's for you."

"You're making excuses," Dane said.

"What are you offering me? You're offering us living together for a little while. You want me to uproot everything to live with you. And... I don't...."

"I'm not talking about for a little while," Dane said. "That isn't what I want. I want to live with you. I want to be with you. Just you, Bea. I know that you spent a lot of years with a crush on me. I know that you spent time fascinated by me. And I didn't have that with you. But you know what I did have? A life. A whole lot of lovers. And it wasn't this. I know that. I know the difference. You don't know how amazing this is. How much it means. How much it matters. Because you haven't slept in bed next to somebody and felt more alone than you did when you were by yourself. I don't feel that way with you. With you I feel like I'm home. With you I finally feel like I can sit still for a little while."

She took a step back, her heart pounding. "I'm glad that I'm comfortable for you. But when comfortable wears off I think that you're just going to want to find someplace new to go."

"That's where you're just going to have to trust me,

Beatrix. I can't show you the future. I can just tell you what I want. I want you."

He was standing there offering her what she had imagined would be her biggest fantasy. Dane was willing to live in her cabin with her. Willing to be her lover. Those were the things she had dreamed about. Okay, maybe when she was younger, she had dreamed about love and marriage and things like that, but she knew better now. She knew those things were one in a million. Fifty-fifty, really. That Lindy had to go through Damien to get Wyatt. That her parents had never even found that.

Dane was offering her something wonderful.

And she didn't know how to take wonderful. Because the only thing she'd ever had in her life that felt wonderful had fallen apart. Betrayed her.

And in the end, only Mabel had been by her side. People failed constantly. That was her experience. It was her life.

And Dane wasn't settled. Not like her. He was at a crossroads in his life. In a position that he'd been forced into by an accident. And what would happen when he got back out there and saw all the options available to him?

Bea and her cabin would seem so small then.

She was what he wanted when he had to be here, but he wouldn't be stuck here forever. She had been great when he'd been eight months celibate and unsure of what he wanted.

And when he had the whole world before him, why would he choose this? Why would he choose her?

"No," she said. "That isn't what I want. I told you

what I wanted. I wanted to have sex until we decided it wasn't fun."

"That's really all you want from me?"

"Yes," Beatrix said, feeling like she was being torn in two. "It's what I need. Some people are better off doing things by themselves, Dane. And I'm one of them."

"So all these months of us existing together on the property, helping each other, that didn't mean anything to you?"

"It did. It was nice, but it's not my life and it isn't going to be."

"Why not? Because it seems to me that you're letting an awful lot of other people decide what your life is going to be, Beatrix. And I thought that you were stronger than that."

His words hit hard, square at the center of her chest, where that hideous ache had already taken root earlier when they'd made love.

"Is that what you think? Or are you just upset because what I want isn't what you want? That doesn't make you any different from any of the other men that have ever been in my life, Dane. That makes you exactly the same. You can't understand why I value what I've created for myself. You can't understand why I want..."

"To protect yourself? Because that's what I see. You get so angry that everyone treats you like a child, but you know that you encourage that. You are the one that hid yourself away in a cabin in the woods and acted like you were some hapless fairy. You want people to under-estimate you because then you don't have to put yourself out there or try to rise up to anything. You want to be able to barricade yourself in that little space you've made. And I get it. I do. Don't tell me that I don't understand. Honey, I see it clearly. From one person trying to protect himself to another. We might have done it in different ways, but it's all for the same reasons. I wanted to set myself up big, so big that I was invincible. And you wanted to make yourself small so that no one would notice. You're like a creature hiding away in a den, and you can call it a choice, Bea, but I don't believe that it is."

"Yeah, because you know me better than I do," she said, the words beginning to fray, beginning to tremble. She hated this. Hated how exposed and raw she felt. Because that's what this was. He was right. He was pulling her out of her den, kicking and screaming, and if there were earth to hold on to she would have done it. Would've ended up with bloodied fingers with dirt wedged under the nails. That's how hard she wanted to hold on to that safety.

She remembered a little over a year ago when she had found Evan. On the side of the road, his mother and brother killed by a car. The way that he had clung to the blanket she had handed him like it might protect him from the world. And maybe that was her in her cabin. But it had protected her. It had. And now she was trying other things. She had tried to do this thing with Dane, and she was terrified. Like a small animal left out in the open with no defenses. It wasn't right, and she hated it. There was no creature in the natural world that would ever subject itself to it.

No creature except for humans. But humans were stupid. They ignored their protective instincts in favor of other things, and it only led to destruction.

Bea knew better.

She knew better because she had watched animals and how they behaved. Because she had observed closely how to survive.

"I want to go home," she said. "I need to be done."

"We don't have to leave for a few hours," Dane said.

"I didn't want to stay here in the first place," she said. "You were the one who thought you could treat me like any other woman. Who thought that I was supposed to melt because you took me to a hotel suite and got me room service. But when have I ever acted like I cared about that?" She clung to that, as thin as it was, because it gave her ammunition. And she wanted to be angry at him. She didn't want to be scared. And she didn't want to be upset at herself. But she was running low on things to accuse him of, and this seemed like as good a thing as any.

"You thought that the same tricks would work with me. That I would give you whatever you wanted because you put me in a big bed with high thread count sheets. Because you fed me strawberries in it. I'm not just done with the hotel. We need to be done."

"Don't you dare do that to me," he said. "I've been honest with you. Honest as hell. More than I've ever been with anyone else. I've never hid the fact that I had other lovers. You know that. I also never hid the fact that I think you're different. You're different with me. For me. Do you think I've ever asked a woman to live with me? What did I just say? I built a life out of being bulletproof. Out of building up a tower for myself that was so high no one could land a hit. I never hid, you're right. I put it all out in the open, but I made myself a tar-

get that no one could land a punch on. Well, I'm down
here now. And I'm letting you land a hit. The idea of
not being able to go back to the rodeo was something
I couldn't stand because I couldn't see another way to
live life. Until you. I am… I am bleeding here. For you.
I bled out in front of a crowd once. Before I passed out,
I remember. The way the blood was pumping out of my
side, soaking into the dirt. And I remember thinking I'm
just watching myself die. That was nothing. That was
nothing compared to this." He took hold of her arms,
his blue eyes blazing into hers. "I'm watching myself
die, Bea. But you're the only one that can stop it."

She didn't know what to do with that. With this man
looking at her like she had some kind of power. Like
he needed something from her. She had always kept
her head down low, and tried not to get hurt. At least,
after that last time. That last pain. That rejection that
had wounded her so mortally. She knew how to hide.
She knew how to put her head down and protect herself.

She didn't know what to do with this gruff, strong
cowboy who had been the center of her fantasies for
so long. She didn't know what to do with him asking
her to save him.

She had saved animals. At no risk to herself. But
what Dane needed was something she didn't know if
she could give.

"I can't be your Band-Aid," she said, her voice husky.
"Because then I'm just here until you heal." She spoke
the words, allowing each one to widen the chasm in
her chest. To make her hurt worse. "Mark my words,
Dane, the minute that you can go back, the minute you
can have those other women, you will."

"That's bullshit," he said.

"Is it? Because you can't prove that it isn't. You can't prove that you won't. I even think that you believe you won't. But I know better. Because I've watched people leave me."

"You should know better because you know me," Dane said.

"All right. If that's how you want it to be. Maybe it is you. Maybe it's you I don't trust, Dane. Because it was sure fun to learn about sex from you, but if I wanted to learn about unending devotion I would've picked anyone else. You were never around. And I attached to you because I was a kid. But I'm not a kid now. And maybe that was my big mistake. Thinking that I could take this the way a kid does. As a learning experience. We are adults. Which means that we just... Please take me home," she said, feeling suddenly flat and defeated.

His face went blank. Flat. "If that's what you want, Beatrix. That's what we'll do."

"It is."

They suffered through the awkwardness of taking a walk of shame through the lobby that wasn't anything like what Bea thought a walk of shame should feel like. Of having to ride in the cab of the truck, while he played country music instead of talking to her. Which was probably for the best, because there really wasn't anything else for her to say.

She had said everything. She had said too many things. Told him everything about her past and about what scared her. Had said all the hurtful things she could think of to say to him so that she could find ways to be angry.

They finally arrived back home, and much to Bea's relief nobody seemed to be there. She didn't quite know what to say to him. Didn't know what to do.

"Beatrix," he said, his voice rough. "I can give you whatever it is you need. I'm going to make something of myself with this agent thing. I know that I can."

"Is that what you think my problem is? You think that I'm saying no because you're not enough?"

"Isn't that it? You adored me when I was in the rodeo."

"Don't give me that. It was never that. And you know it. I adored you when…"

She adored him now. But back then she couldn't have him. And he was safe as a result. Now he was here and he was offering her…well, almost everything. Almost.

But it was that bit he was holding back that scared her the most. All these grand plans of his that had nothing to do with her, but everything to do with him. That hotel, as beautiful as it was, was all about him giving things.

She wanted the things, because they came from him. But that wasn't what he was doing. He was building another platform. And she could see that clearly.

And actually…

It made her think so much of Jamison. Jamison Leighton, who couldn't stand the idea of looking like less, of having his life look out of order. Oh, it wasn't about order or appearances for Dane. Not in the same way.

But it wasn't about love, or choosing to be with someone just because you wanted to be. It was about giving himself a stage to stand on. Putting himself at the center of that performance. Because whatever he had said about leaving bull riding behind, he wasn't ready to leave all of that behind.

"You're the one who doesn't think this is enough," she said. "You don't think I'm enough. And you don't think you're enough. You're still trying to buy affection, and it isn't going to work."

"Because I'm that bad of a proposition to you?"

"No, because I'm not going to be part of anyone's performance anymore. That's all I am to Jamison. A performance."

"You think I'd offer to move in with you because of a performance?"

"No. I think that you would offer me a fancy hotel room and a life that looks like a triumph as a rodeo agent's wife because you think that is going to make you feel like enough."

"You're twisting this up. It's not a hard decision to make. You either want to be with me, or you don't."

"Do you love me?" she asked, exhaustion infused into each word.

She watched as he faltered. "I care about you."

"That's not love."

"What is love, Beatrix? Because let me tell you, I stood in the street and I screamed at my father how much I loved him. As he got in his car for what turned out to be the last time and started to drive away. And you know what he said to me?"

"What?"

"He said he'd see me again if I managed to get myself on TV."

Her heart twisted for him. For the little boy he'd been. But it ached for the woman she was now. "I'm sorry. I'm sorry that he did that to you. I'm sorry that he made you feel like you had to perform to matter. But you don't have to do that with me. Just drop the bullshit, Dane."

"It's not bullshit. It's me."

"It's not. Give me you. And give me love. And then maybe we can find a way to move on from there."

"You don't trust me," he said.

Maybe she didn't. Or maybe she didn't trust the world. But if he'd give her those words…she would trust them.

"You don't trust *me*. You don't trust me to want you enough. You don't trust me… And I'm sorry. If what you're after is glory you aren't going to find it with me."

"I will give you everything I have. I've earned a hell of a lot, Beatrix. I'm proud of that. I can give you the winery house. Help support the sanctuary. After I get my life back on track. After I make myself into something again."

"You'll come to me with all of that. But can you come to me with nothing?"

"No," he said. "I can't. I won't."

"I can't do this," she said. "I can't. I can't live my life as part of someone's performance. Once you get back to that life, you'll have all these things that make you special and I won't be one of them."

Neither of her fathers had been able to offer her love. But Dane didn't seem to be able to offer it either. And that… She was sure if there was a difference to be had in all the world that was it.

No one seemed to be able to give that to her. Not to her.

"I have to go," she said.

"What if I just didn't go away, Bea? What then?"

"You will," she said, and of all the things she had said in the last few hours, this was the thing she was most certain of. "You'll go away, because everyone does. And the only ones who don't are miserable. Go agent, Dane. Find that life again."

"That isn't what I'm trying to do. I have to do something..."

"Do you? Because to me it all just seems like you're planning your exit strategy."

The glare he gave her then was so cold it hurt. And she regretted her words then. Regretted that she'd said anything because those words had been designed to hit their mark and they had.

"When you have all the choices opened up in front of you I don't think you're ever going to be sorry that you didn't stay with the weird girl in the cabin in the woods. And I'll never be sorry that I didn't give up my life."

"Okay, if that's how you feel." He sat in the truck, didn't get out, didn't make a move toward opening the door for her like he usually did. So she opened it herself.

"But to be clear," Dane said. "I never asked you to give up your life. I asked you to add me to it. You're the one who doesn't believe me. You're the one who doesn't trust me. You're the one who's still scared, Beatrix Leighton. But you're stronger than you think you are. And if you ever learn to let go of all that fear, the world is going to tremble at all your strength. Honey, maybe it won't be me that will make you figure that out. But someday you will. I'd like to be around when you do, except I'm afraid that whatever bastard finally unlocks it in you… I'm just gonna want to kill him."

"It won't happen," she said.

"I hope that's not true."

She opened her mouth to say something about how they could still be friends. Because that was what they were supposed to do. It had been the agreement. That they were going to do this and then be friends.

But that had been the rationale of the woman she'd been before. The one who hadn't understood what she was walking into.

As she knew now, that it was impossible. This had been the kind of affair that destroyed more than it built. And that made her desperately sad. Because for a while she had imagined that all of this was just going to open her up, teach her new things about herself.

But she'd been wrong.

It had brought her to the edge of something she was too afraid to step into.

And maybe he was right. Maybe she was afraid. Maybe that's all it was.

But fear kept you alive. That was one thing she knew for sure.

She blinked, trying to alleviate the stinging in her eyes.

"Well, how about you remember that we could have still been together for a while if you weren't so hell-bent on changing me, and so unwilling to change yourself. So unwilling to offer me anything but a rodeo star I didn't even ask for. Maybe you should think about that." She got out, slammed the door and stomped into her cabin. Evan came inside behind her, and she ignored him. She ignored everything. She went into her bedroom and curled up in the center of the mattress and dissolved completely. She cried like she was breaking apart and she didn't know why. Because she had made the choice. She had decided.

And it was the biggest fight of her life not to fling herself out the front door and go after him.

She was safe inside of her cabin. At least that's how it was supposed to feel. But she didn't feel safe at all. Instead, she felt sad.

And she was struck by the realization that her life hadn't changed at all, but something had changed inside of her all the same.

The walls of her cabin no longer felt like a haven—they felt like they were crushing her.

And still, so much of her would rather be crushed by the walls than crushed by Dane.

And she knew that he would crush her eventually. Because if he didn't love her, all the determination and promises in the world wouldn't make this enough.

She had to keep on believing that. Because the alternative was that she'd just walked away from her best chance at happiness. Because she was too afraid. And that was too terrifying to consider.

CHAPTER TWENTY-TWO

"How's this for a plot twist, Lindy," Dane said as he walked into his sister's house without knocking. "She broke my heart."

"She… What?" Lindy came running out from the kitchen and into the main part of the house, her expression one of shock.

"I asked her to move in with me. She told me no. She's fine. She's fine, because she has her animals and her cabin. And I'm not fucking fine. I'm the furthest thing from it."

He walked into the living room and sank down onto the couch, ignoring the twisting pain in his knee that told him he'd been moving too quickly. Hell, it barely matched the pain in his chest. It was a helluva thing.

"So she…"

"She rejected me. I asked her to move in with me and she said no. Because she said that someday I was just going to leave her. That I was going to choose money over her. Can you believe that?"

"Well, what did you offer her?"

He stared at his sister, who clearly thought he was an asshole even when he was heartbroken. Which was just great. "I offered her *everything* I have to give. My life. She's scared, because I said that I was thinking about doing some agent thing in the rodeo, but that…"

Lindy's lips pulled tight. "In fairness to her, she knew somebody who kind of sucks who used to do that."

"I'm not Damien."

"I know you're not. And I think that Bea knows that too. But I would assume growing up in their house she has some other issues. I know Sabrina well enough to know her father was difficult. And as much as I don't want to absolve Damien from his bad behavior, he didn't spring up out of a hole in the ground. Something made him. The same things that made Bea."

"I know she's been through some things, but dammit. I have too."

"And you're expecting her to give up her life for you? What are you giving up for her?"

"Why does anyone have to give anything up?"

"Maybe no one has to. But the fact is, in her situation I would probably be afraid too. You never noticed her until you were stuck here. Until you had no other option but to hang out in Gold Valley for a while. And maybe that's what you needed. But…"

"You're supposed to be on my side," he said.

"I actually am on your side. I believe you. I believe that you're not going to be offering to share your space, to share yourself with somebody unless it's serious. But that's because I know where we come from. And I know… I know that we had a mother who didn't care. And I know what it did to you when our father left. I know what it still does to you. But unless you've told her everything, she doesn't know. What a road it's been for either of us to love someone. To trust them. Dane, I get it. I really get it. But she has to get it."

"I don't know what to do beyond what I already said."

"How committed are you to the life that you would have with her here?"

"What does that mean?"

"Are you willing to not go after the agent job? If she wants you to give it up, could you?"

"What does that leave me with?" he asked. "And I don't mean from the perspective of…fulfilling, like, or whatever bullshit, I mean what does that…make me?"

Lindy looked down, then back up. "What if you only had *you* to offer her? What if you couldn't offer her being married to a big rodeo star? What if you have to accept that none of that is ever going to happen again? What if it's just you, Dane? Can you offer her that? Not a chance at a better life in the way that you see a better life. Not the chance at more money. Not the show. The Dane Parker Show, which I am a particular fan of, but it's a thing. Beatrix doesn't care about that. And you know it. Can you come to her and just offer you?"

Fear slammed through him like a freight train. And it made him feel like a damned coward. But it was like being hunted down and captured, being asked to stare in the face of your worst nightmare.

Standing there, empty-handed, offering love that would never be enough.

"I'm not… I'm a piss-poor prize, Lindy. A busted-up rodeo cowboy with nothing to give. I live in your house. I don't even have a house to offer her. Not one that's mine. Not really."

"What if you're enough? What if it's all the other stuff that's getting in the way?"

"Lindy, if she doesn't want me with all that other stuff…"

"Maybe it's the other stuff that scares her."

"I don't know what else to do. I drove her to her test. I've supported her every step of the way. There is no way that just me… There's no way."

"Why not?"

"Because our own father didn't stay. Our mother… she didn't care. And Lindy, our dad did watch me. That was when he cared. Not when I stood in the driveway crying and saying I loved him and begging him not to leave. But when I made something of myself."

Lindy shook her head. "Dane, the fact the boy crying in the driveway wasn't enough to make Dad stay was a lack in him, not in you."

He thought of what he'd say to Bea on the subject. What he had said. "I…"

"Did you tell Bea you loved her?"

"Why? When everything I have isn't enough, why would those words be?"

"Because they're everything, Dane. They're what separate us from our parents. They're what make us different. We've always loved each other, been there for each other. You thought nothing of dumping Damien as your agent when he hurt me. You know what love looks like. Why don't you think you can have it?"

"You know why."

"Dane, I've watched Bea watch you for the better part of a decade. That girl adores you. Everything about you. And it has nothing to do with money or success.

It has everything to do with the man that you are. But I think you're going to have to bring that to the table. And nothing more."

"I used to think you were right. I used to think that she adored me enough that she would do anything for me."

"Yeah, I think she did. When you were a fantasy. And now you're real. And real is terrifying. Believe me, Dane, I'm well familiar with that. Wyatt was that for me. Unobtainable and out of reach and easy. Easy because I knew that I could never be with him. And then suddenly I could be. That requires compromise and change. And I don't know that Bea has a lot of experience with compromise. You're right. She's a stubborn little thing. I think it's going to take someone just a stubborn to get her to trust."

"I don't know how to do it."

"You have to quit protecting yourself. Everything that's in front of you… You have to let it go. Speaking as someone who's done it, as someone who fully understands where you're at. Who had her heart broken before she reached the happily-ever-after… Believe me. There has to be one person that's willing to give. That's willing to let it all go. To lay it all down. Someone has to move first, Dane. It's a game of chicken that you can't win. It'll just be a stalemate, and everyone's heart will be broken. Offer her everything. The life she wants. Love. Marriage. Offer her every damn thing that you are. I don't even need to know what it is. It's for her. She's what matters."

Dane's heart began to beat faster. Like he was sitting on the back of a bull, waiting to get let out of the chute. He knew that she was right. He knew that he needed to do that. That he needed to let go. Of everything. He couldn't hold Beatrix the way she deserved to be held as long as he was carrying around his own baggage. As long as he had one foot out on the road and one foot home.

He had to be able to answer her every fear, and mean it. Had to be able to prove to her that this was the life he wanted.

"I have some phone calls to make," Dane said.

"Well, feel free to use the extra bedroom."

Dane went into the bedroom and dialed Beatrix. He knew that she shouldn't be his first call, but he couldn't help himself. She didn't answer.

Then he pulled up a number that he had told himself he wasn't going to call.

He expected to get a voice mail. He was surprised when someone on the other end picked up.

"Hello?"

"Hi," Dane said. "Dad. It's Dane."

CHAPTER TWENTY-THREE

THE DAY THAT Beatrix got her test results back she didn't know how to feel. She should feel happy. She had worked so hard for this. And it had been such a whole big thing. A test, not just of her confidence in herself, but of her trust in the people who loved her.

Not Dane though. Dane hadn't said he loved her.

Yeah, you didn't say you loved him either.

She ignored that voice. That voice that was about her, and about what she had done to Dane. Thinking about him made her sick. It made her whole chest hurt. And looking at her test results didn't help. She'd avoided everyone for days. She hadn't wanted to face Lindy, hadn't wanted to face Sabrina, or Kaylee, or anyone else for that matter.

She didn't want to see Jamie and tell her that she'd been wrong. That the sex with Dane wasn't fun, it had torn her heart out of her chest and left her feeling like a terrified weakling.

That it had taken a moment that should have been a triumph for her and turned it into something that didn't seem to mean a damn thing.

And that shouldn't be. She felt reduced.

Her life had been enough for her.

Liar.

She walked out of the cabin and looked around, eyeballing the various trails that led different directions into the woods behind her place. Spiderwebbing out and offering her a million different options for where she might go.

She took one of the trails she rarely ever used, following the rugged path through the woods, over a log that stretched across the narrow part of the creek and out to a small field. A little patch of sunlight offered a tall, weedy square of grass tangled with purple flowers that bloomed along the stem into a range of colors from a pale pastel to a vibrant shade.

This had been enough weeks ago. It had been. And now all she could think of was that this patch of grass felt lonely without Dane sitting next to her. That she would give away the warm sensation of the sun on her skin for a chance to feel his fingertips touching hers.

Maybe it wasn't that this life, that this place, wasn't enough. Maybe it was just that it felt empty without being able to share it with him.

He had called her the other day and she had ignored it. She had let it go straight to voice mail, because she had been too afraid that if she spoke to him she would burst into tears. That she would beg for him to come back, into her life, into her bed. And they would be right where they had left off. Because she would still be too afraid to give him…

To give him her love.

Because one day he would wake up and realize it wasn't enough.

Or maybe he wouldn't. Because maybe it's not about

life being enough. Maybe it's about finding the person you want to share it with, whatever the circumstance.

She gritted her teeth and pushed herself into a standing position, brushing the dirt away from her skirt. A rogue tear tracked down her cheek and she brushed it away angrily, huffing as she did. She tramped straight past her cabin and back toward the winery. She was going to tell Lindy and Sabrina about her triumph. About the way that she had managed to pass her exam, and that she was getting her vet tech certificate.

When she walked into the dining area, it was full of people, a bachelorette party, or something, chatting and enjoying flights of wine, and Bea wandered around the back of them, keeping out of view of the beautifully appointed tables and maneuvering through the restored wooden barn to the back rooms, where she knew she might find Lindy, and possibly her sister.

They were both there, standing in the doorway of Lindy's office, and when Lindy saw her, her face pulled tight, her lips turning down into a frown. And she closed the space between them in a hurry and pulled Beatrix into an overly sympathetic hug.

"How are you?"

"I'm great and so very good," Bea said, offering a fake and toothy smile. "I passed my final. Which is what I came to tell you. Because I got my certification to be a vet tech. So, I am set up to perform minor surgeries even on the animals that come through my sanctuary. So everything is just great."

"It is not great," Lindy said, smacking her on the shoulder with the back of her hand. "You broke up with my brother."

Bea blinked. "Yes, but not everything is about him. I have a thing that's happening that has nothing to do with him, and I'm telling you. Because you're like my sister."

"I can't think about that when the fact that you broke my brother's heart is the primary issue."

"I managed to deal with you even though you broke up with my brother."

"I didn't say I wouldn't deal with you," Lindy said. "I love you. No matter what. But I love Dane too, and it kills me to see him like this. And it's different because your brother is an asshole. Mine cares about you. And he didn't cheat on you. And he would never cheat on you."

Sabrina's lips twitched. "Remember how you just said that you were not going to talk to Beatrix about Dane?"

"I lied," Lindy said. "I didn't mean to lie, but apparently I lied. Bea, I think that I've spent far too long underestimating you. Hello, I know I have. The look on my brother's face when he came to my house the other day… Yes, I have severely underestimated you. But because of that, I'm not going to go easy on you now."

"I don't need you to go hard or easy on me. I made a decision. I did the best thing that I could."

"The best thing that you could to what?"

"To keep myself safe," Beatrix exploded. "I can't go committing myself to a man who doesn't know how to stay in one place. To a man who's still so bound up in the idea of his glory days that the minute he gets a chance to recapture them he's going to do it. Can you promise me that he won't? You know him. He wants… he wants to feel important and someday I might not make him feel important. I don't want to wait around for that day."

"Bea, I know that it's hard. I know that it's hard to love when you've been through stuff. Trust me. But do you really want him to give absolutely everything up to be with you? I think he would. But he helped you realize all of your dreams. He helped you with the animal sanctuary. He might be able to have something for himself, and you don't want him to have it?"

"No," Bea said. "I do want him to have it. Of course I do. But…" She let out a harsh breath. "I didn't ask him to give anything up."

"No," she said. "You just told him that you couldn't trust him and broke up with him."

"I just don't understand why it needed to change. Everything was fine. Then he went and demanded things."

"Because that's love," Lindy said. "It's love to demand things. And to expect somebody to change for you. And to change for someone."

"He didn't say that he loved me."

"Because he's scared. And he needs to change too. But so do you. You can't just live life in a burrow hoping to stay safe."

"But I want to stay safe," Beatrix said, her words small. "I need to stay safe. I just don't want… I don't want to be hurt again. You don't understand. You don't know."

"We won't unless you tell us."

Her throat tightened, panic lancing her. "Sabrina," Bea said, tears stinging her eyes. "I'm not… I'm not a Leighton."

Her sister blinked and drew back. "What?"

"I'm not a Leighton. Jamison… He's not my father. There is a man named Michael Fulsome and he is my father. He used to work at the winery."

"I remember him. He had… He had red hair," Sabrina said frowning.

"Yes," Beatrix said. "He had red hair. And he was the only person who was like me. The only person I'd ever known. And Dad offered him money and paid him and sent him away. He…he left. He took money instead of staying and being my father."

Sabrina looked pale, and visibly upset, and Bea felt terrified, because this was the thing she had been avoiding. Losing any kind of bond with her sister. To know that they didn't share a father might change things, and that scared Bea to death. But…

Hiding wasn't enough anymore. And keeping these things back was all part of hiding.

"I mean, I know a little something about Dad… Jamison…paying people money to go away."

"I know that you do. But you have to understand. Jamison raised me like a daughter because he felt obligated to. And he resented me. He really did. You know he doesn't have any real affection for me. He did it, and he gave me the trust fund and all of that to prove a point. Because it's all part of this weird game that him and Mom play with each other. And he paid the person who loved me to leave. And that person didn't love me more than he loved money. I'm no one's choice. Certainly not their first choice."

"Maybe it was complicated, Bea," Sabrina said. "Maybe it wasn't about him loving money more than you, but maybe he was really convinced that leaving you to the life that Dad said he could give you was the kinder thing to do."

"You don't know that."

"No," Sabrina said, "I don't. But I do know that sometimes people leave for very complicated reasons. I actually had to forgive the person that Dad paid off to leave me, Bea, so don't trick yourself into thinking that I don't understand what you've been through. In a way I do. Liam… I'm married to him now. I love him. He really thought that my life would be better without him in it. And Dad offered him money to go to school. It was his chance to make a better life for himself while leaving me to a life that didn't have him. And he really felt that that was the bigger kindness. Don't you think that maybe Michael thought the bigger kindness was leaving you to your family? Don't you think that he probably felt like the outsider? A man working at a vineyard trying to compete with Jamison Leighton?"

"But he… He was more important to me than money."

"Bea, you're so convinced that Dane would choose a life in the rodeo over you because you don't think that you matter enough. You don't think you matter more than that acclaim, than that glory. And you don't think that maybe your father thought the same thing?"

"But it's not fair. It's not fair to me. He should've asked me… I would've told him that I loved him and that I…"

"Aren't you angry at Dane because he didn't ask you? How is it different?"

Beatrix suddenly felt hideously, horribly small. And

she suddenly realized what a disservice she had done to Dane.

A tear tracked down her cheek, her body beginning to tremble. "But that isn't what I meant to do to him. I'm just so… I'm so scared. I'm so scared because I love him so much. And I don't… I don't even want to think those words. Because I've never loved anyone the way that I do him. He was safe when I couldn't have him. When he couldn't hurt me. But now he could… He could destroy me. And I…"

She took a deep breath. "I want to hide. And I want to be safe. I want to have exactly what I want when I want to and not have to negotiate or argue or explain myself. I want what I've always had except that I… I'm so lonely when I have that. And it's not enough. I know that. Because my cabin doesn't even feel like home anymore because he isn't there. Nothing that I loved before feels like enough because I can't share it with him. And I hate it. I hate it because it's like he carved out an empty space inside of me that wasn't there before. And I can't…live like this. It's terrifying. It's so very terrifying."

"I know," Lindy said. "Believe me. I know."

"Me too," Sabrina said. "I know it very, very well, Bea. How scary it is to love someone like that. To know that you have to let go of the ways that you protect yourself."

"He doesn't need me anymore," she said, her voice small.

"What do you mean, Bea?" Sabrina asked.

"He doesn't need me to take care of him. He's…he's not broken anymore, I am. And I don't know how to be

broken with him. I know how to fix other people. But
he's...he's okay with the fact that his life looks different now. And he doesn't need someone to dote on him
and shove pain pills at him and I don't know... If it
isn't that then I don't know what makes me important.
It's what I do. It's how I... It's how I make people and
things love me."

She found herself being pulled into a fierce hug. Both
Sabrina and Lindy had their arms wrapped around her
and she felt small and fragile.

And cared for.

"Bea," Lindy said, pushing her back. "You do not
have to take care of people in order for them to love you.
You can be broken too. We all are a little bit. I think
that Dane knows that about you."

She had used that. Always. Had given to people,
cared for them, because it gave her a connection while
putting her in a little bit of a position of power. She was
the caregiver. And they needed her.

It was why she had bought McKenna a coat when
they had first met. Not because she didn't genuinely
care about McKenna being warm, she did. But also because she knew it was the fastest way to make someone like you. To give them something. It was the fastest
way to get an animal to bond to you. To save them. To
care for them.

Dane had come into her life and he had started to
care for her. Not in that way that other people did, where
they gave endless advice. But in a real, deep way.

And in the end, that was what scared her.

That he didn't need her, and that she might need him.

That when he was well he would be able to walk

away. Like a bird that was able to fly once its wing had healed.

Once she no longer had more to offer than the wild, free sky. When she wasn't a compelling thing to add to his life, why wouldn't he just leave? If she couldn't keep giving, what then?

"What about Evan?" Sabrina asked. "Evan doesn't need to stay. Evan is completely healthy and healed. Evan chooses to stay."

"Evan is fat," Bea said, stubbornly. "And motivated by food. Which I provide for him. Also, Evan is a raccoon."

"Well, I imagine you provide some things to Dane too," Sabrina said, a smile tugging at the corners of her lips.

"He is my brother," Lindy said, her tone dry. "If we can keep it out of that territory, that would be good for me."

"Well, Beatrix is my sister," Sabrina said, emphasizing the word *sister*, making Bea's heart swell. "And I don't mind it. I would prefer that she was having a satisfying and robust love life to the alternative."

"We're covered there," Beatrix said. "Chemistry is not our problem."

"That's the trouble with really intense chemistry," Sabrina said. "There tends to be something else behind it. Something more than just sex, and that means feelings. Sometimes the chemistry forces you together, and the feelings break you apart. But you can figure that out. God knows Liam and I had to. A whole lot of years of pain. And luckily for you and Dane, I don't think it's going to take thirteen years apart."

"What if it does?" Beatrix said. "What if I ruined it? What if I can't...? What if I can't be brave enough to be with him?"

"I know you pretty well, Bea, and the more I think about it, the more I realize you're the bravest person I know. You have fearlessly navigated life and Dad, doing whatever you wanted. I can't believe you went through finding out your paternity and you didn't even tell any of us. I know you didn't get support from Mom and Dad. The fact that you dealt with all of that on your own... You're strong, but you don't have to be that strong. You can let us in. All it takes is trust."

"That's it?" Beatrix asked.

"That easy and that hard."

"I want him," Beatrix said, her voice small and miserable. "Forever. More than anything."

"Then tell him. And tell him why you're scared. Tell him you need him. You need him to tell you every day how much he loves you. I'm going to be honest with you. About the fact that maybe you're a little bit broken. But trust him to handle that. The way that you trust yourself to handle him."

"What if he doesn't want to? What if he rejects me?"

"Well," Sabrina pointed out, "you don't have him either way."

"Well," Bea countered, "it's different because in one scenario I get to decide. And in the other scenario he rejects me and all that I am."

"And in both you're a miserable beast," Lindy said.

"I don't... I don't know how to be the kind of brave that includes another person."

"I guess you have to decide if he's worth it."

"I dreamed of having him my whole life."

"No, you didn't," Sabrina said. "You fantasized about a man that was out of your reach. And the minute he wasn't, it felt real and scary. It felt like change. And compromise. Dane's not a fantasy. He's a man. But the good news is, you're not a wood sprite. You're a woman. And I think the two of you can find a way to make that work."

Bea sighed and clutched her forgotten test results, nodding and walking out of the winery. Her phone buzzed in her hand and she looked down, and saw that it was Dane. Her fingers hovered over the button, and then she declined it.

Because she was broken. Diminished. And she didn't know what she could do about that.

CHAPTER TWENTY-FOUR

HE HAD HOPED to talk to Beatrix before he walked into the Mustard Seed. But she hadn't picked up. Just like she hadn't picked up any of the times he'd called her over the past couple of days. He couldn't remember ever in his whole life calling a woman like this. He never had. Usually, he was the one declining calls. Beatrix had him acting like a desperate, crazy person. And he wasn't even sure that he minded. It was a strange, painful, giddy space to exist in.

He just had one more thing to do before he turned phone calls into a knock on the front door.

He walked into the diner and looked around. When his eyes fell on the gray, diminished man sitting at the counter, Dane felt hollowed out.

That mountain of a man he remembered was different now. Or maybe, it was Dane who was different. Not small and wiry, and looking up at the man he saw only once a month or so. Not a little boy looking at his dad. Just a man looking at another man, who apparently shared some of the same DNA as him.

"Hi," Dane said, sitting down next to him on one of the benches. "I'm glad you could make it."

His dad looked at him with matching blue eyes, and Dane felt a moment of emotion over that resemblance.

Over that shared feature. But just like that, it was gone when the other man looked down into his cup of coffee. "Sure. Not quite sure why you wanted to meet in person."

"Seemed important," Dane said. "But then, I guess you've seen me lots of times over the past few years. On TV. I can't say the same."

"I don't reckon you can."

"I'm not going back," Dane said. "I'm not going back to the rodeo, and I felt like I should tell you in person."

"Son…"

"No, let me talk. You owe me. Last time we saw each other you left when I was talking, and now you have to hear me out. It was important to me to get on TV. I remembered you watching bull riders. When you would come over and turn the TV on for a while, and that's what you would put on. Those were your heroes, and you were mine." Dane cleared his throat. "I don't know if you remember what you said to me. When you left. I asked if I'd see you again and you said…maybe not. But you could see me if I found a way to get on TV."

"Your mom didn't want me around," he said. As if that absolved him. Simply and easily.

"I know," Dane said. "But let me tell you a little something I've learned over the past few days." He held his phone out and opened up the call log, showing the list of outgoing calls. "That's how many times I've called a certain woman over the past few days. She hasn't picked up. Not once. It's like hell. But I haven't stopped. I haven't given up. Because I love her. I love her, and fighting for her is damn near killing me. But she's worth it. She's got her shit, I have mine. And I sure as hell haven't been perfect. I spent years ignoring what was right in front of me, and I don't blame her for not believing me now that I've got my head out of my ass and I'm asking for forever. I'm fighting for her. I'm fighting for her because she matters to me. And being with her matters more to me than my pride, or my comfort. So you can take that excuse that you've given yourself over all these years and you can add that to it. I fight to be with people I love. That you don't do the same has nothing to do with me. And I just now realized that."

"I didn't have any money," his dad said. "I didn't have anything to offer you."

"You were my father," Dane said. "You didn't have to offer me a damn thing. I never saw you much when I was a kid, not after Mom kicked you out. And then you just took off. But those days that we watched bull riding together shaped my entire life. How the hell can you tell yourself you didn't have anything to offer me? You didn't want to. You didn't want to fight. I spent all those years trying to show you. All those years living at you. I fought harder for that relationship than you ever did."

"Is that why you asked me here? To make me feel bad?"

"I asked you here to clear some things up. I asked you here so that we could both get a little bit of reality. I asked you here because you're unfinished business for me. When I go back to Beatrix, I want to walk up to her as a man with nothing in my arms. Because I just want to hold her. Nothing else. I don't want excuses."

"It's not the rodeo that made you important," his dad said. "It was never that you weren't important. Don't you think I knew that I made a mistake walking away from you and your sister? Of course I did. But your mom didn't want me around, and I figured that there wasn't enough good about me to bother staying. Maybe you're right. Maybe that's weak. But it doesn't surprise me any to know that I'm weak that way. I was always proud of you. I heard how well you did in football, and I used to tell all my friends that. I always said…Dane Parker, that bull rider, yeah. He's my son. I didn't have any pictures in my wallet, but I could show them that."

"Well, I lived a lot of other life too." His chest felt tight, his heart hammering. Anger for himself, for his sister, threatening to choke out his words. "And so did Lindy. She owns a winery. She's fancy. She's…strong and great. And it's not because of you or Mom. It's in spite of you. And I'm not much more than a bull rider, but I'm working on it. I'm working on it. What I want more than anything is to be a strong husband. A strong father. Because I think that's a real achievement. A real damn hard thing that takes a strong man."

"Wait," his father said when Dane started to go. "I'd like to see you sometimes. I'd like to see your sister."

"Why? Because you won't be able to turn on the channel and see me anymore?"

"Because I'm old," his dad said. "When you're old all you do is sit around and think about all the shit you fucked up. I fucked up big. I didn't call you just to ask about the rodeo. I called and I didn't know what else to ask about. Because you're right. I don't know anything else about you. I tried to connect with you in that way that I knew how." It was on the tip of Dane's tongue to tell him the fuck off.

To tell him to go right to hell and not bother.

But he thought he'd come here for one reason. To get rid of the show. Any desire to have it. The Dane Parker Show wasn't what he wanted to offer. He intended to offer Dane Parker, and he'd do what he had to, to be able to do that.

To burn it all down and have his say, and that was what it would look like when he walked to Bea a free man.

But he was wrong.

"I…I can't speak for Lindy," he said. "But I don't know. I might not be totally opposed to figuring something out."

"I don't care if you go back to the rodeo or not," his dad said. "I just want a chance to fix some things."

Dane had fixed things without his father. He had fixed things because of Bea. She had mended things inside of him that he had broken, much worse than his knee or his thigh, or any of the other injuries that he'd sustained.

He didn't need reconciliation with his father. If he could have Bea, that would be enough.

But Dane realized something. That there was strength in accepting what he'd convinced himself he didn't need. That forgiveness was pretty damned powerful when you gave it because you chose to, not because you needed to.

Anger was what you needed when you had to have some fuel to motivate you. It had gotten him this far in life. That whole life that was him demanding his parents face how wrong they were about him. That he mattered.

But suddenly he just felt that he did. Maybe because

Bea thought so. Or maybe it was something deeper. But either way that burning need to prove it was gone.

And with it the need to be angry. The need to perform.

"Maybe I'll call you later," Dane said. "And we can set up another time to meet. Right now I have something very important to take care of."

Dane Parker had never chased after a woman in his life, and he had certainly never been this pathetic for one. But Beatrix had loved him, had had a crush on him for a lot of years and he had done nothing but hang around oblivious to the fact.

So if he had to make an ass of himself a couple of times, he would consider that fair. Yeah. It was more than fair.

He would do anything for her. Crawl across broken glass, maybe. And as someone who'd had a hell of a lot of stitches, he knew exactly what that would mean.

But for her, it was worth it.

For her, anything was worth it.

Risking himself, his heart. It was all worth it.

CHAPTER TWENTY-FIVE

BEA STOPPED OUTSIDE the front of the cabin and eyed it all warily. Usually when she arrived home she felt a sense of peace. This place had been her sanctuary. It had been her escape. For so long. And now it just felt hollow. The place itself didn't have any power at all. Those feelings that she used to have for this place seemed to have been transferred.

To Dane.

As if he was the keeper now. Of her peace. Of her sense of belonging. She needed to see him, suddenly. And she needed him to know. That she felt broken. That everything she had accused him of…of hiding, of being in denial… She wasn't any better.

But she loved him.

Imperfectly. With a bit of fear at the moment. But she did.

She let out a swift breath and flung herself at the door of the cabin, opening it wide and then stopping in her tracks when she saw him standing there at the center of the room.

Broad shouldered, wearing a black T-shirt and a black cowboy hat, a big belt buckle, tight jeans. Dane Parker, her rodeo cowboy fantasy made flesh right there in her living room, where she had discovered that he was as good as a dream, but much better as a reality.

Much better as a man.

"You won't answer my phone calls," he said.

"I'm sorry."

"Evan was at the door, so I figured I should let him in."

Bea frowned deeply. "Evan is the source of much of my sorrows."

"And yet, you haven't gotten rid of him. Unlike me."

"Hey," she said. "That's not fair. Evan didn't accuse me of being a coward while hiding under the furniture. So."

"You're right about that. And I've come to some conclusions. I think having to go be alone and heartbroken helped with that."

"Heartbroken?" She despised the little thing in her voice that sounded slightly hopeful.

"You did a number on me, Beatrix. I haven't had so much to drink since the accident."

"As long as you didn't mix it with pain pills."

"What if I did?" he asked.

"I'll hit you over the head with a stick."

He raised a brow. "Out of great concern for me?"

"Yes," Beatrix said. "Yes. Unfortunately."

"It's unfortunate that you're concerned about me?"

"I think so."

"I recall not that long ago you said you didn't care if I dropped dead where I stood."

"Well. I lied."

"I would love the chance to hear about what a liar you are," he said. "But first, I'm going to have to tell you some things. I don't need to go back to the rodeo. At all. I was worried, Bea, that I wouldn't have anything to offer you if I didn't. No money, no glory. What I understand now is how it looks to you. Like I'm hedging my bets. Like I'm waiting to see if I'm going to become dissatisfied with what I have here. And that's not what it is. I don't want you to think that. And I also… I saw my father today."

"You did?"

"Yes," he said. "I saw my father because I needed things to be said between us. I needed for that to be out of the way so that you wouldn't think I would be tempted to go back because of that. So that you wouldn't think anything I was doing was a reaction to something. I told him. Plain and simple, how I joined the rodeo in hopes that he'd see me. And how I'm over that. Bea, I'm not going to live my life for a man who may or may not care for me anymore. The life that I have here is what matters. And I want to live for you. For us. And I don't know that I'm a particular prize. I think I felt like I might be when I had championships. When I had endorsement deals and money. Those things made me feel real. But you know, being with you… That makes me feel the most important of all. If you could care about me, Beatrix, then I must be all right."

"Oh, Dane…"

"I love you," he said. "I was afraid to say those words before, Bea. But they were always true. I told my father I loved him like those words were magic. Like they'd make it so he wouldn't leave and he did, anyway. And I felt…there's nothing quite like what I felt then. Powerless. I decided to take action. Take control. And I let anger drive me. I was determined to show him. And I think… I think talking to him maybe I did. But knowing that didn't make me happy. It didn't fix anything. Loving you did. You loving me when I had nothing. When I was nothing. I was pretty determined to try not to learn from that, but losing you made me."

Bea's eyes overflowed, tears streaming down her face. She closed the distance between them and wrapped her arms around him. "Dane, I've been such an idiot."

He put his hand on the center of her back, stroking her delicately, whispering in her ear. Sweet words. Dirty words. And she loved them all, because they were all him.

"Why is that?" he asked finally, the words hushed and husky.

"Dane, I like broken things. But it isn't because I'm kind. It's because I'm scared. It's because I know how to mend broken things and make them feel… I don't know. Obligated to me even. Because I didn't trust that anything else could possibly make anyone or anything care about me. And the thing that scares me the most is that I need to be taken care of. I'm afraid to want that. I'm afraid to need that. I'm afraid if I can't give…if I can't give enough why would anyone stay? Because for all I know that's what drove my dad away. Not money. But that he didn't want some needy kid following him around. But Sabrina said…"

She swallowed a choked breath. "She asked what if he didn't feel good enough. And that was why he walked away. And I realize that in some ways that's more awful. Because it's just fear. It's fear and selling the other person short. I also realized it's what I did to you. I took all of my insecurities and I put them on you. I didn't trust you when you said you wanted to be with me. Because I was afraid. But I don't want to be afraid anymore. I want to be yours."

"Beatrix," he whispered, stroking his fingers through her hair, his lips soft and sweet on her temple. "You're mine, princess. There's nothing you can do to change that. And I will live wherever you want to live. I'll stay here forever. I'll be a ranch hand. I don't need anything but you."

She swallowed hard. "But you can have more than me. And that's another thing. Expecting anything else is selfish. And it's a misuse of your feelings for me. I have to trust you enough to believe that if you want to go away sometimes, I have to believe you're going to come back. That you're going to choose me."

"I will," he said. "If every option in the world were laid out before me, you're the one that I'd choose, Beatrix. If my leg was healed tomorrow I wouldn't go back to riding. I want to be here. With you. My dream was never to be the most famous, the richest. At the end of the day, my dream was to be loved. And if I can be loved by you… Honey, that's a better dream than anything else."

Beatrix nodded vigorously, throwing her arms around his neck. "I love you," she said. "Dane, I love you. I don't think I really knew what that meant until you. I thought love meant making yourself more interesting than anything out in the world. I thought love was all about currency. Or obligation. And nothing in between. But it's not. I thought that I could protect myself that way. But I need… I need what you give me," she said. "And that's not me tending to you like a wounded animal and accepting your gratitude. You help me. You came into my life, and you understood me. And you... you helped me with the sanctuary. You believe in me. You don't think I'm insane for having a raccoon in my house."

"Well, more like I tolerate the insanity that comes with you doing things like having a raccoon in your house. But, sure."

"I was so angry at you," she said softly. "Because this place didn't feel like a safe haven anymore. Because I couldn't take shelter here like I once could. It didn't feel like a respite. It felt hollow. Because this cabin, these woods, they are not my shelter anymore. You are, Dane. You are the place where I can be broken. The place where I can be small. The place where I can be me. I didn't know that could ever be a person. But it is. For me, it's you."

He took hold of both of her hands and raised them to his lips, and kissed her. "If I'm your shelter, then honey, you're my glory. You make me feel like the man I always wanted to be. I've got a bum leg, but I can stand taller next to you than I ever could before. *You* are my value. *You* are my heart, Beatrix Leighton. I love you. I love you because you're strong. Because you're determined. Because you care with a force that should terrify the whole world. I love you because you showed me who I was. Because you make me want to be as brave as you are. Do things like call my father, and let go of rodeo dreams that didn't even matter to me anymore."

"I'm not sure that I did all that," she said.

"You did, Beatrix. You did."

"Well, I love you, Dane Parker. Not because you were famous. Or because you're hot. I mean, you are. Hot. And you're not really all that famous unless people watch a lot of bull riding."

"Some people do," he said.

"Not that many."

"Enough."

"But," she said, feeling laughter rise up inside of her. "I love you because you're the reason I'm not hiding anymore. You made me see myself differently. And that made me want to show other people what all I could be. I love you because... I love you because you opened up my world."

"Me? I'm just a broken-up cowboy," he said.

"Yeah, but it took a broken-up cowboy for me to see that maybe it's okay if I'm a little bit broken too. Especially if he can love me, anyway."

"Bea, I don't know if you're broken. Hell, I don't even know if I am. Right now things feel just about perfect. But maybe that's the point. Maybe the point is that all the things we've been through made us fit together perfectly. Maybe we wouldn't have hung out in high school. I don't know. Though, I still think we would have. Because I think we would have found that even then all of our pieces fit."

"You're right. Together, I think we fit so perfect it's like being unbroken."

"All I need is you."

"I feel the same," she said. "Why don't you take me to bed?"

"That sounds exactly perfect." He held her up against him and began to walk them back toward her bedroom.

She pressed her hand against his chest, and he stopped. "I don't mean there."

"Where then?"

"The big house," she said. "The main house."

"Bea," he said frowning. "You don't like it there."

"I didn't like it there. I didn't like all the things that it represented. But you know what it represents to me now?"

"What?"

"Where we got started. My first time being with you. Being with anyone. That house, you staying in it... It's the reason we got closer."

"By that rationale I should find the bull that stomped the hell out of me and make him a pet."

"We could," Bea said.

"We cannot," he responded.

"As I've said many times, Dane. There are no bad animals."

"I don't care for that one," Dane said. "Let's just agree that I don't have to like that particular one."

"Well..."

"Bea," he said. "You are not seeking it out, you are not giving it a spot in our sanctuary."

"Who knows, Dane, who knows? Maybe when you're out agenting you'll run across the bull again and have a change of heart."

"You really don't mind me agenting?"

"I want you to do it," she said. "I want you to do all the things that make you happy."

"I don't need to do it. I don't need it to be happy. But I might like to do it. And it will make it easier for me to buy the house from Lindy."

She blinked. "You're going to buy the house?"

"Hey, if you want to live in it with me, I'm going to make it permanent."

"You don't have to…buy it."

"Sure I do. Because we're not going to take any guff from her on whether or not Evan is allowed inside."

"Really?"

"I'm kinda fond of Evan now."

"Why is that?"

"Because this is his fault."

Beatrix laughed. "I guess… I guess it kind of is."

"All right, Beatrix," Dane said. "Let's go home. To our home. Which will be filled with love, and as many animals as you want."

She wrapped her arms around his neck and kissed him, deep and hard. "That sounds like a deal."

Beatrix Leighton was a friend to all living things. She cared for creatures large and small, domestic and wild, nearly every day of her life.

But the best patient that she'd ever had was one big strong cowboy. Because in the end, she loved him. And he loved her.

And not only did she take care of him, he took care of her right back.

EPILOGUE

A little farther down the road...

BEATRIX'S ANIMAL SANCTUARY was an unquestionable success—as Dane had always known it would be. When his wife wanted something, she got it.

From thriving animal sanctuaries, to a busted-up cowboy...to a bull.

"I really, honestly can't believe you talked me into taking this asshole bull," Dane said, walking up the fence and staring out at the gray-and-white beast that had nearly stomped him to pieces only three years earlier.

And he wasn't angry. Not at all.

His life had changed in a thousand ways because of that accident. Yes, his body had changed, but he couldn't begin to separate those changes from all the others.

From owning his home, sharing a life with Bea, to being around to be an uncle to Lindy and Wyatt's brand-new twins.

He could ride a horse just fine, and he could make love with his wife whenever he wanted. That was enough.

In his estimation, that was more than enough.

"Dane, come back to the house with me," Bea said, her eyes shining. "I have something to show you."

"You don't have a vole in your backpack, do you?"

She scowled and hit him. "No!"

"Do you have a—" he lowered his voice and made a suggestive face "—*vole in your backpack?*"

Bea stared at him blandly. "I don't even know what that could mean."

"I would love to find out."

He followed her back up to the house, through the doors and inside. It had been heavily redecorated in the past few years because neither of them liked the stuffy, starchy quality of the rooms before. And Bea had wanted it to be much more like her cabin.

"It's only a very small thing!" Bea said, disappearing into the living room.

He closed his eyes. "Badger? Smaller? Marmot. Rat. I still think it might be another vole."

"Wrong. Wrong wrong *wrong.*"

He opened his eyes and looked at Bea, who was standing in front of him holding a very small white pair of pajamas.

His stomach hollowed out, the breath in his lungs vanishing.

It was like a whole crowd had stood up around them and cheered. Like the biggest, brightest spotlight was shining right here.

The most important moment. With the most important woman.

And he knew right then that the best years of his life were up ahead. Father to his child. Husband to this woman.

He cleared his throat. "The Dane and Bea Show has been pretty amazing so far."

Bea smiled and wrapped her arms around his neck, kissing him on the cheek. "I think it's only going to get better."

"I went out searching for something. For significance. For glory. A sense of purpose. A feeling of being loved. Looking for the answer. It was here the whole time." He stepped back and looked down at Bea's face. "It was *you* all along."

* * * * *

Return to Gold Valley, Oregon,
where the cowboys are tough to tame, until they
meet the women who can lasso their hearts.
Look for Gabe Dalton's book,
Cowboy to the Core,
from Maisey Yates and HQN Books!
Read on for an exclusive sneak peek...

CHAPTER ONE

> "I ain't afraid to love a man. But I ain't afraid to shoot him either."
>
> —Annie Oakley

"GABE DALTON, THAT is not the way to handle a horse like that."

Jamie Dodge was firing on all cylinders right now, her adrenaline hopped-up from the punishing ride she'd just taken with one of the mares, out on a trail behind the Dalton ranch. She'd pushed the horse and the horse had pushed back, more fire in her system than anyone had suspected.

It made Jamie happy to feel the old girl exhibit so much spirit. A great many of the horses that had recently come to the ranch were—according to Gabe—old and burned-out, or abused.

It was Jamie's first day working at the Dalton ranch, with the legendary Gabe Dalton, who theoretically made women swoon across county and state lines. She had been told—by a breathless woman in the feed store who was clearly a rodeo fan—that Jamie working *under* Gabe made her an object of pure envy.

Jamie had fought to keep from rolling her eyes.

Gabe was perfectly symmetrical. And muscular. If

you were into that kind of thing, and she was… Well, she had other things on her mind.

Today had been perfection in many ways. She'd been feeling increasingly lost on the Get Out of Dodge ranch, not because the work wasn't great. It was. She loved leading trail rides for the guests who came to stay at her family ranch.

It was…the surrounding part of it. Everyone had paired off.

It was like springtime in an old cartoon. Her brothers were all married or engaged, her best friends were in relationships…

And Jamie felt a little bit lost.

But not here. Not right now. And not when it came to horses.

Animals made sense. And to Jamie, horses made the most sense of all.

"You have a problem, Jamie?"

She was doing her best to keep her spiked adrenaline under control. To be…nice. She'd been told, on a few occasions, that her direct manner of communication was off-putting sometimes.

"I just feel," she said, searching for some tact somewhere inside her, "that perhaps you could handle Gus a bit differently."

Gabe looked down at her from his position on the horse, his eyes shadowed by the brim of his cowboy hat. His large, weathered hand pulled back on the reins, and he dismounted, muscles in motion from his forearms down to his denim-clad thighs.

And for just a moment, her confidence faltered.

He was familiar in every way. A cowboy like the

kind she'd grown up with. But when his eyes clashed with hers, there was an unfamiliar echo in her stomach. It made her feel hot underneath her skin, and shaky down in her center.

She didn't like it at all.

Jamie Dodge wasn't a woman who wasted time on insecurity and uncertainty. She'd had to grow up fast, and she'd had to grow up tough. Living in a house populated entirely by men meant learning how to meet them on their level.

And so she'd done that.

Her father had been a man with a ranch to run and four kids to raise, with no wife to help him. Her bothers had been older. Gods, in her estimation, or something a little bit less perfect but no less unbreakable.

She'd wanted to be just like them.

There was no doubt about it, her older brother Wyatt wouldn't be standing there like a guppy starting at Gabe Dalton just because the muscle in his forearm had twitched.

It was normal to appreciate something like that. He was—she thought—a bit like a quality piece of horse-flesh.

Muscular. Agile.

But that was just a little visual appreciation. Nothing more, nothing less. Nothing at all to get wound up about.

"He's sensitive," she said, planting her boot against the bottom rung of the fence. She gripped the top rail, launching herself up over the top, jumping down into the fine arena dirt, a small cloud rising up around her.

One piercing brown gaze wasn't going to turn her

into a giggly feed-store girl. Giggling was for other women. Women who didn't have goals of getting themselves into the rodeo by next season.

Women who'd grown up with mothers, with soft voices and soft embraces. Who could afford to take risks because they knew they had a safe place to land if they fell.

The only thing Jamie knew she could count on if she fell was that no matter how hard the ground she'd pick herself back up.

From the time she could remember, when she had fallen down and scraped her knee, she'd wiped the blood on her palm, and wiped her palm on her jeans. Gone on with her day, not letting a single tear escape. She'd learned to suck it up and to buck up.

"This one is skittish," she said, approaching the horse slowly. "And handling him like you are is just…" She did her best to find some words that weren't overtly confrontational and it was damned hard.

She'd been raised by a man who didn't mince words.

There hadn't been a whole lot of softness in Jamie's life, and that was fine by her. The fact was, she preferred direct methods of communication. Often things like this seemed unnecessary to her. But he was the boss and she was the employee. So she had to figure out some kind of way.

"You need to have a little bit of intuition," she said finally.

"He was doing fine for me," he said, looking at the old gelding that he'd been riding only a few moments before.

She shook her head. "He did a lot better with me

this morning. He's balking. Pulling against your reins. He doesn't like it." Really, there was no point mincing words here. "He doesn't like you."

"All right, what's the problem?" He crossed his arms, and her eyes flickered to his forearms. They were streaked with dirt and muscle, and there was a cut right next to his elbow that was just beginning to heal.

She returned her focus to his face. She could see his eyes now that she was closer. Along with the hard, square cut of his jaw and the firm, set line of his lips.

He was not happy with her.

Too bad. She wasn't happy with him.

"He's got a soft mouth," she said. "You need to be more sensitive to that."

"Horses are big-ass animals who don't need to be babied."

She fought to keep her eyes from visibly rolling back in her head. "In general I agree with you. We are getting horses from all different backgrounds, and some of them will need to be babied. I have a firm hand, and I lay out expectations with my animals. But you also have to know when you need to be a little bit more forgiving. And Gus here needs forgiveness."

Also, a rider who doesn't have his head up his ass.

Biting her tongue through that last part was a personal victory.

"Why is it you think you know better than I do?"

"You're a rodeo cowboy," she said slowly. "What you do is a specific thing. Your type… I know all about your type."

Gabe snorted, pulling his hat off his head and running his hand through his dark hair. "Really?"

"I was raised in a house with cowboys. Believe me. I've had enough exposure to make me immune to your charm, and also give me enough insight to know that a lot of times you're leading with your ego."

"You don't think I could possibly just have a different take than you on what Gus needs?"

Her patience frayed, then snapped. "If so, it's the wrong take."

"Little girl," he said, his eyes going hard, his mouth firm. "I hired you to work for me. I hired you to assist me. I didn't hire you to tell me what to do."

She didn't apologize, because she knew Wyatt wouldn't have. Because she knew it was how he would have talked to someone in this situation. Straight up.

Wyatt wouldn't have ignored being called a little girl. But Jamie figured since he was her boss, she'd let it go. "You've taken on a lot here."

"You don't need to tell me what I already know. But between the horses I had already agreed to take in that were retired from the rodeo, and the horses that came from that farm Bea told me about, I didn't have much choice. I wasn't going to turn them down. They didn't have another place to go."

"And that's real sad, but we have to make sure we can do good by the horses too. I understand that your goal is to make it so they can go to families. Less experienced riders who need gentle mounts. But we are going to have to make gentle mounts out of them."

"Yes," he said dryly. "I am aware of my goals. And that is why I hired you."

"I'm the best you're gonna find," she said confidently. She didn't have any trouble claiming that. That was the thing. If horsemanship were only about training, then she supposed people could assume that at twenty-five she didn't have the necessary experience to back up her confidence. But it wasn't about age or experience, not alone. So much of it was about instinct and a connection to the animal. About having a good sense for how to work with each individual horse.

Her experience had come from barrel racing, from years working the family dude ranch, where she had managed finding and training new horses for experienced and inexperienced riders alike.

From where she was standing, it looked to her like Gabe Dalton only knew how to do one thing. He knew how to ride bucking broncos. Hard and fast. She didn't think he knew how to sense the different personalities of the animals he was working with. Not intuitively.

"Let me ask you a question," she said, crossing her arms and cocking her hip to the side. Her tank top bunched up at the front, her shapeless jeans stiff against the movement.

Her friend Bea often gave her grief for buying unisex clothing at a farm supply store. But Jamie found that it was serviceable enough. Except, for some reason, standing there in front of Gabe, it all felt a little bit ill fitting.

"Why do you want to do this? Why do you want to work with horses like this? I mean, obviously you can ride."

I guess. For eight seconds at a time. If you're lucky.

"I think you and I both know luck is part of it." His words so unerringly mirrored her thoughts for a moment she was afraid she'd said it all out loud. "But, since you asked, I am a damn good rider, thank you very much."

"A certain kind of riding," she said. "This is different. I have a lot of experience with training horses who are older, and who need to be made into safe mounts. A lot of it isn't training so much as evaluation. You have to know who has the temperament. And they won't all. Some horses are just a lot more hot-blooded than others. A lot more skittish. Now, there are still things we can do with them…"

"You're right, Jamie, I don't have experience with that. But it could be argued that there is some intelligence in knowing that, and in hiring you."

"Well," she said, approaching the big horse, Gus, that Gabe had been on. "I think that Gus has a pretty good chance at being made into the perfect horse for someone older. Kids could ride him, I guess, but he's big, and that will be difficult for them, and I imagine parents will be naturally leery of a horse his size. He is skittish, but I think that's circumstantial. More than his temperament. The fact that he has a soft mouth means that he is responsive. And that will also be good for an older, less experienced rider. Actually, when we're through training Gus, I think that we could use him at Get Out of Dodge."

"Is that so?" He was like a wall. Totally unimpressed with her. And also totally not intimidated by her.

She didn't know what to do with that.

"Yes. We get a lot of people coming to the ranch who don't necessarily have experience with horses, but want to learn. A lot of people later in life who've never been on one."

"It must be an interesting job that you have over there."

She blinked, unsure of what to do with the way he'd taken the conversation and turned it to her.

"It's fine." It was a job that she was going to be taking a break from in the next year. After she'd saved enough money to get herself on the road with the rodeo. After she'd found the right horse, and done all the work she needed to do in order to not…humiliate herself barrel racing.

Wyatt was a rodeo legend. A bull rider who'd won the championships four times.

Jamie wanted to make her own mark in the rodeo. Oh, she knew barrel racing didn't command quite the enthusiasm from the crowd the bulls did. But she wanted to succeed on her own. On her own merit.

She wanted to get out and do things on her own. She *needed* to.

She'd been in Gold Valley all this time. The most distance she'd gotten from her family was working at a Western-themed store in town called The Gunslinger. Otherwise, she lived on the ranch, worked on the ranch.

Her life revolved around it. Around them.

She knew that her father and brothers all felt like they took care of her. Right down to Wyatt being completely and utterly disapproving of her taking a job with Gabe Dalton. As if he was going to seduce her, or something.

As if he could.

Hell, she'd grown up in a house full of men just like him, and those men had brought their friends. Had brought other rodeo cowboys around.

They smelled. They left the toilet seat up. They hit on everything that moved. She'd spent her life picking around men's underwear in the clothing baskets, had been rinsing whiskers out of the sink with great distaste since she was ten.

Between her father and her older brothers, men had been pretty thoroughly demystified.

Body odor, constant swearing, jockstraps, asshole behavior…

Gabe was watching her while she mused, his lips tipped up slightly, as if he could read her mind.

"Does Wyatt give you a lot of freedom?"

She snorted, the action loosening some of the tension in her chest. "Wyatt doesn't give me anything. I work at our family ranch. Otherwise I do what I want."

Cowboys were not her type. Not at all. She supposed that in order for them to be interesting at all their behavior had to seem romantic.

And to her, it just wasn't. But then, Jamie wasn't a romantic. She was a practical kind of girl. She was well aware of the way the world worked, well aware of the way cowboys worked.

Her desire to get back into riding had nothing to do with cowboys, as a matter of fact. She was always much less interested in the man on the horse than she was in the horse he was riding.

If she were going to be interested in a man—and someday she supposed she'd find one—it wouldn't be one like that.

Gabe Dalton was exactly the kind of man she was immune to.

But Wyatt worried.

What Wyatt didn't understand was that she had always taken care of herself. But until she wasn't right at home, he was always going to feel like that was his responsibility.

Jamie had learned early on how to be self-sufficient.

Babies didn't *choose* to be born, and they definitely didn't choose the manner in which they were born.

Jamie certainly hadn't chosen to cause a blood clot that led to her mother's death days later.

But the fact of the matter was her mother had essentially traded her life for Jamie's.

The boys and her father had lost her, and gained Jamie.

In return, Jamie had done her best to be tough. To be like them.

Maybe that was the real reason cowboys didn't hold a lot of appeal or mystery to her.

She hadn't just been raised by them. Hadn't just been surrounded by them.

She'd learned to become one of them.

Tough as nails and confident in who she was, in what she knew.

"My work at the ranch is definitely interesting," Jamie said. "But I'm looking forward to this. To a change."

"To getting Wyatt out of your hair a few hours every day?"

Jamie bristled. "My brother is the best man, and the best cowboy, out there. You could probably learn from him." It was one thing for her to think uncharitable thoughts about Wyatt, but she would be damned if she would let Gabe Dalton say anything.

"He's a bull rider," Gabe said.

"Yeah, and he can ride both."

"There's a reason I chose not to," Gabe said. "First of all, I have a brain in my head. Second of all, I like horses."

"I thought you chose to ride saddle bronc because that's what your daddy did." She hadn't meant that to come out quite like it had. And she was actually pretty annoyed with herself for making the comment. Given that she was fighting against that concern herself.

Wanting to join the rodeo, not wanting for everyone to think she was there because of Wyatt.

Something shifted imperceptibly in Gabe's expression. As if he'd injected his face with granite. The whole thing had gone firm, solid. "I chose to do it because that's what I like to do. And now I'm done with that. Now I'm here."

"Well, you're off to a good start."

"I thought you thought I was off to a bad start."

"I meant with hiring me. The rest… I'm not so sure."

He crossed his arms, his eyes taking on a mocking glint. "All right, Jamie Dodge. You going to show me how it's done or what?"

"Gladly." She stuck her left foot in the stirrup and swung herself up onto the back of Gus. "Watch and learn, Gabe Dalton. Watch and learn."

Honorary Westmoreland Thurston "Mac" McRoy delayed a romantic ranch vacation with his wife for too long—she went without him! Now it will take all his skills to rekindle their desire and win back his wife…

Read on for a sneak peek at
His to Claim
by New York Times *bestselling author Brenda Jackson!*

Thurston McRoy, called Mac by all who knew him, still had his arms around his mother's shoulders when he felt her tense up. "Mom? You okay?" he asked, looking down at her.

When his parents glanced over at each other, that uneasy feeling from earlier crept over him again. Not liking it, he turned to go down the hall toward his bedroom when his father reached out to stop him.

"Teri isn't here, Mac."

Mac turned back to his father. His mother had moved to stand beside his dad.

"It's after two in the morning and tomorrow is a school day for the girls. So where is she?"

His mother reached out and touched his arm. "She needed to get away and she asked if we would come keep the girls."

Mac frowned. He knew his wife. She would not have gone anywhere without their daughters. "What do you mean, she needed to get away? Why?"

"She's the one who has to tell you that, Thurston. It's not for us to say."

Mac drew in a deep breath, not understanding any of this. Because his parents were acting so secretive, he felt his confusion and anger escalating. "Fine. Where is she?"

It was his father who spoke. "She left three days ago for the Torchlight Dude Ranch."

Mac's frown deepened. "The Torchlight Dude Ranch? In Wyoming?"

"Yes."

"What the hell did she go there for?"

His father didn't say anything for a minute and then gave Mac an answer. "She said she always wanted to go back there."

Mac rubbed his hand across his face. Yes, Teri had always wanted to go back there, the place he'd taken her on their honeymoon, a little over ten years ago. And he'd always promised to take her back. But between his covert missions and their growing family, there had never been enough time. Teri, who'd been raised on a ranch in Texas, was a cowgirl at heart and had once dreamed of being on the rodeo circuit due to her roping and riding skills. She'd even represented the state of Texas as a rodeo queen years ago.

When they'd married, she had given it all up to travel around the world with her naval husband. She'd said she'd done so gladly. Why in the world would Teri leave their kids and go to a dude ranch by herself?

He knew the only person who could answer that question was Teri.

It was time to go find his wife.

His to Claim
by New York Times *bestselling author Brenda Jackson,*
available June 2019 wherever
Harlequin® Desire books and ebooks are sold.

www.Harlequin.com

Get 4 FREE REWARDS!

We'll send you 2 FREE Books plus 2 FREE Mystery Gifts.

FREE
Value Over
$20

Both the **Romance** and **Suspense** collections feature compelling novels written by many of today's best-selling authors.

YES! Please send me 2 FREE novels from the Essential Romance or Essential Suspense Collection and my 2 FREE gifts (gifts are worth about $10 retail). After receiving them, if I don't wish to receive any more books, I can return the shipping statement marked "cancel." If I don't cancel, I will receive 4 brand-new novels every month and be billed just $6.74 each in the U.S. or $7.24 each in Canada. That's a savings of at least 16% off the cover price. It's quite a bargain! Shipping and handling is just 50¢ per book in the U.S. and 75¢ per book in Canada.* I understand that accepting the 2 free books and gifts places me under no obligation to buy anything. I can always return a shipment and cancel at any time. The free books and gifts are mine to keep no matter what I decide.

Choose one: ☐ **Essential Romance**   ☐ **Essential Suspense**
　　　　　　　 (194/394 MDN GMY7)　　 (191/391 MDN GMY7)

Name (please print)

Address　　　　　　　　　　　　　　　　　　　　　　　　　　　　　　　Apt. #

City　　　　　　　　　　　　State/Province　　　　　　　　　　Zip/Postal Code

Mail to the Reader Service:
IN U.S.A.: P.O. Box 1341, Buffalo, NY 14240-8531
IN CANADA: P.O. Box 603, Fort Erie, Ontario L2A 5X3

Want to try 2 free books from another series! Call 1-800-873-8635 or visit www.ReaderService.com.

---

*Terms and prices subject to change without notice. Prices do not include sales taxes, which will be charged (if applicable) based on your state or country of residence. Canadian residents will be charged applicable taxes. Offer not valid in Quebec. This offer is limited to one order per household. Books received may not be as shown. Not valid for current subscribers to the Essential Romance or Essential Suspense Collection. All orders subject to approval. Credit or debit balances in a customer's account(s) may be offset by any other outstanding balance owed by or to the customer. Please allow 4 to 6 weeks for delivery. Offer available while quantities last.

Your Privacy—The Reader Service is committed to protecting your privacy. Our Privacy Policy is available online at www.ReaderService.com or upon request from the Reader Service. We make a portion of our mailing list available to reputable third parties that offer products we believe may interest you. If you prefer that we not exchange your name with third parties, or if you wish to clarify or modify your communication preferences, please visit us at www.ReaderService.com/consumerchoice or write to us at Reader Service Preference Service, P.O. Box 9062, Buffalo, NY 14240-9062. Include your complete name and address.

STRS19R